P9-CEC-882

TYLER

MONTANA CREEDS

**Center Point
Large Print**

TYLER

MONTANA CREEDS

Book #3

LINDA LAEL MILLER

CENTER POINT PUBLISHING
THORNDIKE, MAINE

This Center Point Large Print edition
is published in the year 2009 by arrangement with
Harlequin Books S.A.

The text of this Large Print edition is unabridged.
In other aspects, this book may vary
from the original edition.
Printed in the United States of America.
Set in 16-point Times New Roman type.

ISBN: 978-1-60285-462-8

Library of Congress Cataloging-in-Publication Data

Miller, Linda Lael.
  [Montana Creeds. Tyler]
  Tyler : Montana Creeds / Linda Lael Miller.
    p. cm.
  Previously published under title: Montana Creeds: Tyler, 2009.
  ISBN 978-1-60285-462-8 (lib. bdg. : alk. paper)
  1. Rodeo performers—Fiction. 2. Ranch life—Fiction. 3. Single mothers—Fiction.
    4. Montana—Fiction. 5. Large type books. I. Title.
  PS3563.I41373M68 2009
  813′.54—dc22
  2009008459

For Katherine "KO" Orr and Marleah Stout,
my pals. Loves ya's.

CHAPTER ONE

TYLER CREED SUPPRESSED a grin as the old guy in the Wal-Mart parking lot stared, dumbfounded, at the fancy set of keys resting in his work-roughened palm. Blinked a couple of times, like somebody trying to shake off an illusion, then gave the brim of his well-worn baseball cap an anxious tug. According to the bright yellow stitching on the hat, his name was Walt and he was the world's greatest dad.

Walt looked at his ten-year-old Chevy truck, the sides streaked with dry dirt, the mud flaps coated, and then shifted to stare at Tyler's shiny white Escalade.

"I thought you was kiddin', mister," he said. "You really want to trade that Cadillac, straight across, for my old rig? It's got near a hundred thousand miles on it, this junker, and every once in a while, a part falls off. Last week, it was the muffler—"

Tyler nodded, weary of Walt's prattle but not about to show it. "That's the idea," he replied quietly.

The aging redneck approached the Cadillac, touched the hood with something like reverence. "Is this thing stolen?" Walt asked, understandably suspicious. After all, Tyler reflected, a man didn't run across a deal like that every day, especially in

Crap Creek, Montana, or whatever the hell that wide spot in the road was called.

Tyler chuckled. "No, sir," he said. "I own it, fair and square. The title's in the glove compartment. You agree, and I'll sign off on it right now, and be on my way."

"Wait till Myrtle comes out with the groceries and sees this," the old fella marveled, hooking his thumbs in the straps of his greasy bib overalls, shaking his head once and finally cutting loose with a gap-toothed smile. Walt needed dental work.

Tyler waited.

"I still don't understand why any sane man would want to make a swap like this," Walt insisted. "Could be, you're not right in the head." He paused, squinted up into Tyler's impassive face. "You look all right, though."

Involuntarily, Tyler glanced at his watch, an expensive number with a twenty-four-karat-gold rodeo cowboy riding a bronc inlaid in the platinum face. Diamonds glittered at the twelve, three, six and nine spots, and the thing was as incongruous with who he was as the pricey SUV he was virtually giving away, but he'd never considered parting with the watch. His late wife, Shawna, had sold her horse trailer and a jeweled saddle she'd won in a barrel racing event to buy it for him, the day he took his first championship.

"I don't know as I'm eager to trade with a man

in a hurry," Walt said astutely, narrowing his weary eyes a little. "You're runnin' from somethin', and it might be the law. I don't need that kind of trouble, I can tell you. Myrtle and me, we got ourselves a nice life—nothin' fancy—I worked at the lumber mill for thirty years—but the double-wide is paid off and we manage to scrape together ten bucks for each of the grandchildren on their birthdays—"

Tyler suppressed a sigh.

"That's some watch," Walt observed, in no particular hurry to finalize the bargain. The wise gaze took in Tyler's jeans and shirt, newly purchased at rollback prices, lingered on his costly boots, handmade in a specialty shop in Texas. Rose again to his black Western hat, pulled low over his eyes. "You win it rodeoin' or somethin'?"

"Or something," Tyler confirmed. His own brothers, Logan and Dylan, didn't know about his marriage to Shawna, or the accident that had killed her; he wasn't about to confide in a stranger he'd met in the parking lot at Wal-Mart.

"You look like a bronc-buster," Walt decided, after another leisurely once-over. "Sorta familiar, too."

You look like a forklift driver, Tyler responded silently. He looped his thumbs in the waistband of his stiff new jeans. "Deal or no deal?" he asked mildly.

"Let me see that title," Walt said, still hedging

9

his bets. "And some identification, if you don't mind."

Knowing it wouldn't matter if he *did* mind, Tyler fetched the requested document from the SUV, pausing to pat the ugly dog he'd found half-starved in another parking lot, in another town, on the long road home.

"Dog part of the swap?" Walt asked, getting cagier now.

"No," Tyler said. "He stays with me."

Walt looked regretful. "That's too bad. Ever since my blue tick hound, Minford, died of old age last winter, I've been hankerin' to get me another dog. They're good company, and with Myrtle waitin' tables every day to bank-roll her bingo habit, I'm alone a lot."

"Plenty of dogs in need of homes," Tyler pointed out. "The shelters are full of them."

"Reckon that's so," Walt agreed. He studied the title Tyler handed over like it was a summons or something. "Looks all right," he said. "Let's see that ID."

Tyler pulled his wallet from his hip pocket and produced a driver's license.

Walt's rheumy eyes widened a little, and he whistled, low and shrill, in exclamation. "Tyler Creed," he said. "I thought I'd heard that name before, when I saw it on the title to this Caddie of yours. Four times world champion bronc-rider. Seen you on ESPN many a time. In some TV commercials, too. Takes guts to stand in front of a camera wearing nothing but boxer-briefs and a shit-eatin' grin the way you done, but you pulled it off, sure as hell. My daughter Margie has a calendar full of pictures of you—two years out of date and she still won't take it down off the wall. Pisses her husband off somethin' fierce."

Inwardly, Tyler sighed. Outwardly, he stayed cool.

"Myrtle and me, we'd be glad to have you come to our place for supper," Walt went on.

"No time," Tyler said, hoping he sounded regretful.

Walt looked him over once more, shook his head again and got his own paperwork out of that rattle-trap truck of his. Signed his name on the dotted line. "Just let me fetch my toolbox out of the back," he said.

"I'll get my own gear while you're doing that," Tyler answered, relieved.

The switch was made. Tyler had his duffel bag, his dog and his guitar case in the Chevy before Walt set his red metal toolbox in the back of the Escalade.

"Sure you won't come to supper?" Walt asked, as a woman emerged from Wal-Mart and headed toward them, pushing a cart and looking puzzled.

"Wish I could," Tyler lied, climbing into the Chevy. If he drove hard, he and Kit Carson, the dog, would be in Stillwater Springs by the time the sun

11

went down. They'd lie low at the cabin overnight, and come morning, he'd find his brother Logan and punch him in the face.

Again.

Maybe he'd put Dylan's lights out, too, for good measure.

But mainly, heading home was about facing up to some things, settling them in his mind.

"See you," he told Walt.

And before the old man could answer, Tyler laid rubber.

Five miles outside Crap Creek, the Chevy's muffler dropped to the blacktop and dragged, with an earsplitting clatter, throwing blue and orange sparks.

"Shit," Tyler said.

Kit Carson gave a sympathetic whine.

Well, he'd wanted to go back and find out who he'd have been without the rodeo, the money and Shawna. This was country life, for regular folks.

And it wasn't as if Walt hadn't warned him, he thought.

With a grimace, Tyler pulled to the side of the road, shut the truck off and scooted underneath the pickup on his back, with damage control on his mind. Just like the bad old days, he reflected, when he and his dad, Jake, had played shade-tree mechanic in the yard at the ranch, trying to keep some piece-of-shit car running until payday.

Whatever Walt's other talents might be, muffler

repair wasn't among them. He'd duct-taped the part in place, and now the tape hung in smoldering shreds and the muffler looked as though somebody had peppered it with buckshot.

Tyler sighed, shimmied out from under the truck again and got to his feet, dusting off his jeans and trying in vain to get a look at the back of his shirt. Kit sat in the driver's seat, nose smudging up the window, panting.

Easing the dog back so he could get his cell phone out of the dirt-crusted cup well in the truck's console, Tyler called 411 and asked to be connected to the nearest towing outfit.

LILY KENYON WASN'T HAVING second thoughts about staying on in Montana to look after her ailing father as she and a nurse muscled him into her rented Taurus in front of Missoula General Hospital. She was having forty-third thoughts, seventy-eighth thoughts; she'd left *second* ones behind about half an hour after she and her six-year-old daughter, Tess, rushed into the admittance office a week before, fresh from the airport.

Lily had remembered her father as a good-natured if somewhat distracted man, even-tempered and funny. Until her teens, she'd spent summers in Stillwater Springs, sticking to his heels like a wad of chewing gum as he saw four-legged patients in his veterinary clinic, trailing him from barn to barn while he made his rounds, tending sick cows, horses, goats and barn cats. He'd been kind, referring to her as his assistant and calling her "Doc Ryder," and it had made her feel proud, because that was what folks in that small Montana community called *him*.

In those little-girl days, Lily had wanted to be just like her dad.

Now, though, she was having a hard time squaring the man she recalled with the one her bitter, angry mother described after the divorce. The one who never showed up on the doorstep, sent Christmas or birthday cards, or even called to ask how she was.

Let alone sent a plane ticket so she could visit.

Now, after seven long days of putting up with his crotchety ways, she understood her mom's attitude a little better, even though it still smarted, the way Lucy Ryder Cook could never speak of her ex-husband without pursing her lips afterward. Hal Ryder, aka Doc, seemed fond of Tess, but every time he looked at Lily, she saw angry, baffled pain in his eyes.

Once her father and daughter were buckled in, Hal in the front and Tess in the special booster seat the law required of anyone under a certain age and height, Lily slid behind the wheel and tried to center herself. The day was hot, even for July; the hospital had been blessedly cool, but the vents on the dashboard of the rental were still huffing out blasts of heat.

Sweat dampened the back of Lily's sleeveless blouse; without even turning a wheel, she was already sticking to the seat.

Not good.

"Can we get hamburgers?" Tess piped from the backseat.

"No," said Lily, who placed great stock in eating healthfully.

"Yes," challenged her curmudgeon of a father, at exactly the same moment.

"Which?" Tess inquired patiently. "Yes or no?" The poor kid was nothing if not pragmatic—stoic, too. She'd had a lot of practice at resigning herself to things since Burke's "accident" a year before. Lily hadn't had the heart to tell her little girl what everyone else knew—that Burke Kenyon, Lily's estranged husband and Tess's father, had crashed his small private plane into a bridge on purpose, in a fit of spiteful melancholy.

"No," Lily said firmly, after glaring eloquently at her dad for a moment. "You're recovering from a heart attack," she reminded him. "You are not supposed to eat fried food."

"There's such a thing as quality of life, you know," Hal Ryder grumped. He looked thin, and there were bluish-gray shadows under his eyes, underlaid by pouches of skin. "And if you think I'm going to live on tofu and sprouts until my dying day, you'd better think again."

Lily shifted the car into gear, and the tires

screeched a little on the sun-softened pavement as she pulled away from the hospital entrance. "Listen," she replied tersely, at her wit's end from stress and lack of sleep, "if you want to clog your arteries with grease and poison your system with preservatives and God only knows what else, that's *your* business. Tess and I intend to live long, healthy lives."

"Long, *boring* lives," Hal complained. Lily had stopped thinking of him as "Dad" years before, when it first dawned on her that he wouldn't be flying her out to Montana for any more small-town, barefoot-and-Popsicle summers. He hadn't approved of her teenage romance with Tyler Creed, and she'd always suspected that was part of the reason he'd cut her out of his life.

"I'd be happy to hire a nurse," Lily said, shoving Tyler to the back of her mind and biting her lip as she navigated thickening late-morning traffic. "Tess and I can go back to Chicago if you'd prefer."

"Don't be mean, Mom," Tess counseled sagely. "Grampa's heart attacked him, remember."

The image of a ticker gone berserk filled Lily's mind. If the subject hadn't been so serious, she'd have smiled.

"Yeah," Hal agreed. "Don't be mean. It reminds me of Lucy, and I like to think about her as little as possible."

Since Lily wasn't on much better terms with her

mother than she was with Hal, she could have done without that last remark. She peeled her back from the seat and fumbled with the air-conditioning, keeping one eye on the road. Her cotton shorts had ridden up, so her thighs were stuck, too, and it would hurt to pull them free.

Another thing to dread.

"Gee, thanks," she muttered.

"Nana's a stinker," Tess commented, her tone cheerful and affectionately tolerant.

"Hush," Lily said, though she secretly agreed. "That wasn't a nice thing to say."

"Well, she *is,*" Tess insisted.

"Amen," Hal added.

"Enough," Lily muttered. "Both of you. I'm trying to drive, here. Keep us all alive."

"Slow down a little, then," Hal grumbled. "This isn't Chicago."

"Don't remind me." Lily hadn't intended to sound sarcastic, but she had.

"Is your house big, Grampa?" Tess asked, bravely trying to steer the conversation onto more amiable ground. "Can I have my mom's old room?"

Lily flashed on the big, rambling Victorian that had once been her home, with its delightful nooks and crannies, its cluttered library stuffed with books, its window seats and alcoves and brick fireplaces. Remembering, she felt the loss afresh, and something squeezed at the back of her heart.

"You can," Hal said, with a gentleness Lily almost envied. She felt his gaze touch her, sidelong and serious. "Is there a man waiting in Chicago, Lily—is that why you want to go back?"

Lily tensed, searching for the freeway on-ramp, wondering if the question had a subtext. After all, Lily's mother had left her father for another man, and he hadn't remarried during the intervening years. Maybe he mistrusted women—his only daughter included. Maybe he expected her to drop everything and run back home to some guy she'd met at Burke's funeral.

She sighed and shoved a hand into her blond, chin-length hair, only to catch her fingers in the plastic clip she'd used to gather it haphazardly on top of her head that morning before leaving the motel for the hospital. She wasn't being fair. Her dad had suffered a serious coronary incident, and the doctors and nurses at Missoula General had warned her that depression was common in patients who suddenly found themselves dependent on other people for their care.

Hal Ryder had been doing what he pleased, at least since the divorce. Now, he needed her, a near stranger, to fix his meals, sort out his prescriptions, which were complicated, and see that he didn't try to mow his lawn or fling himself back into his thriving practice before he was ready.

"Lily?" he prompted.

"No," she said, after thumbing back through her

thoughts for the original question. "There's no man, Hal."

"Mom's a black widow," Tess explained earnestly.

Hal chuckled. "I wouldn't go that far, cupcake," he told his granddaughter.

For a reason Lily couldn't have explained, her eyes filled with sudden, scalding tears—and she blinked them away. Tears were dangerous on a busy freeway, and besides that, they never made things better. "I'm a *widow*," Lily corrected her daughter calmly. "A black widow is a spider."

"Oh," Tess said, digesting the science lesson. She began to thump her sandaled heels against the front of her seat, something she did when she was impatient for the drive to be over.

"Stop," Lily told her.

A few moments of silence passed. Then Tess went on. "My daddy died when I was four," she announced.

"I know, sweetheart," Hal said, his voice tender and a little gruff.

Lily's throat ached. She'd filed for divorce, after a tearful call from Burke's latest girlfriend, whom he'd apparently dropped. Would he still be alive if she'd waited, agreed to more marriage counseling, instead of calling a lawyer right after hanging up with the mistress? Would her child still have a father?

Tess had adored her dad.

"His plane hit a bridge," Tess said.

19

"Tess," Lily said gently, "could we talk about this later, please?"

"You always say that." Tess sighed; she'd been born precocious, but since Burke's death, she'd been wise beyond her years, an adult in a first-grader's body. "But later never comes."

"You can talk to Grampa," Hal said, slanting another look at Lily. "*I'll* listen."

Helpless rage filled Lily; her hands, still damp with perspiration even though the air conditioner had finally kicked in, tightened on the steering wheel. *I listen,* she wanted to protest. *I love my child, unlike* some *people I could name.*

To her surprise, her dad reached across the console and patted her arm. "Maybe you ought to pull over for a few minutes," he said. "Get a grip."

"I have a grip," Lily said stiffly, drawing a very deep breath, letting it out and purposely relaxing her shoulders.

"I'm hungry," Tess said. She never whined, but she was teetering on the verge. No doubt she was picking up on the tension between the adults in the front seat.

Definitely not good.

"We'll be in Stillwater Springs in under an hour," Lily said, keeping her tone light. "Can you hold out till we get there?"

"I guess," Tess said. "But then we'll have to stop at a supermarket and everything. Grampa told me there's no food in the house."

Lily's head began to pound. She glanced into the rearview mirror, to make eye contact with her daughter. "Okay, we'll stop," she said. "We'll get off at the next exit, find one of those salad buffet places."

"Rabbit food," Hal murmured.

"One burger wouldn't kill us," Tess said.

Whose side was the child on, anyway?

"No burgers," Lily said firmly. "Fast-food places don't offer organic beef."

"Oh, for Pete's sake," Hal said.

"Kindly stay out of this," Lily told her father evenly. "My purse is on the seat beside you, Tess. There's a package of crackers inside. Have some, and I'll keep my eye out for a decent market."

Sullenly—Tess was never sullen—the child rummaged through Lily's handbag, found the crackers, tore open the package and munched.

After that, none of them spoke. They were twenty minutes outside Stillwater Springs when they spotted the man and the dog walking alongside the highway.

Something about the man jarred Lily—the set of his shoulders, the way he walked, *something*—tripping all sorts of inner alarms.

"Stop," Hal commanded urgently. "That's Tyler Creed."

And I thought this day couldn't get any worse.

Lily pulled over and put on the brakes, while her father buzzed the passenger-side window down.

"Tyler? Is that you?" he called.

The man turned, flashed that trademark grin, dazzling enough to put a heat mirage to shame. Damn it, it *was* Tyler.

All grown-up, and better-looking than ever.

And here she was, with her back and thighs glued to the car seat and her hair tugged up into a spiky mess.

He approached the car, the dog plodding patiently at his heels. Bent to look in at Hal. When his gaze caught on Lily, then Tess, the grin faded a little.

"Hey, Doc," Tyler said. "I heard you went through a rough spell. You feeling better?"

"I'll be all right, thanks to Dylan and Jim Huntinghorse," Hal replied. "I went toes-up at Logan's place, during a barbecue, and they gave me CPR. I'd be six feet under if it hadn't been for those two."

Tyler gave a low whistle. "Close call," he said. In high school, he'd been cute. Now, he was drop-dead gorgeous. His eyes were the same clear blue, though, and his dark hair still glistened, sleek as a raven's wings. "Lily," he added, in grave greeting.

"Get in," Hal said. "We'll give you a lift to Stillwater Springs."

"Don't you have a car?" Tess ventured, fascinated, straining in the hated "baby seat" to get a look at the dog.

Tyler grinned again, and Lily's stomach dipped

like a roller coaster plunging down steep and very rickety tracks. "It broke down on a side road," he explained. "No tow trucks available, so Kit Carson and I started hoofing it for home."

"Hoofing it?" Tess echoed, confused.

"Walking," Lily translated.

Tyler chuckled.

"Well, get in," Hal said. "That sun's hot enough to bake a man's brain."

Tyler opened the right rear door of the Taurus, and he and Kit Carson took their places alongside Tess, the dog in the middle. Delighted, Tess shared the last of her crackers with Kit.

"Obliged," Tyler said.

"My daddy died when I was four," Tess said. "In a plane crash."

Lily tensed. Oddly, Tess often confided the great tragedy of her short life in strangers. With counselors and well-meaning friends, she tended to clam up.

"I'm sorry to hear that, shortstop," Tyler told her.

"Is hoofing it the same as hitchhiking?" Tess asked. "Because hitchhiking is *very* dangerous. That's what Mom says."

Lily felt Tyler's gaze on the back of her neck, practically branding her sweaty flesh.

"Your mom's right," Tyler answered. "But Kit and I didn't have much choice, as it turned out."

"You could have called Logan or Dylan," Hal said.

Lily wondered at the note of caution in her father's voice, but she was too busy merging back onto the highway to pursue the thought very far.

"Cold day in hell," Tyler said.

Lily cleared her throat.

"Cold day in *heck,* then," he amended wryly.

"Who are Logan and Dylan?" Tess asked.

"My half brothers," Tyler replied, belatedly buckling his seat belt.

"Don't you like them?" Tess wanted to know.

"We had a falling out," Tyler said.

"What's that?" Tess persisted.

Risking a glance in the rearview mirror, Lily saw him ruffle Tess's dark blond hair. She had Burke's green eyes, and his outgoing personality, too. Telling her not to talk to strangers was pretty much a waste of time—not that Tyler Creed was a stranger, strictly speaking.

"A fight," Tyler said.

"Oh," Tess said, sounding intrigued. "I like your dog."

"Me, too."

Lily sat ramrod-straight in the sticky vinyl seat. Concentrated on her driving. She'd thought a lot about Tyler Creed since she'd hurried out to Montana to keep a vigil at her father's bedside, but she hadn't expected to actually run into him. He was a famous rodeo cowboy, after all—a sometime stuntman and actor, and he did commercials, too.

People like that were, well, *transitory.* Weren't they?

Wandering through her kitchen with a basket of laundry one day a few years before, she'd glimpsed him on the countertop TV, hawking boxer-briefs, and had to sit down because of heart palpitations. Burke, an airline pilot by profession, had been between flights, and asked her what was the matter.

She'd said she was getting her period, and felt woozy.

She'd felt woozy, all right, but it had nothing to do with her cycle.

"Grampa and I wanted hamburgers for lunch," Tess informed her fellow passenger, "but she said it would clog our arterials, so now we have to wait and eat salad with *tofu.*"

"Ouch," Tyler commented. "That bites."

Lily pushed down harder on the accelerator.

"Where shall we drop you off?" she asked sunnily, when they finally, *finally* hit the outskirts of Stillwater Springs. The place looked pretty much the same—a little shabbier, a little smaller.

"The car-repair place," Tyler replied.

Lily had forgotten how sparely he used words, never saying two when one would do. She'd also forgotten that he smelled like laundry dried in fresh air and sunlight, even after he'd been loading or unloading hay bales all day. Or walking along a highway under a blazing summer sun. That his mouth tilted up at one corner when he was amused, and his hair was always a shade too long. The way his clothes fit him, and how he seemed so comfortable in his own skin . . .

Do not think about skin, Lily told herself, aware that her father was watching her intently out of the corner of his eye, and that that eye was twinkling.

"Thanks for the ride," Tyler said, when they pulled up to the only mechanic's garage in town. Kit Carson jumped out after him.

"Bye!" Tess called, as though she and Tyler Creed were old friends.

"Anytime," Lily lied.

He walked away, without looking back.

Just as he had that last summer, when Lily, high on teenage passion and exactly half a bottle of light beer, had proposed marriage to him. He'd said they were both too young, and ought to cool it for a while, before they got in too deep.

Lily had been crushed, then mortified.

Tyler had simply walked away. Later, she'd learned that while he was dating her, ending every evening with a chaste peck on the cheek and a "sleep tight," he'd passed what remained of the night in bed with a divorced waitress twice his age.

The memory of that discovery still stung Lily to the quick.

He'd written songs for her, sung them to her in a low vibrato, aching with heart, played them on his guitar.

He'd taken her to movies, and for long walks along moonlit country roads.

He'd won three teddy bears and a four-foot stuffed giraffe at the county fair, and given them to her.

And all the time, he'd been boinking a waitress with a hot body and a Harley-Davidson tattoo on her right forearm.

Lily was a grown woman, a widow, with a young daughter, a sick father and a successful career in merchandising under her belt. And *damn*, it still hurt to remember that the songs and the movies and the romantic walks had meant nothing to him.

Nothing to him, everything to her.

"Water under the bridge," her father commented quietly. "Let's go home, Lily."

Let's go home, Lily.

Hal had said that the night she'd come to the clinic, where he was working late, after the breakup with Tyler, carrying her bleeding, broken heart in her hands. She'd cried, and said she never wanted to see Tyler Creed again as long as she lived. Hal's jaw had tightened, and he'd put an arm around her shoulders, held her close for a few moments.

He's Jake Creed's boy, honey, Hal had said. *They're poison, those Creeds. Every one of them. You're better off without him.*

She'd sobbed, destroyed as only a betrayed seventeen-year-old can be. *But I love him, Dad,* she'd protested.

Let's go home, Lily, he'd repeated. *You'll get over Tyler. You'll see.*

And she *had* gotten over Tyler Creed.

Or at least, she'd thought so, until today.

Now, she sucked it up, for Tess's sake, and her own. Drove toward the house where she'd grown up, a happy kid—until her parents' sudden and acrimonious divorce when she was eleven. Until Tyler shattered her heart, and all the king's horses and all the king's men, plus a certain dashing and very handsome airline pilot, had failed to put it back together again.

The big Victorian hadn't changed, either, except for a few drooping rain gutters and peeling paint on the wooden shutters.

A blond woman in jeans stood on the wrap-around porch, waving and smiling as they pulled up.

"Kristy Madison," Lily said aloud, cheered.

"Creed, now," Hal said. "She married Dylan a while back."

Kristy came down the porch steps, through the open gate in the picket fence, which sagged a little on its hinges. When Hal hauled himself slowly out of the car, Kristy greeted him with a hug.

"We've all missed you," she told him. "Welcome back."

Lily peeled herself off the car seat and got out to stand in the road, while Tess scrambled out of the back.

"Hi, Lily," Kristy said. "It's good to see you again." Her dark blue eyes drifted to Tess, who was just rounding the front of the car. "And you must be Tess."

Tess nodded eagerly, probably pleased that someone in this strange new place knew her. "My daddy died in a plane crash," she said. "When I was four."

"I'm so sorry," Kristy said gently.

"Are there any kids my age in this town?" Tess asked. "I'd sure like to play with some of them, if there are."

Kristy smiled, and her gaze met Lily's for a moment, then went immediately back to Tess's upturned face. "I can think of several," she said. "In the meantime, though, let's get your grandfather inside. Lunch is on the table."

Weary gratitude swept through Lily. Just as she'd forgotten so much about Tyler, she'd also forgotten the nature of small towns like Stillwater Springs. When someone got sick or fell on hard times, people rallied. They aired out rooms and made beds up with clean sheets and set lunch out on the kitchen table.

"I'm plum tuckered," Hal said. "Believe I'll take a nap on my own bed."

He went on inside, while Lily, Kristy and Tess followed at a slower pace.

"I hope you don't mind," Kristy said to Lily. "Briana—that's my sister-in-law, Logan's wife—

29

and I got the keys from your dad's next-door neighbor and spiffed the house up a little."

Again, Lily's eyes burned. In Chicago, she'd had millions of acquaintances and clients, but no close friends. Back in the day, she and Kristy had spent a lot of time together.

"You must be worn-out," Kristy said, reading her face. "After lunch, why don't you lie down and rest for a while, and I'll take Tess over to the library for story hour."

Lily had kept her guard up for so long, living in the big city, coping with all things hectic, that letting it down left her a little dizzy. "Would you like that?" she asked Tess. "To go to the library, I mean?"

"*Yes,*" Tess answered. Not a major surprise; the child had taught herself to read at three.

Lunch turned out to be fresh iced tea, tuna sandwiches and potato salad. Lily fixed a plate for her dad and took it to his room off the kitchen, and when she returned, she sat down with Tess and Kristy in that dearly familiar room and ate, actually tasting her food for the first time since she'd gotten the call about her father's heart attack.

Kristy, she remembered, had gotten in touch soon afterward. And Dylan, an old friend, had come on the line moments later, to reassure her and offer her the use of a private plane.

"You look happy," she told Kristy, when Tess had finished eating and rushed off to explore a little before washing up for the trip to the library.

"I am," Kristy said, glowing. Then she reached across and squeezed Lily's hand briefly. "Things will get better," she promised. "You're home, among friends, and your dad's going to be fine."

Lily laughed, but it was a halfhearted sound, weary and a little—no, a lot—skeptical. "If you say so," she said. "Thanks for everything you did, Kristy. And thank Briana, too. Wherever she is."

Kristy smiled, pushed back her chair and stood to begin clearing the table. "You'll meet her soon enough," she assured Lily. "She and Logan are building on to their house, and she had to go home to talk to the contractor."

Logan was married, and building on to his house. Kristy was obviously happy with Dylan.

And Tyler was probably still sleeping with waitresses—if he hadn't graduated to sexy movie stars and supermodels.

As if she cared.

CHAPTER TWO

IF HIS BRAIN HADN'T SNAGGED on Lily Ryder and then gotten snarled like so much fishing line, Dylan wouldn't have taken Tyler by surprise the way he did, there in the auto-repair shop. A hard slug to his right shoulder jerked him back to the here and now, pronto.

Tyler turned, ready to fight, but drew up when he

31

saw Dylan's side-slanted grin and the bring-it-on glint in his blue eyes.

"That city-slicker rig of yours break down someplace?" Dylan asked.

Tyler unclenched his right fist, let out a breath. Much as he would have liked to punch his middle brother, he figured it might scare Kit Carson, so he didn't. The dog had been through enough. "I swapped it for a truck," he heard himself say. "And *that* broke down."

Dylan raised one eyebrow. "Need a ride?"

Tyler looked down at the mutt, resting watchfully at his feet, brown eyes rolling from one brother to the other. The poor critter looked as though he expected to be smashed between two giant cymbals at any moment.

"Yeah," Tyler said, reluctantly agreeing to Dylan's offer. "The tow truck's out on another call, and I'm fifth in line, so it might be tomorrow before they can haul the Chevy in and fix it."

After he'd told Vance Grant, the only mechanic on duty, that he'd check back in the morning, Tyler and Kit followed Dylan out into the afternoon heat. They made a stop at the supermarket, for dog kibble, coffee and a few other staples, and headed, by tacit agreement, for the ranch. In all that time, barely two words passed between them.

They were a good three miles out of town, in fact, Kit panting happily in the backseat of Dylan's extended-cab pickup, before it occurred to Tyler to wonder how his brother had happened along at just the right—or wrong—time.

Reflecting on the question, Tyler idly rubbed his sore shoulder, where Dylan had slugged him. "Did you come into the shop looking for me?" he asked.

"Yup," Dylan answered easily, without so much as glancing in his direction. The slight tilt of amusement at the corner of his mouth told Tyler he'd seen him nursing that arm, though. "Word gets around. Big news, when a Creed hits the old hometown."

Tyler sighed. "Not much happens around here, if we're news."

"You'd be surprised," Dylan said. "If you ever stuck around long enough to find out what's going on around Stillwater Springs, that is."

They'd run into each other a little over a week before, at the home of a mutual friend, Cassie Greencreek, but it hadn't exactly been a family reunion. Tyler had met Dylan's little girl, Bonnie, and taken a fierce liking to her, even fetched her some medicine when she was sick, but that was the extent of the brotherly bonding.

"Catch me up," Tyler said, because Dylan was bent on talking, evidently. And when Dylan was bent on *anything,* it was easier to just ride it out.

"Well, I got married," Dylan said. "To Kristy Madison."

Tyler absorbed that. "Okay," he said. "Congratulations."

"Gee, thanks. Your enthusiasm is over-whelming."

"She's half again too good for you," Tyler commented, at something of a loss. There was so much bad blood between him and his brothers that he didn't know how to carry on a civil conversation with either of them. "Kristy, I mean."

Dylan laughed. "True," he answered. Then he proceeded to bring Tyler up to speed on all the latest doings in Stillwater Springs, Montana. "They dug up a couple of bodies on the old Madison place," he went on. "And Sheriff Book retired early, a week before the special election. Mike Danvers was running against Jim Huntinghorse, but he dropped out of the race, so Jim's The Man now."

"Bodies?" Tyler echoed. He'd barely untangled himself from the shock of seeing Lily Ryder again, and that little girl of hers, and now Dylan was laying all this stuff on him.

"Murder victims," Dylan confirmed.

"Holy shit," Tyler said. "Anybody we knew?"

"Probably not," Dylan answered, as they bumped off the main road onto one of the old cattle trails snaking through the ranch like a network of ancient tree roots. A muscle tightened in Dylan's jaw. "A drifter who worked for Kristy's dad for a while, and a young girl who went missing during a family camping trip a few years back."

Tyler remembered the media frenzy surrounding

34

the missing girl. Searchers had turned over every rock in that part of Montana, without success, and eventually the hoo-ha had died down and the parents had gone home, defeated and hollow-eyed with despair. "Did Floyd nab the killers?"

"Do you ever read a newspaper?" Dylan countered, sounding semi-irritated now. Now there was a tone Tyler understood.

"No," he snapped back. "My lips move when I read, and that makes me testy."

"*Everything* makes you testy, little brother." Dylan paused, sighed. Went on. "Freida Turlow killed the girl—some kind of jealousy thing. And the drifter—well, that's another story."

"Those Turlows," Tyler said, "are just plain loco."

Dylan laughed again, but it was a raw, gruff sound, without a trace of humor. "Coming from a Creed, that's saying something."

In spite of himself, Tyler laughed, too.

"What brings you back to the home place, little brother?" Dylan asked. He was downright loquacious, old Dylan.

"Stop calling me 'little brother,'" Tyler told him. "I'm a head taller than you are."

"You'll always be the baby of the family. Deal with it." Dylan downshifted, with a grinding of gears, and they jostled up the lake road, toward Tyler's cabin. "Answer my question. What are you doing here?"

Tyler let out a long sigh. "Damned if I know," he admitted. "I guess I'm tired of the open road. I need some time to think a few things through."

"What things?"

Again, Tyler's temper, never far beneath the surface, stirred inside him. "What the fuck do you care?" he asked.

Kit Carson gave a fitful whimper from the backseat.

"I care," Dylan said evenly. "And so does Logan."

"Bullshit," Tyler said flatly.

"Why is that so hard for you to believe?"

The cabin came in sight, nestled up close to the lake. It was more shack than house, his hind-tit inheritance from the old man, but Tyler loved the solitude and the way the light of the sun and moon played over that still water.

Logan, being the eldest, had scored the main ranch house when Jake Creed got himself killed up in the woods, logging, and Dylan, coming in second, got their uncle's old dump on the other side of the orchard. That left Tyler in third place, as always.

Hind-tit.

Tyler unclamped his back molars, reached back to reassure the dog with a ruffling of the ears. Ignoring Dylan's question, he asked about Bonnie instead.

"She's fine," Dylan answered.

36

He brought the truck to a stop in front of the log A-frame, and Tyler had the passenger-side door open before Dylan had shut off the engine. Kit Carson waited, shivering a little, with either anticipation or dread, until Tyler hoisted him down from the backseat.

"Thanks for the lift," Tyler told his brother, reaching over the side of the truck bed for the kibble and the grub they'd picked up in town. *Here's your hat, what's your hurry?*

Dylan got out of the truck, slammed his door.

"Don't you have things to do?" Tyler asked tersely. Kit Carson was sniffing around in the rich, high grass, making himself at home—and he was all the company Tyler wanted at the moment. Once inside, he'd prime the pump, build a fire in the antiquated wood cookstove and brew some coffee. Try to get a little perspective.

"I have all kinds of 'things to do,'" Dylan answered, his mild tone in direct conflict with his go-to-hell manner. "I'm building a house, for one thing. Logan and I are back in the cattle business. But you're at the top of my to-do list today, little brother. Like it or lump it."

Tyler consulted an imaginary list, envisioning a little notebook, like the one his dad had always carried in the pocket of his work shirt, full of timber footage and married women's phone numbers. "You're at the top of mine, too," he replied. "Trouble is, it's a *shit* list."

Dylan leaned against the hood of his truck, watching as Tyler started for the cabin, lugging the kibble under one arm and juggling two grocery bags with the other. Kit Carson hurried after him, though it was most likely the dog food he was after.

"Ty," Dylan said, easy-like but with that steel undercurrent that was pure Creed orneriness, born and bred, "we're brothers, remember? We're blood. Logan and I, we'd like to mend some fences, and I'm not talking about the barbed-wire kind."

"You've obviously mistaken me for somebody who *gives* a rat's ass what you and Logan would like."

Dylan stepped back from the truck, folded his arms. "Look," he said, as Tyler passed him, headed for the front door of the cabin, "we were all messed up after Jake's funeral—"

Messed up? They'd gotten into the mother of all brawls, he and Logan and Dylan, down at Skivvie's Tavern. Wound up in jail, in fact, and gone their separate ways—after saying a lot of things that couldn't be taken back.

Tyler shook his head, shifted to fumble with the doorknob. The thing was so rusted out, he'd never bothered with a lock, but that day, it whisked open and Kit Carson shot over the threshold, growling low, his hackles up.

Dylan was right at Tyler's back, carrying his

guitar case and duffel bag. "What the hell?" he muttered.

Somebody was inside the cabin, that was obvious, and Kit Carson had them cornered in the john.

"Whoa," Tyler told the dog, setting aside the stuff he was carrying.

"Call him off!" a youthful voice squeaked from inside what passed as a bathroom. "Call him off!"

Tyler and Dylan exchanged curious glances, and Tyler eased the dog aside with one knee to stand in the doorway.

A kid huddled on the floor between the pull-chain toilet and the dry sink, staring up at Tyler with wild, rebellious, terrified eyes. Male, as near as Tyler could guess, wearing a long black coat, as if to defy the heat. Three silver rings pierced the boy's right eyebrow, and both his ears and his lower lip sported hardware, too. The tattooed spider clinging to his neck added to the drama.

Tyler winced, just imagining all that needlework. Gripped the door frame with both hands, a human barrier filling the only route of escape, other than the tiny window three feet above the tank on the john. The kid glanced up, wisely ruled out that particular bolt-hole.

"I wasn't hurting anything," he said. His eyes skittered to Kit, who was still trying to squeeze past Tyler's left knee and challenge the trespasser. "Does that dog bite?"

"Depends," Tyler said. "What's your name?"

The boy scowled. "Whether he bites me or not depends on what my *name* is?"

Tyler suppressed a grin. Aside from the piercings and the spider, he reckoned he and the kid were more alike than different. "No," he said. "It depends on whether or not you stop being a smart-ass and tell me who you are and what the hell you're doing in my house."

"This is a *house?* Looks more like a chicken coop to me."

Standing somewhere behind him, Dylan chuckled. He'd set Tyler's guitar case and duffel bag down and, from the clanking and splashing, started working the pump at the main sink.

"Okay, Brutus," Tyler said, looking down at the dog, "get him."

Kit Carson looked up at him in confusion, probably wondering who the hell Brutus was.

"Davie McCullough!" the kid burst out, scrambling to his feet and, at the same time, trying to melt into the bathroom wall, which was papered with old catalog pages and peeling in a lot of places. "All right? My name is *Davie McCullough!*"

"Take a breath, Davie," Tyler told him. "The dog won't hurt you, and neither will I."

Somebody had hurt him, though. Now that the kid was up off the floor, and dusty light from the high window illuminated his face, Tyler saw bruises along his jawline, fading to a yellowish purple.

Again, Tyler flinched. Either Davie McCullough had been in a tussle with some other kid recently, or an adult had beaten the hell out of him. Having had an alcoholic father himself, Tyler tended toward the latter theory.

"What happened to your face?" Dylan asked, poking wood into the stove to boil up some java, as soon as Davie edged out of the bathroom, past both Tyler and the dog.

Davie kept a careful distance from everybody. Quite a trick in a cabin roughly the size of one of those clown cars that spill bozos at the rodeo.

"You're really going to build a fire on a day like this?" Davie countered.

"I asked my question first," Dylan responded, setting the dented enamel coffeepot on the stove with a thump.

Davie scowled. With a temperament that prickly, Tyler thought with grim amusement, he should have been a Creed. "My mom's boyfriend was in a mood," he said, peevish even in an indefensible position. "Okay?"

Tyler felt another pang of sympathy—and an urge to find the boyfriend and see if he was inclined to take on a grown man instead of a skinny kid who'd probably never lifted anything heavier than a laptop computer.

"Okay," Dylan answered affably. He reached

right into one of Tyler's grocery bags, pulled out a package of chocolate cookies and tossed it to Davie. Davie caught the bag and promptly tore into it.

"I ate that canned meat you had in the cupboard," he told Tyler, spewing a few cookie crumbs in the process. "You don't keep much food around here, do you?"

"McCullough," Tyler said, and this time, he didn't bother trying to hold back a grin. "I don't think I've run across that name around Stillwater Springs. You new in town?"

Clearly torn between bolting for the door, which Dylan had opened to let out some of the stove heat, and staying because he didn't have anywhere else to go, Davie hesitated, not sure how to answer, then drew back one of the four rickety chairs at the table in the center of the cabin and plunked down to scarf up cookies in earnest.

He'd obviously been hiding out at the lake for a while, if he'd run through the several dozen cans of congealed "ham" Tyler kept on hand for intermittent visits.

"My mom lived here a long time ago," Davie said, after considerable cookie-noshing. "Before I was born."

"Who is your mom?" Dylan asked mildly. Mr. Subtle. Like an idiot wouldn't know he was planning to find the woman and give her some grief for letting the boyfriend pound on her kid.

42

"You a social worker or something?" Davie asked suspiciously.

"No," Dylan replied, finding mugs on the shelf, peering into them and frowning at whatever was crawling around inside. "Just trying to be neighborly, that's all. Your mom must be pretty worried, though."

"She's too busy schlepping drinks out at the casino to be worried," Davie scoffed. "Roy's been out of work for a year, so she's been pulling double shifts, trying to save up enough to get us our own place."

Another look passed between Dylan and Tyler. Neither of them spoke. Now that the kid had some sugar and preservatives under his belt, he'd turned talkative.

"We live out at the Shady Grove trailer park, with Roy's grandma. It's pretty crowded, especially when he's on the peck."

Jake Creed had been known to throw a punch or two, when he was guzzling down a paycheck, and both Dylan and Tyler had been in Davie's shoes more often than either of them would admit. They'd taken refuge at Cassie's place, sleeping on her living room floor or in the teepee out in her yard. Only Logan had been immune to Jake's temper, maybe because he'd always been the old man's favorite—the one who might "amount to something."

The coffee started to perk.

Kit Carson ambled out onto the porch and lay there letting the sun bake his bones, like an old dog ought to be allowed to do.

"I'll give you a ride back to town," Dylan told Davie, once some time had gone by. "The new sheriff's a friend of mine. There might be something he can do about Roy."

Davie's face seized with fear, quickly controlled, but not quickly enough. "Nothing short of a shotgun blast to the belly is going to fix what's wrong with Roy Fifer," he said. "Why can't I just stay here? I can sleep outside, and I'll work off the food I ate, chopping wood or something."

Tyler knew he couldn't keep the boy; he was a loner, for one thing. And for another, Davie was a minor child, no older than thirteen or fourteen. For good or ill, his living arrangements were up to his mother. "That wouldn't work," he said, with some reluctance.

What would he and Dylan have done, all those nights, if Cassie had turned them away from her door? If she hadn't faced Jake Creed down on her front porch and told him she'd call Sheriff Book and press charges if he didn't go away and sober up?

"I'll work," Davie said, and the desperation in his voice made Tyler's gut clench. "I could take care of the dog and chop firewood and catch all the fish we could eat. I'll stay out of your way—won't be any trouble at all—"

"I might not be around long," Tyler said, his voice hoarse, unable to glance in Dylan's direction. "And you can't stay here alone. You're just a kid."

Davie looked as near tears as pride would allow. "Okay," he said, shoulders sagging a little.

Dylan pushed back his chair, stood. Sighed. He had to be remembering all the things Tyler remembered, and maybe a few more, since he'd been the middle son, not the youngest, like Tyler, or the smart one, like Logan. No, Dylan had been wild, the son who mirrored all the things Jake Creed might have been, if he hadn't been such a waste of skin.

"I'll have a word with Jim," he told Tyler.

Tyler merely nodded, numb with old sorrows. Shared sorrows.

As kids, he and Dylan and Logan had fought plenty, but they'd always had each other's backs, too. Logan, mature beyond his years, had made sure he and Dylan had lunch money, and presents at Christmas.

When had things gone so wrong between the three of them?

Not at Jake's funeral. No, the problem went back further than that.

Passing Tyler's chair, Dylan laid a hand on his shoulder. "You know my cell number," he said quietly. "When your truck's ready to be picked up, give me a call and I'll give you a lift to town."

· · ·

LILY AWAKENED at sunset, to the sound of familiar voices—her daughter's and her father's, a novel combination—chatting in the nearby kitchen. Outside somewhere, perhaps in a neighbor's yard, a lawn sprinkler sang its summer evensong—*ka-chucka-chucka-whoosh, ka-chucka-chucka-whoosh.*

Sitting up on the narrow bed in what had once been her mother's sewing room, Lily smiled, yawned, stretched. Slipped her feet into the sandals she'd kicked off before lying down. She'd intended to rest her eyes; instead, she'd zonked out completely, settling in deeper than even the most vivid dreams could reach.

For a little while, she'd been mercifully free of ordinary reality.

The guilt over Burke's death.

The wide gulf between her and the man she had once called "Daddy."

The gnawing loneliness.

She sat for a few moments, listening to the happy lilt in Tess's voice as she told her grandfather all about story hour at the library. It had been too long since Lily had heard that sweet cadence—Tess was usually so solemn, a little lost soul, soldiering on.

Hal chuckled richly at one of Tess's comments. He'd always been a good listener—until he'd simply decided to *stop* listening, at least to Lily. When she'd called him, after the divorce, desperate for some assurance that things would be all right again, he'd brushed her off, or so it had seemed to a heartbroken child, grieving for so many things she could barely name.

Lily stepped into the kitchen, found Tess and Hal setting the table for supper. Spaghetti casserole—the specialty, Lily recalled, of Janice Baylor, her dad's longtime receptionist. Tess's small face shone with the pleasure of the afternoon's adventure at the library with Kristy.

Lily bit back a comment about the fat and cholesterol content of Janice's casserole and smiled. "Something smells good," she said.

"Mrs. Baylor brought us sketty for supper," Tess said cheerfully.

Hal watched Lily, probably expecting a discourse on the wonders of tofu. "You look a little better," he said. "Not so frazzled."

Lily nodded. She needed a shower and more sleep—would she *ever* catch up?—but she needed a hot meal more, and her father and daughter's company more still.

"How about you?" she asked Hal. "Did you rest this afternoon?"

Hal grinned. Here at home, he didn't look so wan and gaunt as he had in the hospital. The expression of frenzied dismay in his eyes had subsided, too. He'd decided, Lily thought, to live.

"As much as I could, with half the town stopping by with food," he answered. "The doorbell rang at least a dozen times."

Lily was horrified. She hadn't heard a thing. Hadn't stirred on the hard twin bed in the sewing room. What kind of caretaker was she, anyway?

Her thoughts must have shown in her face; Hal winked and said quietly, "Sit down, Lily. You're home now."

You're home now.

Kristy had said something similar, earlier that day.

It was a nice fantasy, Lily supposed, but once her father was well enough to carry on alone, she and Tess would be returning to their old lives in Chicago, to the condo, and Tess's private school, and Lily's job as a buyer for an online retailer of women's clothes.

Burke's mother, Eloise, who doted on Tess, would be lost without their weekly tea parties— just the two of them, if you didn't count Eloise's maid, Dolores. They used the best bone china, Eloise and Tess, and wore flowered hats and white gloves with pearl buttons. Eloise took Tess to museums, and bought her beautiful, handmade dresses, and invited her for long weekends at the Kenyon "cottage" on Nantucket.

The place had three stories, fourteen rooms, each one graced with exquisitely shabby antique furniture. Priceless seascapes graced the walls, and even the rugs were either heirlooms or elegant finds from the finest auction houses in the world.

48

Tess, Eloise never hesitated to point out, was all she had left, with her husband gone and her only son killed in the prime of his life. The accusation went unspoken: if Lily had just been a little more tolerant of Burke's "high spirits," a little more patient—

Lily's own mother seemed to have no time for her, or even for Tess, she was so busy gracing her powerful husband's arm at swanky parties up and down the eastern seaboard.

Resolutely, she shook off the reverie, went to the kitchen sink and washed her hands. Then she sat down to a "sketty" supper with her family.

"I like that man with the dog," Tess announced, midway through the meal.

Lily felt a little jolt at the mere reminder of Tyler.

"Where does he live?" Tess persisted, when neither Lily nor Hal offered a response.

Lily had no idea. Didn't want to know. Everything would be easier if she could just pretend Tyler Creed didn't exist, the way she had since the night he broke her heart, but that was bound to be a tall order in a town as small as Stillwater Springs.

"His family owns a ranch," Hal explained, with a readiness that surprised Lily, given her father's formerly low opinion of the Creeds in general and Tyler in particular. She flashed back to the friendly way he'd greeted Tyler when they found him walking along that lonely road. "It's a big spread.

49

Tyler's cabin is on the lake—best fishing in the county."

"I doubt if he's around much," Lily said moderately.

"He's a busy man, all right," Hal agreed, with quiet admiration. "He's come a long way since he was a kid. So have Logan and Dylan. All of them went to college, with more hindrance than help from Jake, and made their mark in professional rodeo, too. Logan has a law degree, as a matter of fact."

Lily widened her eyes at her father. "Since when are you such a fan of the Creeds?" she asked, careful to keep her tone light. Tess was so bright that she might pick up on the slightest nuance.

"Since one of them saved my life," Hal said quietly. "And, anyway, I admire gumption. They've got it in spades, all three of them."

"Is he married?" Tess asked, just a mite too cagily for Lily's comfort. "Does he have a little girl?"

Lily nearly choked on a forkful of spaghetti casserole.

"Far as I know," Hal said, looking at Lily instead of Tess, "he's single. No children."

"Do you think he'd like a little girl?" Tess persisted, with such a note of hope in her voice that Lily's eyes filled with sudden, scalding tears. "One like me?"

"Honey—" Lily began, but words failed her.

Hal reached over to pat his granddaughter's hand, his smile fond and full of tender understanding. "I think *any* man would be proud to have you for a daughter, cupcake."

"Don't," Lily whispered.

And just then, the wall phone rang.

Lily rushed to answer it, partly because she needed the distraction, and partly because she didn't want Hal rushing off to take care of somebody's sick cow and compromising his fragile health.

"Hello?" she chimed.

"Lily? This is Tyler."

The floor went soft beneath Lily's feet, just the way it had when she was a teenager, and just the sound of Tyler Creed's voice had the power to melt her knees.

"Er—hello—" Lily fumbled.

"I want to see you," Tyler said. *I want to see you.* Just like that.

As if he hadn't sold her out to sleep with a tattooed waitress. As if he hadn't shattered her most cherished dreams, and fostered a cold distance at the center of her marriage that she and Burke had never been able to overcome.

Damn him, he had his nerve. Because he *wanted* to see her, he expected it to happen. It probably hadn't even occurred to him, in his arrogance, that she might refuse.

"Lily?" he prompted, when she was silent too long.

Her face burned, her stomach did flip-flops and she turned her back on Hal and Tess, in a fruitless attempt to hide what she was feeling.

"Lily?" Tyler repeated. "Will you have dinner with me tomorrow night?"

"Okay," Lily said, though she'd meant to say no instead.

When it came to Tyler Creed, she had no backbone at all.

CHAPTER THREE

IF TYLER HAD HAD to explain what made him call Lily and ask her out, he'd have been hard put to find the words. She'd been on his mind ever since they'd run into each other on the road, after his truck broke down, but there was more to it than that—a lot more.

Maybe it was being alone at the cabin, with just Kit Carson for company—although, in truth, solitude had always been one of his favorite things in life. He was a loner for sure—more so than either of his brothers, and that was saying something.

Maybe it was knowing only too well what it was like to be a kid like Davie McCullough—a player in a game of psychological dodgeball, always "it." Never knowing which direction to jump, but always and forever *ready* to sidestep some missile.

And maybe it was the brief time he'd spent with

Dylan that day, reminding him that having brothers could be a good thing.

For some people.

People who weren't Creeds, that is.

In any case, he'd called Lily, without even stopping to think that she might be involved with some lucky bastard. She'd agreed to go out to dinner with him, though, and that was a start.

The question was, of what?

He was sitting on the porch step, looking at the lake, Kit Carson beside him, leaning slightly against his right shoulder as if to anchor him somehow, and sipping strong coffee when his cell phone rang.

His first thought, as he set his cup down to take the phone from his shirt pocket, was that Lily had changed her mind. Come to her senses. She was calling back to tell him she'd thought it over, and thanks, but no thanks. . . .

But the caller, as it turned out, was Dylan.

"The kid's situation is pretty bad," Dylan said. Typical. He never bothered with "hello" but, then, Tyler didn't, either, most of the time. Or Logan. When Tyler got somebody on the horn, it was because he had business with them. He didn't shoot the breeze—a family trait, he reflected, with some amusement. "Davie's, I mean."

Tyler let out the sigh that had been hunkered down inside him, dark and heavy, ever since he'd found Davie McCullough cowering in his john that afternoon. "I figured that," he said. "Did you talk to Jim?"

"I did," Dylan answered. "Our new sheriff is up to his ass in alligators right now. He wanted to call in social services and have the boy put into a foster home. Davie said he'd run away first, and I believe him—so I talked Jim into giving it a few days."

Tyler closed his eyes. "Where's Davie now?"

"I took him to the casino. He's hanging out in one of the restaurants till his mother gets off work." Dylan paused, cleared his throat, and Tyler, who had known something bigger was coming at him since the call began, braced himself. "Ty?" Dylan went on. "The kid's mom—well—she's somebody you know." He stopped again. Tyler had a flash-vision of the bomb doors swaying open in the bay of a fighter jet, of ominous cylinders dropping with slow and deadly grace. "You knew her as Doreen Baron."

"Holy *shit*," Tyler rasped, when he'd absorbed the impact.

Talk about your emotional mushroom cloud.

Doreen had been a waitress when he knew her, back when Skivvie's still had a lunch counter and a few tables. Fifteen years his senior, Doreen, with her network of tattoos and what-the-hell attitude, had taught him everything he needed to know about pleasing a woman—and then some.

Still scrambling for some kind of inner foothold,

Tyler did some frantic counting—backward, from the age he guessed Davie to be.

"Shit," he repeated.

Davie could be his son. And some son of a bitch was beating on him, on a regular basis, it would seem.

"You still there?" Dylan queried, somewhat cautiously, when the taut silence had finally stretched itself to the breaking point.

"Yeah, I'm here," Tyler answered, dizzy with a combination of dread and wild hope. On the one hand, he hoped Davie *was* his. On the other, such a revelation might make it impossible to find any sort of common ground with Lily.

Did he even *want* to find common ground with Lily?

"You thinking what I'm thinking?" Dylan pressed quietly.

"Yes," Tyler said. "Davie's about the right age, I guess." He ducked his head, pinched the bridge of his nose between a thumb and forefinger. The dog gave a little whimper and leaned in harder. "Doreen never pretended I was the only game in town, though, and I think if Davie was mine, she'd have hit me up for money somewhere along the way."

Dylan was silent for a long time. "Look, you're going to need a rig. I've already spoken with Kristy, and she's willing to lend you her Blazer until your truck is back on the road. We could bring it out when she gets off work at the library, if you want."

Pride swelled up inside Tyler, fit to split his hide, but he needed transportation. The auto shop wasn't the kind of place that offered loaners, and rental cars were out, too, unless he wanted to go all the way to Missoula for one—which he didn't.

"Okay," he said, finally. "Thanks."

Dylan laughed. "See? That wasn't so hard, was it?"

It had been *plenty* hard. Dylan, being a Creed himself, had to know that.

"Don't start thinking we're going to buddy-up or something," Tyler warned.

Again, Dylan laughed, more of a chuckle this time, and the sound of it chafed at some raw places in Tyler. He'd sworn he wouldn't be beholden to either of his brothers for anything, after that set-to at Skivvie's following Jake's funeral, and he'd lived by that vow. Now here he was, borrowing a Blazer like some loser who couldn't even manage to come up with a set of wheels on his own.

"God forbid," Dylan said dryly, "that we should 'buddy-up.'"

"Whatever," Tyler shot back, and thumbed the disconnect button.

Two hours later—hours Tyler spent alternately pacing and fiddling around with his guitar—two rigs rolled up to the cabin, Dylan driving one, Kristy at the wheel of the other.

Tyler left the doorway, laid his fancy, custom-made guitar in its case and hoped nobody would comment, but Dylan's gaze swung right to it, as soon as he and Kristy stepped into the house.

Kristy, carrying two-year-old Bonnie on one blue-jeaned hip, went straight over to admire the instrument, giving a low whistle of exclamation.

"A Martin," she said, with suitable reverence.

"I like a girl who knows her guitars," Tyler said, giving his sister-in-law a peck on the cheek and then ruffling Bonnie's blond curls. Kristy was a looker—always had been. Legs that went on forever, and an honest-to-God *brain* behind that angelic face. And she had a particular glow about her, indicating a very recent orgasm, of the cosmic variety.

Dylan, his eyes peaceful, his body moving as though his joints were greased, had, of course, been the lucky guy.

Tyler felt a stab of pure, undiluted envy.

Smiled to hide it, though he suspected Dylan knew exactly what he'd been thinking.

Kristy pulled the keys to her Blazer from a pocket in her perfectly fitted jeans and jangled them under Tyler's nose. "Here you go, cowboy," she said.

"Cowboy," Bonnie repeated exuberantly, straining to come to him.

Tyler had a weakness for kids, and took his niece into his arms. Crouched to introduce her to Kit Carson.

The little girl giggled with delight.

Kit licked her face.

Tyler stood up again.

Kristy laid the keys on the kitchen table, her dark blue eyes alight with goodwill. "It's nice to have you back in Stillwater Springs, Ty," she said. "We're headed over to Logan and Briana's for supper. Care to join us?"

"I'm not ready for that," Tyler said gruffly, after exchanging a glance with Dylan. He *was* curious about Briana and that ready-made family of Logan's—two boys, according to Cassie—and all the work going on over at the home place, too, but Logan would be there, and that was reason enough to stay away.

Again, Dylan's gaze shifted to the guitar. He was probably remembering the incident at Skivvie's, after they'd laid Jake Creed in his grave, just as Tyler was.

"Bygones," Dylan said, "ought to be bygones."

That was easy for him to say, Tyler thought, stung anew by the old fury. He'd written a song about Jake—or the man he'd needed his father to be—and Logan had torn the guitar out of his hands and smashed it to splinters against the bar.

Tyler could still hear the dull hum of the strings.

It had been a mail-order special, that guitar; probably hadn't cost more than twenty or thirty dollars, even when it was brand-new. It had also been the last thing Tyler's mother had given him, before she'd gone off to some seedy motel, evidently too weary of being a Creed wife to go on for even one more day, and swallowed a bottle of pills.

"I'll let you know," Tyler finally responded, his voice tight, "when bygones get to be bygones. In the meantime, don't hold your breath."

Bonnie, picking up on the change in the atmosphere, went back to Kristy, her small face solemn with worry, jamming a thumb into her mouth as she settled against her stepmother's shoulder.

Kristy's expression turned troubled, too.

"Bad vibes," she remarked softly, looking from Tyler to Dylan and back again.

For Kristy's sake, and even more for Bonnie's, Tyler worked up what he hoped was a reassuring smile, not a death grimace. "Thanks for the loan of your car, Kristy," he said. "I do appreciate it."

Dylan lingered near the open door, ready to leave, now that he'd delivered the rig and thus done his good deed for the day. "If you change your mind about supper, you know where we'll be," he told Tyler, and then he went out.

Kristy gave Tyler another puzzled look, then followed with Bonnie.

Tyler waited until they'd all left in Dylan's truck before grabbing up Kristy's keys. "Come on, boy," he said to Kit Carson. "Let's go find out if I'm somebody's dear old dad."

· · ·

TESS FELL INTO THE BED in Lily's old room, the stuffed animals Tyler had won at the carnival so long ago tucked in all around her.

"Can we stay here, Mom?" she asked, when Lily sat down on the edge of the mattress, which was still covered in the ruffly pink-and-white-polka-dot spread she'd received on her eighth birthday. "In Stillwater Springs, I mean, with Grampa?"

Lily stroked a lock of hair, still moist from an after-supper bath, back from her daughter's forehead. Kissed the place she'd bared. "We have a condo in Chicago," she said. "And your grandmother Kenyon would miss you something fierce if we moved away."

"She could visit me here," Tess said, with an expression of resigned hope shining in her eyes.

The thought of Eloise Kenyon roughing it in a cow-town like Stillwater Springs brought a wistful smile to Lily's face—the woman probably didn't own a pair of jeans, let alone the boots or sneakers most people wore. As far as her mother-in-law was concerned, the place might as well have been in a parallel dimension.

"Why do you want to stay in Montana, sweetheart?" Lily asked. "You have so many friends back home—"

"It doesn't feel lonely here," Tess told her. She had a way of making statements like that, of pulling the figurative rug out from under Lily's feet with no warning at all. "I like this house. It feels like it's hugging me. And Grampa said I could help him take care of all the animals, when he goes back to work."

Silently, Lily counted to ten. Of *course* Hal was behind this whole idea of her and Tess moving back to the old hometown—now that he'd come face-to-face with the grim reaper, he was suddenly a family man. Once, he'd taken her, Lily, on his rounds, just as he'd promised to take Tess. Then one day he'd gotten tired of having a daughter, apparently, and written her off, just like that.

By *God,* he wasn't going to do that to Tess. He wasn't going to win the child's love and trust and then shut her out of his life.

"You were lonely in Chicago?" Lily asked help-lessly, because she'd need some time to think before she addressed the other issue. How on earth was she going to warn Tess, a six-year-old child, not to get too attached to her own grandfather? Especially when she so obviously needed a father-figure of some sort?

"It always seemed like Daddy should have been there," Tess said sagely, with a little shrug. "And I could make new friends right here. Kristy *said* there were kids around for me to play with, and I really liked story hour, too."

Lily tried, but tears came to her eyes anyway, and Tess saw them.

She sat up, threw her little arms around Lily's

61

neck and hugged her tightly. Another child might have clung; Tess was *giving* comfort, not taking it.

Now, it was Lily who did the clinging.

"Don't cry, Mom," Tess pleaded, her breath warm against Lily's cheek. "Please don't cry."

Lily sniffled bravely. "I'm sorry," she said. "*I'm* supposed to be the strong one."

Tess settled back on her pillows—the very pillows where Lily had dreamed so many Tyler-dreams—and regarded her mother with that singularly serious, too-adult expression that troubled Lily so much.

"Nobody's strong all the time, Mom," Tess said. There she was again—the Wise Woman, posing as a child. "You can be happy if you'll just let yourself. That's what Grampa said, while you were taking your nap and we were getting supper ready."

Privately, Lily seethed. *Thank you, Parent of the Year,* she told her feckless father silently. "I *am* happy, honey. I've got you, after all. What more could I want?" She fussed with the covers a little, looked around at all the mementos of her childhood, thinking, to distract herself, that the room could use updating. New curtains, fresh wallpaper, a few framed watercolors instead of all those dog-eared rock-star posters from her teens . . .

"You could want a husband," Tess suggested, in answer to Lily's question, which had been rhetorical. Not that a six-year-old—even one as precocious as Tess—could be expected to understand rhetoric. "And more kids."

"I have a job in Chicago, remember?" Lily pointed out. "One I happen to love. And I don't think I want a husband, if it's all the same to you."

Skepticism skewed Tess's freckled face, wrinkling her nose and etching lines into her forehead. "You don't love that job, Mom," she argued. "You're always saying you'd rather have your own company, so you could do things your way and set your own hours. And anyhow, we don't need money, do we? Nana Kenyon says you have plenty, thanks to Daddy's trust fund and the insurance payment."

Behind her motherly smile, Lily added Eloise Kenyon to the mental hit-list headed up by Hal Ryder. Why would Burke's mother mention matters like trust funds and insurance settlements to a child, unless she'd wanted the remark to get back to Lily? *Using* Tess as a go-between was inexcusable, downright passive-aggressive.

As for Burke, whatever his other failings, he *had* kept his will up to date. He'd looked out for his daughter and, to some extent, his wife.

The trust fund was safely tucked away for Tess, and Lily had used the insurance money to pay off Burke's many credit card debts and the mortgage on the condo. Her job, though it sometimes made her want to tear out her hair from sheer frustration, paid well, and she and Tess lived simply, anyway.

Lily was nothing if not sensible.

Except when it came to Tyler Creed, of course.

Why had she agreed to have dinner with him, when she knew no other man on earth, not even her own father, had the power to hurt her the way Tyler could?

Was pain getting to be a way of life with her? Had she started to *like* it?

"We're both tired," she said at last. "Let's talk about this another time."

She saw the protest brewing in Tess's eyes. *You always say that . . . and later never comes.*

Lily laid an index finger to her daughter's lips, to forestall the inevitable challenge.

"We'll talk about it tomorrow," she said. "I promise."

Mollified, though barely so, Tess sighed a little-girl sigh. Relaxed visibly.

Lily kissed her again. "Want me to leave the light on for a while?" she asked. Tess had never been afraid of the dark, but the house was strange to her, after all, however much she claimed to love it, and she'd had a very big day.

"I'm not *scared,* Mom," Tess said. "I *told* you, this is a hugging house."

A hugging house.

For a moment, Lily yearned for the innocence of youth, ached to feel the way Tess did about the old place. As a child, she had—she'd loved living there. Until her parents had torn the concept of home into two jagged pieces, each taking half and leaving her scrambling in midair.

Lily simply nodded, not trusting herself to speak without crying again, and stood. She switched off the bedside lamp, with its time-yellowed, frilly shade, and headed for the hallway.

"You can leave the door open, though," Tess volunteered gamely, from the darkness.

Lily smiled, knowing she was visible to her daughter in the light from the hall. "Good night, pumpkin."

"Night," Tess murmured, in a snuggling-in voice.

A few moments later, Lily joined her father in the living room at the front of the house. He was seated at his ancient rolltop desk, going over what appeared to be a stack of bills.

Lily, who had a bone to pick with him, swallowed. Was her dad all right for money? He ran a small-town veterinary practice, after all, and if she remembered correctly, collecting his fees wasn't a high priority with him. Especially if his clients happened to be hard up.

Times being what they were, folks were scrambling just to hold on.

"I could help," she heard herself say. "If you're a little behind or something—"

Hal smiled and again, something moved in his eyes. Something that seemed to hurt him. "I appreciate the offer," he said, his voice sounding a little hoarse. "But I'm solvent, Lily. No need for you to fret."

Lily nodded, embarrassed now. Kept her face averted as she sat down in an overstuffed armchair that was probably older than she was. "Tess is talking about staying in Stillwater Springs for good," she ventured. "Is that your doing?"

Hal chuckled, sounding wistful. "It's still a fine place to raise a child," he said. "Safe to trick-or-treat at Halloween. You can say 'Merry Christmas' to folks without somebody getting in your face for being politically incorrect, and every Fourth of July, there's a big picnic and fireworks in the park."

Lily's face heated. "So is Chicago," she said, unable to meet her father's gaze, even then. "A good place to bring up a child, I mean."

Hal blew out a breath. "*You* were happy here," he reminded her.

"Yes," she retorted stiffly. "Until I suddenly became persona non grata."

The moment the words were out of her mouth, Lily regretted them. Truthful or not, Hal was recovering from a major heart attack. This was no time for digging up and rattling old bones.

Hal didn't speak for a long time. When he did, his words made Lily's throat tighten painfully. "You were *never* a 'persona non grata,' Lily," he insisted, his tone ragged and weary. "Your mother and I loved you very much. We just didn't love each other anymore, and you took a lot of the fallout. For that, I am truly sorry."

She wanted to ask him right then why he'd shut her out all of a sudden, soon after her breakup with Tyler, but she wasn't sure she was strong enough to hear the answer.

"I guess divorce is never easy on anybody," she said, conceding the obvious. "Adults *or* children."

With a sigh that snagged at Lily's heart, her father hoisted himself up from the desk chair, crossed the room and sat down in the second armchair, facing her. "Tell me about *your* divorce, Lily," he said. "How long were you unhappy with Burke before you finally decided to cut your losses and run?"

Lily lowered her head. "Too long," she whispered.

"He cheated, didn't he? Ran around with other women?"

She swallowed hard, nodded. Looked her father straight in the eye. "Mom claims *you* were 'running around with other women' when she left you. Is that true, Da—Hal?"

Hal's smile was rueful. "It wouldn't throw the earth off its axis, Lily," he said gently, "if you called me 'Dad' again." He shifted in his chair, took a pipe from the holder on the table beside him, and at Lily's fierce expression, put it back. "To answer your question, I was faithful to your mother, at least in the literal sense of the word."

"What does *that* mean?"

"That we were too different from each other, Lucy and me," Hal said slowly. "She liked bright lights and big cities, and I liked being a country veterinarian. She wanted to drive a fancy car, and I refused, even though we could have afforded one, because I didn't like the statement it would have made among people who struggle just to keep food on the table. When it got down to the brass tacks, Lily, the only thing your mother and I had in common was you."

Oh, right, Lily wanted to say, but she bit the words back.

Hal chuckled, but he sounded so tired. It was time he took his medicine and went to bed. Lily started to get up, fetch the bag full of pill bottles the doctor had sent home with them.

"Sit down, Lily," her dad said firmly.

Lily dropped back into her chair.

"I still want to know about Burke. Not the public version. Scion of a great New England family, and all that tripe. What was he really like?"

"Shallow," Lily said, after some thought. "Funny. Smart. Self-assured."

"And very popular with other women?" Hal put the question gently, but at the same time there was no doubt that he expected an answer and wouldn't let her off the hook until she replied honestly. Clearly, he wasn't going to be thrown off the trail.

"Very," Lily agreed. "There were a lot of little

signs, looking back on it—the usual hang-ups on the phone, odd charges on his credit card statements, condoms in his suitcase when we never used them, things like that. I pretended not to notice—I guess I couldn't face the truth about us. But it was almost as though Burke *wanted* me to know he was running around. I'd call his room when he was out of town on a flight, and a woman would answer. He'd say the whole crew was in his room, that they were celebrating somebody's birthday, or anniversary, or retirement. . . ." She stopped, blushed, shook her head at her own naiveté. "Until he crashed his plane, I thought he was trying to maneuver me into making the first move, so he wouldn't have to be the first Kenyon in history to file for divorce. But when I finally did see a lawyer, he—"

"Killed himself," Hal supplied gently.

"Yes."

"You're sure of that? Maybe it was an accident."

"I wish I could believe it was," Lily said, very softly. "There wasn't a note or anything, but he called me a couple of hours before he went up that last time. He was upset, begging for another chance, making all sorts of crazy promises." She stopped, swallowed hard. "He said—he said it wouldn't be right to break up Tess's home—that we should have another child—"

"And?"

"I said I didn't love him anymore. That it was no

use trying, since we'd had counseling after his last affair." Lily bit down so hard on her lower lip that she felt a sting of pain, and half expected to taste blood. She'd wanted more children so badly, but Burke had always refused. One was enough, he'd said. As though Tess were a mortgage with a balloon payment, an *object* of some kind. "What's the old saying? 'Act in haste, repent at leisure'?"

"Even if Burke did crash that plane because you were divorcing him, Lily, it wouldn't be your fault."

"I keep telling myself that," Lily admitted. "But a part of me knows it's a lie." The truth burst out then, all on its own, too big to contain. "I didn't love Burke—I never did. I loved the idea of love, of being someone's wife, someone's mother. Having a home and a family. But deep down, I never cared for Burke the way I should have, and I guess he knew it."

She'd never loved Burke because she'd never stopped loving Tyler, and she was the kind of woman who mated for life.

"You must have had feelings for Burke," her dad reasoned gently. "After all, you married him. You had Tess with him."

"I guess in the beginning, I thought I'd fall in love with him in time. But it didn't happen." A tear slid down Lily's cheek, and she didn't bother to brush it away. "I shouldn't have gone through with the wedding. He might be alive today if I hadn't."

"There's no way of knowing that," Hal told her.

"Let yourself off the hook, Lily, if only because there's no way you can change the past, and because Tess needs a happy mother, one who's looking ahead, not backward."

"I *am* happy," she insisted, for the second time that evening.

Hal's sigh was heavy with bittersweet amusement, and a certain degree of resignation. "No, you're not," he argued. "Your mother was all for the marriage, but I remember looking down into your face, just before I walked you up that church aisle and gave you away, and seeing something in your eyes that made me want to put a stop to the whole shindig, then and there. Tell all those Kenyons and their fancy friends and relations to eat, drink and be merry, but there wouldn't be a ceremony."

Hal Ryder had given his daughter away long before her wedding day, but that was beside the point. Still another old, dusty skeleton that shouldn't be exhumed.

"Why didn't you say anything?" Lily asked softly. "To me, at least?"

Hal sighed again. "Because I didn't have the right. You were a grown woman, with a college education and a good job. And because I'd already interfered in your life once before that." Just when Lily would have asked what he'd meant by that last part, he stood, stretched, yawned. "I'm worn-out, Lily," he confessed. "I need some rest."

"I'll get your pills," Lily said, rising, too.

"Oh, yes," Hal replied, with grim humor. "My pills. Let's not forget those."

In the kitchen, she opened the pharmacy bag, studied the labels on the little brown bottles and carefully counted out the appropriate doses while her father set the coffeepot for morning and locked the back door.

Lily raised an eyebrow at that. "People are locking their doors in Stillwater Springs these days?" she asked.

"I normally don't," Hal admitted. "But I've got you and Tess to think about now. And some things have been happening around here lately—"

He'd just made a speech, in the living room, about what a good place Stillwater Springs was to raise a child—specifically Tess. Knowing he was tired, Lily didn't call him on the contradiction between his words and his actions.

I've got you and Tess to think about now.

Had he convinced himself they would be staying on in Stillwater Springs permanently, after he'd recovered enough to live on his own?

She set the handful of pills on a paper towel, and handed them to him, along with a glass of water. Watched as he forced down his medication.

"Good night, sweetheart," he said, when he'd finished, and set his empty glass in the sink.

When was the last time he'd called her sweetheart?

The night Tyler handed her her heart in fragments, that was when. Had it *really* been that long?

Lily closed her eyes and waited until Hal had left the room. Until she heard his bedroom door close, just down the hall from the kitchen.

And then she cried, for little girls without fathers. And for big ones, too.

CHAPTER FOUR

THE FIFTEEN-YEAR GAP between their ages showed in Doreen's haggard face in ways it hadn't way back when. She looked thin in her casino-waitress uniform, and lines in her forehead were etched deep. She was developing jowls, and her mouth was hard, the lipstick too red and slightly off-center.

Still, her weary eyes softened a little when she recognized Tyler, standing in one of the casino's several restaurants. Davie sat in a booth nearby, nursing a soda and pretending to read one of those glorified comic books that pass as a novel.

He doesn't look much like me, Tyler thought, with distracted regret. But, then, he hadn't looked much like Jake Creed, either. Secretly, he'd fantasized that his mother had been fooling around, conceived him with some lover, but he doubted his own fantasy. Poor Angie didn't seem to have the strength to defy Jake that way. Or maybe she'd just loved her husband too much to cheat.

In the end, that love had destroyed her.

"Tyler," Doreen said, almost breathing the name.

"Doreen," Tyler replied, with a nod. Now that he was face-to-face with the woman who might have borne his child without bothering to let him know, all the things he'd planned to say, all the things he'd rehearsed on the way into town with Kit Carson riding shotgun, deserted him.

"I could take a break in half an hour," she said.

Tyler merely nodded again. He'd left Kit Carson at Cassie's to spare the dog a long wait in the Blazer, so he had time. He could cool his heels awhile.

Doreen hesitated for a few moments, looking from Tyler to Davie and back again. Then she sighed and turned to walk away, take another order for another plate of nachos, another mug of beer.

Everything about her, the way she moved, the way she spoke, said she was miserable. Hated her life, but didn't know how to escape it.

Unlike Angela Creed. *She'd* found a way out, and devil take the grief she'd left behind.

Tyler approached Davie's table.

"Mind if I join you?"

Davie didn't look up. Just shrugged.

The cover of the graphic novel showed a woman being devoured by some hideous beast, and Davie seemed absorbed.

Tyler sat down across from Davie, signaled another waitress, ordered coffee. He liked a beer once in a while, but with Jake Creed for a father and a wild youth not that far behind him, a man tended to moderate his alcohol intake. He wondered briefly if Logan and Dylan took the same care not to overdo the booze.

"Good book?" he asked.

"What do you care?" Davie shot back.

"Do all those hooks and rings hurt?" Tyler persisted, frowning at the eyebrow piercings. The silver ring through Davie's lower lip made him a little queasy, and after some of the bar brawls he'd been in, that was no small matter.

"Hurt when they did it," Davie allowed, sounding defiant and, at the same time, interested. "What are you doing here?"

"I came to talk to your mother," Tyler said.

"About what?"

Tyler wasn't about to bring up the paternity question—not before a word with Doreen, anyway. "Just things. Dylan tells me Sheriff Huntinghorse wanted to send you to a foster home, and you said you'd run off if he did."

There was no humor in the smile Davie gave then, or in his eyes. "Small towns. Word really *does* travel like wildfire."

"Running away would be a bad idea."

"You don't know my mom's boyfriend. The sheriff said he was going to track Roy down and warn him not to hit me anymore." Davie gave a bitter huff of a laugh. "That ought to make things real nice when Mom and I get back to the old trailer after her shift."

Tyler's gut churned just to think of what the boy might be facing, later that night and afterward. And he suddenly knew he couldn't stand it, whether Davie was his or not.

"I've been thinking things over," Tyler said carefully. "Maybe I could use somebody to help out around the cabin."

Davie couldn't hide his interest then, though he tried. He closed the book, set it down with a little thump and frowned at Tyler. "What kind of help?" he asked, almost suspiciously.

This from the kid who'd practically begged to stay.

"You said it yourself, this afternoon. Taking care of Kit Carson, cutting grass, stuff like that."

"That place is small. Where would I sleep?"

"We'd get you a cot and a sleeping bag."

"You don't even have a TV."

Tyler grinned. "You're mighty choosy, all of a sudden, for somebody who wanted to move right in before."

"Would you be a foster parent?" Davie asked, sounding like a lawyer now. "Maybe collect a little check from the county or the state?"

Tyler chuckled, enjoyed a sip of bad casino coffee before answering. "Hell," he said, "no amount of money would be enough to put up with *your* attitude. It's a neighborly offer, that's all. And your mom has to approve, of course."

From the looks of Doreen, she'd been running interference between good ole Roy, the boyfriend, and her son for too long. Letting Davie bunk in at Tyler's for a while would probably be a relief, with all her problems.

"What changed your mind?" Davie asked grudgingly, but with a little less attitude than before. He was afraid to hope—Tyler could see that—and it galled him. Brought back way too many memories.

Life shouldn't be the way it was for Davie, the way it was for a lot of kids.

The way it had been for him.

"I just needed some time to think, that's all," Tyler said. The words felt as lame coming off his tongue as they probably sounded to Davie. "Of course, you screw up and you're out of there."

Davie's eyes widened. They were Doreen's eyes, not Tyler's own, or those of any family member he could recall, but still.

Still.

"You mean it? I could stay at your place?"

"I mean it. Long as you don't cause trouble."

"You'll get a TV?"

Tyler chuckled. "I didn't say that," he pointed out. "But once I see what kind of yard-bird you really are, I might let you use my laptop now and then."

"And all I have to do is take care of the dog and cut some grass?"

"You've seen the grass. It's waist-high. I think there's a lawn under there someplace, but I can't be sure." Tyler paused, considered. "Fact is, I'm thinking of building on to the place." *Had* he been thinking that? Not consciously, but now that the idea had presented itself, most likely prompted by Dylan's mention of razing his old house to put up a new one, and what little he knew about the restorations going on at the main place, under Logan's direction, he kind of cottoned to the prospect. "That would mean some carpentry. Maybe a little plumbing and electrical work, too."

Davie looked worried. Maybe all that hard work would be a deal-breaker. "I don't know anything about construction," he finally said.

"That makes two of us," Tyler said.

Cautious relief replaced the consternation in Davie's face. "I wouldn't mind learning, though. I always thought it would be kind of cool to be able to make bookshelves and stuff like that."

Tyler glanced pointedly at the glorified comic book lying forgotten on the table. "You got a collection of those things?" he asked.

Davie gave a snort of amusement, tinged with bitterness. "No," he said. "I got this one at the library. I mostly go there to use the computers, but Kristy said I ought to give reading a shot, and she never chases me off when I'm just looking for a place to hang out, so I checked this out."

Tyler raised one eyebrow, intrigued. "I suppose

she—Kristy, I mean—suggested something like *White Fang* or *Ivanhoe*," he said.

Davie laughed, and this time it sounded real. Almost normal. "Nope. She chose this one for me herself. Said it would be a good way to get my feet wet, find out how much fun reading can be."

Tyler thought back to Kristy's predecessor, Miss Rooley. She'd been a spinster, tight-mouthed and generally disapproving. She'd allowed him to hide out in the library, too, as a kid, when Jake was having a particularly bad day and Logan and Dylan weren't around to get between him and the old man's fists, but she'd demanded her pound of flesh. He'd been forced to read what Miss Rooley reverently called "The Classics," always capitalizing the term with her tone.

At first, it was agony, slogging through tomes he barely understood. Then, he'd begun to enjoy it, though that was something he'd never wanted anybody to know, particularly his older brothers. Right up there with his secret penchant for Andrea Bocelli's music. He liked the Big Band stuff, too—Glenn Miller, Tommy Dorsey, that crowd.

As secrets went, these were pretty tame, but they were secrets just the same. And they would be harder to hide, with a kid living under the same roof.

"You like Kristy?" Tyler asked, mainly to keep the conversation going.

"She's all right," Davie allowed. "I'm supposed to call her 'Mrs. Creed' at the library."

"Yeah," Tyler said.

Mrs. Creed. There were two of them now, counting Logan's bride.

It just went to show that those who didn't learn from history really were condemned to repeat it.

Kristy had lived outside of Stillwater Springs all her life; she knew what it meant to marry a hell-raiser, which left her with no excuse for taking the risk. Briana, on the other hand, was an innocent victim, a stranger.

Had anybody warned her that the Creeds were notoriously bad at marriage? Showed her the three graves in the old cemetery out beyond the orchard, the final resting places of the *last* generation of Creed wives—all of them dead long before their time?

Watching Davie, Tyler thought the boy studied his face a little too intently, seeing too much. He looked as though he wanted to ask a question, but he gulped it back when they got unexpected company.

A big man loomed over the table, beer-belly straining at his wife-beater shirt. His arms were tattooed from fingertips to shoulder, he needed a shave and the billed cap pulled low over his face looked as though it had been run over by a semi-truck with a serious oil leak.

Davie seemed to shrink in on himself, like he was trying to disappear.

Roy's presence had exactly the opposite effect on Tyler.

He slid out of the booth and stood.

Doreen had always liked tattoos. Maybe that explained why she'd taken up with three hundred pounds of ugly, though some things went beyond reasonable explanation, and this creep was one of them.

Roy's mean little pig eyes widened a little. Evidently, he'd been so focused on Davie, he hadn't noticed that the boy wasn't alone.

Now, he looked Tyler over with belligerent caution.

"Who are you?"

"His name's Tyler Creed, Roy," Davie piped up, obviously terrified. "We were just talking. He wasn't doing any harm—"

Tyler put out one hand to silence the boy.

Roy, being a head shorter but bulky, looked up into Tyler's face.

"A Creed, huh?" he said. "Know all about *that* outfit."

Tyler folded his arms. Waited.

Roy pulled in his horns a little. "Look," he said. "I just came to take the boy home. There's no need for any trouble."

"He's not going anywhere," Tyler answered. "Not at the moment, anyhow."

Roy clearly didn't appreciate being thwarted; like all bullies, he was used to getting his way by acting tough. The trouble with acting tough was, as Jake had often said, the inevitability of running into somebody just a little tougher.

And that could make all the difference.

"I said I didn't want any trouble," Roy reiterated mildly. "I just want to take the boy home, where he belongs."

"We're still figuring out where he belongs," Tyler said, just as mildly but with an undercurrent of Creed steel. "Right now, all I'm sure of is, he's staying right here, and you're not going to lay a hand on him."

A dull crimson flush throbbed in what passed for Roy's neck, though his head seemed to sit pretty much square with his shoulders. He tightened one grubby fist, too, wanting to hit somebody.

"You lookin' for a fight, cowboy?" he asked Tyler.

"Nope," Tyler said. "But I won't run from one if the opportunity happens to present itself."

The flush spread into Roy's hound-dog face.

Evidently, Tyler reflected, Doreen had given up on teaching men how to treat a woman. This guy had no clue how to treat *anybody*.

Roy rubbed his beard-stubbled chin, narrowing his eyes thoughtfully. Thought, Tyler figured, was probably painful for him, and thus avoided except in the most dire circumstances.

"You talked to Jim Huntinghorse," Roy speculated peevishly. He glanced down at Davie, his expression so poisonous that the very atmosphere seemed polluted by it. "The kid lies. I never done nothin' to him he didn't deserve."

Out of the corner of his eye, Tyler spotted Doreen, peering around one of the slot machines edging the restaurant. On the one hand, he felt sorry for her. On the other, he was furious that she wouldn't step up and protect her own child. She'd probably never had two nickels to rub together, but she'd had spirit once, she'd lived by her own rules, and she hadn't just survived, she'd *thrived*. She'd had tattoos, for God's sake, in an era when women simply didn't do things like that. She'd traveled with biker gangs and rock bands. She'd taught him to use his fingers and his tongue in ways that bordered on sacred knowledge that had stood him in good stead ever since.

What the *hell* had happened to her?

The same thing that had happened to his mother, he supposed, in the next moment. Life had simply beaten her down. She'd taken one too many hard knocks, one too many disappointments.

Roy must have seemed like the last train out of town.

Damned if *that* wasn't depressing.

"Come on," Roy barked, gesturing to Davie.

Davie started to get out of the booth. Then, at a glance from Tyler, he stayed where he was.

"He's not going anyplace," Tyler said.

"I ought to knock your teeth down your throat,"

Roy replied. It wasn't clear whether he was addressing Tyler or Davie.

"You're welcome to try," Tyler told him cordially. "You ever fight a *man,* Roy? Or just kids and women?"

Roy looked apoplectic. "You ain't heard the last of me," he said.

"Not only tough," Tyler observed, "but original, too. What's next? 'This town ain't big enough for both of us'?"

Davie ducked his head at that, like he was expecting a blow.

And that made Tyler want to tear Roy's head off, right there in the restaurant. He'd end up as an overnight guest of the sheriff's if he did, a prospect he didn't relish after the last experience five years before, but the temptation was fierce just the same.

Roy grunted, shook his head once, like a man plagued by a swarm of flies, and then turned and lumbered out.

"He'll get you, Tyler," Davie said pragmatically. "He'll get me, too. He's like that."

"I know what he's like," Tyler said, watching Roy disappear.

When he was gone, Doreen came out of hiding. She looked sheepish and scared as hell. Davie didn't have to go home—Tyler would hand-deliver the kid to the child-protection people before he'd see that happen—but *she* did.

"You go back and wait in the employees'

lounge," she told Davie, showing a faint semblance of the old Doreen, the one who'd lived wild and free. "Roy won't be able to get at you there."

Davie hesitated, nodded and left the table, then the restaurant.

Tyler gestured for Doreen to sit down. Both of them could have wished for a more private place to hold the forthcoming conversation, but it wasn't to be, and Tyler, for one, was resigned to that.

Doreen slid into the booth, hunching in the same way Davie had.

Tyler sat down across from her. Drew a deep breath.

"Things are pretty bad, I guess," he said, when Doreen didn't speak.

She nodded. "Worse than bad."

"Is he mine?" The words were out before Tyler had a chance to think them over. Not that thinking would have changed anything, but he might have been more diplomatic.

For a few moments, Doreen pretended not to understand. Tyler simply stared her down.

"No," she finally said. "Davie isn't yours. I wish he was, though. God, how I wish he was."

Tyler felt a combination of relief and disappointment, and he still wasn't fully convinced that Doreen was telling the truth. "How old is Davie?" he asked quietly.

"Thirteen," Doreen admitted, after some lip-biting and some hand-wringing.

"The math works," Tyler said.

Doreen gave a rueful little laugh. Raised and lowered her stooped shoulders. "Yeah," she said. "For a lot of guys, Ty. Not just you. Davie belongs to a trucker who stopped by Skivvie's one summer night, crying in his beer because his wife didn't understand him. I cheered him up. And Davie looks just like him."

"Okay," Tyler said. "So why do you let the boyfriend bounce Davie off walls?"

Tears filled Doreen's eyes. "I've been fighting things all my life," she said. "One day, I just ran out of fight."

"Tough break for Davie," Tyler said evenly.

"You think I don't hate myself for that? For all of it?" Doreen straightened her spine a little—though not enough, unfortunately. "I never expected to end up like this. I could have had an abortion—Davie's father offered to pay for one—but I had this crazy idea that I'd find a good man someday. Davie and I and the prince." She laughed again. "What a fairy tale."

"Let me take Davie home with me. Just for a while. Until you can get things under control."

Doreen stared at him, clearly amazed. "Why? Why would you do that?"

"Because I was a kid once, with a crazy father," Tyler said, as surprised to say what he did as Doreen probably was to hear him admit it. He'd been in denial about Jake Creed all his life, even

86

written songs about him, for Christ's sake. "What you're doing now isn't working, Doreen. Time to try something different."

"You don't understand," Doreen whispered, in a teary rush of words and breath. "Davie's a handful. He has problems, Tyler. And Roy—well, you don't know what Roy's like. He'll lay for you. He'll never forget the run-in you and him had tonight. If he has to wait the rest of his life, he'll find a way to pay you back, and when he does, it won't be pretty."

"I can handle Roy," Tyler said. "Seems to me, the more immediate concern is what he might do to you, or to Davie. Let me drive you someplace, Doreen. Right now, tonight. There are shelters, or you could stay at Cassie's place—"

Doreen's face turned to stone. "I know what those 'shelters' are like. My mother and I were in and out of them when I was a little girl. Church women, looking down their noses at us. Secondhand clothes. It was like being in prison, and all it did was make my dad even meaner, once he caught up with us. And he *always* caught up with us."

"That was then, Doreen, and this is now."

"Take Davie home with you," Doreen said, stiff now, and flushed with shame and fury and frustration and God only knew what else. "You'll want to give him back soon enough."

"Maybe," Tyler agreed. But he was remembering

87

all those times when Cassie had stood toe-to-toe with Jake Creed and refused to let him drag his youngest son home by the hair. What would have happened to him if it hadn't been for Cassie and, to a lesser degree, for Logan and Dylan?

Payback time.

There was a kid in trouble, and he couldn't ignore that.

Doreen looked at her watch. A little of her favorite tattoo showed on her upper arm—a phoenix, rising majestically from the ashes. "Do what you want," she said. "Play hero. You'll be sorry, Tyler. *You will be sorry.* And that's the last warning you're going to get from me."

Tyler reached for a napkin, gestured for Doreen to hand over the pen she used for taking down food and drink orders. Scrawled his cell number on it.

"Call if you need help," he said.

Doreen eyed the number with contempt, but she took it in the end. Stuffed it into her apron pocket in a wad.

Tyler watched her go. Settled up for the coffee. Made his way through the casino to the employees' lounge. He'd gone to high school with the security guard posted in the hallway, and hung out with Jim Huntinghorse when he was still man-aging the place, so nobody got in his way.

Davie sat hunkered down in a chair in the corner, alone in the room, clutching the library book in both hands.

"Time to ride," Tyler said.

"What if he's out there?" Davie asked. "What if Roy's out there?"

"I couldn't get that lucky," Tyler told him, with a grin.

But Roy wasn't waiting in the parking lot. Davie was surprised; Tyler wasn't. Roy *would* strike back, but not when there was a chance of getting his ass kicked in a public parking lot. He was the come-from-behind type. He'd use a tire iron, or maybe even a gun.

Serious business. But Tyler had had a lot of practice at watching his back. A lifetime of it, in fact.

And being a Creed, he didn't have sense enough to be scared.

So he and Davie made a quick stop at Wal-Mart, for a sleeping bag and a cot, the usual personal grooming necessities and a change of clothes for Davie.

"You don't actually expect me to wear these, do you?" Davie protested, once they were back in Kristy's Blazer, headed for Cassie's place to pick up the dog. He was holding up the pair of jeans Tyler had chosen for him. "They are definitely not cool."

"Being cool is the least of your problems," Tyler pointed out. "You'll wear them."

Kit Carson greeted them at the door when they got to Cassie's, probably relieved to learn that he hadn't been dumped there for the duration. Not that Cassie wouldn't have been good to him—she was a little rough around the edges, Cassie was, but she had a gentle soul, a heart for lost dogs. And lost boys.

"Picking up strays now?" she asked, under the bug-flecked cone of light on her porch, watching as Davie hoisted Kit Carson into the back of the borrowed Blazer.

Tyler grinned. "Just carrying on the tradition," he said.

Stillwater Springs was a small town. Cassie, having lived there since before the Battle of the Little Big Horn, had to know Davie, and his mother, too. Maybe she even remembered the summer Tyler had spent in Doreen's bed, in the little room above Skivvie's Tavern, learning to be a man.

"Is he yours?" she asked, proving Tyler's theory.

"Could be," Tyler answered. "His mother denies it, but she could have lots of reasons for doing that."

"Like what?" Cassie countered reasonably.

"Like not wanting me to have a claim on him, back when he was little and she could still handle him," Tyler said. "Doreen was always independent to a fault. Maybe there's still a little of that left in her, even now."

"This is going to complicate your life," Cassie predicted, sounding resigned.

"Maybe my life has gotten too simple," Tyler replied.

"Spoken like a true Creed," Cassie retorted, but she was smiling—with her mouth, anyway. Her dark eyes were serious. "Folks have long memories, Tyler. Everybody—including Lily Ryder—is going to recall what happened between you and Doreen, and put two and two together."

Tyler sighed. He hadn't let on to anybody that Lily was on his mind, but Cassie knew him too well to be fooled by lies of omission. "Is she involved with anybody? Remarried maybe?" he asked, his voice sounding husky. He wouldn't have put that particular question to anyone else on earth, not even Lily. His pride wouldn't have allowed that. But Cassie, a wise middle-aged Native American with a teepee in her yard, was like a grandmother to him.

"No," Cassie said. And she put a hand on his arm, a signal that she was about to say something he wouldn't want to hear. "Her husband was a pilot. He killed himself two years ago."

Suicide.

Tyler closed his eyes, thrust right back into the bad old days as surely and suddenly as if he'd stumbled into a time warp. He might have been a kid again, not a man standing on Cassie's front porch, but a boy hiding on the other side of the kitchen door, out at the home place, listening as Sheriff Floyd Book, Jim Huntinghorse's legendary predecessor, broke the news to Jake.

Angie's dead. I'm so sorry. We found her at the

91

Skylight Motel, on the old state highway. It was an overdose, Jake. . . .

Tyler had heard a wail, primitive and piercing, and thought it was Jake.

He'd only realized the sound was coming from his own throat when Dylan and Logan each took one of his arms and hauled him up off his knees, braced him between them.

Cassie squeezed his arm, hard, brought him back from the abyss, the place where the questions never stopped.

All of them started with the same word.

Why?

"What could be that bad?" he rasped. "A wife like Lily. A little girl like Tess. What would make a man throw them away?"

"You're trying to understand again," Cassie pointed out gently. "And there *is* no understanding, Tyler. People are fragile. They can break. It's as simple—and as complicated—as that."

Don't try to understand.

How many times had he heard that advice, from how many people? Dylan, certainly. Logan, too. Even his late wife, Shawna, when she'd been trying to pull him out of some slump. And it wasn't the first time Cassie had offered it, either.

The problem was, he couldn't help going over the old ground, looking for clues. Analyzing. His mother's suicide was the reason for so many things that had happened—and not happened—in his life.

It drove him half-crazy sometimes, the need to know why she'd done it. Why she hadn't been able to hold on, leave Jake, make a new start somewhere else.

"You'll be seeing Lily, I suppose?" Cassie ventured.

"We're having dinner tomorrow night," Tyler answered, braced for more advice.

Leave it alone, Cassie had told him, after the breakup that summer, when he'd wanted to go back to Lily, beg her to forgive him for sleeping with Doreen, give him another chance.

Forget the girl, Jake had counseled. *She's too good for you, anyway.*

Are you nuts? Logan had demanded, after bouncing him off the back wall of the barn a couple of times. *Rolling in the hay with a waitress twice your age when Lily's crazy about you?*

Sometimes, the voices from the past crowded in like that, made Tyler want to put his hands over his ears. Not that that would have shut them out.

What had happened, had happened.

What was done, was done.

So why couldn't he just let his poor mother rest in peace?

Why couldn't he forgive her for breaking down that final time?

The realization hit him hard.

That was why he'd come home to Stillwater Springs, left the rodeo and the big-money stunt work and photo shoots behind, sold his big, empty house in L.A. and traded his Escalade for a junker that wouldn't even run.

He'd come back to take on all the old ghosts, one by one or in a snarling pack, however they came at him. Win or lose, the fight was on.

Would he still be standing when it was all over? There was only one way to find out.

And he was through running away.

CHAPTER FIVE

AFTER SERVING HER FATHER and daughter a healthy breakfast—grapefruit, whole-wheat toast and scrambled egg whites—Lily sneaked into her dad's study to pick up the phone.

She'd call Tyler—she'd decided that while tossing and turning the night before. Tell him she couldn't go out to dinner with him after all. Backpedal like crazy, tell an outright lie if she had to, say *anything* to get out of that hastily made date.

Except that she didn't have his number.

She could get it from Kristy, of course. Call her or just walk over to the library and ask. Since Tyler was Kristy's brother-in-law now, she'd surely know how to reach him.

Her eyes fell on her dad's tattered address book. Hal had always disapproved of Tyler Creed, but now, after picking Ty up alongside the road the day before, it seemed the man was her dad's new best friend. Maybe the number was right there, within easy reach.

It would be so much easier if she didn't have to contact Kristy, either in person or over the telephone.

Lily had flipped to the *C*s—the book was jammed with tattered sticky notes, names and numbers scrawled helter-skelter on each one, all of them stuck in at odd and dizzying angles—and was scanning for Tyler's contact information, when Hal walked in.

"Need something?" he asked, with a slight smile.

Lily swallowed hard. "Tyler's number," she said. There, it was out there. Let him make of it what he would.

"Don't have it," Hal said, still watching her, but more closely now. "By the way, Tess and I have taken a vote. It's unanimous. Breakfast sucked."

Lily closed the bulging address book, set it aside. Straightened her spine. "I suppose you would have preferred bacon and eggs?" she asked, sounding a little terse because she was embarrassed that he'd caught her going through his address book *and* gotten her to admit that she'd intended to call Tyler, of all people.

"*Preferred* is not the word," Hal said, grinning. "More like *adored*. Why do you want to call Tyler—as if I didn't know?"

Lily's face heated. He didn't know. Hal probably

thought she was jonesing to hear Tyler's voice or something, like a besotted schoolgirl. Or hot to trot. "He asked me out to dinner," she reminded him. "And I've decided not to go."

Hal frowned. "Why?"

Lily countered with a question of her own. A stall tactic, for sure, and one that wouldn't work for very long, if at all. "Weren't you the one who always warned me that the Creeds were bad news, and taking up with them would lead to certain doom and destruction?"

"Lily, this is dinner, not an orgy."

Lily bit back an instinctive response—being one-on-one with Tyler Creed, even in a public place, was the sexual equivalent of spontaneous combustion. The man could probably bring her to orgasm without even touching her—and she'd be a fool to let herself in for that.

Or a fool *not* to.

"My," she said instead, still hedging, "how things have changed."

"I was wrong about Tyler," Hal said, catching her completely off-guard. He'd never been quick to admit to a mistake but, then, neither had she, to be fair about it. "Wrong about a lot of things. Go out with him, Lily. Wear a pretty dress and some perfume and enjoy the evening."

Enjoy the evening. People from her father's generation were so innocent, so naive.

Or were they?

"What about Tess?" she asked.

"She'll be just fine here with me. She's a smart kid. If I go into cardiac arrest, she'll call 911."

"What's cardiac arrest?" Tess asked, appearing in the doorway of the study. She was wearing expensive pink shorts, a flowered sun-top and flip-flops, all gifts acquired on her last visit to Nantucket, with Eloise. A little frown creased the space between her eyebrows. "Is somebody going to put Grampa in jail?"

Lily smiled, in spite of herself. "Nobody's going to put your grandfather in jail," she said, to reassure the child. It was so easy to forget how literal children were. "And you look very pretty today, by the way. Do you have plans?"

"There's a kid playing in the backyard next door," Tess answered, letting the subjects of incarceration and emergency medical intervention lapse, for the moment at least. "I think it's a boy, but I'm going to introduce myself anyhow."

"A nice couple lives there now," Hal put in, at Lily's look of concern. In Chicago, she didn't know a single one of her neighbors, nor did Tess. "They bought the place after the Hendersons retired and moved to Florida." He smiled down at Tess. "The child in question," he added, "is a girl, and her name is Eleanor. She's seven years old, and visiting her aunt and uncle for the summer."

"Is she nice?" Tess asked seriously.

"Well," Hal responded, just as seriously, "she's

never soaped my windows or set fire to the shrubbery or let the air out of my tires. Beyond that, I couldn't tell you. Guess you'll just have to march on over there and find out for yourself."

"Guess so," Tess said, with one of those sudden, dazzling smiles of hers. Lily realized, with some chagrin, that she hadn't seen her daughter light up like that since before Burke's death. "Can I have money for the ice-cream truck? I heard the bell a few minutes ago—it's about three streets over, I think, and headed our way."

"No," Lily said.

"Yes," Hal answered, at exactly the same moment, already reaching into his pocket for the requested loot. His eyes, less weary than the day before, lingered on Lily's face even as he handed Tess a few small bills. "It's summer," he told his daughter quietly. "Tess is six, pretty in pink and hoping to make a friend. Give her a break, Lily."

A speech about processed food and preservatives and questionable hygiene conditions in ice-cream trucks and packaging plants rose into Lily's throat, but she held it back. Her father was right. Surely one cone dipped in chocolate wouldn't compromise the child's health and well-being.

"Okay," Lily agreed, with a smile.

Both Tess and Hal looked so surprised at her acquiescence that Lily wondered what they took her for. Some kind of natural-food fanatic, obviously.

"Have fun," she told Tess. "And don't go any farther than the neighbor's yard or the front sidewalk."

Tess beamed, thanked her grandfather for the cash and fled.

"I'll need a dress," Lily said, thinking aloud. Since she'd come back to Montana to look after her sick father, she hadn't brought any special clothes along—just jeans, T-shirts, shorts and a few nightgowns.

She blushed, realizing how eager she must have sounded. How excited. Cinderella, going to the ball.

"You look good in red," Hal told her, pleased. "There's a little boutique downtown—it caters mostly to tourists, but you ought to be able to find something pretty there."

Lily's native good sense returned. Some of it, anyway. "I'm not leaving you alone. You just got out of the hospital."

"I'm in no danger of keeling over, Lily," Hal said. "In fact, I could use a little solitude, if you want the truth. I'm used to living alone." He paused, looked comically inspired. "And think of the other possibilities. You could pick up something ghastly for lunch. Sprouts, maybe. Or something made of congealed soybeans."

Lily laughed. And it felt strange and new and good—a forgotten skill, just rediscovered.

"I won't be gone long," she warned, "so don't be

seeing any four-legged patients or digging through the freezer for hot dogs or toaster waffles while I'm out. For all you know, one of those magnets on your fridge is really a nanny-cam in disguise."

"I wouldn't put it past you," Hal joked.

Lily went to him, on impulse, and kissed his craggy cheek.

Five minutes later, after skimming a glaze of lip gloss over her mouth and combing her hair, Lily was in her rental car, headed for Main Street.

The boutique Hal had told her about was tiny, and pitiful by Chicago standards, but she found a red sundress with white polka dots in her size, tried it on and liked what she saw in the dressing room mirror. She bought the dress, a lacy little over-sweater of gossamer white lace and a pair of strappy sandals to complete the outfit.

The next stop was the grocery section at Wal-Mart, since the mom-and-pop market had gone out of business years before, and there was no tofu to be found. She'd planned to prove to Hal that tofu could be delicious, but evidently, there wasn't a big market for it in Stillwater Springs, Montana.

So she selected the ingredients for a seafood salad instead, all fresh and touted as organic, added a package of chicken breasts for Tess and Hal's supper, and was rounding a corner, intent on getting to the checkout lines ahead of three women with copious purchases, when she nearly crashed her cart into Tyler's.

Since when did he shop at Wal-Mart in the middle of the morning?

Damn, he looked good though, even at that hour. He wore a white T-shirt and battered jeans, and a lock of his raven-dark hair tumbled, bad-boy style, over his forehead.

His gaze drifted lazily over Lily, and her toes curled inside her sneakers. She even caught herself wishing she'd worn something sexier than jeans and a tank top.

Reality doused her like so much cold water, flung from a bucket.

In a matter of hours, she was going to be alone with this man.

In grave danger of spontaneous combustion—if it didn't happen right there in Wal-Mart, in front of God and everybody.

Heat climbed Lily's neck, pulsed in her cheeks.

She'd tried so hard to make things work with Burke, especially in bed. How many times, though, had she reached the pinnacle by imagining that Tyler Creed, not her husband, was the one fondling her, suckling her breasts, driving deep inside her? Had she cried out *his* name, at the height of her release, instead of Burke's?

Probably.

The thought filled her with shame—and a dense, sultry kind of heat.

She'd never made love with Tyler, though they'd certainly engaged in some heavy petting while they were dating. For all she knew, he was a dud in bed. And why was she even debating such a question, anyway?

"How's your dad?" Tyler asked.

Lily bit her lower lip. Not such a tough thing to answer. It should be easy—as soon as she stopped fighting back the climax already building deep in her center.

"He's—fine. Stubborn. I think he'll be okay."

"Good," Tyler said.

Lily glanced at the contents of his cart. Power tools. Sheets and blankets. Sugary cereal and a big jug of whole milk. A small-screen TV.

Quite a combination.

He grinned, slow-heat style, watching her. Was he imagining her naked?

No, she was the one whose imagination was running wild.

Get a grip, she told herself.

He touched her hand, where she held on to the shopping-cart handle with a death grip. It was a simple, innocent brush of his fingertips, nothing more.

And Lily went over the top.

Smiled determinedly, broke out in a sweat. That special little muscle deep inside her flexed violently, then flexed again. It was all she could do not to groan aloud with the unexpected and purely inappropriate pleasure of it.

She'd just come in Wal-Mart, *for God's sake.*

Fully dressed. In the bright light of day.

Tyler didn't know, did he? He couldn't have guessed.

"The air-conditioning must be on the blink in here," he said, but there was a look in his eyes that said he knew full well what had just happened, or at least suspected. That he'd set the whole thing in motion on purpose.

But that was impossible, of course.

Even for a Creed.

Wasn't it?

"About tonight," she choked out, when the aftershocks began to subside. She still sounded too breathless. "I really shouldn't—"

"No getting out of it now," Tyler broke in easily. "Your dad will be okay, and so will Tess, and it's only dinner, Lily."

It's only dinner. Where had she heard *that* before?

And if Tyler could bring her to climax with a leisurely once-over and a touch of his hand, what would happen if he got her alone? What would happen in the restaurant?

Lily didn't want to find out.

Much.

Desperately, she began making excuses to herself. She simply didn't have random orgasms in public places. No, it was just that she'd gone without sex for so long, that was all, and then she'd let her thoughts head down the wrong road.

No, it would probably never happen again.

Damn it.

Just as Lily was about to press on to the nearest checkout line, neatly skirting any further conversation about their date that night, a barely adolescent boy appeared from two aisles over, sporting a spider tattoo on his neck and various piercings.

"I found the hammer," he told Tyler, holding the tool up as evidence.

Lily felt an odd little quiver of dread in the pit of her stomach, something completely unrelated to the sweet tremors of pure female ecstasy she'd just survived.

"Lily," Tyler said lightly, but with watchful eyes, "this is Davie McCullough. Davie, Lily Ryder."

"Lily *Kenyon,*" Lily corrected primly. Anything to establish some distance between herself and the heat mirage that was Tyler. Talk about shutting the barn door after the horse ran away.

"Hi," Davie said. His obviously new jeans and striped T-shirt were at strange variance with the piercings and the tattoo.

Lily smiled. "Hello," she answered.

"See you at six," Tyler told her.

"Is this the hot date?" Davie asked.

Tyler rolled his eyes, but if he was embarrassed by Davie's remark, it didn't show. He was the legendary Tyler Creed, after all. He probably made women climax in discount stores all the time. No big deal.

"This is the hot date," Tyler confirmed.

Lily blushed again, and then simply bolted, knowing anything she might have said would have been wrong, and probably gotten her in even deeper than she already was.

And Tyler's low, knowing chuckle trailed in her wake.

"THAT," Tyler told Davie, a beat after Lily raced away, "was *not* cool."

Davie grinned unapologetically. "Oh, *well,*" he said. "She is hot. And you *did* warn me that I might have to bunk in at your brother's place if things went down the way you hoped they would."

Tyler watched as Lily chose the longest line, knew she'd done so because it was the farthest away from where he was standing. She looked beyond good in those big-city blue jeans of hers, and it was a damn good thing, by his reckoning, that he had a full shopping cart to stand behind.

He'd seen Lily go over the edge, known by the blush in her cheeks and the dazed expression in her eyes that the mental trick Doreen had taught him had worked, and he'd gone hard as bedrock the moment she'd come undone.

This, along with the current state of his anatomy, came under the heading of Things Davie Didn't Need to Know, so he was careful to stay behind the cart.

"Don't be a smart-ass," he told the kid.

"I have problems," Davie retorted smugly. "I'm a Troubled Teenager. There's no telling what I might say." The kid admired Lily from afar as she lobbed salad greens and a package of what looked like chicken onto the rolling counter, shook his head. "Makes a man wish he was twenty years older."

Tyler had to chuckle at that, even though a part of him wanted to get Davie by the scruff and hustle him out of Lily-viewing range. Which was Creed-crazy. Davie was only a kid, for all his big talk. "Pull your eyeballs back into your head, Cartoon Boy. She's spoken for."

Mercifully, Davie let the subject drop. Maybe because he'd won a round, on their second trip to Wal-Mart in twenty-four hours, by talking Tyler into buying him a TV.

Tyler, on the other hand, couldn't seem to move on from the Lily encounter. Lily was primed, all right. If he could just get her naked, he could untie all those knots inside her. And when she turned loose for real, let herself go beyond the impromptu climax she'd just had to the genuine article, the universe would tremble on its foundations.

Not just for her, but for him, too.

Whoa, cowboy, he told himself silently. Thoughts like that weren't going to make the lodgepole pushing at the front of his jeans go down, and he couldn't hide his hard-on behind that shopping cart forever.

He needed to get some perspective.

Perspective, hell. He was already planning the call he meant to make to Dylan, as soon as he could get out of Davie's earshot. *Would you mind babysitting a thirteen-year-old?*

He was already picturing Lily, crooning in his bed, arching her back under his hands and mouth, already imagining her afterward, when they'd both recovered, stripped to her delectable skin, bobbing in the cool, dark waters of Hidden Lake, just off the end of his ancient swimming dock.

Skinny-dipping with Lily *Kenyon,* as she'd so carefully reminded him.

Oh, yeah.

Welcome home, Tyler Creed.

Welcome home.

"How do I look?" Lily asked nervously, at five-thirty that evening, modeling her red sundress in the kitchen of her dad's house. Tess and her new friend, Eleanor, were sitting at the table, picking at the chicken breasts she'd broiled earlier, for their supper and Hal's.

Both the girls seemed stricken to silence, as though they'd never seen a woman in a dress before, but Hal found words. "That's some getup," he said. Was that a twinkle she saw lurking in his eyes? "I'm glad you took my advice and went with red."

"It's only dinner," Lily said. Hadn't people been telling *her* that all day?

She wasn't eloping with Tyler.

They probably wouldn't even kiss, since they were virtually strangers to each other.

Hal laughed, shook his head.

Had she said something funny? And if so, when?

"My mom has a name for shoes like that," Eleanor said sagely. Eleanor, like Tess, was a miniature adult, disguised as a child. The old-fashioned name suited her perfectly, in fact.

"They're straight out of *Sex and the City*," Tess observed.

"Tess Kenyon," Lily challenged, "what do you know about *Sex and the City*?"

Being no dummy, Tess subsided. "Just that the older girls talk about it at school sometimes," she said sweetly. "And that all the women in the TV show can run in *really* high heels."

"That does it," Lily said. "I'm blocking cable."

"I don't have cable," Hal put in. "So no worries."

"You look beautiful, Mom," Tess said, with such sincerity and even wonder that Lily forgot all about the things her daughter might have been watching on TV when she wasn't around. "Like a princess."

"A princess in sexy shoes," Eleanor said.

Eleanor's parents, Lily had learned over the course of the long, lazy, front-porch afternoon, were going through a bad divorce. It was important to show tolerance and understanding, but there were limits.

"Can Eleanor spend the night?" Tess asked. "Her aunt said it was okay."

"If it's all right with your grandfather, yes," Lily said. Then she turned her gaze to her dad. "No TV," she added ominously. "Unless it's Disney, or educational in some way."

Hal sighed, raised both hands, palms out, in a gesture of benign surrender. "I was planning on a game of cutthroat Monopoly. Is that curmudgeonly enough for you?"

Lily gave him a look.

"Are you driving, or is Tyler picking you up?" Tess asked Lily. From her tone, she might have been forty, not six.

Lily's cheeks felt hot again. She was a fool for even going on this dinner date at all, let alone not taking her rental car, but since she'd been in such a dither from the first encounter with Tyler, the day before yesterday, she hadn't thought to suggest that they meet at the restaurant.

Was she *trying* to get herself seduced?

Did she *want* to let Tyler have his way with her, and to hell with the consequences?

It was a possibility she didn't dare examine too closely.

"Tyler is picking me up," she finally answered.

Eleanor and Tess high-fived each other.

And before Lily could respond to that, the door-bell rang.

Lily's heart shimmied into her throat.

There was still time to back out. She could pretend to be sick, maybe even persuade Hal to lie for her, though the chances of *that* were slim to none.

But what kind of example would she be setting for Tess?

Lily patted her hair, pinned up in a loose twist at the back of her head. Hal smiled, reading the gesture for what it was, and Tess and Eleanor raced for the front of the house, giggling when they nearly wedged themselves into the first doorway.

Lily thought she was going to throw up.

Maybe it *wouldn't* be lying to say she was sick.

The trouble was, no one would believe her. Not her dad, not the little girls who knew too much about sexy shoes, and certainly not Tyler.

She'd just have to go through with the whole thing, that was all.

Hope she could pass a pleasant evening with an old friend without letting her inner hussy come to the fore and climb Tyler's frame like a monkey scrambling up the trunk of a palm tree.

Lily was still dealing with the Freudian aspects of *that* image when she saw Tyler, standing in her father's foyer, wearing jeans and a freshly pressed white shirt, holding a black cowboy hat in one hand and looking shy.

There was something to be said, she decided, for illicit sex.

Something to be said for just getting it over with, out of the way, so she could think straight again. Recover her balance, get some perspective.

After nodding to Hal and the girls, Tyler took the tiny white sweater from her hands and draped it over her shoulders. Leaned to whisper in her ear even as he reached for the doorknob with one hand.

"It's inevitable," he said. "What do you say we skip dinner and get right down to business?"

CHAPTER SIX

LOGAN CREED STOOD with one booted foot braced on the lowest rail of his corral fence, arms resting across the top as he watched the latest stray—a dark-haired kid with piercings, tattoos and plenty of attitude—riding the tamest horse on the place, bareback.

Dylan, right beside him, watched, too, while Kristy, Dylan's bride, supervised the boy's ride from within rein-grabbing distance. Kristy was good with horses, even gifted. After a long hiatus spent grieving for her old partner, a gelding named Sugarfoot, she was training them again.

"Think the kid is Tyler's?" Logan asked quietly. Briana, the love of his life, was in the house, whipping up supper for a crowd, while Bonnie, Dylan's little girl, played on the kitchen floor, and his stepsons, Josh and Alec, worked on the summer lessons their mother had assigned them.

Briana was a stickler for education, and preferred to home-school her sons, but she'd agreed to let them attend normal classes in the fall. In the meantime, she made sure they kept their math and reading skills up to snuff.

Logan's heart bucked like a bronc fresh from the chute, just thinking of her in the house, a ranch wife in blue jeans and a sexy cotton blouse, and the sweet secret they shared.

In roughly eight months, there would be a new Creed on Stillwater Springs Ranch, of the small, messy, noisy variety.

He could barely wait. Thought sometimes he'd burst if he had to keep the secret to himself much longer. But he and Briana had agreed not to spread the word until she was three months along, so he stayed mum.

"According to Ty, Doreen denies it," Dylan answered. A grin cocked up one corner of his mouth, and he adjusted his hat. "I'm not sure Ty's convinced, though. It would be a good thing for him, and for Davie, too, if the kid's one of us."

"One of us," Logan repeated, unable to hide the touch of sorrow that phrase made him feel. "Ty doesn't want to be a Creed, remember? So even if the DNA's right—"

Dylan laid a hand on his brother's shoulder. "Our little brother's back on the ranch," he reminded Logan. "That means something. That he's come home, that he wasted no time asking Lily out. Give him a little time to come around, Logan."

Logan gave a rueful chuckle, part snort. Except for marrying Briana and helping to raise Josh and Alec, he'd never wanted anything as much as he wanted the Creed family restored, and the ranch back in working order.

He and Dylan, once on the outs, were brothers again. They were full partners in the newly formed Tri-Star Cattle Company; they'd bought the start of a herd and doubled the size of the ranch by purchasing Kristy's folks' old place, but there was still a line on the official documents, awaiting Tyler's signature.

The outfit wouldn't be "Tri"-anything until Ty joined up.

And since the last time Logan had seen his youngest brother, at their dad's grave, Ty had sucker punched him, reconciliation didn't seem all that likely.

"If I hadn't busted that damn guitar—" Logan mused, remembering. Regretting. It had happened the day they buried their dad—they'd all been drunk, down at Skivvie's, and Tyler had been singing and strumming some stupid song he'd written, making Jake sound like John Wayne or Roy Rogers, not the hard-drinking, ornery son of a bitch he'd really been.

Logan, full of grief and rage and cheap beer, had suddenly lost it. He'd jerked that guitar out of Tyler's hands and smashed it to splinters against the bar. A second later, he'd have given anything to take back what he'd done, but there was no changing it.

The guitar had belonged to Tyler's dead mother, and it had been her most precious possession.

The damage had been done.

The fight was on.

And all three of them had been thrown into the clink for public drunkenness and brawling and a whole list of other misdemeanors. They'd gone their separate ways the next morning, as soon as Floyd Book turned them loose from the hoosegow, and written each other off.

"That goddamned song," Logan muttered, watching as Davie relaxed a little on the horse, under Kristy's patient tutelage, and started showing some potential as a cow-puncher.

Dylan nodded. "Everything Tyler wanted in a father was in that song," he recalled. "Everything we *all* wanted Jake to be."

"Why didn't I see that?" Logan asked.

"Maybe because you were hurting, too. We all were, Logan. It was a tough day for everybody."

Logan shook his head, not in denial of what Dylan had just said, but out of resignation and remorse. "Pretty crazy," he said. "We hated Jake's drinking and hell-raising, and what did we do? When push came to shove, Dylan, we acted just like he would have. Came straight to Skivvie's from the funeral home and started swilling beer. Got ourselves arrested."

"Jake would have been real proud," Dylan joked. Since Kristy, he'd mellowed out a lot, and developed a halfway decent sense of humor. Must have been all that regular, down-home sex.

Logan knew that because of what he had with Briana. Whenever the kids weren't around, they were doing it—in the barn, in the laundry room, anywhere they happened to be. They'd tear off each other's clothes and collide. Briana liked it fast and wet and hard, liked being bent over things and taken in a single thrust, like a stallion with a mare in heat—hardly any foreplay at all.

Ironically, the foreplay came later, when they'd eased that first ferocious, almost violent need to join their bodies, when Logan would lay his flushed and still-gasping wife down on the nearest soft surface and take his time pleasing her. And in pleasing Briana, he more than pleased himself.

He shifted against the coral fence, lest Dylan spot the instant hard-on thinking about Briana always produced, and shoved a hand through his hair.

"I guess you like being married," Dylan observed dryly.

Damn him, he didn't miss much.

"I like it all right," Logan allowed. "What about you?"

"If I'd known what it was going to be like with Kristy," Dylan answered, "I'd have been the original virgin bridegroom."

Logan gave a hoot of laughter, and some of the gloom over his broken relationship with Tyler let up. "You, a virgin? Hell, were you *ever* a virgin, little brother? This is me you're talking to—I happen to know you did the babysitter when you were barely fifteen."

"'Babysitter'?" Dylan balked, but there was a laugh behind the word. "Are you completely clueless? That woman wasn't a babysitter. She was one of Dad's bar-fly girlfriends—he brought her home from one of his binges and she stayed on when he left for work the next morning."

"And you decided to do her?"

Dylan grinned, the cocky little bastard. "It was mutual. These days, they'd arrest her, but I've got to admit, I enjoyed being taken advantage of."

"Yeah," Logan drawled. "I reached that same conclusion when I came running into Jake's room to rescue you—the way you were howling, I thought somebody was killing you—and there you were, buck-ass naked, with her riding you like a bronc at the rodeo."

"If she'd have had a hat handy," Dylan agreed, "she'd have been waving it in the air."

Logan laughed. Shook his head again. "It's no wonder we're so screwed-up," he said.

Dylan glanced at Kristy, and his expression softened. "Not anymore, brother," he said. "I'm not screwed-up anymore, and neither are you."

"Nothing like the love of a good woman," Logan

conceded, just as Briana appeared on the porch and called out that supper was ready.

"Nothing like it," Dylan said.

Davie swung a leg over and got down, and he and Kristy went into the barn to put the animal up for the night. That was part of learning to ride, as far as Kristy was concerned. You looked after the horse, first, last and always, even if it made you late for supper.

"You think Tyler's serious about Lily, or just looking for a piece of tail?" Logan asked, as he and Dylan headed toward the house. All he really knew was that Kristy and Dylan had agreed to keep an eye on young Davie while Tyler took Doc Ryder's daughter, Lily, out to dinner.

Dylan had explained, in his offhand way, that Davie had an asshole for a stepfather, and needed to live away from home for a while, so he was bunking in at Tyler's place. At the mention of Doreen's name, and Davie's age, Logan had started counting backward, summer by summer, to the most likely scenario.

"I think our little brother is *definitely* looking for a piece of tail," Dylan replied, after some thought. "I also think he never got over Lily, any more than I got over Kristy, but he may not have figured that part out yet. Could be that Lily hasn't, either."

Logan hoped Tyler *would* fall for his high school sweetheart, hoped he'd marry her and get her pregnant and stay right on Stillwater Springs Ranch, where he belonged.

Where all of them belonged.

The Creed brothers ride again, Logan thought, picturing the three of them riding abreast on well-fed horses, driving their own cattle over their own land, justifiably proud of their name because they'd turned things around, made being a Creed mean something good.

Some dreams never died.

No matter how bad the odds against them might be.

"WE ARE *NOT* SKIPPING DINNER," Lily whispered, as soon as the front door had closed behind her and Tyler. "And we're not 'getting right down to business,' either!"

Tyler laughed, damnably confident. Standing there in the first pink and lavender shadows of a Montana sunset, he looked like a character in a Western movie. "You're hungry?" he teased.

Heat surged through her.

There was no way she was going to be able to get so much as a bite of food down, with the air so charged between her and Tyler, and he probably knew that as well as she did.

"I'll fix you some scrambled eggs out at my place," Tyler went on, when she didn't speak. He took her hand and instead of pulling free, turning on one heel, dashing back into the house, slamming and locking the door behind her, like any halfway sensible woman would have done, Lily let him lead her down the steps. "How's that?"

"*Nothing* is going to happen between us," Lily insisted, leaving the scrambled-egg question to dangle and casting an anxious glance over one shoulder. Her dad, Tess and Eleanor were all standing with their noses practically pressed to the glass in the living room window, taking it all in.

"Then what's the harm in scrambled eggs at the cabin?" Tyler asked reasonably, nodding cordially to the spectators. "You're putting on quite a show, you know," he added. "Try to make this look like an ordinary dinner date—as it is, anybody would think you're expecting me to hoist you off your feet and throw you over one shoulder at any second. Carry you off to some cave and lick every part of you until you lose your mind."

More heat, so heavy that it nearly brought Lily to her knees.

"I could still go inside and forget this whole crazy idea, you know!" Lily whispered furiously.

"You won't," Tyler said easily. "Do you think I don't know you got off in Wal-Mart this morning? You are a woman in need of some intense sex, and I'm just the man to give it to you."

"And *you* are *impossible!* And I did *not* 'get off,' as you so crudely put it, in Wal-Mart!"

"Smile and wave," Tyler coached, grinning. "We're still being watched."

She worked up a smile, waved to the delighted onlookers and against all better judgment, against all reason and good sense, let Tyler guide her down the walk to the gate, through it and up to the passenger door of a Blazer. It didn't look like the kind of rig he'd drive, she thought, distracted, but then his truck *had* broken down on some lonely highway, leaving him and his dog afoot, which was part of the reason she was in this mess. Maybe the Blazer was a rental.

"I did not have a climax in Wal-Mart!" she blurted, once she was seated in the spotlessly clean SUV, with her seat belt buckled. Her head wanted to do one thing—go back into her dad's house, where she'd be safe—but her body had staged a mutiny, taken over.

Tyler, still standing on her side of the Blazer, braced one foot on the running board and smiled at her through the open door. "Save it, Lily. Your eyes practically rolled back in your head. You were breathing from the back of your throat, not your lungs, and you broke out in a very fetching orgasmic sweat. You *came.* And if it's the last thing I ever do, I want to see it happen again."

She scowled at him, turned stiffly to face straight forward, glaring through the windshield. "I did *not* sweat!" she fussed.

Tyler laughed, closed the door and started around to the driver's side.

Run for it! her brain warned fitfully.

Take off your underpants, her wanton body countered. *It will save time.*

"You promised me dinner," Lily said, as they pulled away from the last bastion of sanity on earth.

"You don't *want* dinner. You want my head between your legs."

She squirmed, wet enough that taking off her panties began to seem almost practical. "Of all the *arrogant*—"

"Face it, Lily. You're horny as hell. I'm horny as hell. And neither of us is going to be able to think straight until we've tended to business."

She noticed he hadn't said "until we've made love." No, he'd said, "tended to business." There would be no tender kisses, no avowals of lasting affection. What was about to happen between them could only be classified as good old-fashioned *fucking*.

And Lily was stunned at how much she wanted just exactly that.

From Tyler Creed.

In his cabin at Hidden Lake.

If they even got that far.

As it turned out, they made it to the copse of heavy-leafed trees shading his gravel driveway.

By then, Lily had given up all pretense that it wasn't going to happen.

She was furious with herself, and she was furious with Tyler, and even that didn't change a damn thing.

When he pulled that Blazer under those trees, a place made private by the density of the foliage, she unhooked her seat belt and shimmied out of her panties. Angrily rolled down the window and hung them to dry on the passenger-side mirror.

Tyler chuckled at that, a hoarse sound, wholly masculine. He'd won, before he'd even touched her, and she'd made it so ridiculously easy for him that she'd never be able to think about this night again, if she lived to be a hundred, without being embarrassed to tears.

He got out of the Blazer, came around to her side and opened the door.

Lily glared defiantly into his eyes. "Right here?" she asked, with a coolness she certainly didn't feel. "In the grass?"

"And spoil that sexy little dress?" Tyler drawled. "No way."

Oh, Lily thought, strangely detached from the whole thing. *He was going to have her standing up, the way it happened in books and those pay-per-view movies offered in hotel rooms.*

She'd never done that with Burke, but if memory served, all she had to do was wrap her legs around Tyler's lean hips and he'd be inside her and this needing, this *endless,* stupid, primitive *needing* would finally stop.

Then they could both right their clothes, go their separate ways and get on with their lives.

Only it didn't happen that way.

Tyler went to the back of the small SUV and raised the hatch.

Lily turned her head slightly, to watch over one shoulder while he assessed the space, shook out a neatly folded blanket and arranged it carefully over the bare metal of the tailgate. When he came back, he lifted Lily off the seat as easily as if she weighed nothing at all, carried her around behind the rig and laid her down on the blanket like a picnic-spread at a halftime party.

When he slid her dress up around her waist, she realized she had the analogy right, and her eyes widened with anticipation and no little shock.

Back there in Stillwater Springs, when he'd told her she wanted his head between her legs, she'd thought he was just trying to shake her up. Burke had never been willing to do this—had shamed her the few times she'd asked him to—but now that oral sex was definitely in her very near future, Lily didn't know what to do.

Tyler showed her. He coaxed her into bending her knees, set her feet wide apart, slipped her new strappy sandals off and let them fall to the ground, forgotten.

With them went all thought of Burke and what he had and hadn't done, in bed or out.

In those moments, she and Tyler were the only reality.

He made a throaty, anticipatory sound and began tracing the inside of her right thigh with his lips.

With his free hand, he found the nest of moist curls where all her life-force seemed to have gathered, like a new universe about to be born, her own personal Big Bang.

The pun made her give a soft, sobbing laugh.

"It's all right, Lily," Tyler told her, with a gentleness that brought tears swelling into her throat. "It's all right."

She nodded, sniffled, groped with both hands for his hair, his shoulders, any part of him she could touch, and draw near. "What if I—What if I c-come too soon?" she rasped, remembering the spontaneous orgasm she'd had that morning.

Tyler chuckled again, kissing his way down her thigh, nearer and nearer to the apex, to the wet place where she pulsed and ached with the need of him. "There's no time clock, Lily," he told her. "And you're going to come a lot more than once."

In the next instant, he'd parted her, taken her full into his mouth.

The warmth and the wetness, the first flick of his tongue, instantly sent her shooting skyward on a geyser of stars. She groaned, her cries loud and hoarse, completely surrendered to a kind of lust she'd never let herself feel before.

The climax went on and on, buckling Lily like a live wire fallen into deep water, wringing shout after shout of pleasure from her. Tyler stayed with her, relentless, granting no quarter, demanding everything she had to give, and more.

And she gave.

Oh, how she gave.

When she finally collapsed, spent, exhausted and totally satisfied, tears filled her eyes. It was over. She'd had her climax, and she'd had it too soon.

Now, Tyler would take her. Satisfy himself. But for her, it was over.

He leaned over her, kissed away her tears.

"What?" he whispered, nibbling at the length of her neck, slipping one shoulder strap down to uncover her bra and then her bare breast.

"It's over," she murmured. "It happened too fast—I—"

"Shh," he said. "It's *not* over, Lily. It hasn't even begun."

He proceeded to prove his words then, caressing her, sucking at her breasts, tonguing the nipples until she thought she'd go mad if he didn't suck them again.

And when he'd worked her into an even greater frenzy than before, he went down on her again. Held her apart, teased her clitoris with the tip of his tongue, plied her on the inside with his fingers.

She came again.

And then again.

And still Tyler didn't crawl on top of her.

In fact, when she'd recovered from the third orgasm—or was it the fourth?—he bundled her in the blanket and the discarded dress and lifted her into his arms. Snatched her panties off the passenger-side mirror as they passed.

"Aren't you going to—well—you know?" Lily inquired sleepily.

"Do you?" Tyler asked. "Yeah, Lily. I'm going to do you, like you've never been done before. And then I'm going to do you again. And again after that."

Even in her melted state, a state in which Lily could barely imagine being able to have even one more orgasm, as long as she lived, she felt the aching need of him begin. Felt herself expanding to receive him. "Oh," she said, as though he'd just explained every mystery in the universe.

He chuckled, carried her up a set of rickety steps, pushed open a door.

Greeted his dog.

Lily didn't really see the dog, or the cabin itself. She was all sensation, all warm honey and, conversely, achy wanting.

Tyler carried her up a set of stairs, to a loft of some kind.

She couldn't have walked, she reasoned. Her legs were like noodles.

He laid her down on a bed, the covers pleasantly rumpled and smelling distinctly of Tyler and no one else. Downstairs, the dog gave a halfhearted whimper.

Tyler disappeared, and she heard his footsteps on the stairs, heard him speaking quietly to the dog, shaking kibble into a bowl. Still, he returned in what seemed like a flicker of a second, and he was magnificently naked now, his erection almost frighteningly big.

Her eyes widened.

He stretched out on the bed next to her, his body half covering hers, careful not to put his full weight on her. She felt delicate, precious, and at the same time, fiercely feminine.

"Lily—I—If you want to change your mind—"

Lily was lost. She finally pressed her fingers to his mouth and urged him onto her.

The need was back, more ferocious than before, beyond refusal. It was basic biology—man, woman, instinct.

She wanted him inside her now, deep, deep inside her.

And she would die if she didn't have him.

He eased her legs apart. Hesitated for a long, almost unbearable interval, gazing into her eyes. She knew there was some kind of battle going on inside him, one that might have little or nothing to do with her, but she didn't care.

"Do me, Tyler Creed," she told him. *"Do me."*

She'd seen how huge he was, but when he took her, she gasped at the sheer power of his thrust, at the steely hardness and the instant friction. She would have *loved* a spontaneous orgasm then, reveled in the quick relief it would have brought her.

But that wasn't to be.

The build from one level to the next, each one more impossible than the last, was exquisitely slow. At each new place, Tyler stopped, read the play of emotions in Lily's face as though they were holy writ, made her need him and then need him still more.

The friction increased with every long, slow stroke.

Lily began to fret and toss beneath Tyler, sure she couldn't bear another breathless pinnacle, on the verge of orgasm but not quite there.

Every twist of her hips made him groan like a man in agony, but he didn't give in. Several times he stopped, closed his eyes, the muscles in his neck straining as he struggled for control, but he kept her pinned to the mattress, so completely did he fill her.

"Tyler," she finally begged, tossing her head from side to side on the pillow now, nearly delirious with the promise of satisfaction and the withholding of it. "Make me come—Oh God, Tyler, *make me come—*"

Something broke inside him then. He slid his hands under her buttocks and slammed into her with everything he had, driving fast and hard and deep enough to touch her very soul.

Lily splintered, even as Tyler stiffened on her, spilled himself into her. She felt his warmth inside her and sobbed his name as another orgasm tore through her, then another. Through it all, Tyler pleasured her with exquisite skill, even after he'd emptied himself, his hands cupping her face now, buried in her sweat-dampened hair. He kissed her as she convulsed under him, around him, as she called his name again and again, in a throaty wail of pleading and of triumph.

Later, when she was back inside herself, Lily would reflect that never in her life, not with Burke, not even when she'd given birth to Tess, had she felt so completely, gloriously, uncompromisingly female.

She'd surrendered to Tyler.

She'd also conquered him.

But it wasn't lovemaking, she reminded herself, even while she was still clawing at his shoulders and his back, even while she was still shuddering under him, still begging him to have her. It wasn't lovemaking. It was getting off, being *done*.

Nothing less, nothing more.

Finally, he rolled onto his side next to her, breathing hard, and pulled her into his arms. Held her. Murmured the occasional senseless word into her hair.

And in some ways, that part of the encounter was even more satisfying than the shattering climaxes he'd given her only minutes before. The tender, time-out-of-time feeling of it brought fresh tears to Lily's eyes.

Tyler held her more tightly still, and told her to shush, and the two of them drifted off into sleep.

• • •

WHEN LILY AWAKENED, the room was dark, except for a silvery stream of moonlight pouring in through a window that hadn't been washed in a while. Tyler's side of the bed was empty, but as reality coalesced around her, sound by sound, feeling by feeling, sight by sight, she heard his voice.

He was downstairs, talking to the dog.

Lily sat up, felt around for her sundress, started to pull it on and gave up. It was a wrinkled mess—how was she going to go home and face her father and daughter and little Eleanor from next door in a garment that had so obviously spent most of the evening in a crumpled heap?

She began to panic.

What had she *done?*

Tyler started up the stairs; she saw his head first, grinning. Then his T-shirt and misbuttoned jeans. Then his bare feet.

He offered her a jelly glass with wine in it.

"How am I going to explain the state of this dress?" Lily demanded, but she took the glass, and a gulp of the wine, and was a little surprised to realize it was good stuff, not the kind that came out of a spigoted box.

And there was music playing somewhere.

Was that Andrea Bocelli?

"I wouldn't *try* to explain the dress, if I were you," Tyler said, sitting down on the edge of the

130

bed with a satisfied sigh. "A couple of slaps with an iron and it will look okay."

"*You* own an iron?"

Tyler laughed. "Yeah," he said. "A few other luxuries, too."

Lily felt another rush of panic, looked at her wrist, which was bare since she'd forgotten her watch at home, and then all around the room, in hopeless search of a clock. "What time is it?"

"Early enough," he drawled.

"Early enough for what?" Lily demanded, but she knew, of course, and her resolve was already weakening.

She *hadn't* come to her senses, then.

In fact, she was nowhere near them.

"Early enough," Tyler repeated. Then he took the wine out of her hand and set it aside. He stood and peeled the T-shirt off over his head, unbuttoned his jeans and took them off.

Once again, Lily's eyes nearly popped at the size of his erection. He seemed even bigger than before.

How was that possible?

Deftly, he turned her onto her hands and knees, knelt behind her, stroked her belly and her thighs and her breasts until she whimpered.

"You might want to hold on," he murmured, kissing her right shoulder even as he guided her fingers to the rails in the headboard. "This position is hell on the old G-spot."

Lily's palms felt moist and slick where she gripped the rails. She gave another little whimper when she felt him pressing at her vagina, about to ease inside her.

"Have you ever done it this way, Lily?" he asked, gliding his mouth across her back to her left shoulder, weighing her breast with one hand and toying with her clitoris with the other.

She shook her head, nearly hypnotized by the sound of his voice, the hard heat building inside her. She'd thought she needed to get laid, specifically by Tyler Creed, and that was it.

Slam, bam, thank you, sir.

He *had* satisfied her, every time. Oh, satisfaction wasn't even the word for the things he'd made her feel.

But she'd expected to get him out of her system.

Scratch the itch, and be done with it.

Now, here she was, on her knees, bending over for him, holding on to the headboard of his bed like some—some *porn* queen. Even in a whole new fog of lust, she blushed to remember things she'd cried out before—*do me, Tyler—make me come—*

He eased inside her, smooth and slow.

Began a gentle rhythm, rocking her on the bed, murmuring softly to her.

In and out, in and out.

In five minutes, she was begging him again, groaning those same fitful phrases—and some new ones, too.

132

CHAPTER SEVEN

THE HEADLIGHTS of an oncoming car splashed through the windshield of the Blazer, a cruel dazzle to the eyes, as Tyler drove Lily back to her dad's place in Stillwater Springs. She sat huddled in the passenger seat, wearing her crumpled dress, arms clamped around her middle, being very careful not to glance in his direction.

She'd looked fantastic in that dress.

Even better *out* of it.

Now, at a little after one in the morning, remorse was evidently setting in. Lily, helping him pound the headboard against the wall of his sleeping loft only a little while ago, howling like a she-wolf as she came, seemed profoundly miserable now.

It grieved Tyler to know that, because regret was the *last* thing he felt. He was still weak in the knees from the pleasure he'd shared with Lily—it had been the best sex of his life, bar none. And he'd had a *lot* of sex in his life.

"Hey," he said gruffly, hoping she'd pick up the conversational ball and run with it.

"We didn't even use condoms," Lily lamented, thrusting the fingers of one hand into her love-tangled hair.

Tyler *always* wore a condom, but the precaution hadn't even occurred to him with Lily.

"I'm healthy, Lily," he said. "Nothing to worry

about there." He paused, swerved slightly to avoid a doe and a young fawn dashing suddenly across the dark road. "Could you be pregnant?" he asked, after a few moments of recovery from the near-miss with the deer.

She made a strangled sound, part laugh, part sob, but distinctly neither. "No," she said.

"You're on the pill—or something?"

"Or something," she said, with a touch of bitterness. "I can't have any more children, Tyler. Believe me, I tried."

Lily couldn't have kids? The thought opened a hollow place deep inside Tyler, an echoing void.

"You have Tess," he pointed out lamely. Like she might have forgotten.

"There were some problems," she explained, still without looking at him. "After Tess was born, I mean."

Tyler marveled at the scope of his disappointment. It wasn't as if he'd planned to marry Lily and start a family or anything, but the idea that it wasn't possible to have a child with her had struck him hard, like an unexpected punch to the gut. He might have doubled over, if he hadn't been at the wheel of Kristy's Blazer.

"You're sure?" he asked.

"I'm sure. Burke and I wanted more children— or, at least, *I* did. But after Tess was born, I couldn't get pregnant again."

They'd reached the outskirts of Stillwater

Springs, and the place looked less scruffy in the dark. "Were you tested?"

Lily shook her head. "There was no point," she said. "If something hadn't been wrong, I'd have conceived."

"Did it ever cross your mind," Tyler pressed, "that you might not have been the one with the problem?"

She made that sob-sound again. Hugged herself more tightly than before, as though she feared she might fly apart in pieces if she didn't. "Burke Kenyon, the hotshot pilot, the ladies' man, *sterile?* I don't think so. Besides, he used to brag about how many abortions his mother had to pay for while he was in college."

"Nice guy," Tyler commented.

They pulled up in front of Hal Ryder's dark house. Hopefully, the doc and the two little girls were sound asleep by now. The kids were too young to speculate about Lily's dress and the state of her hair and the way her mouth was swollen from too much kissing, but Doc would know the whole story at a glance.

Tyler got out of the Blazer, came around to open Lily's door, only to find her already scrambling off the running board. She stood there in the street, trying to straighten that hopelessly messed-up dress.

He knew she'd probably slap him silly if he tried to kiss her good-night, but he couldn't just dump her in front of her dad's front gate after all that had happened between them out at his place.

He took her by the arm and walked her through the gate, up the walk, onto the porch. Waited while she fumbled with the handle on the screen door. Beyond it, the front door stood open.

"Lily," he said, very quietly, lest he wake the neighbors or Lily's dad.

"What?" she snapped, but she kept her voice down.

"I wouldn't change what we did tonight for any-thing," he answered.

She opened the screen door, and it creaked a little on its hinges.

Lily winced, looking as anxious as a teenager out after curfew. "You got what you wanted," she whispered. "I got what *I* wanted. Now, we'll just act as if it never happened."

"Are you kidding?" Tyler demanded, insulted.

"Shh!" Lily said, putting a finger to her lips. "Do you want to wake everyone up?"

Tyler sighed. If it had been up to him, he'd have woken up the whole damn town, whooping and hollering for joy, in true cowboy style. "Good night," he said instead, as well-mannered as some-body's English butler, holding the screen door for her, so it wouldn't slam when she went inside, the way screen doors tended to do. "I'll call you tomorrow."

Lily didn't answer; she just scowled at him and

136

disappeared into the house, shutting the door decisively between them.

"Hot *damn,*" Tyler said, grinning, as he sprinted back down the walk and through the open gate. He hopped into the Blazer and switched on the engine, sat there at the curb for a long moment, wishing he and Logan and Dylan were still close.

If they had been, he'd have had someone to celebrate with.

He'd have told them he was getting married.

Wait—he was *what?*

He was getting married.

He knew that as surely as he knew the sun would climb up over the eastern hills in a few hours, spilling fiery pink and orange light over the trees and the pastures, the creeks and rivers.

He thrust a hand through his hair. Maybe it was better this way, since he needed some time to adjust to the decision himself, and the prospective bride wasn't in on his plans quite yet.

Still, he couldn't go straight home, knowing what he did, even though he knew poor old Kit Carson would be waiting for him there. The dog definitely suffered from separation anxiety.

He drove back to the ranch, slowly, trying to make sense of everything he was thinking and feeling, and having no luck with it at all. One minute, he'd been his old self. The next, he was suddenly husband material.

He wasn't even sure when the shift had occurred,

but the whole universe seemed to be converging on the concept now—him and Lily, married. It was mind-boggling and, at the same time, entirely natural, as though it had been inevitable from the beginning of time.

Passing by the main ranch house—it was dark, with everybody bedded down for the night—Tyler found himself yearning for the old days, when he and his brothers were still kids.

They hadn't been *all* bad, those times.

When Jake was sober, he'd played driveway basketball with the three of them. There had been a hoop over the garage door, back then. He'd spun yarns, too, most of them about the glory days of the Creeds, when the ranch was one of the biggest and best in the whole state of Montana. Yes, sir, Jake had known all about the "thrilling days of yesteryear," as he'd put it, and when Tyler, puzzled, had asked him to explain the phrase, Jake had shaken his head and said it had to do with the Lone Ranger and you had to be there to understand.

Remembering, Tyler's eyes smarted a little.

He stopped, got out of the Blazer and opened a gate in Logan's fancy new wooden fence, drove the Blazer through and went back to shut the gate again. There were cattle on the place now and, having grown up in the country, Tyler respected ranch etiquette. No matter what, if a gate was closed when you got to it, you made sure it was closed again when you'd passed through it.

He headed for the old cemetery, with the Blazer's headlights switched off. If Logan or Dylan had seen their glow in the pasture, they might come out to investigate.

At the edge of the pioneer graveyard, Tyler parked the rig, shut off the engine and, ignoring Jake's grave, found the one marked with his mother's name.

Someone had been there recently, left a bouquet of pink, purple and yellow wildflowers in a Mason jar by her headstone. A sliver short of being full, the moon spilled a silvery glimmer over the whole place, lending it a strange and potent beauty.

Tyler crouched, touched the flowers in the canning jar and wondered who had left them. He finally concluded that it must have been Logan's wife, Briana. Kristy and Dylan were still staying in town, at her place, while their new house was being built, but Logan and Briana lived within walking distance. And someone had mentioned in passing—Tyler couldn't recall who—that Briana and her boys had taken care of the cemetery long before she and Logan met.

Having no idea what to say to a dead person—he wasn't all that good at talking to *live* ones—Tyler simply sat there on his haunches, remembering, wishing things had been different.

Angela Creed had been a beautiful woman, delicate and spirited and full of music. Until Jake's drinking and womanizing and chronic poverty had gotten to be too much for her, anyhow.

Lots of women lived with worse situations, Tyler reflected. Doreen was a good example. But they didn't just drive off one day, hole up in some fleabag motel on a lonely stretch of highway and down a handful of pills.

Had she even thought about what her death would do to him or, for that matter, to Dylan and Logan? They'd both lost their mothers, and they'd loved Angela. Loved her singing and her guitar-playing on the back porch at night—serenading the fireflies, she'd called it.

Loved her peach cobbler, too, and the way she'd mussed their hair and straightened their collars, treated them like her own boys.

The news the sheriff brought might not have been such a shock if Angela had seemed unhappy. Oh, she and Jake had fought often, and loudly, behind the closed door of their bedroom, and there were other signs that the marriage was on its way down the tubes, but she'd always had a smile for "my boys," no matter how bad things were other-wise.

But she hadn't even said goodbye.

She'd made supper that night, like always, Tyler recalled, and told him and Logan and Dylan to do their chores. She'd seemed distracted and upset, that was true, but she sure hadn't let on that she wouldn't be coming back.

Why? Tyler asked himself silently, for about the millionth time. Why hadn't she turned to Cassie that night, or to some other friend or relation, gone *anywhere* but to that damn dead-end motel? Why hadn't she just divorced Jake Creed?

That, Tyler could have comprehended, young as he'd been at the time.

He would even have understood if she'd said she couldn't take him with her, if she'd left him behind with Logan and Dylan, until she'd found a teaching job someplace, and managed to rent an apartment or a house.

Instead, she'd consigned herself to oblivion.

Permanent solution to a temporary problem, Jake had said, the day of her funeral. He'd worn a suit that didn't fit him, Jake had, and smelled of stale whiskey.

Shut up, Logan had told their father furiously. *Why can't you just shut up?*

Tyler blinked, yanked himself back to the here and now, rose to his full height.

Thought about Lily.

What if whatever it was that had been wrong with Jake was wrong with him, too? What if it was hard-wired into his DNA, and he took up with Lily and then one fine day woke up with a yen for whiskey?

What if.

Both Logan and Dylan must have had similar doubts, similar fears.

And yet Logan had married Briana and taken on a couple of stepchildren in the bargain, and Dylan had made Kristy Madison his wife, set out to raise two-year-old Bonnie, too.

What did his brothers know that he didn't?

Or were Logan and Dylan just whistling in the dark? Taking a chance, throwing the dice, hoping against hope that things would work out—but well aware that, being Creeds, they were a pair of emotional time bombs, programmed to morph into the old man when some mysterious switch was flipped in their brains?

Did they wake up in a cold sweat at night, wondering when it would all come crashing down around them?

Both his brothers had been wild men when they were younger—Logan had been married at least twice before Briana, and Dylan hadn't been a real father to Bonnie until he'd been forced into it, after finding the toddler in his truck one night in Vegas, abandoned by her mother.

Tyler left the graveyard, got back into the Blazer, started the engine and headed for his cabin.

He'd put off going back because he knew Lily's absence would echo in the place, that the sheets would be imprinted with her singular scent. Now, because of the dog, and because Kristy or Dylan or both would be dropping Davie off first thing in the morning, he couldn't wait any longer.

Kit Carson was ridiculously glad to see him.

After some ear-ruffling and reassurances, Tyler took the dog outside. Without Lily to distract him, Tyler heard all the night sounds this time—the frogs croaking at the mossy-green edges of the lake, the crickets, an owl or two. Even fish breaking the surface of the water and splashing as they made re-entry.

For all the burdens he carried, Tyler loved that ramshackle old shack, ugly and small though it was. Jake had rented it out for a fishing cabin while he was growing up, but the old man had promised that when the time came, and the ranch was split between him and Logan and Dylan, Hidden Lake and some three thousand acres surrounding it would be his.

Promise-keeping had been a rare thing for Jake Creed, but he'd kept this one. Six months after his death, and the debacle at Skivvie's that had put an end to so much, an official-looking letter had caught up with Tyler, somewhere on the rodeo circuit, along with a document granting him full title to one-third of Stillwater Springs Ranch.

Tyler and Kit Carson walked to the end of the ancient dock, watched the moonlight dance on the surface of the water. He'd just married Shawna when that letter arrived, and for weeks they'd talked of coming back, spending a "just-the-two-of-us summer," and maybe conceiving a baby.

But before the winter was over, Shawna, returning from a visit with her folks, had hit a patch of ice on the long, twisting road between Carson City, Nevada, and Reno, and rolled her truck. According to the EMTs called to the scene by a passing motorist, Shawna had died on impact.

The one thing that had kept Tyler sane was knowing she hadn't suffered.

But there would be no summer at Hidden Lake.

No baby.

No anything.

Tyler had grieved, not just for Shawna, but for all they'd planned, all the things that would never happen.

The guilt had been even worse than the grief—because while Tyler had *liked* Shawna, he'd soon realized that he'd never really loved her, and the fear that she might have known that all along ate at him whenever he allowed his thoughts to wander down that particular trail.

Which wasn't often.

Although he hadn't consciously recognized it when he'd first met Shawna, behind the chutes at a rodeo in Cheyenne, she'd borne a certain casual similarity to Lily. Same compact but lushly feminine build, same blue eyes and blond hair.

He sat down on the end of the creaky old dock—like everything else on the property, it needed replacing—and Kit Carson huddled up close and leaned in.

Tyler put an arm around the dog, trying to reassure the poor critter. They were together for the duration, him and ole Kit Carson, two veterans of a hard-knock world, home at last.

He tried to pinpoint the moment he'd decided to marry Lily; figured it must have been right around the time she'd hung her damp panties on the passenger-side mirror of Kristy's Blazer. The memory made him smile.

Did he love Lily?

He wasn't sure. Growing up Creed the way he had, he wasn't sure he'd know love—the real thing—if it bit him in the ass.

He sure as hell felt *something,* though. Something deep and undeniable and completely unlike anything he'd ever felt before.

It wasn't just the sex, though God knew *that* was good.

He watched, pondering, as moonlight played on the still, dark water, putting on the kind of show he'd missed in the big city, for all the bright lights. New York, Las Vegas, L.A.—he'd tried to put down roots in all three of those places, but he'd never been able to find a soft spot in all that concrete.

No, he needed rich Montana dirt under his feet, and that fabled Big Sky over his head.

He needed Lily.

Maybe he even needed his brothers, though he wasn't quite prepared to admit that, just yet.

The question was, did Lily need *him?* She'd responded, body and soul, to every touch of his hands, every brush of his lips, every caress and whispered word and hard, deep thrust of his hips. But there was a lot more to the far side of a wedding than sex; even a marriage-challenged Creed like himself knew that much.

It was possible she'd been telling the truth when she'd informed him, in so many words, that she'd only gone along with the whole thing because she wanted to get him out of her system. And she'd seemed pretty adamant, as they drove back to her dad's place: the whole night had been about getting off, to hear her tell it.

In the beginning, Tyler had believed that, too. That taking Lily to bed was a way of scratching an old itch. In retrospect, he knew that during their first simultaneous climax, it hadn't been just their bodies that had connected and then fused in a flash of fire. It had been some other, more elemental dimension of their beings.

Or, at least, that was how it had been for him.

He turned his head, disturbing the leaning tower of dog a little, and looked back at the cabin. From the looks of that house, it might just fall over on one side at any minute, its beams finally giving out under the pressure of too many deep-snow winters weighing down on its roof. Too many hard winds battering its walls, rattling its windows. Too many glaring summer suns warping its timbers.

It was time to tear down and rebuild, the way Dylan was doing on his section of the ranch. Like

146

Dylan, Tyler felt no sentimental attachment to the structure itself; it was the *land* that mattered to him—the land generations of Creeds had walked on. Good Creeds and bad ones, strong ones and weak ones—a long and winding line of them reaching all the way back to old Josiah himself.

Suddenly, it was as if the ghosts of all Tyler's ancestors rose up out of that good Montana soil, a horde of them, demanding their due.

We fought for this land, they seemed to say. *We lived and died and sweated and bled here. We raised our children and buried our dead, and laughed and wept and shook our fists at heaven itself when the crops failed and the cattle died. And like it or not, you're one of us. We're in your blood. No matter where you go or what you do or who you try to turn yourself into, you're still a Creed.*

"Damn it," Tyler muttered, shoving a hand through his hair.

But the words echoed in his mind. *You're still a Creed.*

Kit Carson whimpered, concerned.

"You're going to have to tough up, dog," Tyler told him, ruffling the animal's floppy ears. "You're a Creed now."

Slowly, Tyler got to his feet, made his way back down the dock to the shore, made himself go inside the cabin. He knew he wouldn't sleep in the bed he'd just shared with Lily—those few square yards would feel like an acre of frozen river—so he crashed downstairs on the cot he'd set up for Davie.

He woke to sunlight reddening his eyelids and somebody banging around in the general vicinity of the cookstove.

Raising himself on one elbow, Tyler blinked.

Logan was there, building a pot of coffee, and Kit Carson, who would obviously never go down in the annals of history as one of the great guard dogs, was practically glued to the intruder's heels, tail wagging, tongue lolling, ears perked.

"Mornin', little brother," Logan drawled, as though he had every right to invade another man's house while he was sleeping. "Nice to know you're not dead. You must have had yourself one hell of a night."

"What are you doing here?" Tyler snapped, sitting up, swinging his legs over the side of the cot. He'd hauled off his shirt at some point, and slept in his jeans.

"Well, dumb-ass," Logan answered easily, "what does it *look* like I'm doing?"

"It looks," Tyler snarled, "like you're *trespassing*."

Logan grinned. "That, too," he agreed. "But mainly I'm making coffee. Maybe a cup will restore your friendly attitude." He paused, shook his head. "*That's* right," he corrected himself. "You never *had* a friendly attitude in the first place."

"What the hell *time* is it, anyhow?" Tyler

growled. He'd left his watch upstairs, and there wasn't a clock in the whole damn place.

"Around six," Logan said, rustling up a couple of mugs and setting them on the table. "Half the day's gone. If you were any kind of rancher, you'd know that."

Tyler shook his head. Stumbled into the john, used it, washed his hands at the sink and came out again.

Logan had drawn back a chair and sat down to wait for the java to brew, just as if he was welcome in that house.

"Time we talked," he said.

"We've got nothing to talk *about*," Tyler grumbled. Kit Carson was at the door, so he let him out.

"I'm sorry I busted your guitar," Logan said.

The words were simple ones, but something about the proud, quiet way his brother said them got to Tyler in a way that made him reinforce his anti-Logan force-field.

"Too little, too late," Tyler grumbled, glaring at the coffeepot, willing it to perk so he could get some caffeine flowing through his veins.

Logan rolled his eyes, but the set of his mouth was grim. Determined. "God*damn* you're stubborn," he said. "I'm your *brother,* Ty."

"Spare me the 'I'm your brother' crap," Tyler said. "Five years ago, we decided to go our own ways—with good reason. Let's keep it like that, okay?"

"You plan on staying here on the ranch?" Logan asked, and Tyler would have thought his brother hadn't heard a word he'd said, if it hadn't been for that familiar muscle bunching in Logan's jaw. That always happened when he was annoyed.

"Maybe," Tyler ground out.

"Then how do you expect to avoid Dylan and me?"

"There must be a way," Tyler said.

Logan chuckled. "Haven't you ever done anything you wished you could take back?" he asked.

There were *plenty* of things Tyler regretted, but he wasn't inclined to share them, especially with Logan. "What do you want?" he demanded, clearly enunciating each word, dragging back a chair and sitting down opposite his brother. After all, it was *his* house. Why should he stand, while Logan lounged at his table?

"Another chance," Logan answered. This time, he sounded hoarse.

"Why?" Tyler asked, honestly puzzled.

Logan didn't reply to that. He just folded his arms and sat there looking at Tyler like he was two feet over the border between smart and stupid.

"You're not going to leave this alone, are you?" Tyler rasped.

"Nope," Logan said.

"Okay, I forgive you for smashing the guitar. Are you happy now?"

"I'm *real* happy," Logan shot back. "Don't I *look* happy?"

"You look butt-ugly," Tyler said. "Now, will you please leave? I'm not a morning person."

Logan laughed again, reached out, tapped a stack of papers with the tip of one finger. Tyler hadn't noticed the documents until then. He frowned.

"What—"

"I assume you can read," Logan said.

Smart-ass son of a bitch.

Tyler picked up the documents, scanned the face page. Something about a corporation called Tri-Star Cattle Company.

"We're trying to run a ranch here, Dylan and me," Logan told him. "A third of it's yours. Are you going to sign on or not?"

CHAPTER EIGHT

LILY WAS IN THE LAUNDRY ROOM, peering at the label in her once-beautiful red dress—she went through three different languages before she got to washing instructions in English—when her dad popped his head in through the kitchen doorway.

Blushing a little, Lily stuffed the dress into the washing machine. Barefoot, her hair still damp from the shower, she wore a short cotton bathrobe, tightly cinched at the waist, and nothing else. Except maybe the golden, telling glow of a woman recovering from a night of nonstop orgasms.

"Good morning," Hal said sunnily. "I took the liberty of making breakfast, since you overslept.

We had toaster waffles with jam and canned whipped cream, and there's not a damn thing you can do about it."

In spite of all her misgivings, those concerning her father's diet and those having to do with the way she'd carried on with Tyler the night before, Lily chuckled. Shook her head. "Where is my daughter now? Having her stomach pumped?"

"She and Eleanor are in the backyard, trying to dig their way to China. They'll be pretty dirty by now, I reckon, but they're happy."

Lily raised the washer lid, dumped in a sprinkling of powdered soap and set the dial to Delicate. Pulled the knob and spoke over the ensuing roar of water filling the machine. "A little dirt won't hurt them," she said.

Hal arched a bushy gray eyebrow and grinned. "And here I expected an argument," he teased. His gaze was tender as he studied her, though. "Did you have a good time last night, Lily?" he asked gently. "How was dinner?"

She couldn't tell him the truth, of course—that she and Tyler had never gotten around to eating dinner. They hadn't even had the scrambled eggs he'd promised her. "Fine," she said, as he backed out of the doorway so she could pass him and step into the kitchen. "It was fine."

Fine? taunted her inner hussy.

Oh, Tyler, do me—make me come—

Lily blushed again, ducked into the spare room

152

she'd taken over as a bedroom, and hastily dressed in khaki shorts and a pink-and-white-checked sleeveless blouse.

When she came out, her dad was just plucking a couple of waffles from the toaster. He dumped them on a plate and set them on the table.

"What?" Lily teased, too ravenous to refuse the food. "No tofu?"

"Fresh out," Hal bantered back. He set the jam jar and canned whipped cream on the table. Got Lily some silverware. "I thought I'd stop by the clinic today," he ventured. "See how things are going."

Lily didn't bother to protest; she knew it wouldn't do any good and, besides, she felt too mellow to argue.

Hal joined her at the table. Sipped coffee while he watched her demolish the toaster waffles. He glanced toward the back door once, probably to make sure Tess and Eleanor weren't about to burst on the scene, and cleared his throat. "Be careful, Lily," he said.

So he'd guessed what had happened between her and Tyler, then. Lily was a little embarrassed, but not surprised. After all, the signs were probably all there, and the man hadn't been born yesterday. "Too late," she answered.

Her dad reached across the table, closed his hand over hers. "Is it serious?"

"I don't know," Lily said truthfully. She, too,

glanced toward the door then, but Tess and Eleanor were still in the backyard. The sweet sound of their laughter came through the screen door. She swallowed, moved by the ordinary joy of two little girls enjoying a summer morning. "Is this the part where you remind me that Tyler is a Creed?"

Hal shook his head. "Nobody knows that better than you do," he said.

Lily's throat tightened then, cinched closed so she couldn't speak. Tears stung her eyes.

"I'm your father, Lily," Hal went on hoarsely, his own eyes moist. "I love you, and I want you to be happy. With or without Tyler Creed."

I'm your father—I love you—I want you to be happy.

Since when? Lily wondered.

"I know you don't believe it," Hal persisted, watching her in that vaguely unsettling way again. "That I love you, I mean. But I always did and I always will."

Lily couldn't stand it anymore, couldn't keep the hurt inside. "Then *why?*" she whispered raggedly. "Why did you shut me out the way you did? Why didn't you call or write or let me visit?"

Hal wiped his eyes. Cleared his throat again. Looked everywhere but at Lily and then forced himself, visibly, to meet her gaze. "I didn't want you in Stillwater Springs because Tyler was here," he said finally. "He'd hurt you so badly, fooling around with that waitress."

"But Tyler and I had already broken up—" Lily began, then her voice faltered. She sucked in a shaky breath, stunned by the depth of the pain the mention of Tyler's long-ago lover caused her.

Hal smiled sadly. "You would have forgiven him, Lily," he said. "He would have charmed you into giving him a second chance eventually, and you know it. I grew up with Jake Creed, remember. I saw him buzz-saw his way through three wives, and Tyler and his brothers seemed like chips off the old block back then. I couldn't bear the idea of seeing you destroyed—"

Lily didn't want to believe her father—she'd lived with the grudge for a long time and it had become comfortable in an odd sort of way—but she knew he was telling the truth. He'd been protecting her all along.

From herself, and from Tyler.

"I thought—"

"I know what you thought, sweetheart," Hal said sadly. "But things had to be that way. I couldn't have you coming back to Stillwater Springs for any reason, and there was only one thing that would keep you safe—my letting you believe I didn't want you around anymore."

Lily pushed her plate away, set her elbows on the table and buried her face in her hands. "You came to my wedding," she reminded him, reminded herself, her voice muffled by her palms and fingers.

He patted her shoulder. "I wouldn't have missed

that," he said. "I had my doubts about Burke, like I told you, but I figured you'd be safe from Tyler, with another man's wedding ring on your finger. I hoped you and I could find our way back to each other then, but the damage was done. You wanted nothing to do with me, beyond my walking you down the aisle to your bridegroom, and I can't say I blame you."

"Why did you change your mind? About Tyler, I mean?"

"I saw how Logan and Dylan had grown up," Hal replied. "And I ran into Tyler a few times, when he came back to Stillwater Springs to hide out in that cabin of his. He seemed like a different person. And I realized I'd been unfair, expecting him to turn out the way Jake did."

As kids, Lily and Tyler had had their share of heart-to-heart talks, but Tyler had never been willing to discuss his father. "Was Jake Creed always—well—like he was?"

Hal sighed, remembering. "No," he admitted. "His folks were decent, hardworking people. They raised Jake right. But the summer before we all started high school, Jake's little brother, Pete, drowned in a swimming hole, out there on the ranch. Pete was only ten or so, and he was clowning around. Swam like a fish, that boy, kept up with the rest of us just fine. He went under and got his foot caught between two old logs lying on the bottom, and by the time we missed him and dove to look for him, it was too late. Jake and I pried him loose and hauled him to the bank, tried to revive him, but he was gone."

Lily put a hand over her mouth, horrified.

"Jake's mother went crazy with grief, as you can imagine. Said she'd trusted Jake to look out for his little brother and he'd let him die—and a whole lot of other things she didn't mean. Jake was never quite the same after that—he grew up, joined the army, went to Viet Nam. His folks died in a car wreck right before he would have mustered out. The army discharged him early, and he came home for the funeral. Between Pete's death and the things he'd seen in combat—" Hal stopped, shook his head again. "Jake went wild. That's all I can say. It was as if he was trying to kill himself the hard way."

Lily let all that soak in. Tyler had never said anything about his uncle's drowning, and it was unlikely that he didn't know, since Stillwater Springs was such a small place. "You were *there* when Pete died?" she finally asked, knowing she was a few beats behind. "You never told me—"

"Would you have told Tess, if you'd had an experience like that?" Hal challenged gently. "Like Jake, I thought I should have been able to save that little boy. I was the Eagle Scout. I knew CPR and all the rest. Instead, I was so busy splashing around in the water, trying to impress some girl, that I didn't even notice Pete was missing."

"You were a child yourself," Lily reminded him.

Hal sighed, wiped his eyes again. "I got over it—insofar as you can ever get over a thing like that. Mom and Dad saw me through the worst of it."

Lily's grandparents, like Tyler's, had died before she was born—both had suffered heart attacks, within a month of each other—so she'd never known them. But their influence lingered—the figurines in the antique cabinet in the dining room had belonged to her grandmother, and she'd been lulled to sleep, as an infant, in her grandfather's old rocking chair.

"Did you ever wish you'd had brothers and sisters?" Lily asked her dad. It was the kind of thing she should have known about her own father, would have if she hadn't been so furious with him all these years. Looking back, she knew he wasn't entirely to blame—she'd cut him off, too.

"Yes," Hal answered. "Did you?"

Lily considered. Nodded. "Being an only child had its advantages, though," she added.

They both chuckled.

And Tess bounded in at just that moment, filthy from head to foot, an equally messy Eleanor directly behind her.

"We didn't find China," Tess announced.

Hal laughed, but it was a misty sound, slightly rough. "Well, go figure," he commented. "I thought you'd be checking out the Great Wall by now."

"It must be down there somewhere," Eleanor reasoned solemnly. "China, I mean."

"Go and wash up, both of you," Lily told the girls. "You look like street urchins."

"What's a street urchin?" Eleanor inquired, with great interest.

"It's just a figure of speech," Tess informed her new friend matter-of-factly. "It means our clothes are dirty and our hair is messed up and people will think we don't have anybody to take care of us." She paused, looking thoughtful. "My mom says things like that all the time."

Hal raised an eyebrow.

"I do not," Lily protested.

"Then how come I know what 'street urchin' means?" Tess retorted sagely. "I'm only six, after all. It had to come from *somewhere*."

"Just wash," Lily said, resigned.

In the laundry room, the washer banged to a stop, having completed its spin cycle.

Lily left the table, fetched the dress and took it outside to hang on the clothesline. Tess had gone into the bathroom to clean up and change clothes, and Eleanor crossed the yard to the back gate.

"My aunt is taking me berry-picking today," Eleanor said, in parting. "Can Tess go, too?"

"Not this time," Lily said, as kindly as she could. She would need to know Eleanor's aunt and uncle a while before she'd let Tess go anywhere with them.

Eleanor took the refusal with a shrug and let herself into the adjoining yard, vanishing into the house.

Lily was still standing near the clothesline, one hand shading her eyes as she surveyed the pitiful state of her dad's flower garden, when a flashy pickup truck whipped into the dirt driveway between the two houses.

At first, the pit of her stomach clenched. The equation was: truck=Tyler, and since the vehicle's windows were tinted, she couldn't see who was driving.

She was both relieved and disappointed when Kristy got out of the rig, smiling broadly. "Hey," she said.

"Hey," Lily said back. For a moment, it seemed to Lily that both she and Kristy were kids again, as innocent as Eleanor and Tess.

"Briana is going to teach me to bake bread today," Kristy announced. "I thought you and Tess might want to come along, spend the day out on the ranch with us."

"Don't you have to run the library?" Lily asked, and instantly felt stupid.

Kristy was certainly capable of managing her own schedule.

"Bonnie and I are taking the day off." Kristy grinned, giving a nod toward the truck. "Letting the volunteers take care of things."

Lily nodded, tilted her head to see around the

open door on the driver's side and spotted a little blond girl strapped into a car seat.

Kristy's gaze drifted over Lily's shorts and blouse. "Change into jeans," she said. "And wear boots, too, if you've got any. We could go for a horseback ride while the bread dough is rising."

"I've never been on a horse in my life," Lily said, alarmed. But it wasn't the horse that scared her; as a veterinarian's daughter, she'd been around animals of all shapes and sizes. It was just that Stillwater Springs Ranch was Tyler's home ground, and that made an encounter more likely. She didn't know if she was ready to face him yet.

"Time you tried it," Kristy said.

"A horse! I love horses, and baking stuff, too!" Tess enthused, from just behind Lily. She hadn't heard the child approaching, and almost jumped out of her skin. "Oh, *Mom,* we *have* to go!"

Kristy chuckled, nodded her agreement with Tess.

"Is Tyler—" Lily croaked out, and then felt stupid all over again.

A look of understanding moved in Kristy's face, along with a certain sadness. "It's not likely you'll run into Ty," she said, very quietly. "Come on, Lily. This would be good for you. And I'd really like for you to meet Briana and her boys."

"Please, Mom?" Tess pleaded, standing at Lily's elbow now and looking up at her plaintively. It was as though the little girl's whole future hinged on 1)

161

riding a horse and 2) baking bread. If she'd been a few years older, the boys probably would have been a factor, too. "Please?"

Lily couldn't think of a reason not to go—her father wanted, and probably *needed,* to visit the clinic, look in on his furry patients, make sure the veterinary school student filling in for him was taking care of business. Eleanor would be off berry-picking for the day, leaving Tess at loose ends.

"All right," she said, slipping an arm around Tess's shoulders and squeezing her once against her side. "Why don't you and Bonnie come inside and say hello to my dad while I change."

Tess had already swapped out her China-tunneling gear for blue jeans and a T-shirt.

Kristy's gaze moved past Lily, and her smile brightened. "Hello, Doc," she said, as Lily turned to see her father coming toward the fence. "How are you?"

"I'm doing just fine," Hal said warmly. "Coffee's on. Come on in and visit for a few minutes."

Kristy looked cheerfully regretful. "Maybe next time," she said. "If I take Bonnie out of that car seat, it will be half a day before I can wrestle her back in."

Tess had Lily by the hand by then, tugging her toward the house. "*Hurry,* Mom!" she whispered, as though afraid Kristy would change her mind, rescind the invitation to bake bread and ride horses and go off without them.

Kristy and Hal went on chatting while Tess practically dragged Lily inside.

While Tess waited impatiently in the kitchen, Lily donned a long-sleeved pink T-shirt, hoping to protect herself a little from the fierce summer sun, and insisted that Tess switch out her sandals for a sturdy pair of sneakers.

Neither of them owned a pair of boots.

Within a few minutes, they were buckled into the flashy extended-cab truck waiting in the driveway, Tess in back with Bonnie, Lily up front with Kristy.

"This is quite a rig," Lily said, as they backed out of the driveway, Kristy giving a farewell toot of the horn to Hal, who stood waving in the yard.

"It's Dylan's," Kristy explained, shifting out of Reverse with admirable skill when they'd reached the street. "Tyler has my Blazer."

Tyler.

Lily drew in a breath.

It was pretty bad when even the mention of his name threw her off balance.

"My mom went out to dinner with Tyler last night," Tess piped up, from the back. "She got home *really* late and she wore this pretty red dress—that was it hanging on the clothesline in my grampa's yard—"

"Tess," Lily broke in, closing her eyes.

Kristy merely chuckled.

"Eleanor is going berry-picking with her aunt

today," Tess prattled on. It was as though she'd stored up words and more words, for months or even years, and the dam had finally broken. Tess was at verbal flood tide. "She wanted me to come with them, but I knew my mom would say no because she doesn't let me go places with people unless she's along, too, or she's been friends with them *forever*—Wait till I tell Eleanor that I got to go someplace, too, and even ride a horse and make bread—"

Lily groaned slightly.

Kristy smiled, reached across the console to pat her arm. "It's okay, Lily," she said quietly. "Let her talk."

And talk Tess did—all the way to Stillwater Springs Ranch, some twenty minutes outside of town.

Lily had visited the place once or twice in her teens, while she was dating Tyler, and it had been pretty run-down the last time she'd seen it.

Now, the hand-carved sign over the front gate arched proudly over their heads as Kristy drove beneath it. The barn had been entirely replaced, and the corral fences were in good repair and painted white. The house retained its original rambling Ponderosa-like design, but the fresh-lumber framework of two large new wings jutted out from either side.

The yard seemed full of dogs and little boys, though in reality there were only two of each.

164

Bonnie began clamoring to get out of her car seat and join the fun, and Tess went silent, but not, Lily sensed, because she felt shy. The little girl fairly exuded eager curiosity.

"Stay put, Houdini," Kristy told Bonnie, bringing the rig to a stop between another truck and a BMW. They all waited while the cloud of dust they'd raised subsided a little.

The boys—a little older than Tess—bounded toward the truck, the dogs frolicking behind them. The smaller boy jumped up onto the running board on Kristy's side and gestured for her to roll down the window.

She did, waving some of the still-roiling dust away from her face. "Hey, Alec. Josh. What's happening?"

Alec, it turned out, was the boy standing on the running board. He gave Lily a brief glance, then focused his freckled attention on Tess. "Who's the *girl?*" he asked.

"That's my good friend, Tess," Kristy said, without hesitation. "Tess, this yahoo with his head stuck through the window is Alec. The polite one is his big brother, Josh."

"Hello," Tess said staunchly. Her desire to be part of the afternoon's adventures was almost palpable.

One second after she'd spoken, she was out of the truck, springing to the ground, rushing to join in. Bonnie, trapped in her car seat, wailed with frustration.

165

"I'm coming," Kristy told Bonnie calmly, unhooking her seat belt.

Alec had leaped off the running board by then, so it was safe to open the driver's door. Kristy did so, and went around to set Bonnie free. Lily was the last one out of the rig.

A trim woman came out of the house, smiling. She had vivid green eyes and strawberry-blond hair, pulled back into a tidy French braid. Like Kristy, she wore jeans and a cotton print blouse, and the boots on her feet weren't the for-show kind. They were scuffed, and respectably dirty, with rounded toes and low heels, the kind a rancher's wife would wear.

"You must be Lily," the woman said warmly, putting out a hand in greeting. She had to raise her voice a little to be heard over the gleeful barking of the two dogs and all the kids jabbering at once.

"And you must be Briana," Lily responded, offering her own hand, and a smile, too.

Briana's attention was momentarily diverted to her sons. "Boys," she said. "Settle down a little, and the dogs will, too. All that yapping and yowling is enough to give me a headache."

"We've got lots of horses," Lily heard the older boy, Josh, say to Tess. "Want to see them?"

Lily bit back an automatic be-careful. She didn't know Briana Creed, but Kristy was an old friend, and a responsible person, and she didn't seem one

166

bit worried. Lily took a deep breath, let it out slowly and kept her fears to herself.

Kristy hoisted Bonnie up onto one hip and offered a hand to Tess. "I'll go along, too," she said, and started for the barn.

Lily didn't know whether to follow the gaggle of woman, dogs and children, or stay behind with Briana.

"She's a regular pied piper," Briana commented, smiling as she watched Kristy move away, with a trail of kids and canines straggling behind her. "Come inside, Lily. I just brewed a pitcher of iced tea."

Again, Lily hesitated—everything inside her was geared to watching over Tess in any and all situations—but there was something about Briana, about the very energy of that place, that reassured her.

And she trusted Kristy.

"Your dad gave us quite a scare," Briana said, as she and Lily headed toward the house. "I guess you know the heart attack happened right here, on our patio, during a barbecue we held for Jim Huntinghorse, when he was running for sheriff."

Lily nodded, shuddering a little. The story could so easily have turned out differently—she and Tess might have come back to Stillwater Springs for a funeral, rather than a long summer visit.

"Dylan and Jim did CPR," Briana went on, as they stepped into a cool, old-fashioned kitchen.

The room, like the rest of the house, was obviously being renovated.

"I'd like to thank them both in person," Lily said.

"You'll get your chance," Briana told her, gesturing toward the large round table in the center of the kitchen and heading for the refrigerator. "Have a seat. I'll pour that tea I promised you."

Lily sat down, looking around and trying not to be too obvious about it.

The Creeds were a local legend, so she knew some of their history. According to Hal, except for the five years since Jake Creed's death, that house had been continuously occupied for well over a century.

What would it be like, to live in a place where so many of your ancestors had lived and died?

"We're replacing this god-awful flooring with pegged hardwood," Briana said good-naturedly, arriving at the table with two ice-filled glasses and a pitcher of cold tea. "At the same time, Logan and I don't want to change things too much."

Logan and I.

Lily smiled. In high school, Logan had had the typical Creed reputation: hell-raiser, heartbreaker, fearless rebel. He'd been reckless to a fault. Now, apparently, he was a family man, concerned with things like pegged hardwood and the integrity of old houses. "I see you're building on," she said, mostly because it was her turn to contribute to the conversation.

Briana smiled, poured tea for herself and then for Lily, and sat down across from her at the table. Schoolbooks and tablet paper had been gathered into a semineat pile and shunted over to one side. "We're adding a master suite," she told Lily. "Rooms for the boys, an office for Logan and a big family room."

A big family room implied the expectation of a big *family.* Clearly, Briana and Logan planned to have more children, and Lily felt a swift stab of generous envy. She'd wanted at least four herself, and she and Burke had tried, but after Tess, there had been no more pregnancies.

She supposed it was for the best, but there was still that bruised place in her heart, where the disappointment lived.

She must have made some inane comment, because Briana reacted as though she'd spoken.

Nodding, Briana joked, "At least we're not going to have a room with a mechanical bull in it, like Kristy and Dylan."

"A mechanical bull?" Lily echoed, confused.

"You know." Briana grinned. "Like the ones they have in cowboy bars? A bull-shaped machine that bucks?"

Lily laughed. *Toto,* she said silently, *we're not in Chicago anymore.*

"I remember," she told Briana. "Dylan rode bulls in the rodeo."

Again, Briana nodded. "Logan's event was saddle-bronc riding, and Tyler rode bareback."

Tyler. For about five seconds, she'd forgotten about him.

Silly to think the respite could have lasted. This was Tyler's childhood home; he'd grown up in this house. And even when Lily was dating him, back when she'd barely gotten the braces off her teeth, he'd been entering every rodeo he could.

"I guess they must still have the rodeo in their blood," she said, referring to the mechanical bull Dylan and Kristy were installing.

Briana smiled again. Or had she ever actually *stopped* smiling? She and Kristy were about the happiest women Lily had ever seen, and it wasn't hard to figure out at least one of the reasons. They slept with Creed men, every night of their lives. It figured that they'd glow with perpetual satisfaction, if her own night with Tyler was any indication of what these fabled brothers could do in—or out of—bed.

"They're over it," Briana said, with a note of relief in her voice. "Following the rodeo, I mean. But Logan and Dylan still ride like crazy men when they're herding cattle." She paused and, for the first time, her spirits seemed, if not dampened, not high, either. "Then there's Tyler—"

"Does he still follow the rodeo?" Lily ventured, hoping she sounded casual. The ice cubes in her tea glass rattled a little, though, as she lifted it to her mouth to take a sip.

"I don't think so," Briana answered, after biting

her lower lip and looking away for a moment. "He doesn't come around, and Logan and Dylan don't talk about him much, so I don't know for sure."

"Oh," Lily said, much relieved when Kristy, Bonnie, Tess, the boys and the two dogs all came in from outside.

Kristy carried Bonnie into a nearby bathroom, and when the two of them came out, their faces and hands were scrubbed clean. Briana sent her boys to wash up, and that left Tess standing there in a strange kitchen, looking somewhat at a loss.

The poignant hope in Tess's little face struck Lily like a blow. She got up, went to the kitchen sink and moistened a length of paper towels under the faucet.

"Let's get you washed up, too," she told Tess, as briskly as if she were a Creed wife, like Kristy and Briana, and Tess was as much a part of this boisterous household as Bonnie or Alec or Josh.

Tess's smile was so quick, and so bright, that Lily's throat closed up again.

For a little while, she told herself, she'd let Tess pretend that they both belonged with this family, on this land. And she'd allow herself to pretend a little, too.

CHAPTER NINE

WITH KRISTY AND BRIANA laughing and chattering in that venerable old kitchen, and flour flying everywhere as the makings of bread dough were gathered and assembled, it was all too easy for Lily to go right on pretending.

She imagined what it would be like to be married to Tyler.

For starters, the sex would be cataclysmic.

And Tyler would want her to let Tess take more chances, urge Lily not to be overprotective, and they'd argue about that sometimes.

She was a good cook, so she wouldn't mind fixing the meals, but, like her dad, Tyler probably wouldn't be all that crazy about the quantities of tofu she'd feed him.

They'd probably have words about that, too.

Heated ones, maybe.

And then they'd make up in bed, in the sultry darkness of the room they shared, not just one night, but *every* night, as soon as they were sure Tess was sound asleep and wouldn't overhear.

Imagining the making-up process made Lily's core turn molten and her face burn. She waited until neither Briana nor Kristy was looking, then held her iced tea glass, many times refilled by then, to the base of her throat.

Her heart was beating too fast, and her breath

was shallow. And still she couldn't make herself put an end to the scenarios unfolding in her mind.

Tyler would be good with kids—she knew that. He'd be a father to Tess, love her like his own. Teach her to ride and fish and fix things that were broken.

And Tess would thrive under the warmth of his easy approval, in a way she might never do if it was just her and Lily against the world.

You're on dangerous ground, warned the voice in Lily's head, the one that hadn't wanted her to go out with Tyler the night before. The one that had scolded her for hanging her panties to dry on the side mirror of the Blazer he'd borrowed from Kristy. The one that would never, *ever* say the things Lily had not only said but shouted in the delicious, frenzied, slippery-naked heat of love-making.

The iced tea wasn't helping. And Lily couldn't stop the fantasies.

She imagined Tyler assembling things, late on Christmas Eve, to put under the tree for an ever-more Santa-skeptical Tess.

She imagined washing his back in the shower, even ironing his shirts.

All of it sounded good.

Her practical side tried, yet again, to assert itself. *And none of it is ever going to happen. You're torturing yourself, that's all.*

Her *im*practical side won out.

When the bread dough was finally glimmering, buttery-topped and fragrant, in a row of pans on the counter, and they all trooped outside for the promised horseback ride, Lily pictured Tyler saddling a horse, lifting Tess onto the animal's back, adjusting the stirrups for her, calmly instructing her to hold the reins this way. . . .

And once Tess was safely settled on some gentle creature, Tyler would give Lily a boost into another saddle, on another horse, and swing up behind her. Reach around her to take the reins, enclosing her in the steely circle of his arms.

She could almost feel his erection pressing against her buttocks and lower back, hard with heat and promise.

When we're alone, he might whisper into her ear, *this is what I'm going to do to you. . . .*

"Are you all right?" Kristy asked, breaking into Lily's reverie. "You look flushed. You're not sick or scared or anything, are you?"

Lily wasn't sick or scared, mounted though she was on a real, live, sweaty, dusty horse. The creature was so old it hadn't even moved yet, though all the other horses, Tess's pony included, were moving happily around the grassy pasture just beyond the corral fence.

Even little Bonnie was riding, safely tucked in front of Kristy, grinning and gripping the saddle horn with both her pudgy little hands.

"I'm okay," Lily lied, summoning up a smile. *Just terminally horny, that's all.*

Kristy smiled, believing her. "Good," she said.

They'd finished the ride, and put all the horses away by the time Logan and Dylan arrived, crossing the broad pasture on horses of their own. The boy Lily had seen with Tyler the day before, in Wal-Mart, was with them, riding behind Dylan.

Lily had virtually grown up with Logan and Dylan, and they greeted her exuberantly. Logan sprang down off his horse, picked her up by the waist and spun her around in a circle before planting a smacking kiss on her cheek. She'd barely recovered her equilibrium before Dylan did the same thing.

Logan and Dylan made short work of unsaddling their horses and turning them loose in the corral.

"Where's Tyler?" someone asked as the whole bunch of them headed toward the house. The bread was ready to go into the oven, according to Briana, and Lily knew she and Kristy had planned a huge ranch-style supper to go with it.

By then, Lily had decided to give Tess, and herself, the gift of letting the pretending go on until the day was over and they were back in the real world.

A look passed between Logan and Dylan, and the boy—Davie, if Lily recalled correctly, from their brief meeting at Wal-Mart—was the one who answered the question about Tyler's whereabouts.

"Maybe his truck is fixed," Davie said, sounding a little sad. "And he's gone to pick it up."

Dylan slapped the boy on the shoulder and then said something that made him smile tentatively, though Lily didn't hear what it was.

The bread turned out perfectly, and the meat loaf and several side dishes Briana had prepared tasted as good as anything Lily had ever eaten.

But darkness was gathering outside the windows of that well-lit, noisy kitchen. It was the time of day that had always made her homesick after her mom and dad's divorce; when she was with one, she'd missed the other.

Now, perhaps because of the silly head games she'd been playing with herself all afternoon, it was Tyler she missed.

His absence was a yawning ache inside her.

And she suspected, for all the laughter and the teasing and the second helpings, that some of the others gathered in that enormous kitchen felt it, too.

He should have been there.

She and Tess didn't belong—but he did.

When the evening finally wound down, it was Dylan who drove Lily and Tess back to town. Tess, exhausted from all the fun, had practically fallen asleep on her plate, and Dylan had carried the child to his truck, buckled her in with the easy skill of a veteran father.

Tess was out like the proverbial light before

they'd even passed under the big sign over the gate.

Dylan didn't say much until they'd reached the main road. Then he cleared his throat, glanced into his rearview mirror to make sure Tess was down for the count, and said, just as her father had, "Be careful, Lily."

She stiffened, looked over at him. "What's that supposed to mean?" she asked lightly.

"You know what it means," Dylan told her patiently.

Lily's face heated again, but this time the phenomenon was rooted in mortification, not fantasy. "He told you?"

"That the two of you spent the night together?" Dylan asked. "There was no need for that, Lily. He asked Kristy and me to keep Davie with us until this morning, and it wasn't hard to figure out the rest."

"Dylan, you're a good friend—you saved my father's life and I'll always be grateful—and *I like you.* I especially like your wife. But none of this is any of your business—I hope you know that."

He grinned that crooked-at-the-corner Creed grin that had probably been the ruination of more women than a Chinese merchant could tally up on an abacus. "Take it easy. I'm on your side. All I'm saying is, Tyler's still—Tyler. Of the three of us, he was the wildest. He's got a temper and a grudge against Logan and a few other people in this town, and I don't believe he's thinking straight."

Tyler's still Tyler.

"I don't want to see you get hurt, Lily," Dylan said. "That's all."

Lily bit her lower lip, looked away, changed the subject. Dylan might be satisfied that Tess was actually asleep, but she wasn't. Like all children, Tess played possum when she wanted to listen in on a grown-up conversation.

"I really appreciate what you and Jim Huntinghorse did for my dad," she said. "When he had his heart attack, I mean."

Dylan resettled his hat, kept his gaze straight ahead, on the dark highway. The truck's headlights shone like beacons, but country roads were treacherous—Tyler had barely missed a doe and a fawn early that morning, when he was bringing her home. "I guess the other conversation's over?" he asked.

Lily indicated Tess's presence with a slight motion of her head. "For now," she said.

Dylan didn't say much of anything after that. He delivered Lily and Tess to Hal's house in town. By the time they arrived, Tess was awake, yawning and dusty and a little sun-burned.

He walked both of them to the front door, but as soon as Tess had gone inside, calling for her grandfather and probably intending to give him a blow-by-blow account of the afternoon's events, Dylan stopped Lily on the porch by taking a light grip on her elbow.

178

"I can't let you go in there thinking any of us—the Creeds, I mean—would be unhappy if you and Tyler got together," he said. "We'd be thrilled, Lily. But he's still got a lot of things to work through, and I don't want you or Tess to be caught in the cross fire."

Lily nodded, touched by Dylan's concern. It was almost as if they were already family. "Thank you, Dylan," she said, and she meant it.

He leaned forward, planted a light, brotherly kiss on her forehead. "Come back to the ranch again soon," he told her. "It was real nice having you and Tess around."

More emotion welled up inside Lily, so much that she couldn't speak. She'd felt alone for so long, even before Burke died, and the afternoon on the ranch had been wonderful—like being part of a large, caring family.

Dylan smiled, turned and walked away.

Lily stood on the porch, watching until he drove away, and nearly collided with Hal when she turned to go inside.

"Tess is sleeping in her clothes," Hal reported, with a smile. "She's absolutely worn-out, but she promised to tell me all about her day at breakfast."

Lily swallowed hard, laughed. "I'd better go in and help her change into pajamas at least," she said.

Hal shook his head, urged her toward the rocking chairs at the other end of the porch. "I took her shoes off," he replied, "and one night sleeping in her clothes won't do any harm."

Lily let her father guide her to a chair, and sat down somewhat heavily.

"You're pretty tired, too," Hal observed gently.

Lily nodded. "It was quite a day."

"Especially after such a late night," her dad agreed.

Lily let the remark pass.

"I brought your dress in from the clothesline after I got back from visiting the clinic," Hal told her affably, settling into the second rocking chair. In happier days, before and after the divorce, the two of them had sat on the porch lots of nights, talking about everything in general and nothing in particular. "It was dry and I figured it might fade or something if I left it out there."

Lily nodded her thanks but let the comment pass. "How are things going at the clinic?" she asked. Hal looked rested, as though he might have had a recent nap, so it seemed safe to assume he hadn't overextended himself by visiting his office.

"Great," Hal answered, with a gruff little chuckle. "It's almost as if they don't need me down there at all."

"Have you thought about retiring? Selling the practice and just taking it easy?"

"I'd be dead inside of six months," Hal wasted no time in saying. He wasn't looking at Lily, but out into the spill of light pooling beneath the

180

nearest streetlamp. "Nothing like a heart attack to make a man take stock of his life. My veterinary practice—well—it's about the only thing I've done right in a long, long time."

Don't, Lily pleaded silently. Now that the day on Stillwater Springs Ranch was over, and the fantasy of being a Creed wife had passed—all the things she'd imagined seemed silly now—her emotions were raw, and much too close to the surface for comfort.

It was sinking in now, Dylan's warning.

Tyler was indeed still Tyler, always ready to take chances, tangle with fate, face whatever came his way.

And she was still Lily Ryder Kenyon, basically shy, overly cautious, terrified of so many things.

Hal took her hand, unaware of her thoughts, of course. Chafed her knuckles with his thumb. "I'm sorry, Lily. I'm sorry for the way your mother and I handled the divorce. Sorry for sending you away. I should have had more faith in you—let you live your life, with or without Tyler Creed."

Lily was glad of the relative darkness shrouding that porch, because her eyes filled with tears.

I should have had more faith in you.

Her father had been trying to protect her, just as she tried to protect her own child. Would there be a gulf between her and Tess someday, like the one she and her father were trying to bridge now? Did she have the courage to allow Tess to grow up in

181

confidence instead of the continual fear that something bad would happen? Could she allow Tess to make her own mistakes, and suffer the consequences?

"You did your best," Lily managed to say, though her voice was hardly more than a murmur. "And maybe you were right. Maybe Tyler would have sweet-talked me into forgiving him, way back when—"

"And maybe you would have been happy with him, Lily," Hal broke in quietly.

"I wouldn't have had Tess, then. And I can't imagine that."

"I know. But you wouldn't have known the difference, would you, if your life had taken a different course?" He paused, gave a ragged chortle. "You might have had a son or a daughter with Tyler—maybe several. And then you wouldn't be able to imagine not being the mother of *those* children, either."

As convoluted as it was, Lily got her father's point. And a certain sadness possessed her; for a moment or two, she was struck breathless with the loss of the children who had never been born to her and Tyler. It was as if they'd actually existed somewhere, all this time, just out of reach.

Rowdy, rough-and-tumble boys.

Sweet, spirited girls.

She shook off the strange yearnings her father's words had aroused in her. She had Tess, and Tess was the greatest blessing in her life. It was wrong to want more.

"I guess it's making me crazy," Hal reflected apologetically, after a long, pensive silence. "Recovering from that damn heart attack, that is. I've got too much time to think."

Lily could identify. Before her return to Stillwater Springs, she'd been too busy with Tess and her very demanding job and, until two years ago, Burke, to think about Tyler, and the children and home they might have had together. Except, of course, during those moments when memories would ambush her . . .

Stop, she told herself.

There was no reason to believe that, even if she and Tyler *had* gotten back together, even if she'd married him instead of Burke, things would be all sunshine and roses now.

Like as not, Tyler would have gotten restless and left her alone to go on the rodeo circuit. And he probably would have found himself another wait-ress, eventually, too. Maybe a whole bunch of them.

"Are you planning to see Tyler again, Lily?" Hal asked.

Lily rose slowly out of her chair. Stretched. She was tired to the bone, and she ached, though whether that was because of that afternoon's brief horseback ride or Tyler's lovemaking, she didn't know.

"He hasn't asked," she said.

"He will," Hal said, standing up. "And that isn't an answer."

If Tyler set out to seduce her again, Lily knew, she wouldn't put up much resistance. Where he was concerned, she seemed to have no willpower at all, which was a scary thing, since she was so independent in every other way. But it went deeper than physical need, beyond desire, into something basic and sacred and mostly inexplicable.

She knew this much: There was a certain spectacular freedom in letting herself go, the way she had with Tyler. She'd felt powerful, even in surrender, strong, even in weakness. In Tyler's company, in his arms, in his *bed,* she was a different person. A person who wasn't afraid to *feel.*

She'd swaddled herself in pretended indifference, not long after Burke's first affair. And in the rare instances when that apathy had given way, she'd hated herself for not having the backbone to leave him, right then, and start over somewhere else, just her and Tess.

"Lily?" Hal prompted, rising out of his chair, too. It rocked rhythmically with the motion, as though, in some parallel universe, another Hal was still sitting there.

She sighed. Her father wasn't the only one losing his mind. "I'd go," she admitted, to herself as well as to Hal. "If Tyler asked me out again, I'd say yes."

He patted her shoulder. "That's what I thought," he said.

They went into the house then, father and daughter, and Lily noticed that her dad paused to lock the front door and turn the dead bolt. It hurt, knowing the town she remembered as such a safe place had changed enough to make such measures necessary.

Hal switched off various lights, and Lily went on to the kitchen, to take his pill bottles down from one of the cupboards and carefully count out the night's dose.

Reluctantly, he swallowed the medicine, said good-night, disappeared into his room.

Lily remained in the kitchen for a few minutes, puttering. Setting up the coffeemaker for morning, checking her cell phone, which she'd forgotten to charge the night before.

She plugged it into the cord, switched it on to check for messages.

To her surprise, there were two.

Vaguely unsettled, since no one had called her on the cell phone since the day she left Chicago to rush to her father's bedside in that Missoula hospital, Lily punched in the voice-mail codes.

The first call was from Eloise. She missed Tess—and, oh, yes, Lily, too, of course—and some storage-unit place had called about an overdue bill. Evidently, Burke had stashed some of his belongings there, and did Lily want to go through all that

185

stuff, or should she, Eloise, have it hauled away?

Lily frowned. She'd paid all of Burke's bills after he died, as they came in. If there had been one from this "storage-unit place," as Eloise put it, she would have paid that, too.

Her first instinct was to call her mother-in-law back, as late as it was, and ask her to have some charity haul away whatever Burke had been storing, promising to reimburse her for the storage rental and any other expenses involved. But something besides common courtesy stopped her from dialing the familiar number.

Suppose there were things in that storage unit that Tess would want someday?

That didn't seem likely, once Lily reflected on it for a few moments. If Eloise Kenyon was willing to have "that stuff" hauled away, that meant she had all the important mementos from her son's younger days safely in her possession.

It was all too complicated to think about that night. She'd decide what to do in the morning, when she was rested.

Lily saved her mother-in-law's message and listened to the second one.

Her boss had called.

They were sorry, and they hoped her father was getting better with every passing day, but they couldn't hold her job open for the requested six weeks after all.

If Lily couldn't return to Chicago by the beginning of the following week, they would have to replace her.

Numbed by the knowledge that she could be replaced so easily, Lily saved *that* message, too.

She *couldn't* go back to Chicago so soon.

Hal wasn't out of the woods yet, couldn't be left to fend for himself. He'd be back at work full-time and living on greasy cheeseburgers before she and Tess hit the city limits. And he'd said some things that worried her, while they were talking on the porch earlier.

Nothing like a heart attack to make a man take stock of his life. My veterinary practice—well—it's about the only thing I've done right in a long, long time.

I'd be dead in six months.

Chilled, Lily realized with a wallop how very much she wanted to get to *know* her father, get back to the place where she could comfortably call him "Dad" again.

As she prepared for bed, taking a long bath, pulling on the oversize T-shirt she'd always worn when she needed to feel cosseted and cozy, brushing her teeth, she reviewed her financial situation.

She wasn't rich, but she was a good saver and she had no debt to burden her. The cost of living in a small town like Stillwater Springs was certainly lower than in the Windy City, and if push came to shove, she could always sell her condo.

Maybe it was time to consider starting her own business, as Tess, of all people, had suggested. She'd always wanted to construct a Web site and sell "outsider art" online—clothing, jewelry, collages and paintings, the work of regular people.

"Regular people," in Lily's experience, were incredibly talented, and their creations were unique. In a world of mass manufacturing, handmade items had more appeal.

Of course, she reasoned, throwing back the covers to get into bed, it might be years before the Web site actually showed a profit—if it *ever* did.

On the other hand, her own needs were simple, and thanks to the trust fund Burke had set up before his death, Tess would never want for anything, even if Lily never worked another day in her life.

After switching off the bedside lamp, Lily lay in the dark, her tired mind whirling.

Eloise Kenyon would raise hell if she brought Tess to live in Stillwater Springs.

She recalled Tess's remark about the trust fund and the insurance settlement—an inadvertent relaying of some observation Eloise had made. Lying there in the spare room bed, Lily felt a surge of anger. *Damn,* she hated that kind of passive-aggressive crap.

And Tess was *her* child, not Eloise's.

Where Lily chose to live, and raise her daughter, was flat-out none of her mother-in-law's business.

Eloise could damn well lower herself to visit rural Montana if she wanted to see her grandchild, and of course there would always be the short jaunts to Nantucket and the Kenyon mansion in Oak Park. Whatever her own issues might be with Burke's mother, Lily knew that Eloise took very good care of Tess when the two of them were together, subtle make-sure-your-mother-hears-this comments to the little girl aside.

The first order of business, come morning, Lily decided, would be to call Eloise Kenyon and decide what to do with the contents of Burke's secret storage unit. Once that had been determined, Lily would break the news that she and Tess might be staying on in Stillwater Springs longer than they'd originally planned.

And when *that* conversation was finished, she would give her soon-to-be-former employer a ring. She knew her boss expected her to rush back to Chicago, flushed with chagrin over her absence and desperate to please, and get right back into the old harness.

Surprise, she thought, with a smile.

It was a new day.

And she was a new Lily.

She closed her eyes, relaxing into exhaustion, and when she opened them again, it was morning, and Tess was standing over her with the cordless phone from the kitchen in one hand.

"It's Nana," she said, in a stage whisper. "I told

her you were still sleeping, but she *has* to talk to you, *right now.*"

Exasperated, Lily struggled to wake up, raised herself to a sitting position with the pillows fluffed behind her and took the phone.

Tess lingered, probably curious, but Lily sent her out of the room with a waving motion of one hand.

Reluctantly, Tess left, closing the door behind her.

Lily drew a very deep breath and released it slowly before saying pleasantly, "Hello, Eloise. What's the big emergency?"

Eloise was silent for a moment, and when she spoke, it was with wounded indignation. "Can't I call my own daughter-in-law?" she asked. "Especially when she's taken my only grandchild to some godforsaken burg in *Montana?*"

Lily's temper surged. She tamped it down, forced a smile into her voice. "Tess told you I was sleeping," she said moderately. "When you insisted on talking to me anyway, I assumed it was urgent."

Clearly miffed, Eloise immediately snapped, "I need to know what you want me to do with Burke's things. The ones he was keeping in that storage unit."

"Now?" Lily asked sweetly.

She felt Eloise back off before she heard it in the other woman's voice. "I've been through the stuff," she admitted. "There's nothing that would

190

interest you or Tess—except possibly some medical records."

"Medical records?" Lily asked, sitting up straighter now. Feeling mildly alarmed. Had Burke been suffering from some hereditary disease—one that might have been passed down to Tess?

Eloise let out a long, broken sigh. "He had a vasectomy, Lily," she said. "Right after Tess was born."

Lily's head spun. *"What?"*

Eloise began to cry, very softly. "I know you always wanted more children. I wanted more *grandchildren.* Apparently, Burke deceived us both."

Burke had had a vasectomy—without telling her.

He'd let her go on hoping, go on trying to conceive, knowing all the while that he'd already made that impossible.

"Lily?" Eloise prompted, when Lily didn't respond. "Are you still there, dear?"

Dazed, Lily struggled to find her voice. When she did, she stammered out something incoherent and hung up. She dropped the receiver onto the bed beside her, laid both hands to her abdomen.

Tyler had asked if she could be pregnant.

And she'd said no.

A combination of exultation and fear roiled inside her.

Surprise, she thought. But this time, she wasn't smiling.

191

CHAPTER TEN

LOGAN'S UNSCHEDULED MORNING visit had been brief and to the point, and it stuck in Tyler's mind long after his brother had left the cabin. Soon afterward, Dylan had stopped by, ostensibly to drop Davie off.

As it turned out, Dylan and Logan were planning a trail ride into the foothills—Logan hadn't mentioned that—and they wanted to take Davie with them. The kid looked so hopeful, Tyler never thought of refusing—not that he had any right to say yes or no where Davie was concerned anyway.

"You could come with us," Davie suggested eagerly, stooping to ruffle Kit Carson's ears in belated greeting.

Tyler passed a glance in Dylan's direction. "Apparently, I'm not invited," he said. "Logan didn't say a word about any trail ride when he came by here a little while ago to harass me."

There had been something else Logan had wanted to say, something about Jake, though every time he'd gotten close to spitting out whatever it was, he'd veered off again. He'd mostly yammered on about the Tri-Star Cattle Company and how to err was human but to forgive divine.

Tyler did not aspire to divinity.

Dylan rolled his eyes. "Come on, Ty. What do

you need—a printed invite? You're welcome to ride with us and you damn well know it."

Davie's glance skittered from Dylan to Tyler. "If this is what having a brother is like," he said, "I'm kind of glad I'm an only child."

Tyler chuckled at that, in spite of his sour mood, and slapped the boy on the shoulder. "You go ahead. I'm going to call the repair shop in town—and maybe that truck of mine is ready to roll back onto the highway. It wasn't when I checked before."

Davie tensed, and his eyes narrowed. "You're leaving?"

"No," Tyler said quietly. "I just want my truck back."

"Okay," Davie said, relaxing a little.

Dylan was already moving toward the door. His gaze rested a moment on the Tri-Star papers Logan had left behind on the table, and Tyler wondered if they'd planned that early-morning recruitment effort between them. It seemed like something they'd do, but then again, Dylan wasn't the sort to let someone else handle his dirty work. He'd have been right there, along with Logan, if he'd had any part in the scheme. "Just leave the Blazer at the shop if your truck is running again," he said. "Kristy and I will pick it up later."

Tyler merely nodded.

"You're sure you won't come along?" Dylan pressed.

193

The truth was, Tyler wouldn't have minded a long trail ride up into the foothills, even if it meant spending time with his brothers. It had been too long since he'd been in the saddle, except to perform some lame-brained stunt for a movie camera. But he needed his own rig—he couldn't drive Kristy's Blazer forever. And besides, there were some other things he wanted to do.

"Maybe next time," Tyler said, figuring there probably wouldn't *be* a next time.

Dylan shrugged one shoulder and left the kitchen, headed outside, and Davie followed, though reluctantly, stopping on the threshold to try just once more. "It would sure be cool if you'd go with us," he said.

Tyler's throat tightened. He remembered asking Jake to come to the first basketball game of the season at Stillwater Springs High. It was his sophomore year, and he'd made the varsity team; the coach had promised he'd be on the court from the start, and he'd wanted his dad to be there. To be proud of him, maybe even nudge somebody sitting next to him in the bleachers with his elbow and say something embarrassing, like, "You see Number 22, there? That's my son."

Instead, Jake had blithely replied that he had a game that night himself—a high-stakes pool tournament, down at Skivvie's. As an afterthought, on his way out the back door at the main ranch house, he'd told Tyler, "Break a leg, kid."

Tyler had lost his taste for basketball after that, and taken up rodeoing instead—both Logan and Dylan, though still in high school, were already making more in prize money than they could have earned flipping burgers or sweeping floors someplace. And that was on the local circuit.

Anyhow, Tyler had decided, those shorts basketball players wore were just plain sissified, almost as bad as those stretchy shorts people wore to ride bicycles.

"I can't make it today, Davie," he said quietly, telling himself that it wasn't the same as Jake's refusing to watch a basketball game. Davie wasn't his son—probably. "Tomorrow, you and I will find a couple of horses and saddle up. Take a ride of our own. How's that?"

Davie looked partially appeased, but still disappointed, too. He nodded and left the house without another word. Drove off with Dylan.

"It's just you and me now, dog," Tyler told Kit Carson, as he took his cell phone from the counter, scrolled through his collection of numbers for the one for the auto-repair place in town and pressed the Call button.

Sure enough, the rig was ready. They'd installed a new muffler and done some work on the engine, too, though they recommended a total overhaul.

Tyler figured a trade-in would be easier—and cheaper.

He'd been a damn fool to swap his Escalade—

though for him it was roughly in the same category as basketball shorts and ten-speed gear—for an old wreck of a truck.

He'd done it on impulse, shedding that too-fancy SUV the way a snake shed an old skin.

Now, he'd have to live with the consequences.

With that much settled in his mind, if not much else, Tyler loaded Kit Carson into the back of the Blazer and headed for town.

The bill for the towing, not to mention the repairs, probably exceeded the actual value of the truck. Tyler paid it just the same, chalking it up to penance for rash behavior, locked up the Blazer and gave the keys to the girl working the parts counter for safekeeping and took off.

He and Kit Carson stopped off at the lumberyard on the way out of town, and he ordered enough to shore up some of the stuff that was sagging out at the cabin, figuring he'd have the carpentry thing figured out once he'd replaced the small back porch and laid a new kitchen floor. He took a load home in the back of his pickup, too.

He felt ambitious, and hoped this enterprise wouldn't turn out the way the truck deal had. But he had brand-new power tools, a hammer, a brown bag full of nails, and a lot of gumption. How hard could it be to rebuild the back steps and put in some new floorboards in the kitchen?

He picked up a few more groceries before leaving town, and then cruised casually by Doc Ryder's place, hoping for a glimpse of Lily, but there was no sign of her or the little girl or of Doc himself.

Just call her, he thought.

"Oh, right," he answered himself aloud, drawing a concerned look from Kit Carson, who was riding shotgun as usual. "I can hear it now. 'Hello, Lily. This is Tyler. What do you say we get together and boink each other's brains out again, just for the hell of it?'"

The dog whimpered. Maybe he thought he was getting chewed out for something. Or maybe he just disapproved of the turn the conversation had taken.

Tyler reached over and patted the mutt's head. "You a moralist, Kit?" he asked affably.

He'd been back home for several hours, finding out the hard way that replacing a porch, even a pissant one like he had, was easier to think about than to do, when an old black-and-tan Buick sedan rolled into his driveway around noon, throwing up dust in every direction.

Shirtless, since sawing and hammering was hot work on a sunny day, even that close to the lake, Tyler straightened and wondered who his visitor was.

He didn't have to wonder long.

Doreen got out of the dented Buick, dressed in her waitress getup and wearing a casino ID card pinned to her bodice. She'd troweled on the makeup that day, he saw, as she came closer.

197

"Is Davie around?" she asked, stopping about a dozen yards shy of close-up and eyeing poor old Kit Carson like he might spring at her and tear her throat out. Doreen had ridden with outlaw bikers and traveled with rock bands. And she was afraid of a stray like Kit?

But then Doreen was afraid of a lot of things these days, wasn't she?

Tyler set his hammer aside, reached for his T-shirt and pulled it on over his head. He'd had plenty of vine-swinging, chest-pounding, Tarzan-type sex with this woman, back in the day, but now being half-dressed in front of her seemed wrong.

"Nope," he answered. "He's gone on a trail ride with Dylan and Logan."

Doreen gnawed at her lower lip for a moment, and Tyler wondered if Roy had knocked her around a little the night before, or even that morning, so she had to cover up the bruises with war-paint, or if she'd just been heavy-handed with the stuff, hoping for better tips.

"Is he all right?" she finally asked.

"He's fine," Tyler said, approaching her. He wanted a closer look at her face, and when he got it, his blood stung in his veins like venom. He took a gentle but firm grip on Doreen's chin and said, "The gunk isn't working, Doreen. I can see the bruises."

"Let it go, Tyler," Doreen said. "Roy passed out before he did any real damage."

"Looks to me like he did *plenty* of damage," Tyler said, after unclamping his jaw. He was almost as angry with Doreen for putting up with that kind of treatment as he was with Roy for dishing it out. "When are you going to leave that bastard, Doreen? When are you going to stand up for yourself—and for Davie?"

"You don't understand," Doreen said, shrinking in on herself in that way she'd developed in the years since Tyler had first known her. In that way she'd passed on to Davie.

Tyler let his hand drop from her chin. Shook his head. "Oh, I understand, all right," he told her grimly. "You're going to let him do this again and again until he kills you."

Doreen took a step back, rummaged in her big shoulder bag, brought out a sheaf of papers. Thrust them at Tyler.

"What's this?" Tyler asked, even as he took the documents.

Evidently, this was his day for heavy-duty paperwork.

"I lied before," Doreen said, her voice quivering a little. "Davie *is* yours. Roy says if he's going to live with you, we'll need some kind of compensation. So he had a friend of his draw up these papers, over in Choteau, at one of those legal places."

"Compensation?" Tyler echoed, still absorbing the news that he was a father after all. He hadn't completely believed Doreen before, when she'd said Davie's father was a truck driver she'd "cheered up" one night after a shift at Skivvie's. Contradictory though it was, he didn't believe her this time, either.

"We want a hundred thousand dollars," Doreen said, with all the bravado she could drum up. She was red at the jawline, and tears stood in her eyes. "Roy looked you up on the Internet. You've done real well for yourself, it seems, between the rodeoing and the movie work and all that. In fact, you're flat-out rich."

"And Davie's suddenly mine, because I have money?" Tyler asked dangerously.

Doreen's wet eyes widened, and she retreated another step or two. Kit Carson made that worried sound again, a low whine, far down in his throat. "You can spare a hundred thousand dollars," she insisted.

"And you, obviously," Tyler countered coldly, "can spare *Davie*. Provided the 'compensation' is right."

Doreen swallowed visibly. "You can get blood tests, or whatever they do nowadays, you and Davie both. You'll see that I'm telling the truth."

Doreen *wasn't* telling the truth; Tyler had played a lot of poker, with a lot of amateurs as well as pros, and he knew a stone-desperate bluff when he saw one.

"You don't *know* who Davie's real father is, do

you, Doreen? Roy put you up to this because he smelled money."

"You won't miss it," Doreen said, but for all the attitude she was projecting, she still looked as if she wished the ground would open up at her feet and swallow her whole.

"That isn't the point," Tyler argued. "The point is, Doreen, you're basically offering to *sell* me your child."

"He'd be better off with you."

"He'd be *better off* with just about anybody," Tyler replied, feeling sick to his stomach. "I know you've had it tough, Doreen, and I'm not discounting that. I'm really not. But *how can you* sell *your own child?*"

"Like I said, Davie would have a chance if you kept him," Doreen said, though she was still the personification of misery. "I'd know Roy wouldn't hurt him again, and, well, me and Roy, we could make a new start someplace else. Someplace far away."

"You'd just *leave* Davie? 'So long, good luck, it's been real'?" Tyler knew the exchange was pushing a lot of old buttons that had nothing to do with the kid and everything to do with the way *he'd* been raised, but knowing that didn't change a damn thing. "Doreen, how can you *do* a thing like this?"

"Read those papers," Doreen said, her chin high, but wobbling. "You sign them, and write me a check, and that's the end of it. Davie's your son, from that day forward." With that, she turned and started to walk away, toward the battered old car she'd left running in the driveway.

Tyler stopped her, grabbed her arm and spun her around to face him. This time, he didn't try to be as gentle as before.

"You don't even know me, Doreen," he rasped. "How can you be sure I won't ditch Davie, or knock him around like Roy has? I'm a *Creed,* remember? You've been around Stillwater Springs long enough to figure out what that means."

Doreen pulled free of his grip on her arm. Raised her chin again and looked him straight in the eye. He realized then that, bruised and broken though she was, jaded and disillusioned and barely holding on to the frayed ends of the proverbial rope, she was trying to save Davie. Oh, she wouldn't mind taking the hundred grand she'd asked him for, but this wasn't about the money. Like some wild, cornered animal, she was trying to lure the main threat—Roy—as far from her child as she could.

"Doreen," Tyler said gruffly. "Don't do this. We'll figure out some other way."

"There *is* no other way, Tyler. Don't you think I've tried to come up with one?" She paused, swallowed again. "I've got to have an answer by tomorrow," she finished, sliding behind the wheel of her car.

Tyler folded the documents, stuck them into his hip pocket, gripped the edge of her open car window as he leaned in to look at her. "Suppose I agreed to this—and I'm not saying I will. What would you tell Davie?"

A tear slipped down Doreen's cheek, leaving a jagged trail through the goop she'd hoped would cover up the marks Roy's fist had left. " 'Goodbye,' " she croaked. "I'd say, 'Goodbye.' "

With that, she threw the car into Reverse and backed up, and Tyler was left with a choice between jumping back out of the way or losing some or all of his toes.

He jumped.

The rear wheels of that Buick threw up a lot of dust and gravel as she backed up, turned around and gunned the engine.

He stood there for a long time after she'd gone, watching the dust settle and trying to figure out what the hell he ought to do next.

Call Logan? His eldest brother was a lawyer, and a good one. In addition to winning several world championships during his bronc-busting days, Logan had founded a legal-services Web site that had made him a rich man.

It had fattened Tyler's bank account, too, since he'd invested all the cash he could scrape together, way back when, before the stock-splits and the big sale to some multinational conglomerate. He knew Dylan had done the same thing.

Yep, a sensible man would call his big brother, the legal eagle, and ask for advice.

But where Logan was concerned, Tyler wasn't a sensible man.

He finally turned and started back toward the house. Sat down on what was left of the porch and took Doreen's papers from his back pocket and read them—once, twice, a third time.

It was all there, cut-and-dried. There were no loopholes; as far as he could tell, the agreement was iron-clad—and he'd always had a good head for contracts. No hidden clauses, no ifs, ands or buts that would come back and bite him in the ass in a week or a month or a year.

The plain, sad truth was, a fat check would buy him permanent custody of a troubled, pierced, tattooed kid who might or might not be his. Until Davie turned eighteen, he would be Tyler's ward, at least in the eyes of the law.

His first instinct was to say yes, write the check and never investigate the paternity issue at all. He knew that would sound crazy to anybody who hadn't been raised under Jake Creed's roof, and it probably was crazy. He also knew he couldn't change his own childhood by making things easier for Davie.

He just wanted to make a difference to one kid in trouble, that was all.

A week before, even a couple of days ago, he could have made the decision, for or against, without considering anyone else's opinion. But now there was one person in his life whose opinion mattered a *lot,* and that was Lily.

Davie was Doreen's son, whether he was genetically a Creed or not. And Lily had been badly hurt by that affair, all those years ago. Once she learned who Davie actually was, or might be, and that was only a matter of time, she'd probably decide to cut her losses and run.

Could he handle that, especially after the night before?

He'd have to—he didn't have a choice. He'd handled his mother's suicide, Jake's abuse and the bad blood between him and the two older brothers he'd once nearly worshipped. He'd handled Shawna's death, and a whole lot of other things.

And he'd handle whatever Lily decided, too.

Which didn't mean it wouldn't hurt like hell, if she walked.

In some ways, now that he knew how things *could* be between him and Lily, losing her would be the worst loss of all.

There was nothing to do but tell her, face-to-face, that he might have fathered Davie that long-ago summer, before someone else did. After that, it would be her call: try to make whatever they had work, or call it quits, for good.

Tyler had been thrown from, and chased by, the meanest broncs on the rodeo circuit. He'd been in brawls where the other guy's intention wasn't just to win, it was to kill. Being a Creed, he'd never had the God-given good sense to be scared in *any* of those situations.

But he was scared now.

He was scared as hell.

Of one little woman.

He sighed, got out his cell phone and called Doc Ryder's house. If Lily had a cell, she hadn't given him the number.

The phone at the Ryder place rang six times before voice mail picked up, and a recorded message rattled off numbers for the veterinary clinic and Doc's cell phone.

Since it was Lily Tyler wanted to talk to, not Doc, he didn't follow up on either of the alternate numbers.

He put the phone away, went inside the house, made a bologna sandwich for supper, since it was getting on toward evening by then and he'd forgotten all about lunch. He fed Kit Carson, and when the dog had finished munching his kibble, Tyler rustled up a towel and a bar of soap and, instead of showering inside, headed for the lake.

He was in bed reading a book, Kit Carson curled up beside him, when he heard Davie come in. Switch on that little TV he'd talked Tyler into buying for him the day before.

Since there was no cable and no satellite dish, he'd get mostly static and disembodied voices, but that didn't seem to bother the kid. He banged around downstairs for a while, and finally came up the stairs, just far enough for his head to show above the landing.

Tyler felt a pang, seeing how happy Davie looked. He didn't have a clue that his own mother had just put him on the block with a price tag hanging from around his neck.

"Hey," Tyler said.

"Hey," Davie said. "You should have come along today. We had a lot of fun. And your hot date spent the whole afternoon at the ranch, her and her little girl. We had meat loaf and homemade bread for supper, too."

"Is that right?" Tyler asked, deliberately casual. What he was really thinking was, *Don't call her a "hot date." Her name is Lily.* "How'd you get home?"

The word *home* sort of hung in the air for a moment or so, unsettling and not quite right. But not wrong, either.

"Dylan and Kristy dropped me off," Davie replied, with a slight shrugging motion of one shoulder. "Is that your truck parked outside? If it is, it's a sorry piece of crap, and you were better off driving Kristy's Blazer."

"Thanks," Tyler said dryly, opening his book again. The kid had shattered his concentration—now he'd have to go back to the beginning of the chapter, since he couldn't remember a word of what he'd read so far.

Davie hung around. "Dylan and Logan are rich. How come you're so poor?"

Tyler stifled a grin. "How come you're so damn nosy?" he countered.

Davie laughed. "Guess I'll shut up before I dig myself in any deeper."

"Good idea," Tyler said. "And turn that TV down a little. Static isn't my favorite sound."

Davie, turning away, turned back. "No, you like *Andrea Bocelli*. I saw all those CDs you have. But I won't tell anybody, if you pay me."

That time, Tyler *had* to laugh. He also flung the spare pillow, the one he'd tucked under Lily's delectable backside the night before, to intensify her pleasure as well as his own, and Davie ducked.

Kit Carson barked for joy and leaped right off the bed, probably thinking there was a game on.

"Come on, boy," Davie told the dog. "We'll play tug-of-war for a while and watch some TV."

When the boy and the dog were both gone, Tyler didn't have to hide what he felt—a peculiar combination of dread and hope, faith and fury.

Tomorrow, he would have that talk with Lily.

He'd sign the documents, like Doreen wanted, and write the check.

Doreen might say goodbye to her son, like she'd said she would, or she might just hit the road, with good ole Roy. Either way, Tyler would have some explaining to do; young as he was, Davie had a right to know the truth.

Whatever that was.

Downstairs, Davie and Kit Carson were evidently wrestling, the boy laughing, the dog barking for all he was worth.

It sounded so—well—*normal.*

Too bad it wasn't.

Resigned, Tyler gave up on his book, stretched to switch off the light and lay down on those Lily-scented sheets.

Sleep was a long time coming.

LILY SAT, IMMOBILIZED, in the spare room bed, staring at the wall. Trying to absorb what her mother-in-law had told her on the telephone just a few minutes before.

Burke had had a vasectomy. A *secret* vasectomy.

He'd only pretended to want more children after Tess—obviously, he hadn't. Why hadn't he just told her, though, instead of letting her get her hopes up, over and over again, only to have them shattered every month when her period came?

He'd always acted so sympathetic.

I'm sorry, honey. Maybe next month.

Dazed, Lily heard her father's voice in the kitchen, and Tess's, both of them sounding worried, though she couldn't make out their actual words. They might as well have been speaking some obscure dialect as English.

Presently, Hal opened her door a crack and popped his head in. "Everything okay?" he asked.

For all practical intents and purposes, she'd lost her job.

She'd just learned that Burke's deceit had gone well beyond breaking their marriage vows.

Night before last, she'd engaged in an unprotected sex marathon with a man who was about as likely to be sterile as a jackrabbit.

Oh, yeah. Everything was okay. It was just peachy.

And none of it, Lily reminded herself with an inward sigh, was her father's fault.

She worked up a smile. "I'm just feeling a little lazy this morning," she lied.

"Breakfast is cooking," Hal said. Whether he believed her or not, she couldn't tell.

"Not toaster waffles, I hope," Lily responded.

"Oatmeal," he said, raising both eyebrows and wriggling them a little.

He'd always been able to make Lily laugh by doing that, for as long as she could remember. And that morning was no exception.

In spite of everything, Lily giggled.

And it felt good.

When Tyler pulled into Doc Ryder's driveway, around ten o'clock that morning, Doc and Tess were in the backyard, on their knees, digging dead plants out of a flower bed and tossing them into a wheelbarrow.

Seeing him, they both looked pleased, and Doc

hauled himself to his feet. Dusted off his hands on the legs of his tattered khaki pants.

"Can your dog get out of the truck and play with me?" Tess immediately asked, fairly jumping up and down beside her grandfather while she waited for a yes.

Tyler looked to Doc for the answer.

Doc nodded. Smiled. "I could use a little canine company myself," he said.

Tyler hesitated. Kit Carson had jumped into the driver's seat to paw at the window and yip, wanting to socialize. For a shy dog, he was sure coming out of his shell.

"Is Lily around?" Tyler asked, like he should have done in the first place.

"She's in the kitchen, talking on the phone," Tess volunteered, drawing in close to wait for Tyler to lift the dog down out of the truck.

"Quitting her job and demanding severance pay," Doc elaborated.

As wound up as he was inside, Tyler's spirits lifted a little. Lily was quitting her job? Did that mean she planned to stay on in Stillwater Springs instead of heading back to Chicago?

Tyler's mood took another dive. Considering what he had to say, it might not matter whether Lily stayed in town or not. She might understand—after all, he'd been a kid when he was sneaking around with Doreen, and the whole thing was way back there in the past. But she might tell

211

him to take a flying leap, too, if only because she didn't want to get involved with him or Davie's raising.

"I think this dog needs a walk," Doc announced, after surveying Kit Carson ponderously. "Tess, there's a leash in the pantry, hanging on a hook. Would you mind getting it, please?"

Tess rushed into the house, and Kit Carson bounded after her.

Tyler started to call the dog back, and Doc stopped him.

"It's all right, Tyler," he said. "I'm a veterinarian, you know. I allow dogs in my house."

Tyler wanted to avoid Doc's gaze—but he didn't.

"Is something wrong?" Doc asked.

"I'm not really sure," Tyler answered awkwardly.

"But you need to have a private conversation with Lily, and right away, apparently. Which is why Tess and I are taking the dog for a long walk."

"I appreciate that," Tyler said. He felt as nervous around Doc as he had back when he was walking the razor's edge, dating Lily, saying good-night and then heading straight for Doreen's bed.

Just then, Tess burst out of the house with the looped leash, Kit Carson close on her heels. Lily followed, standing on the porch, shading her eyes with one hand and looking way too good in her jeans and a little yellow blouse with no sleeves.

She had good arms.

Good everything else, too.

Tyler steered his thoughts in another direction, but they doubled back.

Damn, he wanted to take Lily back to bed.

And once he'd said what he'd come there to say, he'd probably have a snowball's chance in hell of doing that, ever again.

Calmly, though he probably felt the lust rolling off Tyler in waves as he watched Lily standing there on the porch, Doc bent and slipped the loop part of the leash around Kit Carson's neck.

"We'll be over at the park if you need us," he said. Then he looked down at Tess and smiled. "Let's go, sugarplum."

Moments later, they were gone.

Tyler was still standing in the same place, like a weed that had sprung up out of the lawn overnight.

"I have something to tell you," Lily blurted, before Tyler could get a word out.

That threw him, since he'd been all geared up to spill his guts about Davie.

"What?" he managed, after untangling his tongue.

Lily came down the steps, crossed the lawn to stand looking up into his face, kept her voice low in case any of the neighbors had their ears pressed to a keyhole.

"The other night, when we—" She stopped, blushed, a study in sweet misery. "When we—*you know*—and I told you I didn't use birth control because I couldn't get pregnant—"

Tyler frowned, confused.

Lily seemed to squirm, though she hadn't actually moved. "It turns out I—" Again, she faltered, but this time she couldn't get going again.

Was she about to tell him she'd peed on one of those sticks drugstores sold in kits, and they were going to be parents? It was too soon to know if they'd conceived a baby—wasn't it? Surely science hadn't come that far since the last time a woman had scared the hell out of him.

Suddenly, Lily started to cry, all soft and sniffly.

Stricken, Tyler pulled her into his arms, held her close against his chest. Propped his chin on top of her head.

"Lily, talk to me," he said.

She spoke into the hollow of his throat. "Burke had a *vasectomy,* Tyler. Without even telling me. All the time I was hoping for another baby, and he knew that, and he let me think—"

Tyler closed his eyes. He hurt because Lily hurt.

And what he couldn't leave without saying might make things infinitely worse.

CHAPTER ELEVEN

WHEN LILY HAD composed herself a little, Tyler steered her toward the back porch, sat her down on the top step. Joined her and took her hand.

He waited while she sniffled, attempted several brave little smiles and finally pulled it all together.

"I'm sorry," she said, avoiding his gaze. "I shouldn't have dumped on you like that, but after the other night—"

Tyler squeezed her hand. "You said you wanted more kids," he reminded her when the moment seemed right. "Isn't this *good* news, Lily?"

"It would be for me," she replied, after thinking a while, staring at the flower bed her dad and daughter had been digging out when Tyler arrived. Then she met his eyes. "But what about you, Tyler? What if we made a baby when we—when we—"

Tyler chuckled, chafed her knuckles gently with the pad of his thumb. "Why is it so hard for you to say we had sex, Lily? While it was going on, you didn't have any trouble calling it what it was—in some pretty graphic terms."

She winced, but she didn't pull her hand away. "Don't remind me," she said, yet a little smile teased one corner of her mouth, even though her eyes were serious as she studied him. "And you didn't answer my question. What if we made a baby night before last, Tyler?"

"I'd insist on making an honest woman out of you," he replied, and though his tone might have indicated that he was kidding, he'd never been more serious about anything in his life. "You wouldn't—well—do anything, would you? To get rid of this theoretical baby?"

Lily drew in a breath that was almost sharp

enough to qualify as a gasp. "Of *course* I wouldn't. And nobody needs to 'make an honest woman' out of me, Tyler Creed, because I'm *already* honest."

Tyler sighed, raked his free hand through his hair. "Now it's my turn," he said gravely, unable to look at her, though he could feel her gaze burning into his flesh. "To be honest, I mean."

She stiffened slightly and might have withdrawn if it hadn't been for the firm grip he had on her hand. Out of the corner of his eye, he saw her open her mouth to say something, then close it again.

He shifted to face her. "Lily—"

"Is this about Davie?" she prompted.

He was too surprised to give a verbal answer, though he did manage a partial nod. His heart hammered at the back of his rib cage and his throat was cinched shut, as if somebody had thrown a noose around his neck and put a foot against his chest before pulling the rope tight.

"Is he yours, Tyler? Yours and Doreen's?"

Tyler swallowed, croaked out a hoarse, "Maybe."

Lily reached up, smoothed a lock of hair back from his forehead. That wasn't the reaction he'd expected, and something powerful moved inside him, making it necessary to look away for a moment or two. Compose himself a little.

"What do you mean, 'maybe'?" Lily asked gently.

"He could be," Tyler said, still sounding like

he'd barely escaped a lynching. "Doreen denied it at first, then she came to me with custody papers and swore by all that was holy that he's mine. She's willing to sign him over, Lily, like a load of firewood—for a price."

"My God," Lily murmured. Like most women, she probably couldn't grasp the concept of selling a child. As a man, Tyler didn't find it any easier to understand. "What are you going to do?"

"Pay her and sign the papers," Tyler answered. "Whether he's mine or not, I can't turn my back on the kid. I'm not sure why—he's a little smart-ass and I've got no place to keep him—but if Doreen is willing to deal, so am I."

Lily looked so deeply into him then that she must have seen all his secrets, even the ones he kept from himself. "Are you still involved with Doreen, Tyler?" she asked. "Because if you are, we're not going any further."

"That's been over since the summer it happened," Tyler answered. "And it was never anything but sex, anyway."

"What is it with *us,* Tyler?" Lily asked, very quietly. "Is it nothing but sex with us, too?"

"It's more and you know it," Tyler heard himself say. He grinned. "Not that there's anything wrong with the sex."

Lily laughed and bumped him hard with her shoulder. "Nope," she agreed. "There's absolutely *nothing* wrong with the sex."

"Does that mean we can have more?" Tyler asked.

And that made her laugh again, and cry again, and the combination of the two carved out places in Tyler and filled them with emotions so new to him they didn't have names.

"First chance we get," she said.

"I'm free right about now," Tyler said, and he was only half kidding.

"Tyler," Lily pointed out primly, "we are sitting on *my* father's back porch. He and my six-year-old daughter will be back any minute. I don't know about you, but I see that as a logistical problem."

"We probably have time for a quickie," Tyler suggested, without much hope. He'd have thrown her over one shoulder and carried her back to his place caveman-style, but he'd promised Davie a horseback ride, after backing out the first time, and the kid had taken off for Logan's place right after breakfast, on foot, he was so eager to ride.

Lily traced his jawline with one fingertip, sending flames searing through him. "No quickies, Tyler," she said, almost purring. "Not yet, anyway. I want it slow and hot and wet. And I want hours and hours of it."

Tyler groaned. Now he had a hard-on the size of a totem pole, and no way to make it better. "That was a dirty trick, Lily Ryder," he growled. "How am I supposed to face your dad with a boner shoving against the front of my pants?"

She wet her lips with the tip of her tongue. And she didn't, he noticed, distracted though he was, correct him by saying she was Lily *Kenyon*. "I guess you'd better wait in the truck," she teased. "That way, he won't see."

"You're sure about that quickie?"

"I'm sure. When I have a climax, Tyler, I glow for hours afterward. In case you haven't noticed."

He groaned again. "Oh, I've noticed, all right," he said miserably, shifting on the porch. He eyed the lawn sprinkler, actually considered unscrewing it and drenching himself with the hose, right there in Doc Ryder's backyard, just to cool off.

"Tell you what," Lily said, close to his ear. "I'll slip out later, and we'll meet somewhere."

"Like where?"

"That old cemetery on your ranch?" Lily suggested. "I've always thought that was such a peaceful place, and there's a lot of deep, soft grass—"

Tyler was in genuine pain by then. Make that agony. He got to his feet, tried in vain to right himself without putting one hand down the front of his jeans. Doc and Tess and Kit Carson were on their way back—he caught the sound of their voices, at the vague periphery of his hearing.

"Eight o'clock?" Lily asked.

"Eight o'clock," Tyler agreed, wondering how the hell he'd wait that long. As it was, he'd have to jump off the end of his dock into the lake before he went to meet Davie for that horseback ride.

"You're going to be thinking about this all day, aren't you?" Lily murmured.

"Yes," Tyler answered. "And you're going to pay, once I lay you down in the grass tonight, lady."

Having said that, he went to the truck, got behind the wheel, half in and half out, because Doc and Tess and the dog were almost to the side gate by then. Doc opened the passenger-side door of the truck, and Kit Carson jumped in on his own, scrambled from the floorboards to the seat and sat there panting and grinning, very pleased with himself.

Tyler was doing a little panting of his own, at least on the inside.

"I hope we were gone long enough," Doc remarked casually, with a twinkle in his eyes.

Not nearly *long enough,* Tyler thought. He supposed it was all for the best, though. He'd have had Lily bent over the nearest waist-high surface by then, if she'd agreed to the quickie, and she'd have shone like a lighthouse on a dark night after she came. And came.

Lily was a multiple-orgasm kind of gal.

And even an old fogy like Doc, who probably hadn't had sex since the first Bush administration, would have known exactly what had happened.

"Thanks for walking my dog, Doc," Tyler said,

amazed at how normal he sounded, starting up the truck. Waving to Tess as he backed out of the driveway.

Conscious that Davie was waiting, and probably impatiently, Tyler meant to make one more stop, nevertheless. Fortunately, by the time he pulled in at the casino on the edge of town, he was no longer at full mast, so he wouldn't have to stop off at home for the planned dip in the lake. Unfortunately, he was still damn uncomfortable.

He'd scanned the custody documents Doreen had given him the day before into his laptop at home, and tucked them into a secondhand manila envelope he'd found in a drawer. Now, sitting in the parking lot, he signed them at all the little x's, pulled his checkbook from the glove compartment and wrote a draft for one hell of a lot of money. Finally, he jammed it into the envelope, along with the documents, and scrawled Doreen's name across the front.

Leaving Kit Carson fretting in the truck, he sprinted toward the side entrance, made his way to the employees' lounge and left the packet with the security guard. When Doreen came in to work her shift, her blood-money would be waiting.

Now, he just had to think of a way to break the news to Davie. The trail ride, just the two of them up in the foothills on horseback, would be a good chance to talk, but Tyler had already decided that he'd wait. Davie would be shook up afterward, of

221

course, and need some putting back together, and that would make meeting Lily at the cemetery all but impossible.

Tyler had just paid a shitload of money to basically adopt a kid who might not even be his, and he'd do right by Davie if it killed him, but there were limits to his nobility—and they were just this side of a deep-grass tryst with Lily Ryder under a summer moon.

Since neither he nor Dylan had any horses, though Dylan was in the process of building a real fancy barn, to hear him tell it, Tyler had had no choice but to borrow a couple from Logan. With luck, his brother wouldn't be around when he got there.

As it turned out, he'd used up his quota of luck for the day when he'd leveled with Lily about Davie and she hadn't told him to hit the road. Logan was in the corral with Davie when he pulled in at the home place, with one horse already saddled and a second just fitted with a bridle.

"I wouldn't have believed it," Lawyer-man said lightly, "if I hadn't seen you pull in here with my own eyes."

"I told you we needed to borrow a couple of horses for a trail ride," Davie reminded Logan, already mounted on the saddled gelding, a pinto who looked like he'd move about as fast as cold honey flowing uphill.

Logan didn't look at the boy. He was too busy

assessing Tyler. "There's something we need to talk about, little brother," he said. "If you can work me into your busy schedule."

Tyler climbed over the corral fence, threw a saddle blanket onto the second horse and the saddle after it. "I'm free next August," he said. "Maybe we could do lunch."

"Very funny," Logan replied, and though he was smiling a little, his eyes were solemn. "It's important, Ty."

Tyler tightened the cinch, unhooked the stirrup from the saddle horn and mounted the black gelding. When Tyler leaned to grab the dangling reins, Logan caught hold of them first and handed them up.

"Then why didn't you get around to it when you were at my place before?" Tyler chided, anxious to be gone.

But it was good to have a horse under him again.

Not half so good as it would be to have *Lily* in the same position, but one pleasure at a time.

Logan ran a hand along the gelding's neck before looking up into Tyler's face. "Because it's not an easy thing to say," he replied quietly. "Especially to somebody who likes to make things as hard as possible, the way you do."

Tyler felt a stab of regret at that, and some dread, too.

Was Logan dying of some disease?

Was the ranch about to go on the auction block for back taxes?

Neither question was answered. Logan had turned, walked away to open the corral gate. Davie rode through first. Tyler hesitated in the gap, looking down at his brother.

"You're okay, right?" he asked Logan. "The ranch is okay?"

Logan tilted up one corner of his mouth, but as grins went, that one was a real bust. "Nothing like that," he said. "It can wait until tomorrow."

"Tomorrow it is," Tyler said. "My place or yours?"

"I'll stop by around six, like before," Logan answered. Then he turned to the boy, waiting to head for the foothills. "Maybe you'd like to spend the night here with us," he added.

Davie rolled his eyes, then gave a long, low whistle after cutting a sly look in Tyler's direction. "Another hot date?"

Tyler felt his neck go red and knew Logan had noticed, even before he grinned.

"Better yet," Logan said.

And they left it at that. He and Logan did, at least.

"I'd appreciate it," Tyler told Davie, catching up as they eased their horses into an easy trot across the pasture, "if you'd stop referring to Lily as a 'hot date.'"

"Well, she's hot," Davie reasoned cheerfully. "And she's a date. Therefore—"

"Therefore, nothing. You're thirteen," Tyler reminded the kid. "Try to keep that in mind, will you?"

Davie was in a chatty mood. He also sat a horse like he'd been born on one—a Creed trait, whether he had the right DNA or not. "Oh, believe me, I never forget. It's a royal pain in the ass, being thirteen, and from what I've seen at school, the only thing worse is being *fourteen*."

In spite of his worries, which were considerable, Tyler had to laugh. He remembered a lot about those ages, and Davie was right. Both of them sucked—they didn't call them the 'tween years for nothing.

For a while, they rode in companionable silence, Davie thinking his own thoughts, Tyler doing the same. Part of him was right there, in the moment, but his mind did some wandering, too. He couldn't help wondering what Logan was about to lay on him, and the anticipation of meeting Lily later was hard to keep under wraps.

They'd reached the lower hills when they stopped, by tacit agreement, to rest the horses.

Davie stood in the stirrups to stretch his legs, and if it hadn't been for that damned spider tattoo and all those piercings, he'd have looked like a regular cowboy.

"You're mighty comfortable on a horse," Tyler observed, looking out over the ranch and enjoying the panorama. "If I didn't know better, I'd think you'd been riding all your life." He could see the main house, with its fancy new barn, and the beginnings of Dylan's construction project, too. There were cattle grazing in the pastures, and sunlight sparkled on the wind-rippled grass, and the way Tyler felt, he might have slipped through a time warp and gone back a hundred years.

Before Jake.

Before his mother.

Before that summer with Doreen.

"Guess I'm just a natural," Davie bragged. "In fact, I've been thinking I might take up rodeoing. Dylan says I could qualify for the junior divisions. I just have to pick my event. Did you know he's got a bull?"

Tyler sat easy in the saddle, glad to be back. While he was away, chasing women and money, he'd come dangerously close to forgetting who he was.

Now, he was settled in his own hide, where he belonged. His hair was a little too long, he was driving an old truck and he had a good dog. He liked all that just fine.

And then there was Lily.

"Forget the bull," Tyler told Davie, in case the kid had any ideas about practicing up for the rodeo on that ornery old white-hided devil. "Cimarron's a mean one, famous for stomping in cowboys' rib cages, among other things. Even Dylan couldn't ride him."

"But I could sign up for the rodeo? Try my hand at it?"

Tyler was touched by the boy's eagerness, and worried because he knew from bitter experience that cowboying was a rough life. If a man wasn't among the top riders on the circuit, he'd have a hard time scratching out a living. It was a winner's game, and losing was the order of the day for most cowboys.

"Not with that tattoo and all those little silver rings in your hide," Tyler said, hedging.

"There's a rule against tattoos?" Davie sounded hesitant now. Which might be a good thing.

"No," Tyler answered. "There's no rule against tattoos, or piercings, either. But the other cowboys would josh you right out of the arena, most places."

"The tattoo's temporary," Davie said. "Good for six months if I don't wash my neck too often."

Again, Tyler laughed.

"And I guess I could quit wearing these rings."

"Guess so," Tyler said moderately. He didn't know a lot about kids, except for what he'd gathered by being one once, but he figured if he showed too much enthusiasm for scrubbing off the spider and letting all those little holes grow shut, Davie would dig in his heels.

Especially if he really was a Creed.

"If I do it—go cowboy, I mean—will you get a satellite hookup so I can watch some decent TV?"

Tyler grinned, shaking his head in mingled admiration and amazement. The kid definitely didn't lack for gall. "That depends on what you mean by 'go cowboy,' I guess," he said.

"Getting rid of the tattoo and the rings and ditching all my Goth gear," Davie said. Mischief danced in his eyes. "Wearing jeans and boots and learning to talk like a hick. *That's* what it means to go cowboy."

"Thanks for clearing that up," Tyler said dryly, realizing how much he liked this kid, and how much he'd have missed him if Doreen had made him go back home.

That was what happened when a man let himself care, Tyler supposed—about a lost dog, a thirteen-year-old boy . . . or a woman. It made him vulnerable, open to the kind of pain he hadn't had to risk when he'd kept his heart closed for business.

Davie was peering at him. "You all right?" he asked.

Tyler realized some of what he felt must have been showing on the outside. That was a new phenomenon, too.

Part of being home again, most likely. And being home meant more than just living on the ranch and getting his mail at the hole-in-the-wall post office in Stillwater Springs.

It meant being Tyler Creed, and nobody else, and taking the good with the bad.

"I'm all right," he said.

"If you're worried about telling me my mom signed me over for a chunk of money, it's okay,"

Davie volunteered. "I know it makes her look bad, but she's really just trying to put as much distance between me and Roy as she can."

Tyler stared at Davie, stunned. "You *knew?*"

"Mom told me," Davie said. "I called her at the casino last night, on your cell phone. She said she and Roy would be leaving town soon—she's giving her two-weeks' notice today—but she'll write to me and e-mail, too, once she gets a computer."

Tyler took all that in, and still didn't know how to sort it out. "And this doesn't bother you?"

"I've been through worse," Davie said. In Tyler's opinion, he was way too philosophical for a thirteen-year-old. "Your cabin is pretty much a dump, but you've got Kit Carson, and that lake, and Logan said I can ride his horses anytime as long as there's somebody around to make sure I don't break my neck. So far, I haven't gone hungry. And living with you is one hell of a lot better than living with Roy."

"What kind of 'worse' have you been through, Davie?" Tyler asked, after a little silence.

Davie shrugged. "Before Roy, there was Marty. He was a world-class jerk. Used to get me by the hair and throw me out the front door when Mom was working. Said just looking at me pissed him off. He died of a heart attack or something—had some kind of fit at supper one night and just keeled over. Boo-hoo."

There was no compassion in Davie's voice, but there was no self-pity, either. He was simply stating the facts of his life, grim as they were.

"Before Marty, Mom shacked up with some old coot with a sheep ranch down in Wyoming. Bill didn't hit me or anything, but he was so cheap he rationed out the food, and when he got tired of buying grub, he said I stole money from his wallet and kicked us out."

"*Did* you steal money from his wallet?" Tyler asked. Life with Jake Creed was beginning to look like a picnic compared to all Davie had experienced.

"Yeah," Davie said, in a no-big-deal tone of voice. "But only enough to get Mom and me some bus tickets after we hitchhiked to the next town. And to get us kicked out in the first place, of course."

"Of course," Tyler said dryly. "You're a piece of work, you know that?"

"So I've been told," Davie replied lightly. He checked the position of the sun, like he was John Wayne leading the thirsty survivors of an Indian attack out of the desert or something. "We ought to get these horses back to the barn," he said. "And I promised Josh and Alec they could watch me take out my eyebrow ring."

"You were already planning that?"

"Not unless you agreed to the satellite-TV thing, I wasn't." Davie stretched his legs again, smiled. "Do we have a deal or not?"

Tyler sighed. "We have a deal," he said. "And if I ever catch you going through *my* wallet—"

Davie nudged his horse into motion, passed Tyler on the narrow trail leading down onto the plain. "You'll do what?" he asked casually. "Go postal? Beat me up? Drag me behind your truck for a few miles?"

"Ground you until you're thirty-seven," Tyler answered. "*And* throw that damn TV of yours in the lake for good measure."

Turning to look back at Tyler, Davie whistled in exclamation. He was still grinning, but he looked like what he should have been allowed to be all along: a kid. "Damn," he said. "You play hardball. You'd really throw a perfectly good TV *in the lake?*"

"In a heartbeat," Tyler said. "Satellite dish and all."

"Can I sign up for the rodeo?"

"One thing at a time, kid. You got the TV. You got the satellite dish. Whether or not you can rodeo will depend on how you do in school this fall, and your general attitude between now and then."

"Oh, here we go with the 'attitude' thing," Davie scoffed good-naturedly. He and Tyler rode side by side then, since the trail was wider. "What's wrong with my attitude?"

"Beyond being a smart-ass, you're doing okay in that department," Tyler allowed.

"You'd be a smart-ass, too, if you'd had a childhood like mine."

"Save it, Davie. I *did* have a childhood like yours, except for all the road trips."

"You want to talk about it?"

"No, Dr. Phil, I do not want to talk about it. Not right now, anyway."

"Because you've got a hot date?"

"Attitude alert," Tyler warned.

"Excuse *me,*" Davie replied.

Tyler gave him a look.

Davie was undaunted. "If you're going to marry Miss Lily, Marshal," he drawled, doing a pretty good imitation of a character in a late-night Western, "you'd better fancy up the ole homestead. The lady's a class act. The kind who likes indoor plumbing."

"I *have* indoor plumbing."

"Which is why you bathe in the lake."

"Do you ever shut up?"

"Not unless I'm asleep. Even then, I probably talk. It's a wonder I don't sleepwalk, too, the way I've been abused."

Tyler wrapped the reins loosely around his saddle horn just long enough to play a few notes on an invisible violin.

Davie laughed. "I guess the old sympathy ploy won't work with you."

"Guess not," Tyler said.

They rode the rest of the way in cordial silence, and when they got back to Logan's place, two little boys—Josh and Alec, Tyler presumed—were perched on the top rail of the corral fence, waiting.

"Is he going to get satellite TV?" the smaller one called to Davie.

"Yep," Davie answered, pretending to take a bow, even though he was still in the saddle. "I *told* you I was the master."

"So we get to watch you take the hardware out of your face, like you said?" the bigger boy asked, sounding both thrilled and wary.

"Yeah," Davie responded, happily generous, leaning from his horse to work the latch on the corral gate. "And it's only going to cost you five bucks. Apiece."

"It'll be a free show," Tyler interceded.

"Good," the younger boy crowed, lighting up. "Because we're *broke*."

Tyler chuckled, swung down off his horse and led it into the barn.

Both boys followed, though whether they were tagging after him or Davie he didn't know.

"I guess you're sort of our uncle," the little one said eagerly, "since Logan's our stepdad and you're his brother."

"Guess so," Tyler said, amused. "Are you Josh or Alec?"

"I'm Alec," the kid said, jutting a thumb toward the other kid. "And he's Josh."

"Pleased to make your acquaintance," Tyler said, hauling the saddle off the horse he'd ridden and handing it to Davie to put away.

"My mom said you'd come around eventually," Josh informed him. The shyer of the two, apparently, he'd taken his time closing the distance.

"But *Logan* said hell would freeze over first," Alec supplied.

Tyler grinned to himself. Ruffled the boy's hair. "Did he, now?"

CHAPTER TWELVE

WAS SHE *CRAZY?*

Lily stared at her reflection in the bathroom mirror, at her carefully applied makeup and just-washed hair, tumbling in loose curls around her face the way it always did if she didn't tame it with gel. In the kitchen, Hal and Tess were chatting happily as they cleared away the supper dishes.

Neither one of them had murmured a word of complaint when she'd served them tacos made with soybean crumbles, a meat substitute she'd bought on a quick run to the store after Tyler left.

She'd pressed the red polka-dot sundress as soon as she got back from shopping, and told her father and Tess she was meeting Tyler for a drink over at Skivvie's and might be home late.

Now here she was, all dolled-up and hot to trot. *Again.*

She *was* crazy, she decided. She'd basically thrown herself at Tyler Creed, invited him to have his way with her in the old cemetery, of all places, and pregnancy *was* an issue.

Along with the soybean crumbles, she'd picked up a box of condoms, blushing as she paid for them at the checkout counter, praying the clerk wouldn't hold the box up for everybody to see and loudly ask for a price-check.

The woman who had the spontaneous orgasm in aisle two the other day needs condoms, she'd imagined the woman bellowing into the PA system.

None of that had happened, of course. The clerk, a nice middle-aged lady with thick glasses and the name Connie stitched onto her vest, had simply rung up Lily's purchases and told her to have a good day.

The condoms, Lily reminded herself firmly, as she left the bathroom to face her family, were proof that she still had a *few* tattered shreds of sanity left.

"You look pretty, Mom," Tess said innocently, admiring the dress.

"Yes," Hal agreed, and though his expression indicated that he'd like to add to that brief comment, he refrained.

Bless him.

"Thanks." Lily took her purse and the keys to her rental car from the counter. That afternoon, she'd made plans to drop the Taurus off in Missoula and then fly on to Chicago from there. Tess would be able to spend a few days with Eloise, while Lily emptied her desk at work, made arrangements to lease or sell the condo and packed up some things she'd need when they all returned to Stillwater Springs.

Hal had agreed to make the trip, too, probably well aware that Lily had asked him along so she could keep an eye on his food intake and make sure he took his medicine on time. Of course the idea would have to be cleared with his doctors first, but he didn't seem to anticipate any problem there.

The flight out would be easy enough, barring the always-possible airline snafus, and if the drive back to Montana proved too tiring for him, they could always stop somewhere along the way and buy him a plane ticket.

He and Tess had immediately high-fived each other and shouted, in comical unison, "Road trip!"

"One way," Lily reminded them.

They'd be gone two weeks at the longest, allowing time to do all the things that needed doing and drive home again at a sensible pace.

Maybe by going away, she could get some perspective where Tyler was concerned. Stop wanting to jump the man's bones every time she got within a five-mile radius of him.

Fat chance. After being away from him that long, she'd probably be doing well just to slow down long enough to drop Tess and Hal off at the house before she raced off over several bumpy country roads to find Tyler and screw him silly on the spot.

The prospect flooded her face with heat all over again, heat her dad clearly noticed, though thank God, Tess didn't.

"I'll just walk your mom out to her car," Hal told Tess mildly. "You finish loading the dishwasher, and then I'll beat you at a game of checkers."

"You mean *I'll* beat *you*," Tess responded. "Just like the *last* time we played."

Hal chuckled at that, and even though Lily gave him a look that said she could get to the Taurus just fine on her own, thank you very much, he put a fatherly hand to the small of her back and steered her out onto the porch and over the grass to the car. He didn't say anything at all until Lily had unlocked the Taurus and he'd opened the driver's-side door for her.

"Try to keep the dress clean, Lily," he said, with kindly amusement. "It'll be pretty obvious what you've been up to if you have to wash it and hang it on the clothesline again so soon."

Lily plunked herself into the car seat, took a couple of jabs at the ignition with the key before she managed to hit her mark. "Thanks for bringing that up, Dad," she said. "As if I'm not embarrassed enough already."

"You're a grown woman," Hal reminded her. "If you want to spend the night with Tyler Creed, or anybody else, that's your business. No need to be embarrassed."

"Now you're going to warn me to be careful, right?"

"Already did that," Hal answered lightly. "And, anyway, I think maybe you've been a little too careful, up to now." He paused, leaned in when she buzzed the window down. "What I'm trying to say, Lily, in my own awkward way, is that it's okay to cut loose a little. Stay out all night if you want to. Tess and I will be just fine."

Lily swallowed. Nodded.

Hal smiled. "And thanks for calling me 'Dad' just now. I like the sound of that."

"I've got my cell phone," Lily said, wanting to look away from the earnest love she saw in her father's eyes, but unable to do so. "It's all charged, and I wrote the number on a sticky-note—"

"Lily, just go."

"If you need anything—anything at all—"

"Go."

A nervous little chuckle erupted from Lily's throat. "We're not really going to Skivvie's," she confessed, in a near whisper. "I just said that to throw you off."

Hal grinned again. "Didn't work," he said. Then he stepped back, so she could drive away into the waiting night, headed for a rendezvous a smarter woman would have avoided.

TYLER WAITED near the cemetery gate, leaning back against his truck with his arms folded. He

238

was going for casual, appearance-wise, but when Lily zoomed in, the headlights of her car splashing over him as she parked, his heart pounded and his mouth went dry and he nearly lost what little cool he'd been able to muster up.

He realized, as he pushed off from the truck, that he hadn't really expected her to show up at all. One of these days, she was bound to come to her senses, remember that he was a Creed and upload all the memories of that summer when he'd broken her heart.

"This is kind of kinky," he said, referring to the location, when Lily got out of the car and started toward him.

She stopped instantly, and since her face was in shadow, he couldn't gauge her reaction to the dumb-ass thing he'd just said. Like as not, she'd bolt for the Taurus now, and lay rubber getting out of there.

Smooth, Creed, he told himself. *Real smooth.*

Lily didn't move, either to flee or come any closer.

"I don't think it's kinky," she said tentatively. "I've always liked this place."

Tyler walked toward her, looked down into her face. Up close, he could see that she'd taken some trouble with her appearance, not that she wouldn't have looked good covered in coal dust from head to foot, and he took the effort she'd made as a favorable omen.

"Me, too," he said. "Never thought it was spooky, like most graveyards would be, especially at night."

Keep on diggin', Creed. You'll run her off yet.

The moonlight touched her face and he saw that she was smiling, though just a little, and kind of cautiously. The faint scent of her perfume made him dizzy.

"I brought you a present," she said, with a twinkle in her eyes. She reached into her handbag and brought out a box, extended it to him.

Condoms.

Tyler laughed. "Thanks," he said. "But I brought some along myself." He had blankets, too, old but clean, in case the ground was too cold for her, or too hard, or a little damp.

She took the box back, dropped it into her purse again. Swallowed visibly. The motion of her neck muscles made him want to nibble at the hollow of her throat, make his way to her earlobe—

"What happens now?" he asked, when she didn't say anything. Damn, but he was batting a thousand tonight. *What happens now?* Why didn't he just ask what her sign was, or some other stupid question, and be done with it? Consign himself to the Fool's Hall of Fame once and for all?

Lily chuckled, sounding a mite less nervous than before, but not by much. "I really thought you'd have that part all figured out," she teased, almost shyly. She looked around a little, hugged herself, even though it was a warm night. "Nobody else is likely to show up, right?"

"We're alone, except for a few ghosts." Tyler moved in, drawn to her like steel filings to a magnet, tucked a blond curl behind her right ear. Wondered if she had any idea that she looked just like a moon goddess with her hair like that, and all awash in silvery light. "Are you cold? I've got a jacket in the truck."

She shook her head, rubbed her palms up and down her bare arms once more, then dropped her hands to her sides. "Just feeling a little shy."

"I think you need to get over that," Tyler said. His voice was hoarse now, with the need of her. With the things she made him feel, even with both of them standing there like a couple of kids about to step out on a dance floor together for the first time.

They weren't even touching, for God's sake.

"I think so, too," she replied. "I'm just not sure where to start."

"Here's an idea." He drew her close, bent his head, kissed her. Lightly at first, then with tongue.

When it ended, they were both breathless.

"That works," Lily said.

Tyler chuckled and took her hand then, led her to the spot he'd chosen, after considering several. He'd already spread the blankets on the ground, in the softest place he'd been able to find, under a gnarled but beautiful old maple tree with stars caught in its branches.

Lily stepped onto the thick nest of blankets, tossed her handbag aside and kicked off her sexy sandals. Hauled that little red dress right off over her head and stood there in her lacy underpants and a bra that barely covered her nipples.

"I guess foreplay's out," Tyler said, stricken stupid by the sight of her.

Lily unhooked her bra, slipped out of it, freeing those lush, perfect breasts of hers. "*Waiting* was foreplay," she said, shedding the panties next. "I haven't been able to think about much of anything else all day."

She was a moon goddess, all right. She might be offering herself up to him, but there was an elemental power in that, ancient and irresistible.

Tyler just stood there, staring at her, wondering when he'd gotten to be such a lucky son of a bitch.

Still, power or no power, if Lily thought he was going to play this game her way, after the way she'd made him sweat on her father's back porch that morning, she was mistaken. He'd meant what he'd said about paying her back.

He was going to kiss and caress every inch of her.

He was going to suck her breasts and part that nest of moist curls at the junction of her thighs and do some sucking there, too. He'd bring her within a heartbeat of orgasm, as many times as he could, and then let her settle slowly back down into the wanting again.

When he finally had her in earnest, she'd be way past ready, and so would he.

"You're not going to get off that easy," he told her, watching with appreciation as she lowered herself onto the blankets and reached her arms out for him. He hadn't planned the double-entendre, but it worked.

She blushed, and it was quite a sight, since the color swept, pearly pink in the moonlight, from the top of her head to the tips of her toes. There was some mighty nice territory in between, in need of some careful—and close—attention.

"Tyler," she murmured.

He took off his shirt, got out of his boots, unbuckled his belt and worked the buttons on his jeans. When he was as naked as she was, she looked him over with frank hunger and some trepidation, but her arms were still out.

Tyler knelt on the blankets first, relishing the view. Her nipples stood up like pink pebbles, and though she'd been shivering earlier, a fine sheen of perspiration glistened around her hairline now, between her breasts, on her flat belly.

He cupped his hand around those private curls of hers, slipped a couple of fingers inside her, worked her clitoris with a slow circling of the heel of his palm.

She gasped in welcome; her eyes rolled back and closed, and she arched her back. Parted her legs, ready to take him in.

Prim and proper in public, Lily Ryder was another kind of woman altogether in private.

Oh, yeah. He was one *lucky* son of a bitch.

"Damn you, Tyler," she whimpered, her head still back and her eyes still closed, as he continued to play with her. She was getting wetter by the moment, and he could feel her expanding to accommodate him. *"Take me. I've been waiting for this since—Oh God—"* Her hips bucked high off the bed of blankets, but Tyler kept pace with her. Withdrew his hand when he felt the first quivering flex of a climax close around his fingers.

She made a strangled sound of frustration and brewing fury. "Don't tease," she pleaded.

"Lady, I'm going to tease you within an inch of your life," Tyler vowed gruffly. "And then I'm going to tease you some more."

"Just this once, Ty—*please—*"

Slowly, he stroked the insides of her thighs, enjoying the silken tremor he stirred beneath her flesh with every light pass of his fingertips.

"I can *make* you want me, you know," she sputtered, trying to sit up and then falling back again, with a long, low groan, as he intensified his efforts.

"Oh, I already want you," Tyler assured her. "No question about that. But I'm a patient man. I can wait until you beg—and for a long time after that."

Her eyes widened and sparked fire in the moonlight. The goddess was purely pissed off now, and Amazon-strong. She caught hold of him with one hand and stroked, and he did some groaning of his own.

When she went down on him, he gave a strangled shout, buried his hands in her hair, meant to lift her away but held her to him instead.

She was greedy, took him into the back of her throat, then tongued him until he was literally blind with need. Just when he would have let go, he managed to gather enough willpower to raise her off him, but just barely.

He sat there, on his haunches, all the blood in his body pulsing in his pecker. He gasped, struggling for breath, still holding Lily's head in his hands.

The temptation to let her finish was almost overwhelming.

Almost, but not quite.

"Is that enough foreplay for you, Tyler?" she challenged.

"Not—even—close," he ground out. He used the last of his strength to roll onto his back, catching her by the waist and bringing her with him. She wound up right where he wanted her—straddling his face.

He used his tongue to burrow through to her clitoris, flicked at her.

She cried out his name, began to move in an involuntary, instinctive rhythm, as old as the bright moon shining down on both of them. He gripped her hips, keeping pace, took her full in his mouth and sucked.

Until he knew she was about to come.

Then he lifted her off him. Breathed his way back from wherever he'd been, the taste of her still on his lips.

"Please," she whispered, after a tremor of what must have been rage went through her, a little earthquake following a fault line deep inside her. "Oh God, Tyler, *please!*"

"You're going to have to do better than that," he murmured, and kissed and nibbled at the insides of her thighs, slick with wanting now, tiny muscles rippling under the skin, until she sagged back onto him.

He gave her another ride, this one even wilder than the last, but stopped just short of letting her come unwound.

Not that she'd be satisfied with one orgasm, no matter how ferocious it was—he knew that much about Lily, though a lot of other things were still a tantalizing mystery. Oral sex didn't sate her, it only increased her need. She was a woman who needed to be rode hard and put away wet.

With Lily, sex was anything but tentative. The harder, faster and deeper, the better.

She might come a hundred times, but until he drove into her, until he gave her what she wanted, with no holding back, every flick of his tongue and touch of his fingers would only make her want him more.

No matter how many times they were together,

Tyler realized, with a kind of crazy, beleaguered joy, it would always be that way.

They could get married and have a houseful of kids.

They could raise those kids and turn gray-haired and stiff in the joints.

And even after all that, when he laid Lily down, she'd still want it X-rated, just the way she did tonight.

The knowledge did something new to Tyler, changed the whole terrain of his mind and his body and his soul. Again.

"Marry me, Lily," he heard himself say, even as he nuzzled at her, ready to let her go over the top this time. Then, more raggedly, "Marry me?"

"Yes," she choked out. *"Yes!"*

"Yes, you'll marry me, or yes, you like what I'm doing to you right now?" He made a slow circle around her clitoris with his tongue, causing her to give another throaty cry. "Which is it, Lily?"

"It's—*oh, dear God*—it's both! *Tyler*—"

He sent her over the edge then. Held her hips while she bucked, convulsing, alternately whimpering and yelling his name.

When she'd finally finished, and spent several minutes getting her breath back, she shifted onto her back, lay trembling on the blankets beside him, and said what he'd known she'd say.

He did what she asked, what she *commanded* him to do.

And they'd repeated the whole scenario at least three times before he remembered the condoms he'd brought along.

Hell of a lot of good they were doing in the glove compartment of his truck, he reflected happily, still in the throes of a kind of satisfaction he'd never known with any woman but Lily.

WOBBLY-KNEED, Lily finally recovered enough to reach for the dress she'd discarded so readily earlier in the evening. She examined it carefully, was relieved to see it didn't need to be laundered again, and smoothed the fabric with the palms of both hands, once again embarrassed by the shameless way she'd carried on while Tyler was loving her.

Tyler curled a finger under her chin, made her look at him.

"Promise me something," he said.

Her lower lip trembled, and tears burned in her eyes. "What?"

"That you'll never change."

She blinked, bit her lower lip, not knowing what to say.

Tyler went on. "I like the way you act when we make love, Lily. I like the things you say and the noises you make and the way you ride me like you're going for a world championship on the wildest bronc ever to come out of the chute."

Lily's brain was fogged. None of the circuits were connecting.

I like the way you act when we make love . . .

He'd said "make love." Did that mean anything?

She continued to grope her way toward some kind of normalcy, but neither her mind nor her body wanted to cooperate. He'd asked her to marry him earlier—or had she just imagined that in the heat of passion?

"Lily?" Tyler prompted, one corner of his mouth tilted up in a grin so sultry it fell just short of being cocky. He reached for his jeans while he waited for her to answer, put them back on. But he was still bare-chested, and the moonlight played in his ebony hair.

"I've never done w-what I did to—*with* you—"

Tyler chuckled, found her panties and her bra and gave them to her. "It was good, Lily," he told her. "*Really* good."

She absorbed that, pleased and at the same time even more embarrassed than before. Got into her panties and her bra and pulled the dress back on. Smoothed it anxiously when she got to her feet.

Tyler, still kneeling on the blankets, eased the hem of that dress up to the top of her thighs, hooked a finger at the waist of her panties, and pulled them down again. Fondled her.

Lily moaned and moved her feet apart by a fraction of an inch. "Tyler—"

"Once more for the road," he said. "Tilt your head back a little, so I can see the moonlight on your face. . . ."

He slid his fingers inside her.

She tightened around him, quivered as he awakened all those needs all over again.

His thumb made gentle revolutions around her slick, pleasure-swollen clitoris.

"Oh," she whimpered. She thought her knees would give out, but she was already climbing—climbing. "Tyler—"

"Shh," he said, raspy-voiced, looking up at her, watching every change of expression as the surrender began, softly this time. Oh, yes, this time, it was soft—soft and slow and infinitely sweet. "Let it happen, Lily. Just let it happen."

She threw back her head.

"Look at me," Tyler told her.

She obeyed. She would have obeyed practically any order he gave her, under the circumstances. Done anything for the precious release she craved.

A faint gasp escaped her as she caught on a silky, dreamlike climax, as she flowed with it, flexed with it, let it carry her along like some velvet river.

When it was over, she would have collapsed if Tyler hadn't grasped her hips again, the way he had so many times that night, and held her upright.

Once he was standing, facing her, he kissed her lightly on the mouth.

"You're in no condition to drive," he told her, when he drew back. "So we're spending the rest of the night at the cabin."

"Okay," Lily said, leaning into him, letting him slip a strong arm around her waist and guide her to the passenger side of his truck. "But what about Davie?"

"He's at Logan and Briana's for the night," Tyler answered, hoisting her onto the seat and buckling her in. A grin played on his mouth. "Kit Carson will be around, but he's discreet."

Lily giggled, put a hand over her mouth and burst into tears.

She'd felt too much, and she was about to feel more.

Could she stand it, after years and years of holding it all in?

She was practically a puddle now. What kind of shape would she be in if she spent the rest of the night in Tyler Creed's bed? What if he played with her until she went stone-crazy, like he had on those blankets under the tree, making her come again and again but withholding what she needed most until she was too weak even to beg?

Evidently reading her face, Tyler chuckled. He looked like some cowboy Adonis, standing there in the moonlight, naked from the waist up and soft-eyed with satisfaction. Already, though, some new mischief was brewing in those impossibly blue eyes.

"Relax," he said. "The night is young."

That was what she was afraid of.

She was wrung out, spent. She didn't have

another orgasm in her—she would have been superhuman if she had.

Still grinning, Tyler left her long enough to put his shirt and boots on, collect the blankets and her purse, bring them back to the truck. All the while, she sat there like a lump, sated into a near stupor.

And yet that tiny, magical muscle was awakening again.

Getting ready.

"Did you ask me to marry you?" she inquired, as they were jostling over country roads toward his lake place.

"Yeah," Tyler answered, reaching over to lay a hand on her knee and slide it slowly, skillfully up under her dress, along her bare thigh. "And you said yes."

"I thought so," Lily said. She should push his hand away, she knew she should, but it felt too good, resting on her skin, just short of her panties.

He laughed.

Lily knew he was seducing her, slowly and surely, that she'd be lucky to make it as far as the man's bed before he had her acting like a hussy again. But there was no resistance in her, anywhere.

Tyler had untied all the knots inside her.

And he was tying them back up again, moment by moment.

Lily struggled for balance.

He hadn't said he loved her, she reminded herself.

Maybe he never would.

Would that matter?

Eventually, it probably would, she decided, enjoying the weight and warmth of his hand, squirming a little, needing to be touched where he wasn't quite touching. But that night, it didn't.

Much.

There was always the danger, of course, that she'd blurt out the words—*I love you, Tyler*—in the throes of some violent orgasm.

Maybe he'd say them back to her.

And maybe he'd pretend he hadn't heard.

"Where will we live?" she asked, as they turned into his driveway. Her practical side was *trying* to reassert itself, though obviously without much success.

"We'll figure that out," Tyler promised, parking the truck.

The cabin was dark, though she could hear Kit Carson inside, barking out a welcome.

Tyler got out of the truck, walked around to open her door for her. Helped her down.

She swayed a little.

He steadied her.

"We forgot to use the condoms," she said.

"Yeah," Tyler agreed lightly. "We sure did."

And then he took her into his house, where Kit Carson greeted them in a frenzy of welcome. He cooked an omelet, and they shared it, and the dog got some, too.

They bathed each other in the lake after that, and made love again, on the end of the dock, with only the moonlight for covers.

Lily was purely happy, content in a way she'd never thought possible.

And that should have been a warning.

CHAPTER THIRTEEN

"TWO WEEKS?" Tyler echoed, when they pulled up beside Lily's Taurus, the first orange light of the rising sun just rimming the tops of the mountains. "You're going to be gone for—"

"Two weeks," Lily confirmed gently. "That's not very long, Tyler."

She should have broken the news about her upcoming trip to Chicago sooner, she supposed, but when would she have had the opportunity, before now?

Should she have brought the subject up thirty minutes ago, perhaps, when she and Tyler had both crowded into his ridiculously small shower at the cabin, and he'd taken her, standing up? Even after the howling, train-wreck orgasms she'd had, delicious aftershocks still rocked her, little echo-climaxes that made her catch her breath to keep from moaning aloud.

No, she'd told him about her plans as soon as it became possible to string two words together with any vestige of coherence.

Tyler braked the truck beside the Taurus. Gave a low, raw chuckle and shook his head once. "I guess I might have overreacted a little," he admitted.

Lily smiled. "Ya think?"

He was quiet for a while, struggling with something. "You're coming back?" he asked finally.

"Of course I'm coming back," Lily said, surprised and, at the same time, not so much. "We're getting married, aren't we?"

At last Tyler looked her way. Grinned slightly. "If you still want to, after you've had the time to think about what you're getting yourself into."

The sun was about to rise, and Lily wanted to get back to her dad's place before Tess woke up and realized her mother wasn't around. But she hated leaving Tyler, especially when she knew she'd be getting on an airplane soon.

"I'll still want to," she said softly. She could speak with certainty because she knew now what some part of her had known since she and Tyler dated in high school. She'd *always* wanted to be his wife, even after they broke up over Doreen, and all during her marriage to Burke.

He shifted in the seat, turned to her, took her face gently between his hands and kissed her. It wasn't a passionate kiss, like the ones they'd shared in the shower, or any time before that. It was tender, a sort of communion, and it moved Lily to the very ground of her being.

She loved him.

She could finally admit that to herself, if not to him.

She loved Tyler Creed, with her whole heart and certainly her newly awakened body, now and forever, amen.

When the kiss ended, Lily couldn't speak.

"Would you mind living in a double-wide for a while?" Tyler asked, his lips still almost touching hers.

Confused, Lily blinked. "What?"

Tyler chuckled, shoved a hand through his hair. "I guess some kind of segue would have been good right about there," he said. "What I'm asking, Lily, is if you'd be willing to live in a trailer until we could tear down the cabin and build a proper house. It would be a nice one, not like those rentals in town, I promise—"

She'd have lived in a tent, if it meant she had Tyler Creed's wedding band on her finger, all the sex she could handle, which, apparently, was considerable, and the ultimate: a little brother or sister for Tess growing under her heart.

"Sure," she said. "I'd live in a trailer."

"There's an outfit in Missoula that leases them out, short-term," Tyler went on, looking anxious in a way that made her heart pinch. "If it's okay with you, I'll go ahead and pick one out myself, since you're not going to be here to do the choosing, and have everything hooked up by the time you get back. We'll get a license, throw a wedding, and you and Tess can move in."

Mobile homes, in Lily's experience, were small. With her and Tess there, along with Davie and Tyler and, of course, Kit Carson, the quarters would be a little close.

Right then, fresh from a night of cataclysmic climaxes in Tyler's arms, it sounded cozy, but the reality might be less than fabulous. Still, the benefits would outweigh the liabilities; she was certain of that.

She'd never been—had never expected to be—as happy as she was at that moment in time. Wouldn't have believed it possible. But here it was, this staggering, all-encompassing joy, this absolute confidence that she and Tyler, together, could make it all work.

"There *is* one thing I'd like to ask for, though," she said, with a note of mischief in her voice, already working the lever on the door to get out, make her way to the Taurus and head for town.

"What?" Tyler asked, looking puzzled and a touch wary.

Lily leaned across the console and kissed him again. "Have our bedroom soundproofed," she said. "And make sure there's a strong foundation under that trailer, so it doesn't rock when we—" she dropped her voice to a murmur, licked her lips once, very slowly, because she knew it would drive Tyler mad "—do it."

Tyler laughed, but he also shifted uncomfortably on the seat. He was hard again, and if she didn't get out of there, she'd end up doing something about that, and there was no time. "Done," he promised. He started to open his door, planning to walk her to her car.

Lily stopped him with a smile and a shake of her head. The Taurus was ten feet away, if that, and she didn't need an escort to get to it. "See you in two weeks, cowboy," she said. "You just sit right here in this truck and let that magnificent hard-on go down. If some other woman sees it, she might try to stake a claim."

Again, he laughed, and maybe it was wishful thinking, but Lily dared to hope that new softness she saw in his eyes meant he was at peace. Tyler had always been troubled, but now he looked as though he might have laid the worst of his demons to rest.

She'd certainly sent some of her own running for the hills. She wasn't sure when—and it really didn't matter—but for the first time in years, she wasn't afraid to let herself be happy. She wasn't waiting for the other shoe to drop—the way it always had with Burke.

Humming to herself, she dashed to the Taurus, got inside and sped off toward town.

TWO WEEKS, TYLER THOUGHT glumly, as he watched Lily drive away, disappear around the bend.

A lot could change in two weeks.

For one thing, all those orgasms would wear off, and that telling glow, rimming Lily like an all-over halo, would fade.

Once she was back in Chicago, Lily would probably look around and ask herself why she was marrying a Creed, giving up big-city life to live in a double-wide trailer out in the dingle-berries.

She'd have lunch with her friends, at some elegant bistro the likes of which Stillwater Springs couldn't offer, and word would get around that she was back. Someone would offer her a better, more glamorous job than the one she'd lost. Beautiful as she was, all pink-cheeked and bright-eyed and shimmery as a Christmas angel, with her hair fluffed out instead of tamed with hair goop, some smooth type in a suit was sure to spot her and zero in.

In no time at all, she'd be calling him to say she was sorry, and she hoped he hadn't spent too much money soundproofing the bedroom of that double-wide they'd discussed, because she'd changed her mind about all of it.

She wouldn't be coming back to Stillwater Springs.

She wouldn't be coming back to him.

Oh, there was Doc to consider, but she'd talk him into retiring—he was way past the age anyhow—and pretty soon he'd be living in Chicago, too, in one of those fancy independent-living places for senior citizens.

Tyler clenched his right fist to pound the steering wheel once, but stopped himself short when the very atmosphere around him suddenly altered at a quantum level.

The change, intangible as it was, seemed to permeate his very cells.

Jake was there.

He couldn't see him, or hear his voice, but it was as if the old man had wafted right up out of his nearby grave and plunked himself in the passenger seat.

Jake's words came from inside Tyler's own head and nowhere else, he knew that, and yet the sense of being haunted by his father was as strong as any hunch Tyler had ever had.

And hunches were a way of life for Tyler. A survival mechanism, developed early on and honed during the rodeo years. Without them, he'd have been dead, buried in this graveyard with all the other Creeds.

Let Lily go, Ty. Let her go before she gets hurt again.

"Like you ever gave a damn if anybody got hurt," Tyler said aloud. "And I'm going to take care of Lily, because I'm not you. Damn it, you son of a bitch, *I'm not you.*"

Blood is blood, Jake's invisible ghost insisted. *And a Creed's a Creed. If I were in any position to make a bet, I'd wager all I know of heaven and half I know of hell that you'll be bedding down*

with that waitress, or somebody just like her,
before poor sweet Lily's plane touches down at
O'Hare.

"You know *all* about hell, if there's any justice in
this world or the next one," Tyler growled. It was
crazy to be sitting there, talking out loud to a dead
man, and one he couldn't see at that, but he made
no move to start up the rig, head home, get on with
the million and one things he needed to do to make
a real home for Lily and Davie and Tess. For himself, too. Because this was something that had to
be settled—now. "Get out of my truck. Get out of
my *head.*"

Jake was as intractable in death as he had been in
life. *I'm trying to* help *you, boy. Spare you the kind
of grief your brothers are bound to run into. Spare*
Lily *some heartache, too. Listen to me. You're a
Creed. Dylan and Logan are Creeds, and that's the
fact of the matter. They might think they can fancy
the old place up and make a new start with that
cattle outfit of theirs, but they are who they are,
and there's no changing that. We're poison, us
Creeds, every last one of us.*

Tyler felt sick. God knew, he had his problems
with Logan and with Dylan, too. But damn it, they
were trying, both of them. They deserved a shot at
hauling the Creed name up out of the mud and
building lives for themselves.

They deserved to be happy.

"Let them be," Tyler warned his father. "If

you're real, and not a figment of my imagination like I think you are, *you let Logan and Dylan and their women alone.* You've caused enough pain—even you ought to be satisfied."

He'd have sworn he heard Jake laugh, though it was a feeling, not a sound. *What do you figure you can do about it if I don't let them be?*

"I can hunt you to the farthest corner of hell, when my time comes," Tyler said. "That's what I can do. And *by God, old man, I will.* If it's a hundred years before I kick the bucket, or five minutes, I'll find you, you sorry son of a bitch. And when I get through with you, you'll be running to the devil for pity, because after me, he's going to look real good to you."

The soundless laugh seemed to fill the cab of that battered truck.

Tyler half expected the windshield to shatter with the force of it.

Tough guy, Jake mocked. *All three of you think you're so damn tough, just because you won a few buckles at the big rodeo.*

"That's more than *you* ever did," Tyler answered.

You don't know what tough is, boy. And I did plenty.

Something in that last statement sent a weird chill snaking down Tyler's spine, and his hand trembled a little when he reached for the keys, turned them to start the rig. He was making up this entire scenario, processing a lot of old crap he'd always tried to deny, no question about it—but it seemed just a shade too real now.

And I did plenty.

What the hell did *that* mean?

"I'm done, old man," Tyler said, slamming the truck into Reverse and hurling up gravel and dirt in every direction as he peeled out. "*I am done with you,* and all your bullshit, so get the hell out of here and leave me alone."

Well, I'm not done with you, Jake told him, stone-serious. *Angie was going to meet another man at that motel, did you know that? You were just a snot-nosed kid, but she might have told you. She was planning to run off with him. I killed her for it. I made her take those pills.*

Bile surged into the back of Tyler's throat; he stomped on the brakes, shoved the door open, leaned out to get sick.

It didn't happen, but he still felt as though he'd been kicked in the gut and then trampled. Dazed, he slumped forward, laid his forehead on the steering wheel and breathed. Just breathed, as slowly and deeply as he could.

Relentlessly, Jake's words echoed through his mind, like some devil's litany, though he knew the old man's ghost, or whatever the hell he'd been dealing with, had gone.

There was a tremor in the air, something clean and clear and new.

I killed her for it—I killed her—I killed her.

"Ty?"

Tyler nearly jumped out of his skin at the sound of his name; he hadn't heard a rig drive up. Hadn't heard anything, except for Jake's taunts, until Logan spoke.

Standing in the space gap made by the open door of the truck, he laid a hand on Tyler's shoulder. "You all right?"

Tyler straightened. Nodded. Couldn't quite bring himself to face his brother, because Logan had to know he was lying, and Tyler didn't want to see the certainty of that in his eyes. "What are you doing here, Logan?" he ground out.

Logan leaned in, reached between Tyler and the steering wheel, pulled the keys from the ignition. "We were supposed to meet up at six o'clock, at your place, remember? I was on my way there when I saw Lily pull out of the cemetery road." He paused, and there was a grin in his voice, if a flimsy one. "Two and two still adds up to four, so I figured you must be around someplace, too. I waited a few minutes, in case you were hunting around the countryside for your clothes or something, but when I heard the engine of this old truck whine like it was going to blow all eight cylinders, I thought I'd better investigate."

"He killed her," Tyler said.

Logan thrust out a sigh. Had he even registered what Tyler had just said? "Get out of the driver's seat, Ty," he said. "I'm taking the wheel."

"He killed her," Tyler repeated.

"What the hell are you talking about?"

Tyler got out of the truck, forcing Logan to take a step back. Stood there trying to root himself in the real world while his older brother stared, paler than Tyler had ever seen him. He probably thought his little brother had finally gone around the bend for good.

What was the sense of trying to convince Logan or anybody else that a dead man had confessed to murdering a woman the whole world believed had committed suicide?

Yeah, Logan would think he was crazy, and he'd probably be right.

Once Tyler was out of the way, Logan got behind the wheel, waited. He looked like hell—even in his own state of mind, Tyler noticed that. What was going on?

At the moment, he had his hands full with his own problems. He couldn't stretch his brain around Logan's.

"What do you remember about the year my mother died?" Tyler asked, after sitting there in silence for a long time, trying to figure out how to phrase what he needed to ask without sounding like more of a lunatic than he'd already shown himself to be.

Logan let out a raspy breath. "That was kind of what I wanted to talk to you about," he said. He made no move to start up the truck.

Tyler had been looking straight ahead, through the windshield, a part of his brain counting gravestones; he knew all the inscriptions by heart, who was buried here, who was buried there, when they'd died and in some cases, though not many, how they'd died. Now, because of something in Logan's tone, Tyler turned to face him.

"I've been doing some research," Logan said. "There were some old pictures up in the attic—some diaries and other stuff, too. That's how I found Jake's suicide note, though you didn't give me a chance to tell you that when I broke the news."

Of course Tyler recalled the incident—it hadn't been that long ago and he didn't forget much, which wasn't entirely a good thing. He'd seen Logan heading in the direction of the cemetery that day, guessed which grave he planned to visit and followed. He'd sucker punched Logan, knocked him on his ass, expecting a fight, *needing* a fight.

Logan hadn't given him one, though, which should have been a sign, though of what, God knew.

He'd gotten to his feet, dusted himself off and calmly told Tyler that Jake's death hadn't been an accident, or a murder. It had been suicide.

Even now, Tyler was surprised by his own reaction.

He'd felt—nothing. Nothing at all.

He'd called Logan a liar, more out of habit than anything else, turned and walked away.

"I guess you must have found something else, besides a suicide note written by dear old dad," Tyler said, when Logan didn't say anything more.

"Letters," Logan said, very quietly. "I found some letters. I didn't read all of them—just part of the first one."

In a way, Tyler felt more unsettled, sitting there in that truck with his big brother, than he had when Jake was there.

"What *kind* of letters?" Tyler forced himself to ask.

"They were addressed to Angela, Ty," Logan said. He sounded reluctant, now that he'd finally gotten started, and Tyler knew this was about the last thing in the universe Logan wanted to do.

Once again, Jake's voice grated against Tyler's mind. *Angie was going to meet another man at that motel, did you know that?*

"Love letters," Tyler said, to save Logan the trouble.

Logan's eyes narrowed. "You knew?"

"Not until about five minutes ago. My mother was seeing somebody, wasn't she? Planning to run away, leave Jake and the ranch—"

"Yeah," Logan said. "She was going to leave."

"Who wrote the letters, Logan? Who was he, this man?"

"Nobody you know," Logan answered, after

another lengthy silence. God, for a lawyer, he had a hard time keeping a conversation moving. "Like I said, I only read part of the first one, and there wasn't a return address."

"After all these years," Tyler began, getting angry all over again, "you decide I need to know my mother wasn't just a suicide, she was fooling around, too?"

What little color he had left drained out of Logan's face, and his jawline looked hard enough to strike sparks off of with a rock. "No," he ground out. "I'm telling you because ever since I found those letters, I've been wondering if Angie killed herself or if someone else did."

"It was Jake," Tyler said. "That's what I meant when you were talking about seeing Lily leave here and all that, and I said, 'He killed her.'"

"Holy Christ," Logan rasped.

"You know he was capable of it," Tyler insisted.

Logan gave one brief, sharp nod of his head, now in profile again. Tyler saw him swallow and knew there was something else, something he was having one hell of a time spitting out.

"I knew, Tyler," he said.

"You knew what?" Tyler snapped.

"I knew Angie was seeing somebody else. Way back, when it was happening."

"What?"

"It was a couple of weeks before she died," Logan replied. "You'd gone fishing with Dylan. I was supposed to go, too, but I had some lawns to mow in town. When I was finished, I hitchhiked home, figuring I'd get my gear from the house and catch up with the two of you. There was a strange car parked in the yard, but I didn't think anything about that—until I got inside. They were in the kitchen, Angie and this man I'd never seen before, and the radio was playing. They were—"

Tyler didn't want to think about where *that* sentence was headed, and he must have made some kind of sound indicating that.

"They were *dancing*," Logan finished, with a sort of mirthless chuckle.

"Oh," Tyler said, and immediately felt stupid.

"They hadn't noticed me, and I was trying to figure out how to get out of there before they did, when all of the sudden Jake came busting into the house. He came up behind me, threw me to one side and yelled at me to get the hell away and stay gone, and then he went into the kitchen."

Tyler closed his eyes.

I've done plenty, he heard Jake say.

I killed her.

"What happened then, Logan?"

"Jake had Angie by the hair, and she was screaming, and the guy—whoever he was—pulled a gun on Jake. I knew he meant to kill him and, God help me, I wished he would, Tyler. *I wished he would.* But Angie begged him not to. He wanted her to go with him, and she said she couldn't

269

because—because Jake would take it out on you, and on Dylan and me, if she did."

Tyler stared at his brother, full of amazed fury and no little sympathy for the kid Logan had been. He must have been scared shitless, watching a scene like that, knowing there was nothing he could do to make it stop.

"What happened after that?" Tyler asked slowly, after another long silence had descended on that truck like a cold, wet shroud.

Logan looked haunted. "I don't know," he said gruffly. "I ran, Ty."

"You were a kid," Tyler reminded him. "You couldn't have changed anything by staying."

Logan was back in the past, unhooked from the present. "Jake caught up with me hours later, at Cassie's," he went on, almost as though Tyler hadn't said anything. "She was out of town, as it turned out, so I hid in that teepee of hers, but he found me."

Tyler ached inside. Jake would have been roaring drunk by then; he'd been backed down, humiliated in his own house, and Logan had had the misfortune to witness it.

"He beat the hell out of you, didn't he?"

To Tyler's surprise, Logan shook his head. "It was worse than that," he answered. "He told me that if I ever said a word to anybody about what I'd seen, he'd kill the whole family, like in one of those slaughter movies, with all the axes and chain saws, and I believed it."

Inwardly, Tyler shuddered. He'd have believed it, too.

Even now, years later, the story brought blood-splashed images to his mind.

"And you never told anybody?" Tyler marveled hoarsely. "You held a thing like that inside, all this time?"

"Yeah," Logan said bleakly, coming back from the long-ago and not-so-far away. "I had my suspicions when your mom died, but Jake was meaner than ever after that, and I was afraid of what he might do to you and Dylan, to all three of us, so I pretended like I didn't remember." He paused to clear his throat, blink a couple of times. "I'm sorry, Tyler. *Christ,* if only I'd told someone—Cassie or Floyd Book or *someone*—about the man dancing in the kitchen with Angie, and all the rest of it—"

"Jake might not have caught up to Mom at that motel and forced her to swallow a bottle of pills?" Tyler asked quietly, when Logan's voice fell away into a miserable, pulsing silence. "You couldn't have prevented that. You were a *kid,* Logan."

Logan nodded, started up the truck. Neither of them spoke as he shifted it into gear and they left the graveyard.

Tyler didn't ask where they were headed, and Logan didn't say.

But when they pulled in at the main ranch house, Tyler wasn't surprised.

"They weren't like Jake, the people who lived

here before us," Logan said, after staring at the old place in silence for a long time. "I've read their letters, and a lot of old news clippings, and a few of their diaries, too. It doesn't have to be a curse to be a Creed, that's what I'm trying to say. You and Dylan and I, we can be like they were—good, honest, hardworking people, most of them. Proud of the Creed name."

In that moment, Tyler did something he'd thought he'd never do. He reached over and slapped Logan on the shoulder. "Most of them?" he joked, grinning.

Logan chuckled, but it wasn't a broken sound, like back at the cemetery. There was a quiet joy in it, and a sort of relief. "Everybody has a few bastards creeping around in the branches of their family tree," he said.

Tyler couldn't quite manage a laugh—the grin had been a stretch—but he nodded. "What now, Logan?" he asked. "Jake's dead and gone, and so is my mother. Even if we could prove he forced her to take those pills, what would it change?"

"Maybe nothing," Logan said, getting out of the truck. Since his own rig was parked over by the barn, he must have planned on hoofing it to the lake cabin that day, before he got side-lined at the cemetery. "Maybe everything."

Maybe nothing, maybe everything.

That about sized it all up, in Tyler's opinion.

Jake couldn't be executed for the crime—he

was already rotting in his grave. Still, Angie's memory mattered. All those Creeds, who'd lived out their lives doing the best they could, they mattered, too.

"You want to come inside?" Logan asked. "Briana will have the coffee on, and breakfast started."

Tyler shook his head. He wasn't ready to set foot in that house, after all that had happened within its walls, though he knew Logan and Briana had changed it, not just superficially, but by loving each other there. "I'd like to see those letters, though."

Logan hesitated, then nodded. "I'll get them," he said.

A few minutes later, he was back with a little stack of yellowed envelopes, tied with a ribbon, faded to a pinkish ivory.

"You're sure you want to read these?" Logan asked. "You know what you needed to know—that your mother didn't abandon you on purpose. As for the rest of it, well, maybe some things are better just left alone."

"I'm sure," Tyler said. "But I'd appreciate it if you'd keep Davie here for a while." Reading the letters, he suspected, would be like walking through an emotional firestorm, and a man needed privacy for things like that.

"I can drive him to your place later," Logan agreed. "Just give me a call when you're ready."

Looking down at those letters, holding them in his hands, Tyler couldn't speak. Couldn't even raise his eyes to Logan. "Thanks," he said.

"For—?"

"For not giving up on me, on the three of us—"

"I'm a Creed," Logan said, before he turned to head for the house. "I don't know *how* to give up."

CHAPTER FOURTEEN

LILY HAD BEEN HOME barely five minutes when Tess padded into the kitchen, looking rumpled and sleep-flushed in her pajamas.

"You're still wearing your red dress?" Tess immediately inquired. "Did you sleep in it?"

Lily, busy setting up a pot of coffee, took a moment to come up with a logical explanation. She hated lying to Tess, or anyone else for that matter, but in this instance, of course, there was no other choice. "I just like it, that's all," she said. "The way you like your pink shirt with the sparkly butterflies on it."

"Oh," Tess said, but she looked puzzled just the same.

Before Lily had to carry the conversation any further, her father appeared from the direction of his study, looking spiffy. Clearly, he'd been up for a while.

"My doctor e-mailed me back," he said. "I'm good to go for the Chicago junket."

Mercifully, Tess was distracted. "Road trip!" she chimed.

"Road trip!" Hal confirmed, jutting up a thumb.

"One way," Lily reminded them both, and then laughed at the expressions on their faces.

"Nice dress," Hal said.

Full-circle, hello, square one.

"I'd like to call as little attention to that as possible," she said brightly, almost singing the words. "Thanks for nothing, Daddy-o."

Hal arched an eyebrow, grinning.

"You called him Daddy-o!" Tess crowed, triumphant. "Instead of 'Hal'!"

"Will wonders never cease," Lily said. "Are you both packed for the trip?" They were taking an evening flight out of Missoula; with luck, she'd be able to grab a few hours of sleep in the meantime.

"Ready to roll," her dad said, indicating his best casual outfit. He was obviously looking forward— *way* forward—to a little break in his routine.

Tess beamed. "Are you going to wear that dress?" she asked Lily innocently.

Hal laughed, and Lily blushed a little.

"I think I'll branch out and put on something else," Lily answered. "And it will be *hours* before we leave for the airport, everybody."

"I'll make breakfast," Hal offered, letting the reminder pass and watching his daughter with such fondness in his face that she almost hated herself for calling him by his first name ever since she'd arrived—and before that, too, when she'd addressed him at all. "You get some rest."

"But it's *morning!*" Tess protested.

"Get dressed, young lady," Hal told his granddaughter mildly. "You and I will walk down to the Birdhouse Café and order the special."

"No specials," Lily said darkly, thinking bacon and eggs, or corned-beef hash, two of the nutritional disasters her father liked best. Then, to soften the order, she added, "I mean it, Dad."

He crossed to her and kissed her forehead while Tess scampered off to switch out her pajamas for an outfit more suited to a big occasion like breakfast at the Birdhouse Café.

"No specials," Hal promised. "And it's good to see you looking so happy."

Lily peeked around her father's shoulder to make sure Tess was safely out of earshot. "Tyler asked me to marry him, Dad," she said, braced for an immediate objection, even though she knew Hal had changed his opinion of Jake Creed's boys, Tyler included.

"Did you say yes?" Hal asked quietly, his eyes shining.

She nodded, biting her lower lip. Then, unable to hold in her joy, she did a little victory dance around the kitchen.

Hal laughed with delight.

Tess, a lightning-quick dresser, reappeared in

jean shorts and a red T-shirt, just in time to see Lily's last whirl.

"How come everybody's so happy?" she demanded.

Hal gave Lily a verbal nudge. "Maybe you ought to go ahead and answer that question."

Lily looked at him, looked at her daughter—the little girl who was in danger of growing up too fast. She crossed the room, crouched to look up into Tess's face and took both the child's hands in hers.

"I hope you're not about to say we're going to stay in Chicago," Tess said, "because I don't want to."

Lily laughed, though her eyes burned with sudden tears. "Tyler Creed—you remember, the man with the dog? The one we picked up alongside the highway when his car broke down?"

Hal cleared his throat expressively.

"Okay," Lily admitted, glancing back briefly over one shoulder to acknowledge his point. "Not the best choice of words."

"Of course I remember," Tess said. "Geez, it was *only* a couple of days ago."

"I've known Tyler for a long time," Lily said softly. "We were—friends, even before I met your dad. And he and I—Well—"

Tess's face lit up as the possibilities registered. With uncanny perception, even for a child-genius, she blurted, "You're going to get *married?* You and Tyler Creed?"

Lily swallowed hard, nodded.

And Tess flung herself into her mother's arms with a whoop of delight and such force that they both toppled over onto the kitchen floor, in a giggling, teary heap of celebration.

"I'd say she's okay with the idea," Hal commented, his own eyes glistening a little. "Let's go, Tess. If there's a run on oatmeal down at the Birdhouse, we'll be out of luck."

Tess got back on her feet, solemnly helped Lily up, too.

"Is there going to be a baby?" the little girl asked, evidently not ready to move on to the prospect of oatmeal.

Lily laid a hand on her daughter's hair. "Maybe sometime," she said, thick-throated. Not wanting to get Tess's hopes up any more than she already had. What if something went wrong? Should she have waited until they got back from Chicago to tell Tess about the wedding?

Her dad must have seen the doubts in her face, because he responded to them as surely as if she'd voiced them aloud. "Life is uncertain, Lily. Young or old, we have to learn to take it as it comes."

Lily nodded.

Watched with her heart in her throat as Hal took Tess's hand and the two of them set out for the Birdhouse Café.

Lily stood rooted to the floor of that sunny kitchen for a long time, wanting guarantees from

God—and knowing she wasn't going to get any such thing.

Finally, exhausted, she went into the spare room, took off the red dress, pulled on her old standby, the T-shirt, and toppled into bed.

She was asleep within moments.

TYLER SET the forlorn little packet of letters, with their faded pink ribbon, in the middle of his table.

Now that he was home, much to Kit Carson's delight, he wasn't so sure he wanted to read them after all.

Maybe Logan had been right, stopping after the first paragraph or two. Maybe it was better to just leave things alone—especially his mother's private dreams, reflected in the words of her unknown lover, for a better life than she'd had with Jake Creed.

God knew, that wouldn't have taken much.

A part of Tyler wanted to prove to the whole world that she hadn't committed suicide, that Jake had killed her, in a fit of jealous revenge. But why rake all that up? Why not let the dust settle, once and for all?

The last thing Logan and Dylan needed now, with all their efforts at starting over—the last thing he needed—was a scandal.

Tyler shoved a hand through his hair.

At the moment, he was too tired to make a decision, one way or the other.

He'd made love to Lily all night.

He'd experienced his first—and, he hoped, his *last*—haunting, and he and Logan had made a beginning at reconciling their many differences.

Enough high drama, already.

He needed sleep.

So he went upstairs, stripped off his clothes and fell face-first onto the bed.

He woke, several hours later, to the sound of voices downstairs, on the main floor of the cabin.

One by one, he registered them in his sleep-fogged brain.

Dylan.

Logan.

Davie.

Tyler hoisted himself up onto one elbow, grumbling to himself.

What was this? A family reunion?

A smile crept onto his mouth and stuck.

Maybe that was *exactly* what it was.

"It's about time you rolled out of the sack," Dylan told him a few minutes later, when he'd pulled on yesterday's jeans, a T-shirt, socks and boots, and made his way down the stairs, finger-combing his hair as he went. "Damn, brother, it's the middle of the afternoon."

Tyler grinned. Looked from Dylan to Logan to Davie. Leaned down to scratch Kit Carson's scruff when the dog leaned into his right leg. "Is this a party?" he asked.

"We're going fishing," Davie announced. The holes in his face, where the hardware had been, were already starting to heal over, and the wash-off spider tattoo on his neck was a ghost of its former self. "Briana said she'd cook up whatever we caught for supper."

Logan's gaze, he noticed, had dropped to the thin stack of letters on the table and gotten stuck there. With some effort, he met Tyler's eyes.

Tyler addressed himself to Davie. "Suppose all we catch," he joked, "is an old tire or part of a dead tree? What do you suppose Briana will serve for supper then?"

Davie laughed, and there was relief in the sound, because he'd expected Tyler to refuse to go fishing with his brothers, the way he'd refused the first trail ride. "She could probably make those things taste good, too," he said.

"Why don't you go on out to the truck and fetch those new fishing poles we just bought in town?" Dylan asked, resting a hand on Davie's shoulder.

Davie nodded, skillfully dismissed and none the wiser for it, and hurried out, Kit Carson following close behind him.

That left the three of them, brothers who hadn't talked to each other all that much, at least in a friendly way, for a very long time.

"Logan told me about the letters," Dylan said quietly, watching Tyler. "And about the other thing, too."

Tyler nodded, rubbed his chin. His beard was coming in; he needed a shave. But since he didn't have to worry about giving Lily whisker burn in some delicate places, the razor could wait.

"What do you want to do, Ty?" Logan asked, after clearing his throat.

"For right now?" Tyler answered. "Go fishing with my brothers and the kid who might be mine."

"What about the letters?" Dylan pressed, though, like Logan, he looked a little confused. Like as not, they'd both expected him to run them off with a shotgun or something.

"I think they belong at the bottom of the lake," Tyler said. "And while we're at it, let's toss the hatchet in, too. Next best thing to burying it."

Relief moved in Logan's face, and in Dylan's, too.

"Brothers again?" Dylan asked.

"Brothers again," Tyler agreed huskily. "Until one of you screws up and pisses me off, anyway."

Logan and Dylan exchanged glances.

"I think we ought to throw him in the lake," Logan said. "Like we used to do."

Dylan nodded. "For old times' sake," he agreed.

And they both came at him then.

The struggle went all the way to the end of the dock, with Davie and Kit Carson right on the fringe of it.

Between the three of them, Davie laughing, and the dog barking, excited by the scuffle, they raised one hell of a din.

And it ended with a splash, though Tyler wasn't the only one who ended up in the lake. Dylan and Logan went right in with him—he made sure of that.

When Logan surfaced, he shook his wet hair out of his face and laughed in a way that brought back a lot of Jake-free memories. Times up at the swimming hole, and right there in that lake, the three of them together, having fun.

"Little brother's tougher than he used to be," Logan told Dylan.

Dylan spat out a mouthful of lake water. "Yeah," he agreed.

Right then, Davie jumped in, too, with a whoop, clothes and all.

Kit Carson hesitated on the end of the dock, haunches bunched for the leap.

"Come on, boy," Tyler told him. "You might as well be as wet as the rest of us."

The dog took the plunge, paddled around in happy circles and swam ashore to haul himself up the bank and sit, panting and dripping, in the grass.

"Guess we'd better catch some fish," Logan said presently, hoisting himself up onto the dock with both arms. "Think Briana would know the difference if we went back to town and bought a mess of trout?"

"The plastic packaging might be a tip-off," Dylan said.

Tyler got out of the water, and so did Davie and Dylan.

After that, they each took a pole, baited the hooks with worms Davie had dug while they were waiting for Tyler to wake up, and they fished, content in their wet clothes, nobody saying much.

Slowly, the warm Montana sun dried their jeans and their shirts, and the trout were biting, too.

When they'd all caught their limit, it was nearly sunset.

"You should have brought Alec and Josh along," Tyler told Logan.

"Next time," Logan said. "They spent the day in town with their dad."

"Next time," Tyler agreed, watching as Davie gathered up their fishing poles.

"You'll join the rest of us for supper?" Logan asked. He knew—he had to—that the home place gave Tyler the heebie-jeebies. He'd never set foot in it, never intended to, since the morning of Jake's funeral.

He'd felt something else besides grief that day, he realized now.

Relief.

"I'll be along," Tyler promised, after swallowing. "I've got something I need to do first."

Logan nodded, though he wouldn't have needed to, because Tyler saw the understanding in his eyes and in his bearing.

Davie hurried inside the cabin to stash the poles. Dylan and Logan left, taking the fish with them.

"We're going, too, right?" Davie asked anxiously, when Tyler stepped into the kitchen. "To the main house, I mean?"

The kid must have thought he was going to change his mind.

"We're going, too," Tyler confirmed. "Change your clothes first."

Davie nodded, watched as Tyler picked up the bundle of letters he'd left lying on the table. Weighed them thoughtfully in his hand, tightened his fingers around them for a moment.

"Are you going to change, too?" Davie wanted to know. "You're looking pretty scruffy yourself."

"In a few minutes," Tyler said, very quietly, amused.

Then, taking the letters with him, he went back outside, walked to the end of the dock, hesitated for a moment and then tossed the packet into the lake. Watched as the ribbon came loose and they sank slowly beneath the surface, a few at a time.

He'd never know what had been in those letters now, but that was okay.

He didn't need to know.

Twenty minutes later, after Tyler had grabbed a quick shower and put on clean clothes, he and Davie and Kit Carson pulled in at the main ranch house.

Everybody was crowded into the kitchen—kids, wives, dogs—and the smell of frying fish filled the air.

Tyler hesitated on the threshold, waiting for the

old urge to bolt and run to hit him, and was a little surprised when it didn't.

Briana and Kristy watched him with smiles on their faces and tears shining in their eyes.

Women. The way they were looking at him, you'd have thought he'd been away at war or something.

Then again, he guessed he *had,* though most of the battles had been fought inside his own mind and heart, not on some pile of sand on the other side of the world.

Dylan and Logan, both seated at the table and still in their sun-dried clothes, looked solemn, because both of them knew what was going through his mind. They were giving him space to deal with whatever private devils might be lying in wait for him in that old house, and he appreciated that.

Finally, he stepped inside, unclogging the doorway, and Davie and Kit Carson immediately pushed past him, tired of waiting.

The place was the same, and yet different, Tyler reflected, looking around.

Dylan used one foot to slide a chair back at the table.

Waited.

Tyler crossed the room, sat down between his brothers.

Logan grinned, looked up at the ceiling, back down again. "Damn," he drawled. "Here we are, the three of us, and the *roof* didn't even fall in."

"Go figure," Dylan said, and then he laughed, and the laughter swept through the room, from one grown-up to another, dispelling the last of the tension.

Making everything okay.

It was okay to be together.

It was okay to be home.

The women served up supper, and everybody ate their fill, and then the kids and the dogs migrated to the living room to watch TV, and Briana and Kristy went out for a short horseback ride, leaving the men to clean up.

Fair was fair—the wives had done the cooking.

The only thing that gathering lacked, as far as Tyler was concerned, was Lily and her little girl and her dad. If they'd been there, it would have been perfect.

Tyler glanced at the clock hanging on the wall above the sink, just like it always had. Was Lily on that plane to Chicago?

Already there, maybe, and asking herself what she'd been thinking, agreeing to marry a Creed and live in a double-wide trailer?

Dylan snapped him with a dish towel, like in the old days, and grinned. "Thinking about Lily?" he asked.

"Hell yes, I was thinking about Lily," Tyler answered.

Logan, up to his elbows in suds at the sink

because the new dishwasher hadn't been installed yet, chuckled. "What exactly were you two doing in the cemetery at that hour of the morning, anyway?" he asked, knowing damn well what they'd been doing.

"If that was any of your business," Tyler said, jerking the dish towel out of Dylan's hands and retaliating with a pretty good snap of his own, "I'd tell you."

Logan laughed.

So did Dylan.

And, in his own good time, Tyler did, too.

LILY DROPPED OFF HER DAD and Tess and their suitcases at the airport, returned the rental car and rode back on the shuttle. She hadn't wanted to come back to Montana, even after she got the call about Hal's heart attack. Now, she didn't want to leave.

Not even for two weeks.

After all, a lot could go wrong in two weeks.

Tyler could change his mind. Decide he missed the rodeo, or the movies, or doing print ads for magazines.

He could hook up with a waitress.

"Lily," Hal said, as she worried her way through the security line. "Why the long face?"

She summoned up a smile, grateful that Tess was apparently too busy absorbing the preflight gauntlet to notice her mother's wistful mood. "Just thinking about things I need to do when we get there," she said.

The list *was* dauntingly long.

And it would be after midnight, Chicago time, when they landed at O'Hare.

Eloise, alerted to their arrival by telephone a few hours before, had insisted on sending a car and driver to meet them. She'd wanted Tess delivered to her house, right away, but reluctantly agreed to wait when Lily insisted that she could see her granddaughter in the morning.

Eloise.

Lily wasn't looking forward to that encounter. She'd have to break the news that she and Tess were moving to Stillwater Springs permanently, and she knew her mother-in-law wouldn't take it well.

"Like what?" Hal asked, as the line inched forward.

Lily glanced down at Tess, who was chatting with another little girl.

"Like telling Eloise we won't be living in Chicago anymore," Lily whispered.

"She'll adjust," Hal said.

"You don't know Eloise," Lily replied.

They got through the checkpoint—Tess, an obvious threat to national security, if there ever was one, was wanded, much to her delight—and made their way to the appropriate gate.

Lily considered calling Tyler on her cell phone,

just to hear his voice, and decided it would be *way* codependent. They'd only been apart for a few hours, after all.

Tess and Hal checked out the gift shop.

When it was finally time to board the plane, Lily was relieved. The sooner she got to Chicago, the sooner she'd be back.

Back with Tyler.

"Do I get to have my own room in the trailer house?" Tess asked loudly, as soon as they were settled in their seats.

The flight attendant, checking for renegades who had yet to buckle their seat belts, arched one eyebrow.

Burke had flown for this airline. Lily wondered uncharitably if the woman smirking in the aisle had been one of his many conquests.

Which only went to prove she hadn't had nearly enough sleep.

"Sure," she said cheerfully, looking at the flight attendant as she replied, not at Tess. "We might even put in a lawn, so the chickens can peck for worms, and get Grandma a new set of teeth for Christmas."

Hal, taking the whole thing in from the window seat, chuckled.

Tess tugged at Lily's sleeve, brow furrowed in confusion. "Nana has teeth," she said. "And we *never* call her 'Grandma.' She'd have a cow!"

The flight attendant had moved on.

Lily smiled and ruffled her daughter's hair. "Darned if you aren't right on all counts," she said.

Tess rolled her eyes. "You're *silly,* Mom." She paused, brightened. "I *like* it when you're silly. You're too serious, most of the time."

"Amen," Hal said.

"Well," Lily said, "from now on, I'll try to be silly more often."

She settled back, closed her eyes.

Tess held her hand during takeoff, though whether she needed reassurance herself or was offering it to Lily, there was no knowing.

The moment they came out of the boarding area in Chicago nearly four hours later, however, Lily knew being silly, as much as it pleased her dad and Tess, wasn't going to be an option.

Eloise, looking stately and patrician and well-put-together, late as it was, was waiting beside the driver when Lily, Tess and Hal appeared.

So much for waiting until tomorrow to see Tess, Lily thought.

Tess, for her part, was tired from the flight, and inclined to be cranky. Seeing Eloise, she refused to go to her grandmother and huddled close to Hal, clinging to his pant leg.

"I'm *not* staying in Chicago," she said sturdily, though nobody had asked. "I'm going back to Montana, and marrying Tyler Creed and we're going to live with him in a trailer."

Eloise went pale, even put a hand to her heart.

"She's very tired," Lily said, though she could see her words didn't reassure Eloise.

"Who," Eloise demanded, "is *Tyler Creed?*"

"We'll talk about it tomorrow," Lily said, not knowing whether to be grateful or annoyed when her father went off with Eloise's driver to collect the bags, taking Tess along with him.

"I want to know *now,*" Eloise said.

"Well, Eloise," Lily responded quietly, "I don't want to tell you now."

"I *knew* this would happen!"

"Tomorrow," Lily reiterated wearily.

To her amazement, Eloise subsided. The bags were all present and accounted for, and while the driver went to fetch the car from a nearby parking garage, taking the luggage with him, Hal and Lily and Eloise and Tess all stood waiting on the curb, none of them making eye contact or speaking.

Lily suspected Hal had counseled Tess to be quiet about Tyler and their planned return to Montana, while they were off at the baggage carousel. She'd ask him later, at the condo, after Eloise and the driver were gone and Tess was tucked up in her own bed.

The ride to Lily's condo, with its partial view of the lake, seemed endless.

Eloise remained in the car, stiff-backed, while the driver took the bags out of the back and Lily, Hal and Tess piled onto the sidewalk.

"I'll be coming by first thing in the morning,"

Eloise said tightly. "And I *expect* an explanation."

"Not too early, Eloise," Lily said, firmly though not unkindly. She knew how much Tess meant to Eloise, especially now that Burke was gone, and she felt a lot of sympathy for the woman. "We've all had a long day—including you."

Eloise didn't answer. She was too busy seething.

Lily rummaged through her handbag for her key, and she and Hal and Tess said hello to the doorman, Salvatore—aka Sal—as they entered the building. Eloise's driver left the bags with Sal and made a hasty exit.

Inside the familiar elevator, Lily tilted her head back against the wall, closed her eyes, and ordered "*Nobody* say *anything*."

The condo felt strange when Lily stepped over the threshold, flipped on the lights. There was dust on every surface, and she nearly tripped over the pile of mail just inside the door.

Hal went to the windows, opened the drapes and took in the semiview, while Tess plunked herself down on the sofa, folded her arms and stuck out her lower lip, obstinacy personified.

"Nana," she said, "is in a *snit*."

"So is somebody else I know," Lily commented. "Go to bed, Tess."

"We've been gone a long time," Tess said, though she did get off the couch and meander toward her room. "What if there are *cooties* in the sheets?"

"There are no cooties," Lily said, exhausted.

"There *could* be."

"Good *night, Tess.*"

"Let me know when you're jammied up, kiddo," Hal told Tess, "and I'll come and tuck you in."

Jammied up. It was a phrase Lily remembered from her own childhood, when she'd hated to go to bed, so even putting on her pajamas seemed like a trial. Hal had jollied her into "jammying up," just as he had Tess.

"Thanks," she said, when Tess finally went into her room.

Sal's arrival with the bags coincided exactly with the eloquent slam of Tess's door.

Hal handled the tip while Lily, sighing, went to have a little chat with her daughter.

Tess was sitting on the side of her bed, stony faced, arms folded.

"What's gotten into you?" Lily asked, with as much patience as she could muster.

"She'll make us stay here," Tess fretted. "Nana, I mean. We'll *never* get to go back to Montana and marry Tyler."

Hiding a smile, Lily sat down beside Tess and slipped an arm around her stiff little shoulders. "We're going back, Tess," she said.

"You promise?"

"I promise."

"No matter what?"

"No matter what."

Tess relaxed a little, let Lily hold her close against her side, something she allowed less and less often, the older she got. "Do I have to go to Nantucket with Nana?"

"Probably," Lily said. "But only for a few days."

Tess made a face.

"You *love* Nantucket," Lily reminded her gently. "*And* you love your grandmother. Be nice to her, sweetie—she adores you, you know that."

Tess gave a tremulous little sigh that bruised Lily's heart. "Okay," she said. "I'll be nice to Nana."

"Thank you," Lily said. "I appreciate that." She stood up, crossed to Tess's bureau and pulled out a favorite pair of pajamas and brought them to Tess. "Better jammy up," she added, bending to kiss the top of her daughter's head, "so Grampa can tuck you in."

Tess took the pajamas, examined them with forensic care.

"No cooties," she said, sounding almost disappointed.

CHAPTER FIFTEEN

LILY WAS IN HER ROBE the next morning, squinting at the sticky-note her father had fixed to the cupboard above the coffeemaker—*Just push the button. Tess is showing me the neighborhood— we'll bring breakfast back with us—bagels? Home soon. Dad*—when Orlando, the day doorman, buzzed from downstairs to announce Eloise's arrival.

Grateful to Hal for getting Tess out of the line of fire, not to mention ferreting through the freezer for coffee beans, grinding them and setting up the pot, Lily mimicked the smiley face her dad had drawn at the bottom of his note.

"Send Mrs. Kenyon right up, please," she said cheerfully, because she knew her mother-in-law would be standing practically at Orlando's elbow, ears perked for any nuance of reluctance or irritation that might be evident in her tone of voice.

Lily felt *both* those things—more like *pissed off* and *for God's sake, not now,* in fact, but she didn't want to hurt Eloise, either deliberately or by accident. In her own snooty way, Eloise had been generous from the very beginning.

It would have been nice to have time to get dressed, though, Lily thought sourly, as she took her finger off the intercom button and tried to hand-comb her tangled hair. She'd barely slept the night before, tired as she was, and when she did, she had red-hot dreams about Tyler that left her aching for things she couldn't have.

A quick peek in the refrigerator told her what she already knew—no food until Hal and Tess returned with bagels and whatever else they could find in the plethora of well-stocked delis the neighborhood boasted. Unless, of course, she wanted a tasty mix of baking soda, Dijon mustard and wrinkly green olives for breakfast.

The repast might, she had to admit, have suited her mood.

A minute or so after she'd reached this conclusion, the doorbell rang.

Lily started the coffee, left the kitchen and headed for the front door, smiling as happily as she could, given the ordeal she was about to face. God bless her dad—he'd keep Tess out of range as long as he could, but time was of the essence, just the same.

"Coffee?" Lily asked, stepping back to admit Eloise. The brew wasn't ready, but she knew her mother-in-law would refuse the offer.

Early as it was, the woman was impeccably dressed, in full makeup, high heels, nylons and an expensive navy suit with white piping. Her eyes moved disapprovingly over Lily's ratty robe, turned bleak when she recognized it as an old one of Burke's.

"No, *thank you,*" Eloise bit out. Dear God, the makeup. It was *perfect,* at an hour when Lily wouldn't have trusted herself to apply mascara without putting out an eye. Had Eloise visited the cosmetics department at Neiman Marcus, her favorite, before breezing on over?

Lily suppressed a sigh. Kept her smile in place— and it felt like a pair of those wax lips kids wear at Halloween. "Come in," she said, as Eloise swept regally past, took in the dusty, unlived-in state of the condo and settled herself somewhat warily on the very edge of the sofa cushions.

"What did Tess mean last night," Eloise snapped, never one for preambles, "when she said you were going to marry someone named . . . Tiger whatever-it-was and *live in a trailer?*"

"His name is Tyler Creed." Just saying the name made Lily feel a little stronger, a little steadier. She tightened the belt of her robe and sat down in the easy chair facing Eloise. "We *are* planning on getting married."

We've just been too busy having maniacal sex to set a date yet.

Eloise closed her eyes and paled a little, as though absorbing a physical blow. Obviously she'd cherished illusions that Tess might have had the wedding part wrong. "I *see,*" she said, looking at Lily again. Drilling a hole right into her with her gaze. "And you're going to live in a *mobile home,* if I understood my granddaughter correctly?"

Distantly, the coffeemaker chortled busily away.

It was a comforting sound, and the aroma made Lily's dry mouth suddenly water.

"Temporarily," Lily said mildly, chin up, smile still fixed in place. Inside, though, she wanted to counter with, *What's so terrible about a mobile home? And what gives you the right to be such an insufferable snob?* "Tyler and I intend to build a house. The trailer is temporary."

"You can't be serious," Eloise said, aghast.

"I'm quite serious," Lily said evenly. "About marrying Tyler and about raising Tess in Stillwater Springs. It's a very nice little town, you know."

Eloise actually shuddered, perhaps still thinking about the *mobile home,* or maybe small towns in general. "I can't believe you would do this, Lily, take my *only grandchild*—all I have left of my son—so far away—"

Lily felt a pang of sympathy, and would have reached out to touch Eloise's hand if she hadn't expected the gesture to be slapped away. It wasn't hard to imagine herself in her mother-in-law's position, at least where Tess was concerned. If *she* were grown-up, getting married and moving someplace far away, Lily would be devastated.

The difference was, she'd accept that the decision was Tess's to make.

"You can visit as often as you want to, Eloise," she offered gently. "Montana *is* on the North American continent, you know."

Eloise fanned herself with her tasteful alligator-skin clutch, dyed to match the navy suit. "And stay in a *trailer? That* would be cozy, with you and your new—husband."

Lily bit the inside of her lower lip, something she did when she needed a second or two's delay before she spoke. "Eloise, Burke has been gone a while," she said, when she thought she could trust herself to speak in a civil manner, "and we were getting a divorce, remember?"

Eloise waved off the divorce, along with the decent interval since Burke's death, presumably. "You would have worked things out," she said, maddeningly certain of something she knew nothing about. In the next moment, though, she closed her mouth tightly, as if to stanch things she didn't want to say, and was about to go on when she registered the expression on Lily's face.

"No," Lily said. "We *wouldn't* have 'worked things out,' Eloise. Burke was having an affair—the latest in a long line of them—"

"Boys—" Eloise began.

"Don't you *dare* say 'boys will be boys,'" Lily broke in furiously. No more Mrs. Nice-guy, or whatever. "Burke *wasn't* a boy, Eloise. He was a man. He should have acted more like one—thought about how all that self-indulgence might affect his daughter, if not his wife."

Eloise reddened, but managed, perhaps by generations of good breeding, to hold her temper. The effort was only partially successful. "If you'd been a *real wife* to him—"

Lily stood up, jerked her robe belt even tighter around her waist and then sat down again, because there was no escaping Eloise, or the topic of conversation. "We're not going there," she said, deadly calm. "We are not going there, Eloise."

Eloise seemed to wilt a little then, even backpedal.

"I'm sorry," she said, with what might have been sincerity but probably wasn't. "It's just that I don't know what I'll do without Tess nearby, and it will give me *fits* of anxiety, worrying about what might be happening to her in that godforsaken place—"

"Stillwater Springs," Lily broke in, "is *beautiful*—breathtakingly so. In fact, we call it God's country."

Eloise wasn't listening; she'd made up her mind about Montana *and* about Tyler. "This man you've taken up with, he'll be her stepfather—"

"I happen to *love* 'this man I've taken up with,'" Lily said. "Very much."

The coffeemaker, which always sounded as though it were circling the kitchen, came in for a steamy landing.

"How do you know he'll be good to Tess—this Tyler person?"

Lily seethed. "Do you think I'd marry him if I thought he wouldn't be?"

Just then, a key scraped in the lock. Lily heard her father's voice on the other side of the door, and Tess answering, and then they were both in the living room, Hal carrying a couple of deli bags, their eyes full of trepidation.

Eloise's driver must have been circling the block; otherwise, they'd have spotted the limo.

Hal's gaze moved warily between the two women. "I guess we weren't gone long enough," he said.

301

Tess, on her best behavior, remarkably, approached her flushed grandmother, wrapped both arms around the woman's neck and kissed her loudly on the cheek.

"If we're going to Nantucket," she chimed, "let's leave right now and get it over with."

Eloise flinched. "Get it *over with?*"

Hal cleared his throat and looked away.

And Lily closed her eyes, waiting for the explosion.

"I thought you *liked* going to Nantucket," Eloise said to Tess, pumping some grandmotherly cheer into her voice and still sounding wounded.

"I do," Tess replied philosophically, bouncing once before settling onto the sofa cushions beside her grandmother. "But I'd rather be in Stillwater Springs. My mom's getting married, and I think there might even be a baby coming. I asked her, and she said 'maybe sometime,' but when people get married, they usually have babies—"

Lily groaned and buried her face in both hands.

"So *that's* how it is," Eloise steamed, though to give her credit, she was obviously trying not to blow up in front of Tess.

"Eloise," Lily said wearily, "that is *not* how it is."

Eloise got to her feet, shaking on her high heels, and gave Tess a distracted pat on top of the head. "We'll talk about Nantucket later," she said. "Right now, Nana needs to be by herself for a while, so she can think."

"How come grown-ups always want to be by themselves when they think?" Tess asked her grandfather. "I'm only a kid, and I can *think* just fine, whether anybody else is around or not."

"Tess," Hal said, as Eloise whisked past him, opened the door and stormed into the corridor beyond, *"be quiet."*

"Don't you think that advice came a little *late?"* Lily asked her father miserably. When she'd had a few moments to recover, she turned to Tess and added, "You knew exactly what you were doing, didn't you, young lady? You *wanted* to upset your grandmother so you wouldn't have to go to Nantucket."

Tess's eyes widened in guileless surprise.

Lily was not fooled. "Go to your room," she said.

Tess flung a pleading glance in her grandfather's direction. "What about the bagels and the strawberries and stuff?" she asked plaintively. "I'll *starve* if I have to go to my room."

"Not to mention being devoured by cooties," Lily sniped, and instantly hated herself.

"Better mind your mother," Hal responded, after tossing a quelling glance in Lily's direction. "I'll do what I can to calm her down, and bring provisions if it looks like you're going to be stranded for any length of time."

Tess fled to her room, slammed the door behind her.

303

"Lily," Hal reasoned, sitting down in the place Eloise had so recently vacated and taking one of her hands, "Tess is *six years old*. She didn't set out to upset Eloise—or you."

"That," Lily said, "is what *you* think." She could just picture Eloise, whipping down to the lobby in the elevator, sweeping past poor, friendly Orlando without a word of acknowledgment, angrily gesturing for her waiting driver to get out of the limo and open the door for her—if he wasn't still circling the block while he waited for Madam to appear. As soon as Eloise got back to her mansion in Oak Park, if she didn't stop off at some private investigator's office to start the process before then, she'd find out everything there was to know about Tyler—and all the Creeds.

And so much of it wasn't good.

Eloise had contacts, and she had money. She probably had Tyler pegged for some toothless redneck with a drinking problem. Suppose she decided to sue for custody of Tess? Suppose—

Hal vanished into the kitchen, with the deli bags he'd set on the floor when he sat down, and returned with coffee for Lily—her first of the day, and critically needed—and he held it out to her, didn't let go of the handle until she'd gripped the mug with both hands.

"If it wasn't so early in the day," he remarked, "I'd have dosed this java with Jack Daniel's. That woman is something else."

"I don't have any Jack Daniel's," Lily said, quite unnecessarily.

Hal chuckled. "What kind of place are you running here?"

Lily managed a brief smile, but she was shaken, and there was no hiding it. She didn't even try—this was her dad she was talking to, after all. "Eloise is going to type 'Creed' into some search engine as soon as she gets home and fires up her computer," she muttered, after a few steadying sips, "and when she sees what comes up, all hell is going to break loose."

"Honey," Hal reasoned gently, "if Tyler were a saint, she *still* wouldn't spit on him if he caught fire. He's going to be helping to raise her granddaughter, and he's not Burke, and that's all it takes to piss off somebody like Eloise."

Lily glanced nervously in the direction of Tess's room, dropped her voice to a whisper. "Dad, what if she—Eloise—what if she hires a bunch of lawyers and tries to take away my baby?"

Hal had returned to his seat on the couch, now that he'd brought Lily the coffee, and his face turned granite-hard. "We'll fight, if we have to," he said, and he seemed so serious, and so upset, that Lily was instantly afraid he'd have another heart attack.

She had to get herself—and the situation—under control. And fast. So she did an emotional 180 and tried to look and sound confident. "I'm sure it won't come to that," she said. "I just got a little carried away."

"No wonder Burke was such a piece of work," Hal said. After pulling in some deep, slow breaths, he was still riled, but settling down by visible degrees. "I never liked Eloise Kenyon, and that was when she was a mere acquaintance. Now that I've seen her in action, up close and personal, I think I could hate her without half trying."

"She's really not so bad," Lily insisted, and she meant it. "She *did* spoil Burke—he was her only child and she's a widow and, well, I know how I'd feel, in her position."

Hal smiled, albeit a little glumly. "I suppose it's natural that she's bent out of shape, after the way Tess sprang all this on her before you had a chance to smooth the lady's feathers."

Lily nodded gloomily.

"So what else is on the schedule for today?" Hal asked, determinedly positive. "Whatever it is, it can't be worse than your mother-in-law."

That made Lily laugh. "The first order of business," she said, setting her cup down on the cocktail table and standing, "is to get dressed. The second is to deal with my daughter—preferably over breakfast. And the third, well, I've got to go over to my—*the* office and empty my desk."

"Need any moral support?"

Lily paused to rest a hand on her dad's shoulder before heading for her room to get ready for the day. "Yeah," she said. "I do. But this is something I have to do on my own."

Hal nodded. "I'll look after the munchkin while you're gone," he said, with another grin. "Try to get the concept of diplomacy across to her."

"Good luck with that," Lily replied.

"YOU WANT TO STOP BY the casino?" Tyler asked Davie quietly, as the two of them, and Kit Carson, drove toward Stillwater Springs. "Say hello to your mother?"

Davie shook his head. Wouldn't meet any of the several glances Tyler sent his way. "She's busy," he said. "Let's just go on to Missoula, like we planned, and pick out that redneck castle you promised Miss Lily."

Tyler hurt for the boy, but he had to chuckle at the colorful description of the trailer they were about to lease. Dan Phillips was lining up a crew to bulldoze the cabin and set up some kind of temporary rigging to hold up the trailer, once it arrived. Tyler, Davie and good old Kit would be holing up at the Holiday Inn in the interim.

Both Dylan and Logan had offered them a place to stay between the destruction of the cabin and the delivery and hookup of the trailer, but Tyler hadn't wanted to impose. Logan had a houseful as it was, and there was construction going on at his place, on top of that. Dylan and Kristy had plenty of room in that big Victorian monstrosity in town, but

307

Kristy had already loaned him her Blazer. Asking her to take in two guys and a dog, even briefly, was over the line. Besides, she and Dylan were still newlyweds, like Logan and Briana, and they were building a house, too. They needed what privacy they could scrape together.

In fact, it seemed to him, things were moving pretty fast, all around.

Not fast enough, though, when it came to marrying Lily, he thought ruefully, missing her the way he would have missed an arm or a leg after an amputation. But he'd been at odds with his brothers for a long time, and getting back on solid ground would take a while.

It was doable, anyway. And that was miracle enough.

One thing at a time, cowboy, he told himself. Fishing with Dylan and Logan was one thing, and that trout supper at the main ranch house the night before hadn't been half bad, either. But signing on the dotted line and becoming a partner in the Tri-Star Cattle Company—well, that was something he needed to think about.

They made good time getting to Missoula, stopping for cheeseburgers on the way and cleaning up the mess after Kit Carson hurled his share all over the floorboards.

By noon, they'd looked at every trailer the outfit had to offer—the salesman called them "manufactured homes"—and settled on a four-bedroom triple-wide that was fancier than most of the houses in and around Stillwater Springs. The kitchen even had a special refrigerator for wine, and the cabinets were solid oak.

The living room boasted a TV that came down out of the ceiling at the push of a button—that was a hit with Davie—and the master bedroom wasn't just a bedroom, it was a suite, with a "garden" tub in the bathroom. The whole place was wired for sound, another plus in Davie's opinion, and the "bonus room" was big enough to accommodate a pool table—with no danger of bumping the back end of a cue stick against the wall on a wild shot.

Tyler signed papers and wrote a whopping check, and he and Davie rejoined Kit Carson, who'd barfed in the truck again.

"You're sure you want to build a house?" Davie asked, making faces as he cleaned up the tattered seat with a wad of paper towels. "I wouldn't mind living in *that* place for the rest of my life."

Tyler chuckled. Wondered how much the smell of dog vomit would lower the trade-in value of the rig. "I'm sure," he said.

Davie disposed of the paper towels and sprinted back to the sales office to wash his hands in the john.

Kit gave an apologetic whine, sounding ashamed of himself.

"It's all right, boy," Tyler told him. "But when it

comes to cheeseburgers from now on, it sucks to be you."

Davie returned, turned in the passenger seat before hooking up his belt to ruffle Kit Carson's floppy ears and tell him he wasn't mad at him for throwing up—again—and grinned at Tyler. "Where to now?" he asked.

"I guess we'd better get ourselves a new truck," Tyler said. Lily would be back in two weeks—thirteen days, actually—and he couldn't haul her and her little girl around in a rig that smelled like dog puke.

"We must be rich," Davie said cheerfully. "First you paid off my mom, then you leased that triple-wide and now you're going to buy a brand-new truck—"

"*I'm* rich," Tyler told him. "*You* don't have a dime to your name."

"Speaking of which," Davie replied, without missing a beat. "I need an allowance."

"Mow some lawns," Tyler suggested, thinking of Logan. He'd delivered newspapers, shoveled snow, anything he could do to make a buck, right up until he started rodeoing.

"We live in the *country,*" Davie reminded him, with good-natured indignation, as they pulled back out onto the road, which was lined on both sides with car places advertising *Deals, Deals, Deals!* "As far as I can tell, nobody even *has* a lawn."

Tyler hid a grin. Whipped into a lot when he

310

heard a blue Chevy extended-cab pickup with excess chrome calling his name. "I think there's one under all that grass you promised to cut out at the cabin," he said.

"All you've got is that old push mower," Davie lamented. "And it's rusted out. Anyhow, the grass is waist-high. I need a machete, not a lawn mower."

"Cry me a river," Tyler said.

"You're not very sympathetic, are you?"

Tyler laughed. "Nope," he said, bringing the truck to a stop next to the blue Chevy. "If you want money, kid, you're going to have to get off your backside and earn it."

"How am I supposed to be a normal kid if I don't even get an allowance?" Davie persisted. He was enjoying the banter, that much was obvious— probably because it was a lot like having a father.

"Figure it out," Tyler said.

"Figure it out," Davie mimicked. "There are limited employment opportunities in our area, you know. Especially for thirteen-year-olds."

"Dig down to the lawn, then," Tyler retorted, as an eager salesman approached. He wondered how long the guy's trust-me-I'm-on-your-side smile would last once he got a whiff of the trade-in.

"Buy me a machete," Davie shot back.

"Use the push mower," Tyler told him.

And so it went.

They bought the truck—Tyler took a financial

bath on the old one, since it was clearly a junker and stunk like a roadhouse john—and headed back for Stillwater Springs. Davie bitched the whole time about being forced to live under the poverty line, and Kit Carson, riding in the spacious back-seat, managed not to upchuck all over the leather upholstery.

All in all, Tyler thought, it was a good day.

One down, thirteen to go.

DENISE SUMMERS, Lily's longtime boss, stood in the doorway of Lily's office, looking pained. The company sold upscale clothes, accessories and jewelry by catalog and online, along with a growing number of household decorating items, and they'd done so well over the past few years that there was talk of building a few flagship stores around the country, on the model of Chico's and Coldwater Creek.

"I didn't think you'd really *quit,*" Denise said, watching as Lily tucked the last of her things into a single box. Funny how years of hard work and buying trips could boil down to so little. "Lily, *nobody* has your eye for product. *Please* reconsider. I think we could swing a substantial raise, even profit-sharing—"

Lily smiled. She wasn't angry with Denise; they'd been friends, after a fashion. "I'm sorry," she said pleasantly. "Things change."

Denise's carefully made-up face stiffened

slightly. "Remember, you signed an agreement. You can't go to work for the competition within two years without forfeiting your severance package and compromising your retirement plan."

Two years, Lily reflected happily. Time enough to have at least one baby with Tyler, and a second one if they were lucky.

And the "competition" probably wasn't planning to set up branch offices *or* build stores in Stillwater Springs, Montana.

"I won't break the contract, Denise," she assured the other woman calmly, hoisting the box into both arms and waiting politely for the doorway to clear so she could leave. As for her tentative plans to start an online business of her own, well, she hadn't even discussed those with Tyler or her dad yet; she wasn't about to run the fledgling idea up Denise's flagpole.

It wasn't likely she'd salute, anyhow.

Reluctantly, Denise stepped back out Lily's way. "At least let us throw a going-away party," she pleaded, all but wringing her hands as she followed Lily through the crowded but stone-silent reception area.

Lily juggled the box to push the elevator button with her left elbow. "A going-away party?" she echoed. "Denise, you basically fired me, remember?"

"I was bluffing! Trying to get you to come back to Chicago, where you belong. I know your father's sick, but we *do* have heart specialists here, you know."

The elevator doors opened, and Lily stepped inside.

Denise dropped the act. She'd probably assured the board of directors that Lily would cave when she offered a raise and profit-sharing. Now, she'd have to face them with the news that they needed a new buyer—fast. Red from the neck up, she blurted, "Don't think you can come waltzing back here when you come to your senses!"

"Denise?" Lily countered sweetly, as the doors began to close.

"Yes?" Denise asked, looking pleased.

Lily smiled again, warmly. Winningly. Like the Potato Queen at the state fair, or whatever kind of queen Montana might coronate. She'd already collected her severance check, and arranged for her 401(k) to roll over. "May I offer you a little advice?"

"Okay," Denise said, sounding as lame as she looked. The whole company, it seemed, had collected in the reception area to watch the show.

"Never screw around with a country girl," Lily answered.

Right on cue, like in a movie, the doors closed.

Alone in the elevator, the last ride out of Dodge, she did a little jig.

Reaching the parking garage, she stashed the box in the trunk of her car, got behind the wheel, locked the doors and fished her cell phone out of her purse.

Her dad, still hanging out at the condo with Tess, answered on the second ring.

"I'm so out of there," Lily told Hal, fairly bursting with the exhilaration of it all. She hadn't even realized she was in prison, and now she was *free*. "How are things going on your end?"

Hal laughed. "We're doing okay. We had something reasonably healthy for lunch. There hasn't been a single Eloise sighting, and I've sat through *The Princess Diaries* twice. Tell me you're going to be home soon, because I think we're gearing up for an encore."

Lily beamed. "I'll be there within half an hour, if the traffic isn't too bad," she answered. "Put on your dancing shoes, Daddy-o. You and Tess and I are going out to celebrate!"

CHAPTER SIXTEEN

THE SON OF A BITCH WAS PASSED out drunk, but Doreen McCullough double-checked to make sure. Standing over him, she considered holding a pillow over Roy's butt-ugly face, but it wasn't worth the risk. He was bull-strong, after all; he'd throw her off him for sure, sloshed as he was, and then there'd be hell to pay. Besides, the old lady had only gone next door to feed the neighbors' cats, since the pair of pensioners were away taking care of a sick relative. Granny would make short work of dumping dry food in a bowl for the felines, snooping through the accumulated mail and probably a few drawers and dashing back home to catch her favorite soap opera on the postage-stamp-size TV.

No, she had to get out of there—pronto.

She'd stashed the few things she could pack without making Roy or Granny suspicious in a thrift-store suitcase the night before, stuck the bag in the trunk of her car, under some stuff she'd been trying to get her bastard boyfriend to haul to the dump for a week.

Roy was in the money now, or so he figured it. Taking trash to the landfill outside of town was beneath a man of his means. In his head, he had most of it spent already—a flashy RV so he and his lowlife friends could party on the road, a new hunting rifle or two, a big-screen TV, things like that.

Doreen would have laughed out loud if she'd dared take the chance, and if she hadn't felt so much like crying. How had she gone from teaching a young stud like Tyler how to keep a woman happy, in or out of bed—and a damn fine student he'd been, too—to letting a fat slob like Roy spend her paychecks, drain the gas out of her car and use his fists on her?

Oh, but things were about to change.

Doreen's spirits rose, just to think of the welcome waiting for her when she got where she was going. And good ole Roy was SOL—shit out of luck. She almost wished she'd be around to see the look on his face when he realized he hadn't hit the lottery after all. He'd been shafted, and it couldn't have happened to a more deserving guy.

Slowly, Doreen backed out of the cramped, cluttered little box of a room, jammed in the ass-end of Granny's trailer and always smelling of dirty laundry, stale booze and sweat, no matter how often she sprayed it down.

Everything depended on the getaway; she didn't dare make a sound.

When she came up hard against whoever was standing behind her in the narrow hallway, she about went through the ceiling.

Turned out, it was the old woman she'd collided with.

Doreen put her finger to her lips and made a whispery, "Shh" sound.

"What are you up to?" Granny demanded, ignoring the shushing. Her actual name was Stella, but Doreen always called her Granny, just like Roy did, because it pissed her off. Stella, with her shit-heel trailer and her pitiful Social Security check crawling in every month, thought she was better than Doreen. Better than Davie, too.

Doreen and Roy hadn't told her about the money.

They hadn't told her jack-shit, and that was a good thing—Doreen knew that now. The old biddy was suspicious enough by nature—and right now she was acting as if she'd caught Doreen trying to sneak out with her stupid collection of commemorative plates or something.

Every month, another one of them came in the mail, showcasing somebody famous and dead, like Princess Diana or Frank Sinatra. If Stella had been lucky at bingo, or managed to cadge a few dollars out of Doreen or the Deadbeat before the thirty-day trial was up, she found a space on the trailer wall and hung that new plate up like it was fine art.

How she always found room for another one was beyond Doreen.

"I'm not up to anything," Doreen breathed, not even daring to whisper, taking Stella by the elbow and hustling her back down the hall, away from Roy, who would screw everything up royal—and put her in the hospital—if he came out of his boozy stupor too soon. "And be quiet, will you? Roy's got himself a job at the lumber mill as of today, working swing shift. He needs to sleep all day if he can."

Stella looked so pleased at the prospect of a paycheck coming in, even it wasn't hers, that Doreen almost felt sorry for telling the first whopper that came to mind. Hallelujah, Stella must be thinking, now she could keep every plate, every month, whether the bingo gods had been good to her or not.

"Really?" she asked, sounding almost girlish. "I

told Roy he ought to apply at the mill—his daddy *and* his granddaddy both worked there until they dropped in their tracks. Sure, we lived away for a while, Roy and me, but the name Fifer still *means* something around there." By then, she was nearly clapping her hands. "I just never thought he'd want to lower himself to pulling lumber off the green chain, since he went through trucking school and everything—"

Lower himself? Doreen thought, grabbing up her keys and purse, easing toward the front door, the only way out, as fast as she could. *How was it possible for Roy Fifer III to get any lower than he already was? Numerals after his name, too, like the Fifers were blue bloods instead of trailer trash.*

"You're going somewhere?" Stella asked, as if they'd been friends all along, as if she hadn't treated Doreen like a slut trying to sneak into a palace every time she set foot in the Hall of Stupid Plates.

Like she hadn't called Davie a freak a million times, because of his tattoo and his piercings and those weird clothes he wore.

But Davie would be okay now; she didn't have to worry about him anymore.

The Creeds, at least this new generation, anyway, did right by their own.

"I've got a chance to put in some overtime at the casino," Doreen explained, making herself sound eager. "They're shorthanded today, and there's a tour bus coming in for a slot tournament."

Doreen put her hand on the screen-door handle.

Down the hall, in the room she'd never set foot in again if there was a God in heaven, Roy let out a bellow and then yelled that he had a belly ache.

Stella's papery face went pale.

"He's just having a bad dream," Doreen assured her, pushing open the screen door and bolting.

"But what if he's sick?" Stella called after her, from the little porch in front of the door. "Shouldn't we call a doctor or—"

Doreen didn't even wait for her to finish the sentence.

She just beat it—ran across the lawn to the curb, her keys slippery in the palm of her hand. She hadn't been able to resist a few moments of gloating, and now she was out of time.

She'd been so sure Roy was down for the count, after all he'd drunk during the night and then the little bonus she'd put in his Bloody Mary when he got home, saying he needed some "hair of the dog." Even from the yard, though, she could hear him raging and wailing and carrying on.

As soon as she was inside the Buick, with the engine running and the doors locked, though, she knew she was safe.

Roy Fifer's old beater of a car had been junked months ago; he'd driven Doreen's when he couldn't borrow a rig from one of his drinking buddies, and left her stranded at work more than once, too, so she'd had to bum a ride home from one of the other waitresses.

Anxious, but still needing one more look, Doreen glanced toward the door of the trailer, saw Roy standing on the threshold, whale-big and sick as he deserved to be.

Don't you worry, she told him silently, as she sped away. *Soon as they pump your stomach, you'll be right as rain.*

DAVIE FROWNED, laid the phone at the cabin back in its cradle.

Tyler was at the table, prying open one of the two buckets of take-out chicken they'd picked up for supper coming back from Missoula. "Problem?" he asked mildly.

Kit Carson, knowing he wasn't going to get any of the extra-spicy—with his delicate stomach, Tyler had decided, the dog would have to stick with kibble for the duration—had slunk away to lie, woebegone, on his bed in the corner.

"Mom told me to call her at six, straight up, no matter what," Davie said. "But there's no answer at the trailer."

"Did you try her cell phone?"

"She doesn't have one," Davie answered, with a shake of his head. "She made such a big deal about how I had to remember to call her just when she said—"

Tyler didn't offer a reply. Davie was probably thinking the same thing he was: that Doreen hadn't been able to last out her final two weeks at the casino after all, with that money burning a hole in her pocket. She and Roy had boogied for the Bright Lights, most likely, and saying goodbye to Davie evidently hadn't been a priority.

"What if Roy did something to her?" Davie fretted, after a long time. "You know, so he wouldn't have to share the money?"

The chances of Roy harming Doreen in some way were all too good, especially if he'd talked her into putting his name on the bank account, but Tyler didn't see any point in saying so. "Why don't you wait a little while, until after supper, anyhow, and try calling her again. She's probably just gone to the store or something." Tyler paused. "If you still can't reach her, we'll head into town and look her up, make sure everything's okay. Fair enough?"

Davie looked somewhat mollified, but he didn't go the whole way with it, or he'd have put away more of the chicken than he did. That whole second bucket, extra-crispy, was his.

"I wanted to tell her about the triple-wide," Davie confided, pacing, shoving his hand through his hair every once in a while, a habit he'd probably picked up from Tyler. "And the new truck."

"You can do that later," Tyler said, wondering if he shouldn't give Jim Huntinghorse a call, have the sheriff send a deputy by old Stella Fifer's trailer to make sure Doreen was all right. At least, as all right as anybody could be, living in that kind of setup.

In that strange way things sometimes happen, the phone rang right then, and Davie scrambled for it, practically yelled his hello.

Tyler watched as the color drained out of the kid's face. "It's for you," he said, after listening for a few seconds and gulping hard. "Sheriff Huntinghorse."

Tyler took the receiver. What if something had happened to Lily and her little girl? Or to Dylan or Logan or—

"Jim?" He practically barked the name.

The lawman had barely been in office a week, if that long, and he already sounded as though he was looking forward to a quiet retirement. "Ty, have you seen Doreen McCullough today, by any chance?"

The first thing Tyler felt was relief. It wasn't a sorry-to-inform-you call.

Sighing once, Tyler put a hand on Davie's shoulder and pressed him back into his chair at the table, afraid the kid's knees would buckle if he didn't sit down. Obviously, even if Doreen was just fine, this whole parental changing of the guard thing was harder on Davie than he'd been letting on.

"No," Tyler said, shifting his attention back to Jim. "Is anything wrong?"

"Plenty," Jim answered. "Roy Fifer's down at the clinic, in the emergency room. They pumped his stomach a little while ago, and he swears up and down Doreen tried to kill him with some kind of poison and lit out with a whole lot of money that belonged to both of them."

Tyler frowned.

Something Davie had said recently snagged in his mind—the boy had been telling him about past stepfathers and boyfriends, and he'd said one of them had some kind of fit at supper one night and died right there at the table.

Boo-hoo. That had been the extent of Davie's sympathy.

"Ty?" Jim prompted, when the silence stretched on too long. "You still there?"

Davie's eyes were the size of the lids on the chicken buckets.

"I'm here," Tyler confirmed. Then, for Davie's benefit, he added, "Doreen's all right."

"Is that a personal endorsement," Jim asked, conveying a little amusement and a lot of controlled frustration, "or are you telling me you've seen her after all?"

"I haven't seen her," Tyler reiterated, with an edge in his voice now. "I presume you tried the casino already?"

"Gee," Jim retorted, "why didn't *I* think of that, since I used to manage the place and hired her myself, so I know that's where she works?"

"Maybe she lit out early," Tyler said, tired of the bickering, good-natured or otherwise. "She was planning to start over someplace else, that's all I know."

"And the boy is staying with you, according to Roy."

"Yeah," Tyler answered, bristling a little and spacing his words out wide. "The boy is staying with me."

"I'll need to have a word with him," Jim said wearily. "He might know where she's gone."

"And he might or might not tell you," Tyler pointed out, watching Davie closely. The kid had gotten the gist by now, knew Jim hadn't called to say Doreen had been hurt, or worse. "Shall I bring him to town, or are you coming out here?"

Davie had been busy looking disinterested until then; now, he was gaping at Tyler and pale again.

"I'll come out there," Jim decided, after a moment's thought. "I could use a little of that fresh country air."

"We'll be here," Tyler said.

Jim gave his ETA as fifteen minutes and hung up.

"Why does the sheriff want to talk to me?" Davie immediately demanded.

Tyler drew back his chair, sat down at the table again. Pushed his plate away. "Roy's at the clinic, Davie. They pumped his stomach a little while ago. He claims your mother poisoned him, and evidently, she's nowhere to be found. Jim figures you might know where she went."

"Why can't they just let her go?"

There was no way to sugarcoat the situation. "Worst-case scenario? Because if she *did* poison Roy, she could be charged with attempted murder."

"And that jerk sheriff thinks I'd tell him where to find her—*if* I knew—so he could throw her in jail for the rest of her life?"

"That 'jerk sheriff' is one of my best friends," Tyler said quietly. "When you refer to him around me, I'll thank you to remember that."

Davie drew in his horns a little. "I don't *know* where she is," he said, almost in a whisper.

"Any wild guesses?"

Davie flushed, and the ghost of the spider on his neck glowed pink. *"No,"* he said, a little too quickly. His eyes blazed. "Next thing, you'll be saying this whole thing was a scam, that Mom and I planned it this way from the first—"

"Was it a scam, Davie? Were you supposed to call your mother at six so the two of you could meet up somewhere later and take off, say at the end of that road right out there?" He cocked his thumb toward the long, winding driveway. "After I was asleep, maybe?"

"No!" Davie yelled. He seemed about to surge up out of his chair in a fit of rage, but in the end, he either didn't have the energy or the courage.

"Tell me more about that poor bastard who

croaked at the supper table," Tyler pressed quietly. "I think you called him Marty. What was his last name, Davie?"

Tears welled in Davie's eyes. "You think Mom killed him? Maybe that we *both* did?"

"I didn't say that. I just want his name."

To Tyler's surprise, and considerable relief, Davie reeled it off, along with a rural address outside of San Antonio. Then he got to his feet, started gathering up his few belongings, like he was planning on hitting the road.

Tyler didn't move from his chair, didn't speak.

"Aren't you going to ask me where the hell I think I'm going?" Davie finally demanded, running an angry arm across his face.

"Okay," Tyler said easily. "Where the hell do you think you're going?"

"Well, I'm going *someplace!*"

Tyler suppressed a humorless chuckle. He'd never seen a kid in so much pain, and with his background, that was a wonder. "Like where?"

Apparently stumped, Davie sagged onto the edge of his cot, sat there with his head hanging. Kit Carson got up off his blanket-pile and ambled over to lick the kid's face.

"I'm probably not your kid anyway," Davie sniffled, after a long time.

Tyler gave a sigh. "You've got all the signs," he said.

Davie looked up. "Of what?"

"Of being a Creed. You've got a temper like a woodstove burning nuclear waste, and you're ready to rush off half-cocked to no place in particular." Tyler sighed again. "I'm not accusing you of anything, Davie. But if you know where your mother is, you need to tell Jim when he gets here."

"It's not like she has anyplace to go," Davie said, and the words stuck in Tyler's heart like a barrage of tiny needles, hitting all the bruised places and quivering there. "You think we'd have stayed with Roy Fifer, or any of the others, if we'd had a *choice?*"

"Your mother's always had a choice," Tyler answered. "You didn't."

Davie ducked his head again, and his shoulders stooped. "She always said if she could live anywhere she wanted, she'd pick Vegas," he said, his voice so small Tyler could barely hear it. "We tried to make it there once, but things were too expensive. Mom said a person had to have a lot of money to live in Vegas. It was too depressing if you were broke, like us."

Tyler heard a car pull up outside, knew it was Jim. Left his friend to let himself in, since he knew the way. "Did you have friends there?" he asked. "Family, maybe?"

Davie shook his head. "Just another of her crap boyfriends," he said. Then, with a bitter laugh, he met Tyler's gaze again. "*That* lasted about five minutes. Mom was crazy about him, but he didn't want to get involved with a woman who had kids. As in, *me*."

Las Vegas, Tyler thought, hearing Jim step up onto the porch, tap at the door frame before entering. It would be a depressing place for a single mother running her feet off for a paycheck. But Doreen wasn't broke anymore, was she? And she didn't have to worry about Davie now, either.

Which probably meant she'd be looking up the kid-free boyfriend.

Jim walked in, drew back a chair at the table and sat himself down. After a nod to Tyler, he turned to Davie.

"Hey," he said.

"Hey," Davie said, albeit reluctantly.

Jim was tall and lean, a good man in a fight, as Tyler had ample cause to know, having grown up with him. Jim Huntinghorse had been as wild as all three of the Creed brothers put together once upon a time, but now he was the pride of the tribal council.

"How are Sam and Caroline?" Tyler asked.

Sam was Jim's son, four or five years old, and the light of the man's life. "Sam's growing up fast," Jim answered. "And Caroline—well, she's still Caroline."

Tyler gave a partial grin at that. Jim and Caroline Huntinghorse went all the way back to elementary school, and it had been a tempestuous relationship from day one. They'd divorced but reconciled later on. Tyler would have bet his brand-new-and-shiny-blue pickup that when they weren't fighting, Jim and Caroline, they were tearing each other's clothes off.

"Things have a way of working out," Tyler said easily, for Davie's benefit as much as Jim's.

"If you say so." Jim sighed. "I hear you and Lily are back together."

"Word does get around," Tyler confirmed. "She's in Chicago and I'm here, so 'together' isn't the operative word."

Jim threw his own words back at him. "Things have a way of working out," he said, watching Davie. Sizing him up. After years of managing a casino, Jim was real good at reading people. Now, his face softened a little. "Where's your mother, Davie?" he asked.

"Probably on her way to Las Vegas," Davie said.

Tyler felt a surge of hope.

Jim gave a slight nod, doing his inscrutable routine. He'd played the noble savage to the hilt, all his life. "You planning on meeting up with her later?"

Davie flushed, flung a rebellious glance at Tyler. "I'd rather go to a foster home," he snapped.

Jim raised his eyebrows. "I see," he said.

"You're not going anywhere," Tyler told Davie.

Jim took a little memo book, the kind that comes with its own pencil, from the pocket of his spiffy uniform shirt. "If I were your mother, and I was on my way to Vegas," he mused thoughtfully, "where would I light when I got there?"

"The guy might have moved by now," Davie said, looking at Tyler again, but without so much defiance this time.

"Or not," Jim said mildly.

Davie, it turned out, had a remarkable memory for names and addresses.

Jim wrote down the lead the kid gave up.

"Marty," Tyler prompted, when Davie didn't volunteer the story about the boo-hoo guy.

Davie looked furious again, but he spilled that, too.

"Is Roy gonna die?" he asked Jim, looking as though he expected to be slapped into a pair of handcuffs when the sheriff closed the notebook and stood to go.

"No," Jim answered.

"Too bad," Davie said.

Jim and Tyler exchanged weary glances.

"I was young once," Jim said, with a philosophical sigh.

"Me, too," Tyler answered.

"What was that supposed to mean?" Davie asked carefully, the minute Jim had gotten into his squad car and started backing down the dirt driveway. Until then, he'd stayed stubbornly silent. "All that stuff about being young once, I mean?"

"It meant," Tyler said, rising from his chair to gather up the remains of the chicken dinner, shaking his head once when Kit Carson gave him a hopeful muzzle-nudge to the knee, "that we both understand what it means to be a thirteen-year-old smart-ass and are therefore willing to cut you a little slack by not assuming you think watching a man die at the supper table is funny."

"It wasn't funny," Davie said. "It was awful." After a few beats, though, a grin quirked up a corner of the kid's mouth, so familiar that it gave Tyler a pang. He grinned like that, and so did his brothers. "Can we talk about an allowance now?" he asked.

"Sure," Tyler replied. "I'll even write the script for you. You say, 'Can I have one?' and *I* say, 'Hell, no, not until you find the lawn.' There. Conversation over. Wasn't that easy?"

"Are you always such a hard-ass?"

"Pretty much. Today, I happen to be having one of my *cordial* days."

Davie didn't grin this time. "Did you mean it when you said I'm not going anywhere?"

"I meant it," Tyler confirmed.

Davie was almost giddy with relief, but some of the glow faded as he watched Tyler wedge the pair of chicken buckets into a fridge meant to hold bait and a six-pack and not much else. "What's going to happen to my mom?" he asked. There was no bravado now, no tough guy with piercings and a major attitude.

Tyler knew Davie was asking if Doreen would

be going to jail and, upon further reflection, that seemed unlikely, especially if Roy made a full recovery and became his normal whiskey-drinking, woman-beating self again. On the other hand, if rat poison, for example, turned up in the lab results after the tests the folks down at the clinic would inevitably run, the attempted-murder rap might stick.

Tyler shoved a hand through his hair. "The truth is, Davie, I don't know."

As far as it went, that *was* the truth, but Davie had asked what was going to happen to his mother, and the answer to that was a whole lot more complicated and a whole lot *less* encouraging.

Given her history, Doreen would probably run through all the money Tyler had given her, with the help of a bad boyfriend or two, and end up either dead or shacked up with some new version of Roy Fifer.

"I don't want to be like her," Davie murmured, and then looked startled, as though he hadn't meant to voice the thought at all.

Tyler's mind shifted to Jake. He remembered one of the many occasions when the old man had come home stinking drunk, long after supper was over and the dishes were washed, and demanded a meal. Tyler's mother had filled a plate for him earlier, kept it warm in the oven, carefully covered with foil, even brought it to him at the table. Anxious to avoid a fight that Tyler and Dylan and Logan had all known couldn't *be* avoided, she'd said something like, "It's your favorite, Jake. Pork chops."

Jake had lifted the foil off the plate, gingerly, like he expected something to jump out at him, then bellowed that a man shouldn't be expected to eat shriveled-up food after a hard day felling trees in the woods to support his family, and flung the whole works, plate, food and silverware, all over the kitchen.

Then he'd scraped his chair back so hard it tipped over, Jake had, and stood. He'd started toward Angela, now cowering against a counter, but Logan, barely older than Davie was now—had stepped square in front of him, fists clenched at his sides.

"No," he'd said, and his voice had been the voice of a man, not a boy. He'd looked straight into Jake's eyes, like he'd have a prayer against him in a fight, and repeated, *"No."*

Dylan and Tyler, huddled in the doorway, had been terrified.

Miraculously, after a long interval of heart-stopping suspense, Jake had suddenly laughed, turned on one heel and said he was going somewhere where people appreciated him.

Where was that, old man? Tyler asked silently, back in the present again. *Skivvie's, maybe? Some whore's bed? Was that where people "appreciated" you, you evil old son of a bitch?*

His throat shut tight against the recollection of

that night and so many others, so tight it hurt. He closed his eyes, dealing with it, opened them again.

I don't want to be like her, Davie had said.

Now, belatedly, Tyler answered him. Answered himself. "You don't have to be like your mother," he said. And *he* didn't have to be like Jake. "All you have to do is make the best choices you can, and your life can be anything you want it to."

Davie looked so hopeful that Tyler wanted to go out and clear a path through the world for the kid. He supposed that made him a father, and DNA be damned.

He waited until Davie had gone outside with Kit Carson to sit at the end of the dock with a fishing pole, gathered his composure a little and got out his cell phone.

Lily answered on the first ring. "Tyler?" she said, instead of hello.

It was one word, but it poured over his spirit like a warm, soothing balm. "Yeah," he said, wishing he could bounce up to the satellite, along with the signal from his phone, and bounce down again in Chicago, stand face-to-face with her. "It's me."

"I miss you," she said softly.

Tyler closed his eyes, let the tenderness of that statement penetrate every part of him. It felt like healing light, slipping through some crack between heaven and earth. "Two weeks is too long," he told her.

"Don't I know it," she replied. "I'll start packing

things up tomorrow, and the real estate agent will be by in the afternoon—probably armed with a list of things I'll have to do to the place." She paused. "Did you choose a trailer?"

He smiled at the word *trailer*—it didn't accurately describe the structure, but it was the easiest word, the one country folks used most readily. "Sure did," he said. "Dan's going to bulldoze the cabin day after tomorrow, and set up some kind of temporary foundation, so Davie and I will be moving into the Holiday Inn for a couple of days."

When Lily didn't ask if he'd had the bedroom soundproofed, he knew for sure she was with her dad and Tess.

Sure enough, she said, "Wait a second," and Tyler listened as she asked Doc some question, her voice just hushed enough that he couldn't catch the words.

"Dad says to stay at his place. The key's under the pot with the dead flowers in it, on the back porch."

Tyler knew he couldn't accept, any more than he could move in with Dylan and Kristy, or Logan and Briana, but the offer meant a lot. He and Doc hadn't always been on the best terms. "Thanks," he said, "but we'll be okay at the hotel."

"I want you to be more than just okay, Tyler."

"Not possible, with you in another state," he said. Then he smiled to himself. Another state? Hell, another *room* would have been too far away.

"Is Davie all right?" Lily asked. "And Kit Carson?"

"They're okay, too." There was no point in telling her about Doreen's shenanigan—she'd only worry that they were all going to wind up on an episode of *Forensic Files*. "Right now, they're down on the dock, fishing."

That sounded normal, didn't it? A dog and a boy with a fishing pole, braving the mosquitoes to sit out under a blanket of stars splashed across a navy sky?

"Just okay," Lily repeated fretfully.

Tyler chuckled. "Lily?"

"What?"

"We're fabulous. We're so happy, Davie and Kit Carson and me, we can't contain ourselves. Is that better?"

She laughed. "No," she said. "I want you to miss me a *little*."

"No problem there," Tyler answered, and his voice sounded gruff again. "Come home soon, okay?"

"It can't be soon enough to suit me," she answered.

"Of course I'm going to take you down, or bend you over something and screw your socks off, the minute we're alone."

"No fair," she said sunnily.

He could just see her squirming, maybe blushing a little.

The image did a lot to cheer him up.

337

It also gave him an instant hard-on, which meant a cold shower or a header into the lake, if he didn't want to suffer the whole night.

"Oh, trust me," he said, "I'm paying the price."

"Good," she replied brightly, as though they'd been discussing carpet colors for the triple-wide or something. "That's *wonderful,* Tyler."

He laughed. "You'll pay," he promised.

"So will *you,*" she chimed in response.

He didn't want to let her go, but the conversation had about run its course, unless he went on to tell her that Kit Carson had barfed in the truck twice that day and Sheriff Jim had stopped by to question Davie about what might turn out to be an attempted murder. And he wasn't about to do that.

There *was* one thing he wanted to say, but you didn't tell somebody you were ninety-nine percent certain you were in love with them over the phone. Best wait until she was home again, and he had her alone and could peel off her clothes and lick everything he uncovered.

The hard-on progressed from uncomfortable to downright painful. Tyler bit back a groan and asked, "Can I call you tomorrow?"

"Sure," Lily answered. "If you think you can behave yourself."

"No phone sex? You don't want me to tell you everything I'm going to do to you, and then do again until you lose your mind and come like you've never come before?"

Her answer made him laugh.

"I didn't say that, now, did I?"

"What time, Lily?"

"What time?" She *was* flustered, then.

Good.

"What time shall I call you and make love to you with my voice," he clarified. "Remember that day in Wal-Mart? It's going to happen again, Lily, only long-distance this time."

There was just the slightest tremor in her voice when she answered. "Dad and Tess are going to the Museum of Natural History tomorrow morning," she said. "Suppose *I* call *you?*"

CHAPTER SEVENTEEN

AFTER A PLUNGE INTO THE LAKE, long after Davie had fallen asleep on his cot downstairs, Kit Carson balanced on the teetery rigging right along with him, Tyler's raging body calmed down.

Mostly.

But his mind just wouldn't stop; it was like a bronc at the rodeo, evading the pick-up men the way broncs-on-adrenaline sometimes did, still bucking, reins dangling, long after the buzzer sounded and the cowboy had scrambled over the fence to safety.

Davie had said he and Doreen hadn't set him up for a scam and the story had some credibility with Tyler; after all, *he'd* been the one to do the paternal math and then hogtie the obvious conclusion and run with it. Doreen had denied that Davie was his, that night at the casino, when they discussed the situation, and with considerable regret. She'd said she wished it was true, but Davie's biological father was some truck driver, long out of the picture.

It had sounded reasonable at the time, even a little noble, given that Doreen could have been collecting child support for the past thirteen years—money she'd obviously needed. But con artists made a specialty of seeming reasonable, didn't they?

Of *course* they were convincing. They were masters of the art of bullshit—they had to be.

Tyler couldn't overlook that possibility. It was all too easy to imagine Doreen following his career on ESPN, in the tabloids, where he'd kicked up a deliberate fuss more than once, and in the movies. At some point, she might have decided to bide her time and go for lump sum when the opportunity was at its prime.

It seemed likely now that he'd been carefully led, managed, from the time he came back to Stillwater Springs. And it wasn't inconceivable—it wasn't even all that big a stretch—to think Roy might have been in on the whole thing, too.

He could just hear the planning they must have done—Doreen and Roy and possibly Davie, gathered around some scratched-up table, somewhere in the wonderful world of low-income housing.

340

You act scared, Doreen might have told Davie. *Tell Tyler Roy beats you up, regular. Roy, I'll call you when the right moment comes. You put on a show for the pigeon. Act real mean. Tyler will buy that, it's a hot button with him, after all he went through with* his *old man—*

Lying there in his loft bed, with Lily conspicuously absent, sleepless and feeling like a rube, it was no trick at all to believe he'd been suckered, taken in.

And yet whenever Tyler was around Davie, he definitely picked up Creed vibes. He'd learned to trust his instincts over the years, rarely had a hunch that didn't prove right—and several of them had saved his life. Deep down, he'd still have bet his share of the ranch that Davie *was* his son.

Or was that just wishful thinking, plain and simple? His childhood had been hell, and after the old man died, he'd been estranged from Dylan and Logan for five long years. And he'd lost Shawna— his best friend if not the love of his life, like she should have been.

Back then, still broken, Tyler hadn't been *able* to love a woman full-out, no holds barred, the way he was starting to love Lily. He hadn't had a clue what was going on in the dark recesses of his psyche, when it would have counted, when he might have given Shawna a fighting chance to get past all the walls he'd put up.

Tyler rolled onto his side, slammed a fist into his

pillow, as if pounding it to fit his thick-skulled Creed head would make a difference.

Nothing was going to make a difference now—not to Shawna. She'd been anything but stupid, so she must have known the score from day one, but she'd carried on anyhow, cowgirl-style. Put a brave face on things, done everything she could to make him happy, and to be happy herself.

I'm sorry, Shawna. God, I'm so sorry.

The best—and worst—part was knowing Shawna would have forgiven him if he'd 'fessed up, said she knew he'd been doing the best he could. Shawna's family, hardscrabble ranchers, had been so much healthier than his, and she'd grown up whole. In a better world, *he* would have been the one to slide off the side of a slick Nevada mountain, not her.

Shawna would have mourned, but those folks of hers, parents and brothers and sisters and aunts and uncles and cousins, would have gathered her in, too. Kept her safe in the center of a warm circle, seen her through the worst of it, encouraged her to go on with her life when she'd had time enough to grieve.

By now, she'd be remarried, with a couple of kids, and he'd only be a memory that gave her a pang to the heart sometimes when it snowed in the night and she woke up to a pristine landscape outside her window, or when she heard their song on the radio. . . .

"Stop," Tyler growled, thrusting himself onto his elbows.

He'd done everything but cry at his own funeral, imagining the parallel-universe scenario, and that made him feel like the damn fool he was. There was no changing the past, and he had to stop trying.

He'd had his chance with Shawna, and he'd blown it.

Now, he had a chance with Lily.

Twice in a lifetime, cowboy, he thought. *That's two more chances than a lot of people get, so don't screw this up.*

He sat upright, thrust the splayed fingers of one hand through his hair. *Don't screw this up?* Hadn't he *already* screwed it up, by getting involved with Doreen and Davie the way he had?

What if he was plain-old, flat-out wrong about Davie?

A man had *died* in the kid's presence, and telling about it later, he'd finished with *boo-hoo?* The kid could be a sociopath, if not worse.

Or simply a thirteen-year-old boy, used to making the best of situations most *adults* never had to deal with.

On the plus side, Davie was good to the dog—he seemed to love Kit Carson as much as Kit loved him. Not typical sociopathic, or *psycho*pathic, behavior. But did it preclude the possibility that Doreen might have purposely offed poor old

Marty, and that Davie might have helped her cover it up? Even helped her do it?

Jesus.

What in hell might he be letting Lily and Tess in for, bringing them to live under the same roof with Davie? The little girl would be vulnerable to Davie in ways Tyler couldn't stand to think about, and couldn't ignore, either.

On the other hand, all he really had to go on was his imagination, which happened to be running wild at the moment. It wouldn't be right to turn his back on Davie on the strength of midnight suppositions.

And it had to be after midnight.

He groped for his watch on the upended fruit crate that served as a bedside table, held it in the shaft of moonlight beaming in through the window. Seeing the golden cowboy on the face of that watch, riding a bronc and holding one arm high, certain to make the critical eight seconds, Tyler's eyes burned. *Shawna.* She'd been so proud when she gave him that watch to celebrate his first championship, probably never even regretted selling her horse trailer and prize saddle to raise the money.

He'd planned on buying her a bigger, better trailer and another fancy saddle, too, but like so many good intentions, that one had been a paved road to hell.

Tyler blinked a couple of times. Squinted to read the dial.

Quarter after eleven? That was *all?* Hell, it felt as though he'd been tossing and turning on that painfully empty bed for a whole night, and he hadn't even turned in until ten.

Frick, he was getting old.

He got up, pulled on some jeans, tugged a T-shirt over his head, threw a flannel work shirt on over that. Pulled on socks and boots and descended the stairs as quietly as he could, in case Davie was having better luck in the sleep department. Grabbing up his laptop, along with his cell phone, he hushed Kit Carson, who stirred on the cot, and went outside.

Closing the door behind him, he sat down on the porch steps and looked up at the bright Montana stars. Millions of them, close enough to touch.

They roused a sweet loneliness in Tyler, those stars.

It would have been his salvation to call Lily—it was two hours later in Chicago, so he'd wake her up—and her voice would be all sleepy and warm. She'd be ripe for a little phone sex. . . .

He shook off the fantasy. Lily was wrapping things up back there; she had a lot to do. She had a child and an ailing father to look after, a condo to clean, things to pack up.

She needed her rest.

So he'd wait, as agreed, until she called him.

If it killed him.

He would have liked to talk to Logan about all

this, or Dylan, or both of them. But they had wives, kids—*lives*. He could have put aside his pride and leveled with either one of his brothers—and that was undeniably progress—but he wasn't about to wake them up, or interrupt something more intimate than sleep. Most likely, they were doing some headboard-slamming with their beautiful ladies.

That made him smile.

Cassie? She'd listen, if he let her know he needed to talk. She'd always been a rock, a refuge. She'd steered him through a lot of things, including some dark days after Shawna's accident. But Cassie's magic only worked in person, not over the phone, and he couldn't drive over to her place and knock on the door at that hour. For one thing, he'd probably get her out of bed, and for another, leaving Davie home alone, at least at night, wasn't an option.

The kid might be thirteen, and street-wise—he might even be a psychopath—but it was a sure bet he'd spent more than his share of nights in an empty house or apartment as it was.

And too many things could happen. What if there was a fire? What if his appendix ruptured?

Tyler shook his head, flipped open the lightweight, superpowered laptop, logged on.

If he couldn't sleep, he'd do a little detective work instead.

First stop, his favorite search engine. His mailbox was jammed, but that could wait.

He typed in "Doreen McCullough," expecting to wade through a hundred different Doreen McCulloughs, if not a thousand, before he found Davie's mom and his first lover.

The first few were strangers, as expected, but then he hit pay dirt—if a mug shot could be called pay dirt.

There was Doreen, face bare of makeup, wearing an orange jail outfit and holding up a sign with numbers on it.

Feeling sick, Tyler scanned page after page of a whole *other* kind of dirt. Doreen hadn't hit bottom with Roy Fifer—she'd come *up* in the world.

She'd been busted for soliciting in Vegas, not once but three times. She'd tried her hand at shoplifting, and done a year for credit-card fraud.

Where had Davie been, when she was sent up?

In a foster home? With the truck driver Doreen had originally named as Davie's father?

"Okay, so she has a rap sheet," Davie said, from just behind him.

Tyler hadn't heard the kid get out of bed, let alone approach, but he wasn't really surprised. Davie probably hadn't been able to sleep any more than he had. He'd been playing possum when Tyler passed through the kitchen a little while before.

"Want to tell me about it?" Tyler asked quietly. Evenly.

Davie stepped around him, wearing the ratty pair

of sweatpants he slept in. Sat down on the step next to Tyler.

"What's to tell?" he finally said. "It's all right there, on the Internet. Most of it, anyway."

Tyler wondered if Jim Huntinghorse had already reviewed all this stuff and, if so, why he hadn't mentioned it during his visit earlier in the evening. "Where did you stay, Davie, when Doreen was doing her time for credit-card theft?"

Davie was a long time answering. He didn't look at Tyler or at the computer screen, but straight out into a darkness that must have seemed dense enough to swallow him whole and then digest him right into oblivion.

"With my grandmother," he finally admitted. "Scroll a little farther—she's on there."

Instead, Tyler closed the laptop, set it aside on the newly repaired porch. Kit Carson squeezed between him and Davie and trotted out into the high grass to lift a leg against the right rear tire of the new Chevy. It gleamed in the thin light of a waning moon, that pickup, a thing of beauty. The kind of rig he should have bought in the first place. "I'd rather hear it from you," he said.

Davie sighed. "Gramma plays bingo all the time, so she wasn't much interested in me—I just got in her way, mostly." The boy gave Tyler a sidelong look and did the Creed grin again, flawlessly. "Not what you were expecting, huh? You thought I was going to say I was taken in by wolves while Mom was in the slammer, or maybe a band of outlaw bikers—"

While Mom was in the slammer.

How many kids had to cope with something like that?

"I thought you were probably in a foster home," Tyler said.

"That would have been better. Mom is the greatest disappointment of my Gramma's life—not counting me, of course. She had two other kids before I came along and, not being married at the time, or particularly flush, gave them both up for adoption." Davie paused, shrugged in a way that made Tyler's heart crawl right up into the back of his throat and pound there. "For whatever reason—my best guess would be that I was a financial ace in the hole, if there was any chance I was yours—she kept me. Came and picked me up as soon as she got out of jail—and was I ever glad to see her."

"I'm going to have to call her, Davie. Your grandmother, I mean."

"Good luck dumping me on *her,*" Davie said, with heartbreaking bravado. "Like I said, I'm not Gramma's favorite person."

Somewhere out in the gloom, Kit Carson began to bark.

Thinking of coyotes, or the bears that sometimes roamed the ranch in search of a meal, Tyler gave a shrill whistle to call the dog back.

After that, things happened so fast that he never got a chance to tell Davie he hadn't intended to foist him off on anybody.

Lights swung through the trees, coming up the driveway, and the roar of a big engine driven too fast in too low a gear made the air vibrate.

Tyler got to his feet. "What the hell?"

"Kit!" Davie yelled, in an instant panic. "Kit!"

Kit was only a shadow, darting along the edge of the tree line between the cabin and the lake, and he'd evidently dropped out of obedience school, because he stayed clear.

The roar got louder, and the ground began to shake.

"Get out of here!" Tyler yelled, fairly pushing Davie off the porch. "Run!"

"Run where?" Davie shouted back.

The headlights were high off the ground, and coming straight at them now, jostling and jumping like the eyeballs of some gigantic monster sprung up out of the earth and bent on destruction.

Tyler grabbed Davie by the back of the neck and flung him to one side, dived after him. They both hit the ground face-first, scrambled back to their feet.

There was a crash, loud enough to rattle the stars overhead, and Tyler looked back to see the big rig pushing his new truck in front of it like a cow-catcher on a freight train. The semi's engine was screaming now, rising toward a shrill crescendo.

"Shit!" Tyler hollered furiously. *"I just bought that truck!"*

Now Davie was the one taking the lead. He had Tyler by the arm and was trying to drag him out of the crazy, swaying beams of those headlights.

"If he sees us," Davie shouted, pulling for all he was worth, "we're dead meat!"

They'd only covered about a dozen yards when the demon semi from hell rammed Tyler's truck into the side of the cabin, and then straight through the wall.

And not just the front wall, but the back one, too.

Dust billowed, fit to choke everything that breathed.

The semi motor gave one last excruciating whine of agonized protest and then died, with a series of metallic clunks. The hand-hewn timbers of the cabin roof groaned and finally gave way with an uncanny grace, smashing down on top of the big truck. On top of Tyler's pickup.

"Christ," he murmured, not sure if he was praying or cursing.

"It was just like in that Stephen King movie," Davie piped up. "The one with the crazy car that went around crushing people against walls—"

"Davie," Tyler said quietly, plucking his cell phone from his pocket. *"Shut up."*

Logan got there first, tearing up the driveway in his truck. He'd heard the crash all the way over at his place, he yelled up to Tyler, who was already on the roof, tossing down boards.

Big brother had hit the ground running—hadn't even shut off his pickup or closed the door behind him. But the scene brought him to a standstill. He shook it off, climbed up to join Tyler. "Holy *shit*," he said, looking around.

It said something about Logan, and the kind of brother he was, Tyler figured, that he got right in and started flinging away shingles, without even asking what they were digging for.

Davie, meanwhile, was trying to round up a very freaked-out Kit Carson, shouting his name, whistling.

Finally, the boy called out exuberantly, "Kit's all right! I caught him!"

Tyler kept pawing at the debris of the cabin roof, hurling chunks of wood aside. He was pretty sure who he'd find behind the wheel of that buried semi, once he and Logan finally got down to it, but not so sure what condition Roy Fifer would be in by then.

In the distance, sirens tore slashes in the otherwise silent country night.

Jim and his crew were on their way, in response to Tyler's 911 call, and since Logan had called Dylan soon before he left his place, brother number two was probably right behind them. If not ahead by a lap or two.

"Do you want to tell me what happened here?"

Logan asked, a little breathless from the exertion of trying to move a house with his bare hands.

"I think that's kind of obvious, don't you?" Tyler countered, and he started to laugh. It started as a low, rumbling chuckle and gathered force until it was a roar. Sweat running down his face, covered in dirt, his house a wreck and his new truck a goner after one day in his possession, he didn't know what else to do but laugh.

The sirens grew louder.

Briana pulled in, driving her BMW and wearing jeans under her nightgown, Alec and Josh in tow.

"I think I heard something," Logan said, after noting his wife's arrival and giving a slight shake of his head. "From down there—"

Tyler stopped laughing to listen.

Sure enough, there was a voice rising from the depths of all that wreckage, like a faint curl of smoke, unintelligible but definitely human in origin.

They dug a little farther, and the words came clear.

"Somebody—help me—"

Logan and Tyler dug harder.

"What's going on here?" Briana called up, from the yard.

Logan chuckled and even in the darkness, Tyler saw the look of tender amusement move in his brother's eyes. "Briana," he called back, "get that flashlight out of my truck and throw it up here. Then *go home!* And take Davie and the dog with you."

"But I want to know—" Briana's protest was cut off by the arrival of all three of Stillwater Springs' squad cars and an ambulance. The din was deafening.

Dylan was there, too—he took the flashlight from Briana's hands and scrambled up onto the pile. Handed the light to Logan and started moving timber.

"What *happened?*" Briana insisted, when some of the noise had subsided.

Jim and two of his deputies were on the roof now, while the EMTs prepared for whatever the night might bring. Within a few minutes, the roof of the semi was in sight—the beam of the flashlight bounced off it.

"Davie will tell you all about it," Logan shouted down to his wife, in belated reply, *"on the way home!"*

Briana finally gave up and left, taking the three boys and Kit Carson with her.

"She'll be waiting up with hot coffee and a lot of questions when we get to the other house," Logan said, pausing to drag an arm across his forehead and wipe some of the sweat away.

"I'd rather have whiskey," Dylan put in.

"There won't be any shortage of questions," Jim huffed. "I've got about a thousand of them."

They'd created an opening, but the timbers weren't stable and now that they'd done enough digging to get down to the truck, Jim ordered everybody off the roof.

The deputies left, but Logan, Dylan and Tyler stayed put, along with Jim.

Tyler started for the hole. This was his house and his truck, after all. He'd be the one to climb down there and see if the crazy man was alive.

Dylan stopped him by taking hold of his left arm. "I'm the bull-rider in this crew," he said. The rodeo reference wasn't lost on the other three men—bull-riders tended to be leaner, shorter and more agile than their counterparts in the other events, though of course there were always exceptions. Dylan was by no means a small man, but Logan, Tyler and Jim were all taller, heavier and broader through the shoulders.

And that hole was going to be a tight fit.

"Be careful," Logan said, with a sigh.

Dylan nodded, glanced Tyler's way.

Reluctantly, Tyler nodded back.

Nimble, like he'd always been, Dylan made his way down some ten feet, easing himself from beam to beam, going still when the timbers groaned and shimmied.

"Everybody down," Jim ordered, for the second time, when the quake subsided.

"Not a chance," Logan said flatly.

"That's our *brother* down there," Tyler added.

"Did it ever occur to either of you knot-heads," Jim bit out, crescents of sweat staining the underarms of his once-spiffy uniform shirt, dust dulling his badge, "that you might be putting Dylan in *more* danger, standing up here arguing with me?" He paused, swallowed hard. "I *am* the sheriff of this county, you know. I expect my orders to be obeyed."

"Expect away," Logan said.

"Give it your best shot," Tyler put in.

"It's Roy Fifer," Dylan called up from the hole.

"Now *there's* news," Jim said sarcastically.

"The cab seems pretty sturdy," Dylan told them. They heard him talking to Roy in a low, easy tone, though the words weren't clear. Then he started back up through the network of shaky beams. "I think he's all right," he said, popping his head into view like a gopher out of a tunnel. "Shaken up, that's all."

Although a big part of him wanted to shinny down that shaft and get Roy Fifer by the throat, Tyler was relieved. Determining Roy's condition had been paramount, but lifting him out of there was going to be a challenge.

"You said the cab of that truck was sturdy," Jim said, watching Dylan. "You think it will hold until we can get Dan Phillips over here with some heavy equipment to move these beams out of the way?"

"It'll hold," Dylan said, his filthy face breaking into a grin. "Now, what do you say we all get our asses down off this roof before we get ourselves killed?"

• • •

IT TOOK DAN the better part of an hour to get out to the ranch, pick up the bulldozer he'd left at Dylan's building site, and drive it over the fields, through the woods and up Tyler's driveway.

Dawn was breaking before they got close enough to the driver's-side door to see Roy staring pitifully out at them through a web of broken window glass.

"I think he might have sobered up," Jim quipped. "First stop, the emergency room. Second stop, my jail."

Dylan let out a long, low whistle of exclamation when what was left of the blue Chevy pickup came into view.

"It had eight cylinders," Tyler lamented. "Leather seats and a sound system like you wouldn't believe."

Logan slapped him on the back. "Easy come, easy go," he said, in big-brother speak.

"Gee," Tyler said. *"Thanks."*

"You want to come along to the clinic and sit in while I question Roy?" Jim asked Tyler, already starting the careful climb down to the ground.

"Fill me in tomorrow," Tyler answered. "Right now, I need some of my sister-in-law's coffee."

The main ranch house was all lit up when they pulled in, fifteen minutes later, Tyler riding with Logan, Dylan following in his truck.

"Quite a night," Logan remarked, like it had been a party or something.

Easy for *him* to be cheerful—Dylan, too. *They* still had their trucks.

Stepping over the threshold into the kitchen, Tyler once again marveled at how much the place had changed. It was the love, he supposed. Logan and Briana were *happy* in that house, and their feelings for each other and the kids had somehow seeped into the walls, the floors, the ceilings.

If houses could be healed, that one had.

Reflecting on all this, Tyler figured he must be in shock or something, since he didn't usually think in lines from greeting cards.

Nevertheless, the bad mojo was gone.

The old man had been exorcised—for good.

Naturally, Davie had already told Briana what he knew about the one-man demolition derby, before he and Kit bedded down in Tyler's old room for the night. He'd guessed, being a sharp kid, that they'd find Roy Fifer at the wheel when they uncovered the truck.

Half rummy from the night's adventures, Tyler ate the fried eggs, potatoes and ham Briana cooked up for all of them. He swilled coffee, but it didn't wake him up. Finally, he accepted the loan of some sweatpants and a T-shirt from Logan, took a hot shower and crashed on the living room couch.

Even under these circumstances, it was good to be home.

"IS HE DEAD?" a young voice asked, breathless. Alec, no doubt.

Sunlight glowed, orange, through Tyler's eyelids.

"No, dumb-ass, he's just *sleeping* like he is." That would be Josh, the older and more serious of the two. "If you'd *pay attention* once in a while, you'd know that Logan said he was *sleeping like a dead man,* not that he is one!"

It struck Tyler then that he *could* have been a dead man, with Davie lying on the next slab and Kit Carson a goner, too, if he'd been able to shut his mind off last night and drift off. He and Davie would have heard the truck coming, given the god-awful racket it was making, but as for getting out of the cabin before the crash—probably not.

Tyler opened his eyes, glad he still had the option.

Josh and Alec were standing next to him, like mourners at a viewing, while Davie sat in a big leather chair nearby, looking a little the worse for the busy night just past but grinning that trademark Creed grin.

"Miss Lily called," he said, nodding toward Tyler's jeans, which lay in a heap at the other end of the couch. "Hope you don't mind, but when your pants pocket rang, I answered."

Lily. Sweet, chronically orgasmic Lily.

He hoped the gap in her schedule hadn't closed,

because he'd been looking forward to that phone sex he'd promised her.

"What did she say?"

"That you're a hunka-hunka burnin' love," Davie joked.

At least, Tyler *hoped* he was joking.

"Woooowwww," Josh and Alec chorused, in unison, their eyes wide with admiration.

Davie made a smoochy sound, and the younger boys broke up laughing.

Tyler, not quite as amused as his nephews, scowled a warning at Davie.

Briana popped her head in from the kitchen, smiled at Tyler with sisterly fondness and said, "Boys. Chores. Now."

Alec and Josh left, groaning.

Briana ducked back into the kitchen.

"What," Tyler repeated, sitting up and pinning Davie with a look, "did Lily say?"

"Before or after I told her what happened to the cabin?"

Tyler closed his eyes.

"Just kidding," Davie said cheerfully. "Basically, she said don't call her, she'll call you. Oh, and she's cutting the trip short, too. Because her car is boring."

"What?" Tyler asked.

Davie grinned, and he grinned Creed. "She's going to sell it there and fly home. Because it's boring, and she wants to buy another one when she gets back here. Something snazzy. She has a sever-ance check, and it's burning a hole in her pocket."

Tyler liked the change in plans—a lot. He'd wait until Lily called if it killed him, and do his damnedest to be alone when she did. Get her all hot and bothered and send her right over the edge.

When she flew in from Chicago, he'd be there to meet the plane. As soon as they'd dropped Tess and Hal off at the house in town, he'd take her somewhere private and make love to her for real.

Then, and only then, he'd break the news that they had to postpone the wedding.

CHAPTER EIGHTEEN

THE PHONE SEX HADN'T HAPPENED, and Lily was feeling the loss of it, a sort of vague, dis-jointed ache, centered more in her heart than in her body, as she drove alone toward the mansion in Oak Park. She'd put off the meeting with the real estate agent until the next day, after packing the surprisingly few things she wanted to take back to Stillwater Springs with her, and sent her dad and Tess off to a matinee at the neighbor-hood cinema.

Getting squared away with Eloise, she figured, was more important than sorting books and dishes, sheets and towels, deciding what to give away and what to keep. There had always been a wide breach between her and Eloise, although they'd managed it better than they were now, but Lily didn't want the problem to become Tess's.

Pulling up to the massive iron gates at the bottom of Eloise's long, crushed-clamshell driveway, a lot of old memories, accompanied by a rush of corresponding emotions, welled up inside Lily.

She remembered her first visit to her late husband's ancestral home, after someone she'd gone to high school with in Stillwater Springs e-mailed her about Tyler's marriage to a pretty blond barrel-racer named Shawna. In a fit of frantic optimism, and because Burke had been shoving his great-grandmother's diamond engagement ring under her nose at regular intervals and telling her how happy they'd be together, she'd accepted his proposal.

He'd brought her here, excited to tell his mother the good news.

The big gates whirred open, just as they'd done that long-ago day.

Lily had been beyond intimidated back then, and nothing in Eloise's coolly polite reception had helped the situation. It had been all she could do not to run across those Italian marble floors, out through the eighteen-foot hand-painted front doors, and scramble over the high stone walls to jump on the first bus out of the neighborhood.

Do not pass go.

Do not collect $200.

She'd have done that, headed straight for Stillwater Springs and taken a job at Skivvie's if the new Wal-Mart wasn't hiring, except that Burke had held tightly to her hand, and whispered that his mother would come around if they just gave her a little time. But that, Lily saw in grim retrospect, was only part of the problem—she hadn't gone home, let herself be the small-town girl she really was, because she wasn't getting along with her dad *and* because she was terrified that she'd run into Tyler and the barrel-racer once she got there.

She'd really believed, deep down, that she didn't have a home anymore.

Why not try to *make* one, with Burke?

The clamshells crunched under the wheels of Lily's sedate sedan—Burke had chosen it for her—with its hand-lettered For Sale sign in the back window.

She smiled as the latest in a long line of gardeners stopped to watch her go past. Turnover was high at Chez Eloise, and he was a stranger—probably thinking she'd come to apply for a job. Maid? Social secretary? Personal assistant?

Emotional punching bag?

Pulling up in front of the Grecian portico, Lily shut off the engine and unclamped her fingers from the steering wheel. It was silly to feel so much dread, she told herself sternly. She'd been to this house a thousand times with Burke, and later, after his death, dropping Tess off for visits, picking her up again when some long, lonely weekend or foray to Nantucket finally ended.

It wasn't the house, of course—Lily was way past feeling like an out-of-place country kid mistakenly invited to high tea at the garden club. She and Eloise were about to have a confrontation, that was the fact of the matter, and it probably wouldn't end well.

Lily got out of the car, drew a deep breath and marched up the beautifully chiseled limestone steps to the front door. The place was a far cry from the trailer she and Tyler would be living in after the wedding, that was for sure.

Oddly comforted by that contrast, Lily relaxed enough to ring the doorbell.

Stately chimes sounded within the hallowed halls, and one of the doors swung open. Eloise herself stood in the entryway, pale and stiff-shouldered.

Either it was the maid's day off, Lily concluded, or Eloise had been watching for her through one of the tall mullioned windows at the front of the house. Quite possibly, after Lily had called an hour before and asked if she could stop in, Eloise had dismissed the staff for the duration.

"Come in," Eloise said stonily, stepping back to admit Lily.

The place was mausoleum-silent, and ridiculously grand.

Lily paused to take in the frescoed ceilings of the two-story entry hall, the graceful curves of the twin staircases, the elaborate grandfather clock, hand-made in Switzerland for one of Eloise's distant ancestors. No quartz-movement there—the thing had been tick-tick-ticking for over a hundred years.

"I thought you'd bring Tess," Eloise said, standing there in yet another pair of high heels, yet another suit. This one was funeral-black.

"We agreed that I wouldn't," Lily reminded her mother-in-law. Eloise had the home-court advantage, but that didn't mean Lily was going to be backed into any corners.

Eloise let the comment pass. Led the way into the "parlor"—which would have been the living room in a regular house. A silver tea service gleamed on the elegant antique table situated between two snow-white suede couches, set to face each other, perpendicular to the imposing fireplace.

"Please sit down," Eloise said.

Lily took her usual seat.

Eloise perched across from her, on the other couch, leaned a little to pour tea. Someone—definitely not Eloise—had prepared small, crustless sandwiches, scones and tiny bowls of diced fruit.

As if.

"Your Tyler," Eloise said, cutting right to the chase, "has quite a family history."

Lily straightened her backbone. "Yes," she answered. If Eloise had expected to take her by surprise, she was bound to be disappointed. "Did you use a search engine to check him out, Eloise, or just hire a detective?"

Eloise's hand trembled slightly as she lifted a delicate china cup to her mouth for a sip, but otherwise, she didn't react. She didn't answer, either. She might even have been a little embarrassed, though that was probably a reach.

It struck Lily, not for the first time, but with more impact than on previous occasions, how lonely this huge house must be in common hours. No husband, no Burke, and now, at least as things stood, no Tess.

"I love him, Eloise," Lily said. How strange to say that to a woman she barely liked, when she hadn't even told Tyler yet.

"Oh, your sort always thinks they're 'in love,'" Eloise said smoothly.

"'My sort'?" Lily inquired.

"Small-town girls," Eloise expanded generously, trying hard to smile but falling far short. "People from a certain—well, *unsophisticated* background."

"There is nothing wrong with my background." *And if this is "sophistication," you can stick it where the sun don't shine.*

"Probably not," Eloise responded, in her own good time. "But there's plenty wrong with Tyler Creed's."

"That's your opinion."

"His mother committed suicide. His father was a

366

drunken lunatic. And Tyler himself, along with his two brothers, was arrested for drunk and disorderly conduct following a family funeral. But I presume you know all that."

"All that," Lily said calmly, "and a lot more. Things that wouldn't mean a thing to you, but mean everything to me."

"Frankly," Eloise retorted, "I don't *care* if you want to marry a cowboy and live in a mobile home on Rural Route Whatever. That's your business. But I care a *great deal* about my granddaughter's well-being."

Lily hadn't touched the tea, of course, or the little sandwiches. She sat rigidly on that pristine couch, her hands knotted together in her lap. Once, she'd have forgone the mini-meal out of a fear of spilling something and staining the couch or the exquisite rug beneath her feet. Now, it was because if she'd tried to swallow anything, she'd have been sick.

"I am perfectly capable of taking care of my daughter," she said carefully.

"*Burke's* daughter, too," Eloise pointed out.

Lily bit back a scathing reminder that Burke was dead. Obviously, Eloise knew that all too well—anybody could have seen that her son's absence was like a black hole at the center of the woman's life, always pulling at her, trying to drag her in.

"Eloise," Lily said, in the most reasonable tone she could manage, "what do you want?"

"I want," Eloise responded, with the most damnable attitude of entitlement Lily had ever encountered, "to raise Tess."

Again, this was a development Lily had anticipated, but hearing Eloise actually say the words was a slap in the face just the same.

"No," she said flatly.

"I thought you'd say that," Eloise replied lightly, still bone-certain that whatever Eloise Kenyon wanted, Eloise Kenyon was supposed to *get.*

"Then why did you ask?"

"It seemed kinder than simply having my lawyers get in touch with you," Eloise said. "Don't force me to sue you, Lily—if only out of respect for Burke's memory. You and I both know Tess would be better off here with me, that she'd have every advantage—"

"Except a mother," Lily broke in, rising to her feet to leave. Her face was hot and she was dizzy. "Go ahead, Eloise. Sic your attorneys on me—they'll be glad to rake in the fees, I'm sure. But you can't win and somewhere in that shriveled, selfish, *snobby* little heart of yours, you know it."

Eloise stood, too, less confident now, but evidently determined to brazen the whole thing out to the bitter end. "Be reasonable, Lily. I have so much to offer Tess that you don't, and Burke would want it this way."

Suddenly, furious tears all but blinded Lily.

"Don't you get it, Eloise? I don't *give a damn* what Burke would want. He was a liar and a cheat and the *second* most self-indulgent person I've ever run across. And here's another news flash for you. For all of that, he *did* love Tess, and the last thing—*the last thing,* Eloise—he would have allowed to happen was for her to grow up the way he did." Lily stopped then, tried to regain her composure, but she was only partially successful. "*Think* before you call the legal eagles, Eloise, because if you try to take her away from me, Tess will *hate* you for the rest of her life!"

Eloise flinched; Lily had finally struck a nerve. Was it remotely possible that the woman hadn't even *considered* how Tess would react to all this? Was she *that* selfish?

Cracks began to appear in Eloise's facade. So much for the lady of the grand manor, hail Eloise, full of grace. "Lily, please sit down—Pull yourself together—"

Lily kept going. Her sneakers made no sound on the marble floor of the entryway, but Eloise's heels clicked rapidly, the sound echoing off the walls, as she gave chase.

Lily jerked open the door. "Go to hell, Eloise!" she cried.

"Please," Eloise pleaded. "Wait—I've handled this badly. I—"

The words almost made Lily stay.

Almost, but not quite.

She stormed across the porch, down the steps, jerked open the door of her car to get in.

Eloise crunched after her, mincing through the clamshells in her spike heels. "Wait!" she repeated, more desperately this time. "Lily, *please* wait—"

It wasn't Eloise's pleas that made Lily sag forward in the car seat without turning the key, rest her forehead on the steering wheel. It was her complete certainty that if she drove anywhere now, she'd be a danger to herself and others.

"I'm sorry," Eloise said, standing beside the car now, reaching through the open door to touch Lily's shoulder. "It's just—Oh, Lily, *please* don't take Tess away from me—Give me another chance—"

Slowly, Lily raised her head, turned, looked straight into Eloise's face. "How can I?" she asked. "How can I ever trust you to be alone with my child after—after—"

A tear slipped down Eloise's cheek. Tears were rare with her—she hadn't even cried at Burke's funeral. "Lily, give me another chance," she whispered. "I'm begging you. I lost Burke. I can't lose Tess, too. *I can't.*"

Lily dried her eyes, sat up straight, took a few deep breaths. "Visit anytime," she said very quietly. "We'll be in Stillwater Springs, Montana." She'd be all right now. All right to drive, all right for the rest of her life. "First trailer on your right."

With that, she closed the car door, started the

engine and drove slowly down the clamshell driveway for what she knew would be the very last time.

And it was all she could do not to shout out a hallelujah.

DAN PHILLIPS ARRIVED at Tyler's place that afternoon, with a crew. Since his bulldozer was already on the premises, he made short work of clearing away the remains of the cabin. Tow trucks arrived to haul off the smashed semi and Tyler's pickup.

Together, Dan and Tyler paced off the place where the foundation would be poured, and the digging started right away.

Spotting a glimmer in the crushed grass, Tyler squatted, picked up the small hunk of metal that had once been his watch. His last gift from Shawna.

Holding it in his palm, closing his fingers around it, Tyler shut his eyes.

Let go, Ty, he heard Shawna say, in his head, as clearly as he'd heard Jake's taunts at the cemetery. *It's time to let go.*

Tyler opened his eyes first, then his fingers. Dylan was standing close by, watching him.

"It's creepy," Tyler said, straightening, "the way you and Logan seem to pop up out of the ground when I'm not expecting you."

And just when I need a brother.

"I called your name a couple of times," Dylan

said quietly. "But with the bulldozer running and you off in another world someplace, I guess you didn't hear me."

Tyler managed a grin, probably more of a grimace, and didn't answer.

"Is the watch special?" Dylan asked. His tone was careful.

Tyler swallowed, nodded. Heard the echo of Shawna's gentle admonition whispering in his mind again. *Let go, Ty. It's time to let go.*

"I'll tell you all about it one day soon," he promised hoarsely.

"Whenever you're ready," Dylan replied. Then he gestured toward the driveway. "Brought the Blazer back," he said. "You're going to need wheels."

Tyler chuckled. "Thanks," he said, as Dylan laid the keys in his hand. The one that wasn't still gripping Shawna's watch, gripping Shawna herself.

Let go.

"Davie and the dog still over at Logan's?" Dylan asked, keeping pace as Tyler headed for the Blazer, intent on the next order of business.

"Yeah," Tyler answered. "I got a call from Jim Huntinghorse a few minutes ago. Roy's out of the hospital, and locked up in a cell in town. Thought I'd drop by and say howdy."

Dylan nodded. "And you don't want the kid around for that," he guessed.

"Nope," Tyler said, waving to Dan Phillips as he opened the driver's-side door of the Blazer.

"Or me, either," Dylan supposed, looking affable and worried at the same time.

Tyler grinned. Slapped his brother on the shoulder. "Nope," he repeated.

Dylan chuckled. Nodded. "Kristy and I are throwing a party for Floyd Book tonight, at our place. Bon voyage kind of thing—our former sheriff and his wife are leaving on a cruise to Alaska tomorrow morning. With all that's been going on, I didn't get around to mentioning it, but I'd really like it if you'd come by. So would Kristy."

Tyler got into the Blazer, rested his arm on the frame of the open window. "I guess I could fit that into my busy social calendar," he said. Then, with a quirk at one corner of his mouth, he added, "Need a lift somewhere?"

Dylan had driven the Blazer out to the ranch, so he'd be on foot if he didn't accept.

"My place," he answered. "The new one, I mean."

When they arrived on Dylan's part of the ranch, Tyler let out a low whistle of exclamation. Workers were everywhere—where had Dan gotten them all?—and both the house and the barn were framed in.

"Impressive," Tyler said. "The house is going to cover an acre, all by itself."

Dylan surveyed the progress with a light of pride in his eyes. "It's a whole new start," he said quietly. "A place to raise up a whole flock of Creeds, starting with Bonnie."

Tyler was choked up, all of a sudden. Again, he remembered the weird incident with Jake, over at the graveyard, remembered the old man's brutal certainty that all Logan and Dylan were trying to build would fall apart.

He expected a chill, but it didn't come.

Instead, he felt peace.

"A whole new start," Tyler confirmed.

Dylan's expression was serious when he turned to face Tyler. "Ty, there are letters, diaries—"

"So I'm told," Tyler said, when Dylan fell silent.

"They were mostly good people. The Creeds, I mean."

Tyler nodded.

Dylan cleared his throat. "Read up on them, will you? The family, the people who carved this place out of the wilderness with their bare hands and held it for us, generation after generation. When you do, you'll know we've got a lot to be proud of."

Tyler figured they had a lot to be proud of, even without the letters and diaries, but he wasn't ready to say that yet, so he just nodded, tacitly agreeing to take a look at the archives.

"See you tonight?" Dylan asked. "At the party?"

"I'll be there," Tyler said. "What time?"

Dylan's legendary grin flashed again. He'd been a heartbreaker, out there on the rodeo circuit, a different rodeo groupie in his bed every night of the week. Now, Kristy had him roped and tied for good, and he'd never looked happier. "*Any*time, Ty," he said. And then he walked away.

Tyler spent the drive into town sorting through all the things it made him feel, having brothers again. Between them and what he had with Lily, he felt something that had been missing from his life for a long time—hope.

JIM WAS SHUFFLING PAPERS in the front office when Tyler arrived at the sheriff's office, and Floyd Book was there, too, wearing civilian clothes and looking mighty pleased that he'd been replaced.

"I hear you and Dorothy are leaving on a honeymoon cruise tomorrow," Tyler remarked, shaking hands with the older man.

"Dorothy's really perked up at the prospect," Floyd said, beaming.

Life, Tyler thought, goes on.

There had been a funeral in town, he knew, marking the end of a long ordeal for Floyd Book and a lot of other people, including Kristy. Seemed like folks were making fresh starts all over the place, not just on Stillwater Springs Ranch.

"That's good, Floyd," Tyler said. Since he didn't know if tonight's party was a surprise or not, he didn't mention it. "Did Jim bring you up to speed on the goings on out at my cabin?"

Floyd nodded, frowned. "Hell of a thing," he said. Then, with a glance at Jim, he added, "Glad *I'm* not going to have to unravel this mess."

Jim threw him a mock glare, then laughed. Jutted his thumb toward the back of the office, where the cells were. "I guess you know the way, Ty," he said, getting a chuckle out of Floyd.

"Guess I do," Tyler said. "Floyd here gave me a guided tour once, a long time ago."

"Twice," Floyd corrected good-naturedly. "There was that time I caught you and Jim and a bunch of other yahoos spinning didos in the parking lot over at the high school, one fine winter night. All of you were tanked up on beer, and the whole county was under an inch of ice, and since I didn't want to drive the lot of you to your separate domiciles, I just threw you all in the clink for the night."

"I remember." Tyler grinned.

Jim chuckled ruefully. "Me, too."

Floyd started for the front door. "I'm getting out of here before somebody slaps a badge on my chest," he said. "See you both at the party tonight?"

"I wouldn't miss it," Jim said.

"Me, either," Tyler added.

"Good," Floyd said, in parting. "Because when I look at you two, I know I did a *couple* of things right, anyway, during my long and illustrious career in law enforcement."

Jim grinned, straightened his shoulders a little.

Tyler felt good, too, as he headed back to see Roy Fifer.

A word of praise from Floyd Book, however offhanded, was as good as a compliment could get. Floyd had been Tyler's childhood hero, and Jim's, too, for all the trouble they'd gotten into with him.

Roy was in the last cell on the right, sitting hangdog on the edge of his cot, wearing a jail-orange jumpsuit. All dressed up, and nowhere to go.

Seeing Tyler, he looked as if he'd leap to his feet and try to squirm between the bars over the window.

"Why'd you do it, Roy?" Tyler asked.

Roy's Adam's apple bobbed along the length of his neck, though there wasn't much distance to cover. Roy didn't really *have* a neck. "I was drunked up," he said. "Mad at Doreen. You going to press charges?"

"That's not up to me," Tyler answered, drawing on what Logan had told him in the ranch house kitchen early that morning, over ham and eggs and a lot of coffee. "You could have killed us, Roy. Davie and me and the dog, too. Since that appears to be what you intended, I guess the county prosecutor will decide what happens now."

"I wasn't after you," Roy said, as though that would make a difference. "I was after that damn kid. He's the whole reason Doreen came back here and messed up my life."

"So you figured *killing* him made sense?"

Roy heaved a great, quivering sigh, shook his head. Stared down at the cement floor of his new residence. "I never thought as far as anybody dyin'," he said. "Like I told you, I'd had a few too many beers over at Skivvie's."

"A great way to cap off getting your stomach pumped," Tyler observed. "Head for Skivvie's and start swilling brew."

"I might have a little drinking problem," Roy confessed gloomily.

"Think so?"

"Kind of like your old man did," Roy said, pushing the envelope. "I'd expect you, of all people, to understand."

"Would you?" Tyler replied lightly.

"Give me a chance, here," Roy went on. There was a whiny note in his voice now, and he was pale as a bottom-feeder's belly. "A word from you, and the prosecutor might give me a stint in rehab and probation, instead of a prison sentence."

Tyler wanted to turn around and walk out, but he knew this was his one chance to get the truth out of Roy Fifer. The man thought he, Tyler, could influence the prosecutor—fat chance, according to Logan—and because of that, Roy might be willing to spill some of the details.

"Did you and Doreen and Davie plan this whole paternity thing, Roy?" Tyler asked, careful to keep his voice light, as though none of it really mattered, one way or the other. "Was it a scam?"

To Tyler's relief, Roy looked genuinely surprised. "Plan it?" he echoed stupidly.

"Saying Davie was mine," Tyler prompted carefully, not wanting to put words in Roy's mouth. "Hitting me up for a lot of money."

Roy blinked. "No," he said. "Doreen had Davie take a blood test, down at the clinic. Fed-Exed it to some guy she used to know, and he e-mailed her a few days later—she used one of the computers over at the library—said he'd followed up with some medical outfit wherever he lived, and the results were negative. I swear to God, that's all she told me."

Tyler closed his eyes.

The truck driver. Doreen had contacted the man she'd believed to be Davie's father, sent him Davie's lab results, and the mystery man had had them compared to his own.

"Are those results around someplace, Roy?" Tyler asked, very quietly.

"There's a copy in the bill drawer, over at Granny's," Roy said, looking baffled. "If Doreen didn't take them with her after she doctored my Bloody Mary and lit out."

"What was in that Bloody Mary?" Tyler asked, almost casually. He even folded his arms, like he was in no big hurry to get out of there. "The hospital must have told you by now."

Roy sighed. Shrugged. "Nobody tells me nothin'," he said. "Ask Jim. He might know."

"I'll do that," Tyler said, turning to leave.

"Wait a second," Roy called after him. "You going to put in a good word for me, with the prosecutor?"

Tyler saw no reason to hold out false hope. "Actually," he answered, opening the door that led into Jim's office, "no."

Jim was waiting when Tyler entered his office, leaving behind a crimson-faced Roy, like he knew what was coming.

"What was in the drink Doreen gave Roy?" Tyler asked bluntly.

Jim looked relieved. "That stuff they give kids when they need to throw up," he said.

"And the man Davie told you about, the boyfriend who bit the dust at the supper table? Did you follow up on that?"

Jim flushed a little, under his bronze skin. "I'm still waiting for the coroner's report," he said. "I did talk to local law enforcement, though, and they said this Marty character had a history of health problems."

"And you didn't bother to mention all this?"

Jim's jawline tightened. "Hell, Tyler," he growled, when he'd unclamped his back teeth. "I just got the call about Roy's lab work an hour ago. I barely glanced at it. Same with the other thing. In case you haven't noticed, I'm up to my Native American ass in problems here."

Tyler relented a little, focused on what mattered.

Doreen hadn't intended to kill Roy, only to slow him down so she could make a getaway. And Davie hadn't been part of any scheme—Roy would have been quick to implicate him if he had.

Tyler headed toward the main doors.

"Where are you going in such a hurry?" Jim asked, worried now.

Tyler didn't take the time to answer.

There were some things he wanted to follow up on.

Now.

CHAPTER NINETEEN

LILY HAD CALMED DOWN by the time she got back to the condo. She'd even stopped by her favorite organic food store on the way, bought the makings for her specialty—a casserole Tess had waggishly dubbed "tofu surprise."

Her dad and Tess weren't back from the movies yet, and she had the place to herself. She considered calling Tyler, but not for phone sex. She just needed to hear his voice.

In the end, though, she decided to start supper instead.

If she accomplished nothing else that day, she'd convince her father and daughter that healthy food could be delicious. She needed to get them back on track—last night's celebration meal had consisted of cheesy pizza.

The casserole was in the oven when the rain started. Lily hadn't noticed that the skies were cloudy either on her way to Eloise's or on the way back, but now a clap of thunder shook the whole complex. The storm must have been brewing for a while.

She switched on the gas fireplace and was on the verge of worrying when the movie-goers returned, laughing, their clothes and hair soaked by the downpour.

Lily sent them both off to change into dry things and started setting the table.

Tess was unusually tired and, after picking at her tofu surprise for a while, she actually volunteered to go to bed.

"Is she all right?" Lily asked her father, once they were alone.

Hal squeezed Lily's hand, smiled a little. His hair was still damp from the shower he'd taken after being caught in the rain. "She's homesick for Stillwater Springs, and convinced Eleanor is going to dig through to the Great Wall before she can get back."

Lily smiled. She'd give Tess a few minutes to settle in, then go in and say good-night. Make sure her little girl wasn't coming down with something. "I'm pretty homesick myself," she admitted.

"Missing Tyler?" Hal asked, smiling.

"Oh, yeah," Lily confessed.

"How did the visit with Eloise go?" He'd probably been waiting all afternoon to present *that* question, and with Tess in her room, the coast was clear.

Lily glanced in that direction anyway, in case her daughter had doubled back to listen in. "It was a disaster," she admitted, as another roar of thunder shook the building. She left her chair, went to the hallway to make sure Tess wasn't hiding there, just out of sight. But she was in her room, with the TV—a gift from Eloise, given over Lily's objections the previous Christmas—blaring. Still, Lily was careful to keep her voice down when she returned to the table. "She threatened to take Tess away from me."

"And?"

"And I told her to go to hell."

"Good girl," Hal said. "That's how it ended?"

Lily sighed, pushed her plate away. Hal had eaten even less of his tofu surprise than Tess had, and Lily herself had only managed a few bites. So the healthy-food gambit was a bust. "Pretty much," she replied wearily. "Eloise backed down a little, once she realized just how far over the line she was. I said she could visit Tess anytime she wanted—in Stillwater Springs."

"That's fair and reasonable, Lily," Hal assured her gently, probably reading her expression again. "You do know, don't you, that no judge in the country would take a perfectly happy, well-adjusted child like Tess away from her mother?"

Lily nodded. "I admit I was a little paranoid at first, but I'm over that." It was time to change the subject—where Eloise was concerned, she was on emotional overload—so she looked down at Hal's plate. It was then that she realized she'd been had. "Did you and Tess eat before you came home from the movies?" she demanded, but she couldn't help smiling a little.

Hal lifted his right hand like a man swearing an oath in a court of law. "No," he said. Then he lowered his hand, and his eyes twinkled. "But we did consume more than our share of popcorn. As God is my witness, we skipped the butter, and the stuff is high in fiber—"

Lily laughed, but her throat felt thick and suddenly she started to cry. Tyler was so far away, she'd had that fight with Eloise and rain sheeted the windows, making it seem as if the normal world beyond had simply vanished.

"Oh, honey," Hal whispered, when he saw the tears in her eyes. He took her hand, squeezed it. "You're tired. Why don't you go in and jammy up?"

Lily's throat closed.

She got up, started to clear the table, just to be busy.

Hal stopped her. "I'll do this," he said. "Go look in on Tess."

Lily gave in, set down the plates and silverware she'd gathered. She felt spent, used up, and she needed a few minutes with her daughter. "Don't throw out the tofu surprise," she said, as she turned to leave. "We can have it for lunch tomorrow."

Hal laughed. "I wouldn't think of doing that," he lied.

Lily wiped her eyes, kissed his cheek and hurried to Tess's door. Knocked lightly.

"Come in, Mom," Tess called. The TV went silent.

Catching a glimpse of the remote, hastily and only partially hidden under the bedspread, Lily decided to forgo the speech Tess was probably expecting—no TV without permission, that was the rule—when she saw the child's forlorn expression.

Immediately, she sat down on the edge of Tess's bed, touched her forehead in that time-honored way of mothers everywhere, was relieved to find no indication of a fever.

"What's the matter, honey?" she asked.

"Nana's mad at us," Tess said sadly.

"She's only mad at me," Lily replied gently. "Because we're moving to Stillwater Springs and it will be harder for her to see you."

"Is she going to steal me?"

Lily's heart splintered. *"No,"* she said, gathering the frightened child into her arms and holding her tightly. Obviously, despite Lily's efforts, Tess had overheard something, somewhere along the line— or simply jumped to a conclusion. "Nobody's going to steal you, baby. Ever."

"Nana said I should come to live with her," Tess

said, her face buried in Lily's shoulder. She was trembling. "So I wouldn't have to grow up in a trailer!"

"You're staying with me," Lily said, and a new and much deeper sadness filled her as she finally faced facts. Tess had been through a lot of changes lately, and although she loved living in Stillwater Springs, she surely wasn't ready for yet another move, for a stepfather. And, Lily realized, she hadn't even told Tess about Davie, who'd be living with them, as well. "You're staying with Grampa and me."

Tess pulled back far enough to look up at Lily, her small face serious and a little pale. "What about Tyler?" she asked. "What about the wedding and the baby and—"

There were times when Lily wished her daughter were a little less perceptive, and this was one of them. ·

She cupped a hand under Tess's chin. "Things have been happening too fast lately," she said softly. "We need to slow down a little."

Tess's eyes filled with tears. "You're going to divorce Tyler before we even marry him," she murmured, crestfallen.

"No," Lily said, crying herself now. "No, sweetheart. I love Tyler. I still want us to marry him. And I still want a baby. But wouldn't it be fun to plan a real wedding? Pick out dresses and decide what flowers we'd like and—"

"No!" Tess broke in.

"No?" Lily echoed, drying her eyes.

"I *like* Tyler. I want him to be my daddy."

Lily's tired heart turned over in her chest. "Baby, there's more to it than that. I know you like Tyler, and I know you want a daddy, but—"

"This is *Nana's* fault!" Tess accused, burrowing down in her covers and trying to cover her head—a tactic Lily gently prevented. "*She* made you change your mind!"

"I haven't changed my mind, Tess. I just think—"

"You *have* changed your mind," Tess insisted. She could be stubborn, but she came by it honestly, there was no denying that. "You're just trying to make me think you haven't!"

"Hush," Lily said, as the door opened behind her.

"Is everything all right in here?" Hal asked.

"No!" Tess blurted.

"Yes," Lily replied, at exactly the same moment.

"Get your stories straight," Hal said.

"Mom isn't going to marry Tyler," Tess announced, "because Nana made her scared."

Lily sighed. "Tess, that simply isn't true."

Tess was immovable. "Yes, it is!"

"Out of the mouths of babes," Hal commented.

Lily turned to him. "Don't help," she warned.

He held up both hands, palms out, in a gesture of benign surrender, and backed out of the room.

"I *hate* Nana," Tess spouted.

Lily held back the automatic, "No, you don't"

that rose to the tip of her tongue. The whole conversation was going nowhere fast, and any response she made would only escalate hostilities.

"Good night," she said instead, kissing her daughter's forehead.

"I want to go home," Tess said.

Lily went to the door, blew Tess a second kiss. "Me, too," she said. "Me, too."

And then she stepped out into the hall and closed the door softly but firmly behind her.

She didn't want to deal with her dad at the moment.

She didn't want to deal with anything.

So she went straight to her bathroom, started a bath running, poured half a bottle of bubbly stuff in and stripped.

High overhead, the thunder rolled and boomed, fit to split the planet into fragments.

It wasn't often, Lily thought philosophically, sinking to her chin in hot water and scented suds, that the weather exactly suited her mood, but that night, it did.

DAVIE PROUDLY SHOWED the cotton ball, stuck to the inside of his forearm with a Band-Aid, to Kristy, as soon as he and Tyler arrived at the party that night. "We had blood tests this afternoon," he said. "Both of us."

Kristy's eyes shone as she smiled at Tyler. "Well, well, well," she said. "How long till you know?"

Tyler felt pretty pleased himself, though he'd long since tossed his own cotton-ball-and-Band-Aid combo. "A week," he answered. "Maybe two."

The Victorian house was crowded with folks gathered to wish the Books well on their retirement and much-anticipated cruise to Alaska. Dylan wended his way through, Bonnie riding on his right hip, to greet the newcomers.

"Where's the dog?" he asked. "Did I forget to mention that he was invited, too?"

Kristy chuckled, shook her head and walked away.

"He's over at the Holiday Inn," Davie hastened to explain. "We had to sneak him in, so I hope he doesn't start barking or something."

"You could stay here," Dylan pointed out, addressing Tyler, not Davie.

Bonnie squirmed in Dylan's arms, wanting to go to the boy and check out the spider ghost on his neck.

Tyler didn't miss the careful way Davie held her. She might have been a doll, made of thin glass.

"Bug!" she said, touching the spider.

Davie laughed. "Can you say 'cootie'?"

"Cootie!" Bonnie repeated, in gleeful triumph. Then she scrambled back to Dylan. "Cootie!"

Tyler gave Davie a look.

Davie laughed again and vanished into the crowd, probably looking for Josh and Alec. Tyler watched him go, found Dylan watching him when he turned back to his brother.

"He's yours," Dylan said, grinning.

"I hope so," Tyler said. "I sure as hell hope so."

JIM HUNTINGHORSE'S DEPUTY admitted Doreen to the holding area at the sheriff's office, but not without reluctance. Clearly, without Jim there, he didn't like doing it, but Doreen had always been a persuasive type.

"How'd you find out?" Roy asked dismally.

"That you tried to kill my kid with a semi?" Doreen retorted furiously, well aware of the nervous deputy hovering in the doorway to the office. Did he think she was going to try to spring the prisoner or something? "About the first thing I did when I left here was buy me a computer. It's all over the Internet, Roy. What the *hell* were you thinking, anyhow?"

Roy looked shame-faced, and hopeful. "I *wasn't* thinking, Doreen," he said. "You broke my heart, and I guess it got the best of me for a little while." He paused, his eyes going watery. "You come back here to bail me out?"

"No," Doreen said, "*I didn't come back to bail your sorry ass out.* And spare me that bullshit about your broken heart, Roy, because as far as I know, you ain't *got* a heart."

Her grammar always went to hell when she was around Roy's kind of people. Once she got away from that place for good, made a fresh start, she'd work on that. Maybe take some night courses.

"Then why?" Roy whined. He swallowed hard. "You've got all that money—You could go any-where—"

"I came back because I didn't say goodbye to Davie," Doreen answered, not that she owed Roy any explanations. She'd only set foot in that shit-hole jail—God knew, the hoosegow brought back bad memories—to see for herself that the bastard was behind bars, where he belonged.

No, her return to Stillwater Springs was all about squaring things away with her son—and with Jim Huntinghorse. She didn't want anybody, least of all Davie, believing she'd meant to kill Roy Fifer, however much he needed killing.

Roy got up off his cot, waddled over and gripped the bars in both hands. "You gotta get me out of here. Granny doesn't have the money to post bail or hire lawyers."

"I don't have to do anything but die and pay taxes," Doreen countered. "And why would I want to spend a cent on you, anyhow?"

"Because I *love* you, Doreen."

That made her laugh out loud.

"Don't make me puke," she said.

And then she sailed right out of there, past the worried deputy, out into the office and straight for the door.

"You tell Jim Huntinghorse," she told the deputy

in parting, "that I'm staying over at the Holiday Inn. Room 322."

With that, Doreen bolted.

Jails, she thought, shuddering. They flat-out gave her the heebie-jeebies—no two ways about it.

THE PARTY RAN LATE, and it was the next morning before Tyler knew Doreen was back. She was sitting in the coffee shop, big as life, when he and Davie came in for the free breakfast, part of which the kid intended to smuggle back to their adjoining rooms, so he could share it with Kit Carson.

"Mom?" Davie said, stopping so quickly that Tyler, walking behind, nearly collided with him.

Doreen smiled and set aside the tattered copy of *People* she'd been reading. "Hello, Davie-boy," she said, in a perfectly ordinary tone of voice. Then, with a nod, "Tyler."

Tyler didn't know whether to stay or go. He'd expected this, on some level, but he was surprised, too.

"Join me?" Doreen asked. They had the place to themselves, at least.

That was something.

Davie sat down eagerly. Tyler held back.

"I want you to hear this, too," Doreen said, beckoning.

Since he was afraid Doreen might make a run for it, taking the kid with her, Tyler gave in. Joined the trio.

He'd been starved when he woke up.

Now, he couldn't have eaten for anything.

"We got blood tests," Davie told Doreen, showing her the cotton ball and Band-Aid. "Pretty soon, we'll know if Tyler's really my dad."

Doreen took Davie's hand, squeezed it. "Tyler's really your dad," she said softly. She raised her eyes to Tyler's face, smiled mistily. "And that makes you one lucky kid."

Tyler wanted to believe her—wanted to take the bait, hook, line and sinker. But he'd aged a little since his return to Stillwater Springs, and he was a little wiser. So he held back, didn't speak, didn't let what he was feeling show in his face.

He hoped.

"You know that for sure?" Davie asked. He was no fool, either. At thirteen, he understood the powerful motivation that settlement was to Doreen. "How?"

"Process of elimination," Doreen answered. "I thought it was Carl—a truck driver I knew once upon a time—but he had some tests run and they came back negative." She looked at Tyler again, her eyes guileless and full of bright hopes. "There was only one other possibility."

"*That's* why you made me get that blood test," Davie said. "Mom, you *said* it was for when school starts in the fall. So I could sign up for the junior rodeo program."

Doreen chuckled, took a sip of her coffee and set

the cup down again. "There are times," she said, "when a fib comes in handy."

Tyler felt dazed. Exuberant, but still cautious, too.

After all, Doreen was the mistress of the handy fib. Even now, she might have a game going, with Tyler as the designated mark.

She seemed to know what he was thinking, and it didn't appear to bother her much. She handed Davie a slip of paper.

"This is where I'll be," she said. "My e-mail address, anyhow. Once I light somewhere, I'll let you know, so we can stay in touch. I want to know all about school, Davie. Don't you get so busy with the rodeo that you let the math and English slide, all right?"

Davie swallowed, took the paper, glanced at Tyler. "All right," he said, choking out the words.

"You're about the only good thing that ever happened to me, Davie," Doreen went on, and damned if she didn't sound sincere. "I made lots of mistakes in my life, but you weren't one of them, and I want you to remember that."

"You didn't really mean to kill Roy, did you?" Davie asked, his voice small and shaky now. Carefully, he folded the paper with Doreen's e-mail address scrawled on it and tucked it into his pocket.

Doreen leaned to touch her forehead to her son's. "If I'd meant to kill Roy Fifer," she said, "he'd be *dead*."

Davie didn't laugh at the joke. Didn't even smile.

Tyler found that more than encouraging.

Doreen stood. Bent to kiss the top of Davie's head.

The boy trembled, but didn't look up at her.

"You behave yourself," she told him hoarsely. "And when you're eighteen, if you're so inclined, you come and see me."

Davie nodded.

Doreen touched Tyler's shoulder as she passed—and then she was gone.

They sat in silence for a long time, Davie and Tyler.

Finally, Tyler said, "Davie?"

"Wh-What?" the boy asked.

"It's okay to cry."

Davie wouldn't look at him, but his shoulders began to shake. "I thought Creeds were supposed to be tough," he said.

Tyler's mouth quirked up at one corner. "Creeds are tough," he agreed. "Tough enough to cry, when that's the only thing there is to do."

Davie cried.

Hard, and for a long time.

Tyler waited it out, his own eyes damp.

But in that way he had, Davie eventually came around. He sniffled, lifted his head, swiped a forearm across his face.

"Can I change my name?" he asked.

Tyler frowned. "To Creed? Sure. You *are* a Creed."

"I meant the Davie part," the boy said.

"What's wrong with 'Davie'?"

"It sounds like a kid."

"Hello? You *are* a kid."

"I kind of like Kit Carson, but that's taken," Davie mused. "Nobody strong is named 'Davie.'"

Tyler thought. "Davy Crockett?" he suggested.

"Yeah," Davie said, nonplussed. "Well."

Tyler's appetite was back. He got up, went to the buffet, filled a plate. A gaggle of cheerful gray-haired tourists wandered in.

"Tom?" Davie said, when Tyler rejoined him at the table.

A woman in a uniform came and cleared away Doreen's plate, pocketed the decent tip she'd left underneath.

"What?" Tyler asked.

"Keep up," Davie told him. "I'm talking names. What about Joe? That's a good one."

"Your name," Tyler said, "is Davie. Get over it."

"You're being a hard-ass again," Davie said.

"Adjust," Tyler answered.

Davie got up, went to the buffet table, returned with a plate of his own. "Mike?" he persisted. "Jack?"

"Dave?" Tyler suggested.

"Lame," Davie said. Things were peaceful for a while, both of them scarfing up the "free" break-fast. When they'd finished, Tyler left a tip and Davie started loading up a plate for Kit Carson.

"I kind of like living in a hotel," he said. "Except for the part about the dog being a stowaway."

Tyler laughed. "Easy on the sausage," he said. "Kit Carson has a delicate stomach."

"Yeah," Davie agreed. "He might puke, and that would blow our cover."

"All too true," Tyler said.

They left the dining room, headed for the elevators, Davie carrying Kit's plate with care.

The doors whisked shut.

Davie's eyes took on a shy expression. "While we're on the subject of names—"

"*Are* we on the subject of names?" Tyler grinned. "I thought we were past that."

Davie swallowed. Made himself meet Tyler's gaze.

"Things we call people, I mean," Davie said.

Tyler waited, raised one eyebrow.

"Would it be okay—" Davie stopped, gulped. "Would it be okay if I called you Dad?"

CHAPTER TWENTY

"THIS ISN'T A TRAILER, it's a palace," Lily said, a week later, standing beside Tyler out at his place, still weak-kneed from the private welcome-home he'd given her.

He'd picked her and her dad and Tess up at the airport, as promised, driving a brand-new green pickup with an extended cab and a top-of-the-line sound system. They'd dropped Tess and Hal off at home, with barely a see-you-later, and he'd headed straight for their special place—the cemetery on Stillwater Springs Ranch.

There, Tyler had laid her down in the backseat of that fancy truck—she hadn't resisted, she blushed to recall—relieved her of her jeans and panties, draped her bare legs over his shoulders and burrowed through to take her into his mouth. Made her come until she didn't think she could come any more.

But he'd withheld the thing she'd wanted, *needed,* most.

The thing she *still* needed.

He smiled at her assessment of the triple-wide, took her hand. "Care for a tour?"

She grinned. "Could we start with the bedroom?"

Tyler laughed. It was a rich, thoroughly masculine sound, and Lily loved it. Loved him.

"Let's save that for last," he said.

"You love to torture me," she accused, smiling.

He stopped, turned to her, touched the tip of her nose with one finger. "No, Lily," he said seriously, his voice gruff. "I love *you.*"

She blinked. That was *her* line. She'd been practicing it for days. Bracing herself to let it be all right, not hearing Tyler say it back. To let it be enough, knowing he'd say it when he was ready.

And now he'd beaten her to the punch.

"You do?" she asked, stunned.

"I do," he said.

She laughed, startling him a little. Then she leaped at him, flung her arms around his neck. "I love you, Tyler Creed!" she yelled. "I love you, I love you, I love you!"

He wrapped his arms around her, held her close, kissed her.

When it was over, and they were both breathless, he led her inside.

He showed her the state-of-the-art kitchen, Tess's room and Davie's. The family room. He made the big-screen TV whir down out of the ceiling in the living room.

"Forget the house," Lily said, impressed. "This place is good enough."

Tyler grinned. "That's what Davie said," he told her. Then he chuckled. "He's calling himself 'Pete' this week, so play along."

Lily's heart fluttered. "He's yours, Tyler?" she asked, very softly.

He looked deep into her eyes, into her very soul. "He's mine," he affirmed, reassured by what he'd seen there. "It's official."

"That's *wonderful*," Lily whispered.

"You don't know how glad I am that you think so," Tyler answered, taking her hand again. Pulling her along. "Now, for the bedroom," he said.

"It's about time," Lily retorted.

"You are one horny little hellcat," Tyler told her. "I like it."

The bedroom was massive—it was fully furnished, and even had a chandelier. The adjoining bathroom, with its huge sunken tub and enormous shower, would have accommodated a crowd, never mind the two of them.

But Lily was only interested in the bed.

She was out of her clothes in no time.

Tyler chuckled, hauled off his T-shirt, undid his jeans.

He was magnificent when he was fully dressed. Naked, he was downright formidable.

And he was ready for her, she could see that by his erection.

"No foreplay, Tyler," Lily said. "You had your way in the back of the truck. Now, I want mine."

He laid her down, not on her back, but on her stomach.

Knelt behind her and raised her onto her knees.

Slammed into her in a long, slow, deep thrust that made her cry out in the first throes of ecstasy.

"Not so fast, Lily," he crooned, pausing to nibble at the back of her neck, weighing her breasts gently in his hands. "Not so fast."

"It's been so long," Lily protested, gasping out the words. "Oh, Tyler, it's been so long—"

"We've got all the time in the world," he told her. His tone was soothing, but it only ignited her desire more—she was rapidly reaching flashpoint.

"Do me," she pleaded.

"Oh, I intend to," he murmured, giving her a little friction, but not quite enough.

Lily's whole body quivered, went damp with perspiration. "I meant now," she whimpered.

He chuckled, and teased her a little more, pulling back until he was almost out of her, but not quite.

She thrust her hips back, took him inside her, deep inside, where she wanted him, where she had to have him.

And in that moment, his control was gone.

He stopped fooling around. He didn't make love to her. He *did* her and did her hard, until they both caught fire, and fused together at the deepest levels of their bodies and their beings.

When it was over, they both collapsed, gasping, lying entwined in each other's arms.

"Is this room soundproof?" Lily asked, after a long, long time.

Tyler laughed, hooked an arm around her neck, pulled her close to kiss the top of her head. "No, oh, horny one, it isn't," he answered. "You'll just have to control yourself a little, at least when the kids are around."

The kids.

Davie and Tess.

And maybe—just maybe—since she was a week late for her period, a third child. It was too soon to tell him, of course—she'd barely dared to tell herself.

How could she have thought she needed time?

She needed *Tyler*. And so, in a completely different way, did Tess.

"When's the wedding, cowboy?" she asked.

WHEN'S THE WEDDING, COWBOY?

Tyler took a few moments to savor those words. He could hardly believe he'd even thought about postponing the beginning of their life together, even though he'd had good reason at the time.

Since then, though, he'd gotten to know Davie a lot better.

Davie. *His son.*

They'd had a lot of long talks, he and Davie, since Doreen left town, after her interview with Jim Huntinghorse. And Davie had let down his guard, shown Tyler who he really was.

A scared kid who'd had it tough from day one, and still had the guts to hope for something better. Nothing more than that, and nothing less.

"You're sure you want to sign on with this bunch?" he asked, playing with a tendril of Lily's soft, sunshine-scented hair. She smelled like Montana—clean and open and fresh—the kind of place where a person could always make a new start. "We're pretty wild, we Creeds."

She raised herself onto one elbow, to look down into his face, and her eyes were serious. "I'm sure," she said, looking and sounding a little worried. "Are you?"

He kissed her, slowly, gently.

"I've never been more sure of anything in my life," he said. And then he rolled her onto her back, eased on top of her. "Except maybe how much I want to have you again—right now."

EPILOGUE

One year later . . .

THEY WERE ALL GATHERED at the main ranch house, and there was so much noise—so much *love*—in that place that Lily half expected the walls to burst.

The kitchen was bigger now, since the renovations were finally finished, and it was still the heart of the house, just as it had always been.

"You come right in and tell us when you see them coming," Briana told Alec, for about the third time that morning. It was Logan's birthday, and they were planning a major celebration, as soon as he and Tyler and Dylan got back from riding the fence lines.

Along with Josh, Alec had been hovering over the antique cradle Logan had rescued from the attic during Briana's last trimester, admiring his new baby sister.

There was a lot to admire about four-month-old Maggie Creed. She had her mother's strawberry-blond hair and her father's dark, solemn eyes—a winning combination.

Dylan and Kristy's boy, Tim, born a week after Maggie's arrival, was already trying to sit up. His blue eyes went round whenever he saw his big sister, Bonnie, and he'd reach for her with his chubby little arms.

Three years old now, Bonnie was a miniature lady—when she wasn't getting into mischief. And she adored her baby brother. If Kristy hadn't been keeping a close eye on her, in fact, she probably would have climbed right into his playpen with him.

Last, but not least, there were Tyler and Lily's own twins, a boy and a girl. Davie had named his brother Michael, and Tess had chosen Molly's name—after Lily had dissuaded Tess from calling her Eleanor.

Her heart full, Lily admired her babies, sleeping cozily in the bassinette they shared. They'd come along a week after Tim's birth, without a problem. Delivered so quickly, in fact, that Lily had almost had them in the truck.

Over at the sink, Eloise was busy peeling potatoes for a salad. It still amused Lily, seeing the woman in jeans, working away in a ranch house kitchen like she'd been raised in the country.

Six months into Lily and Tyler's marriage, Eloise had called to ask, in a shy and hopeful voice Lily hardly recognized, if she could come to Stillwater Springs and visit Tess.

Lily had agreed almost immediately.

Her relationship with Eloise was still a little tentative—maybe it always would be—but Tess had a grandmother again, and that was the important thing.

There had been no visits to Nantucket, or the mansion in Oak Park, but Lily supposed that was coming. She might never be ready herself, but when Tess was ready, they'd discuss it.

The back door sprang open just then, and Lily's gaze swung to the opening, expecting Alec to burst in and report that the men were back.

But it was her dad, standing on the threshold. Her dad and his soon-to-be bride, Madeline. She'd been singing in the choir at his church for years, and they'd always been friends. Then, a few months ago, Madeline's cat had taken sick in the middle of the night, and she'd called Hal in a panic.

He'd rushed over, played big-strong-veterinarian, and the cat had survived.

Since then, the romance had been hot and heavy.

Lily smiled. Her dad was like a new man. He'd cut back his practice to part-time and, after hearing stellar reports from Floyd and Dorothy Book on their cruise to Alaska, he and Madeline spent a lot of time poring over travel brochures.

Lily had already agreed to mind the cat while they were away.

"Jim and Caroline just pulled up," Hal said, to the gathering at large. "They have a present. Were we supposed to bring a present?"

Briana, being closest to the door, greeted him with a kiss on the cheek. "No presents," she said. "Just come in and make yourselves at home."

Jim and Caroline came in next, with their little boy, Sam, between them. Caroline was expecting, at any minute from the looks of things, and she glowed with joy. Jim, the proud father-to-be, looked cocky as a rooster.

Everybody exchanged greetings, all the babies were carefully inspected, and then Alec shot into the room like a bullet.

"They're coming!" he yelled. "They're coming!"

Lily got to her feet.

Briana and Kristy beamed.

"Go," Hal said, to the three of them. "There are enough of us here to keep an eye on the baby crop."

Lily, Briana and Kristy all hurried outside, quick-stepped it to the rail fence.

Their husbands rode toward them on sturdy Montana horses, three abreast, making the kind of picture a woman never forgets.

Lily bumped shoulders with Briana, and Briana did the same with Kristy.

"Aren't they something?" Briana asked.

"More than something," Kristy agreed.

Lily smiled, and tears of happiness welled in her eyes.

As the men drew nearer, her gaze went straight to Tyler's face.

She knew Briana was looking at Logan, and Kristy at Dylan.

Three husbands.

Three fathers.

Three brothers.

Strong. Happy.

And together.

This time, for good.

Center Point Publishing

600 Brooks Road • PO Box 1
Thorndike ME 04986-0001 USA

(207) 568-3717

US & Canada:
1 800 929-9108
www.centerpointlargeprint.com